The Persistent Buccaneer

By Dana Kester-McCabe

ISBN 978-1-0878-7825-6

Published by Moonshell Productions
Bishopville, Maryland

Contents

Introduction

I first read about Anne Toft while researching local history for a radio show I produced. I became fascinated as much with what was written about her, as with what was not. The historical record of 17th century colonial Virginia's Eastern Shore contains almost three decades of Anne's business affairs. Her relationship with a notorious aristocrat, Colonel Edmund Scarborough, is documented through real estate dealings, indentured servitude contracts, and a variety of her witness testimonies.

Court documents describe Anne as a widow with three daughters, all born during the time that she and Scarborough lived together on their luxurious plantation Gargaphia. There is little doubt that an actual first husband never existed. Genealogists acknowledge Scarborough as the girls' father. The couple was suspected of working with pirates, running a brothel, and fomenting armed conflict between their neighbors and local native tribes. They put almost everything in Anne's name, making her the greatest landholder in the region during that era.

Anne's paper trail ends after Edmund's death and after she had signed her vast real estate holdings over to a new husband on the condition that dowries be provided for her three daughters. Despite these and other details found in colonial archives, Anne's place of birth and parentage are unknown. Also missing is any record of her passing. By the age of 44, she seems to have left this world as mysteriously as she entered it.

Was Anne Toft simply a pretty girl who just happened to be in the right place to catch the eye of a wealthy and generous man? Or was she an integral part of a colonial crime syndicate run by an influential yet mercurial aristocrat?

This book is an imagining of Anne's story inspired by bits and pieces found in centuries' old ledgers. For dramatic effect some of the dates and names have been changed, and a few fictional characters have been added. This is an exploration of what life may have been like for people, especially women, trying to build a new country in the likeness of their homeland an ocean away, all while pushing the boundaries of their newfound freedoms. This is an amazing setting in which to weave fiction from an already fascinating tapestry of existing facts. Here's hoping that Anne herself would have appreciated the way truth gets tangled up in the tall tales told here.

Dana Kester-McCabe

1653

Once A Smuggler

There had been a storm the night before little Anne and her Granny went beachcombing, so even though the tide was low everything smelled fresh and clean. Beyond the sandy beach were slick mossy rocks and shallow pools. The sun had just come up. Everything seemed to sparkle in its light.

"Now remember love, them that glitters when they is wet aint always so pretty when they is dry. Bring back them that aint broke or cracked. Maybe look for them that has holes in 'em sos that we can string 'em up."

Granny sent the ten-year-old off to search for seashells and other possible treasures. The little girl's light brown curls were already lying flat and wet against her neck from the ocean spray. Soon she would be soaked to her knees.

"Don't go any further than that big rock and stay with the other children where's I can see ye!" Granny called out. The whole town had come out to inspect the wreckage of a small ship that had blown ashore in the gale.

Anne could see her Granny make the sign of the cross before she loaded her wheelbarrow with scraps of wood, rope, and anything else that looked useful. No bodies, nor valuables, were found so the adults simply salvaged anything that they could easily carry off. It was probably a fishing vessel that had become unmoored up the coast somewhere.

In 1653 this post storm salvage ritual was a common occurrence along Robin Hood's Bay. The steep streets and stone cottages of this small village on the north east coast of England looked like they had been carved from the cliffs they were nestled between. Just as easily as the North Sea provided its bounty, it rose up and attacked with mighty wind and waves.

The people there were a tough, tight knit community. They had to be because they lived at the edge of a country that conveniently forgot about them most of the time. That is, of course, until something was wanted from them. It was not a wealthy region. When the nobles came to demand tribute, it was usually expected in the form of their men being pressed into slave service as laborers or soldiers. This caused longstanding resentment against those in power, by those left behind.

Legend has it that the region's name was inspired by the famed outlaw Robin Hood who led his band of thieves in a defensive raid there against French pirates who were pillaging towns in the area. Robin's gang made friends with the pirates, persuading them to give all their loot back to the townspeople. The villagers, in turn, were so grateful that they named their bay for the fabled rascal and joined ranks with him and the pirates. Ever since then, the story goes, the quiet fishing community had been the front for a not so secret black market of smuggled and stolen goods. Royal neglect made it easy to get away with.

Granny told Anne that Robin was the name given elves who were enchanted mischief makers and thieves. She said that since the time of Bad King Henry, when their churches had been taken from them, many townspeople had returned to the old ways of listening to the fairy folk. They made up their own laws and looked after their own, because they were the only ones who cared to do so. Flouting the official church canon and a healthy hate for noble authority were deeply ingrained in the way of life on Robin Hood's Bay. Even at such an early age Anne had been indoctrinated into this tradition.

Granny was the only real family little Anne ever knew, though she did not even know what her name was. Everyone she knew called her Granny. She had white hair and was otherwise still a good-looking woman for her fifty years of age. People treated her with great respect. Granny could often be seen giving advice to neighbors, men and women alike. She was, in fact, the ring leader of one of the town's smuggling gangs. Granny took no guff and gave orders with a steely calm that few would argue with. She inspired great loyalty because she had steered her cohorts through many sticky situations.

A few weeks before the storm, she had even negotiated a deal with the local lord of the manor, Sir William Strickland, whom Granny called a "Puritan prig." He, like almost everyone in the region, was aware of the smuggling trade. Despite his pious reputation, he didn't want it to stop. He wanted a cut of the profits in exchange for looking the other way. When he gathered the people reputed to be heads of the gangs and told them so, it was Granny who talked him into a reasonable percentage that would allow the smugglers to still make a decent living.

Granny was Anne's father's mother. Anne's mother had died of a fever when the girl was an infant. Not long after that, Anne's father was sent to jail for some reason. She was never told why. He was never heard from again. Anne's parents were gone so early in her life that it actually did not occur to her to be curious about them. All that Granny did say about them was that Anne looked like her father and acted like her mother. Born in 1643, Anne was a slender child with light brown wavy hair and bright blue eyes.

She had celebrated her tenth name day a few days ago, in mid-August. For one so young she was often quiet and somewhat serious. Her reserved demeanor was in part caused by her precarious life with her grandmother, living in a room behind the notorious Toft's Tavern on the southern end of the cliffside town. From the time she was about five years old, Anne's job was to sit outside the tavern by an open window, watching for the appearance of the authorities.

Whenever any strangers came into sight Anne dutifully banged on a pot, signaling Granny and her friends to be on the alert.

In the days following this the storm, the sheriff and three soldiers barged into the tavern despite Anne loudly drumming as they came thundering down the street. Once inside the tavern, there were raised voices and the troubling sounds of a scuffle. When they came out again, they had Sam the bartender, and Granny in shackles. That was the last time Anne saw her Granny who did not even look back as they led her away. She never said goodbye. One of the bar wenches, Auntie Margo, held tightly onto Anne to keep her from chasing after Granny.

Auntie Margo wasn't really Anne's aunt, just a friend of Granny's. She was a big woman with stringy brown hair and ruddy, pockmarked cheeks. She was missing her two front teeth. She was quick to giggle and make snide remarks, which was probably why Granny liked her. Along with other more illicit duties, they kept the guest rooms clean at Toft's Tavern in Robin Hood's Bay.

Over the course of the next few days there were hushed whispers but no explanations. Why did the sheriff take Granny away? Where did they take Granny? No one would talk to Anne or even look at her when she begged them to tell her what was going on. The clientele of Toft's Tavern was too worried about whether Granny and Sam would reveal their own illegal activities. It seems that Lord Strickland had gone back on his word and had arrested Granny and Sam to make examples of them. The gangs would now report and pay tribute directly to his steward. This would give him plausible deniability and greater control over the smuggling.

Meanwhile, Auntie Margo was busy plotting with the other prostitutes who worked in the tavern. They would need to act quickly if they were to take it over and run it for themselves. They were like crabs on the beach consuming the carcass of a fish that had washed up. In very little time they would gobble up the tavern, making it their own, as if Granny and Sam had never been there.

After days of constant crying following her grandmother's arrest, Auntie Margo finally told Anne that Granny was never coming back and that she was taking her down the coast to Scarborough Fair. Now Anne was really terrified. She had heard the grownups making jokes about people who got into trouble and were sent to the fair never to come back. What did that mean? What happened there? Were they given to goblins to be chopped up and eaten? Were they sold to vicious foreign slavers?

"What will become of me? How can I escape?" Anne wondered.

The day Auntie Margo took Anne to Scarborough Fair, she told the orphaned child, "Yer Granny's gone. The tavern is no place for a lass as young as ye. Some brute will have his way with you before yer even a woman and I won't have that on me conscience. Besides, yer Auntie Margo barely has enough for herself. Dem people at the fair find homes for lost one's like you. You'll be better off wit dem."

It took them a good part of the day to hike the path through the moors southward to the town of Scarborough. The heather was blooming in patches of tiny pinkish flowers here and there along the way. The moor seemed to go on for miles in every direction. As the sun rose higher in the sky, it got hotter and hotter.

Auntie Margo kept a strong grip around Anne's wrist and avoided any further conversation with the little girl by singing "Rattlin' Bog." Anne remembered the bar wenches learning the song from an Irishman staying at the tavern last winter. At first it was fun to sing because anyone could add yet another silly verse. It became tiresome as it droned on and on. Auntie Margo had been singing it constantly for months, much to the annoyance of everyone else in the tavern. The walk and the song seemed to go on forever.

When she wasn't caterwauling, Auntie Margo told Anne over and over again that she should never forget her Granny and try her best to make her proud. She could not think of anything else to say except that she should never forget where she came from. She made Anne repeat it several times through her tears: "No matter where I go, no matter if I become a grand lady or a lowly washer woman, I will always be a smuggler from Robin Hood's Bay."

Smugglers make their living showing one face to the world while hiding their true self. Some are merely transporters of ill-gotten goods profiting by turning a blind eye to the crimes of others. Anne had been taught that smugglers were heroes like Robin Hood. They helped ordinary people who were suffering at the hands of bullies. Though Anne did not know it, it was in her bones to live a smuggler's life long before that sad summer day when she told Auntie Margo what she wanted to hear, fully intending to do the opposite. If she had not been sold into servitude, she probably would have just been a Robin Hood's Bay smuggler. Unknowingly, by taking her to Scarborough Fair, Auntie Margo had guaranteed that Anne would live that kind of life in the colonies.

When they finally came down from the moor into town, there were dozens of screeching seagulls whirling above them. A steady breeze off the nearby North Sea helped ease the sun burned faces they had gotten on their trek. They followed other travelers who were all headed toward the fairgrounds.

Scarborough Fair was probably one of the oldest country markets in England, though it had faded somewhat from its earlier glory. Auntie Margo had said that they would find a fantastic place there, where delicious sweets and colorful silks were sold, and where dancers entertained the fairgoers. When they got there, however, there were no dancers, just a pitiful juggler in tattered rags tossing pebbles in the air. He dropped them every few throws. The place looked a lot like the fish market at Robin Hood's Bay where people sold their catch or handiwork. A few vendor stalls were mixed in among several tables where men sat writing in big books. Each had a line of people waiting in front of it.

Anne was hungry, but Auntie Margo had not time nor money to buy them a meal. She took the child by the hand and got in the first line she saw. When they arrived at the table, she began relaying a story to the man seated there.

"This be Anne. She's no one in the world to care for her. I promised her Granny on her death bed I'd find her a place."

"Wait, what did she just say?" Anne wondered in horror, "Is Granny dead?"

The man began scribbling in his book. "That's it? Just Anne?"

"Toft, Anne Toft." Auntie Margo lied. Toft was the name of the tavern where she and Granny worked back in Robin Hood's Bay. Anne thought, "I don't think I ever had a last name before. Anyway, no one ever told me I had one."

"Her age?"

"Thirteen, sir."

Another lie. Anne was skinny and small. Her breasts had not yet blossomed. She certainly did not look thirteen. The man did not even look up to see that Anne could not possibly be any older than ten.

"You understand she will be indentured for seven years to a plantation in the Virginia Colony and in all likelihood, you'll not see her again?"

Auntie Margo tried unconvincingly to look sad. "Well, it does break me heart, but the Lord is good, so I know it's what's best for her."

"You girl, do you accept this indenture? Answer me and make your mark here."

Auntie Margo gave Anne a little push. "Say: Yes sir. And, thank the nice man."

"Yes, sir. Thank you, sir." Anne replied timidly.

He showed the girl how to sign his ledger. He guided her hand and together they wrote the letter X.

"Here is sixpence for your trouble. Take her over to the wagon by the south fair gate and show them this tag."

He gave Auntie Margo the paper with a string attached and a few coins then pointed to his left. Auntie Margo looked at the money as if it was a fortune. She pushed the tag into the pocket of Anne's smock.

"That was easier'n I thought. Now we eat."

They walked over to one of the food booths and she bought them each a hot roll. It was stale, but Anne was glad to get it, gobbling up every crumb of the warm chewy bread.

"Annie girl, I'm a wonderin' if those indenture clerks talk to each other. Let's see if Auntie Margo can make another sixpence off ya. We'll pick a different table and just see what happens." She snickered and pulled Anne to another line.

The routine was almost identical to the first one, except after Anne signed the book. This time the clerk immediately tied a tag around her neck and said gruffly, "Say your goodbyes."

Auntie Margo put both hands on her shoulders and spoke sternly: "Well Annie girl, I guess yer on yer way. What did I tell ye to always re.."

Anne rolled her eyes and responded before she could finish, "…make my Granny proud and no matter where I go, no matter if I become a grand lady or a lowly washer woman, to remember that I come from Robin Hood's Bay." She knew not to say the word smuggler in front of officials. Auntie Margo knew what she meant.

"That's good. That's good. Yer Granny, she was a wise old girl. You try to be like her. Work hard, and be smart, and ye'll do alright. Now off with ya and don't forget yer Auntie Margo neither, ya hear now?"

Anne nodded and before she knew it, she was being tossed into a large wagon with about twenty other people and pushed towards a small group of children. She found a place along the cart wall to grab on to as it began to move. Holding tight to the rough wood with both hands as she tried to keep her footing, she could barely see over the side. Auntie Margo was nowhere in sight. There was nothing she could do except ask forlornly: "Where are we going?" The other passengers just looked away.

In a short time, everyone in the wagon was herded down one plank and up another. All Anne could see were the backs of the other people from the wagon. Next, they were led down a set of stairs. The walls were not whitewashed, just raw planking. This was not a house. It was, in fact, the hold of a ship.

Anne was pushed along with the crowd. As they were directed to sit down on the floor, she could feel the boat gently swaying. A bell rang several times as the crew above them on deck began shouting. Their footsteps started to drown out the squawking gulls until finally there was little noise at all, just an occasional creaking sound.

Suddenly, a girl sitting next to Anne began to wail uncontrollably. "Papa! Papa! Where is my Papa?" The wide-eyed adults looked blankly at each other. Anne was surprised to see a child more frightened than she as. She put her arm around her and tried to comfort her and herself a little too.

"Maybe he's goin' ta meet ye when we get where we's going."

Anne's eyes filled with tears. She needed one of Granny's "bucking up" stories. Without much thought she began talking, not knowing what was going to come out of her mouth.

"My name's Anne. What's yer name?" She did not wait for a reply but began to prattle on for the other girl as much as for herself.

"Did ye know that the sea is full of the fairy folk? My Granny says that if sailors pray to our Lord Jesus and Mother Mary - and promise to be very, very good - they will tell the fairy folk to protect them on the sea. She says that tis why the best sailors are good Christians. Let's try prayin'. Maybe that will help us. Dear Jesus, we promise to always be good obedient girls. Our dear Lady Mary, we promise to be kind to little children, and the weak, and the old. We promise in yer names Jesus and Mary. Amen."

"My Granny taught me that. She says the fairies in Robin Hood's Bay are the most magical in all the world. They dance along rainbows. They sprinkle magic dust in the air to make the sunrise pink. And they can tell a good person from a bad person the minute they see them. They look after the good ones, making their work easier. And the bad ones - they make their feet smell to punish them for complaining. So, we mustn't complain, see, or our feet will smell terrible, and no one'll talk to us…"

Anne went on nonsensically for some time until the little bit of light they had from the grate in the ceiling faded and she fell asleep in the now dark cabin. When she awoke the next day, she saw the other girl had moved across the room. She gave Anne a dirty look. Perhaps she did not like Anne's stories. Thankfully she had stopped her wailing. That was probably the best Anne could have hoped for.

The next day, the ship landed in Bristol and took on more passengers who joined the others in the hold of the ship, which was now very full. There was little room to move about. People had to take turns standing up to stretch and walk a few steps. These close quarters were uncomfortable. Anne wondered how long they would be stuck there. Where were they going and what would happen when they got there?

Two days later, the entire group in the hold was led up to the ship's deck. Anne peeked through an opening in a gunnel. There was no land in sight, just water. The sun was bright and hot, but a slight breeze felt good against her skin.

The ship's captain gave them a speech laying out the rules for their voyage. They were instructed to follow orders given by the sailors and guards without question. They were not to leave the hold of the ship unless told to do so. They must eat and drink what they were given and not try to trade rations for favors or anything else. And everyone must keep the tag they were given at the fair visible at all times. If they did these things, the captain said they would reach their destination safely. Anyone who caused trouble would be put in chains and lose a day's rations.

While the passengers were ushered back to the hold, some of them tried to make small talk with each other. The guards told them to shut up. People who talked back or did not follow orders quickly got a whack on the side of their heads. So, Anne kept to herself and tried to stay out of trouble. She kept thinking about her Granny. What had become of her?

Anne felt alone even though she was confined with about fifty other people in that tight space. She was frightened. She tried to remember her Granny's face. She wanted very badly to see it and to hear her voice. All she could imagine was the sight of her hands: their skin was thin, red, and cracked with large brown spots on the back of them. Granny's nails had no dirt under them, but they were split and stained brown from washing clothes and scrubbing floors. Anne tried to cheer herself up by thinking of her earliest memory of her Granny. That was the time they went to the ruins of Whitby Abbey.

Anne did not know how old she was then, but she must have been small because she remembered that her grandmother carried her most of the way. When they got to Whitby, they had to climb a great hill. The tall grass tickled Anne's feet as Granny waded through it with the child on her hip. As the sun set behind the stone arches of the old cathedral, a campfire lit the faces of other pilgrims who told stories about Jesus.

Anne remembered hearing how he came to save the sinners of the world, and how he once turned a single basket of fish and a loaf of bread into enough food to feed a thousand people. That night all those years ago, as Anne drifted off to sleep, she could hear laughter, singing, and the soft who-whoing of a little owl perched somewhere above her on the ancient stone walls. It was her earliest experience of feeling safe and cherished.

Granny loved the ruins at Whitby. She told Anne that her own Granny had lived there for a short time as a small girl. The nuns there had taken her in when she was orphaned during the Great Northern Rebellion. She lived there until Bad King Henry had the abbey burned and looted when he started his new church. Granny said that the fairies loved his daughter Queen Elizabeth and kept her safe, so that she could rule for a long time and make up for all that Bad Henry had done.

Granny used to say that the stories people tell are precious gifts. "No matter how many times we share 'em, they'll always belong to us. No one can take 'em from us."

She said that would be Anne's great inheritance, the stories she told her every night before bedtime. She had nothing else to pass down. No name. No dowry. Just stories. She said that so long as Anne remembered them and shared them freely, they would bring her good fortune. She was right. Those stories stayed with Anne, and she put them to good use all through her life.

Trying to remember Granny's stories one by one helped Anne endure the voyage which seemed to go on forever. One man was keeping track of the number of days they had been at sea. He scratched hash marks into the floor and proclaimed the number each morning.

In later years, Anne would hear stories of terrible storms, sickness, and violence on other ships making this same journey to the colonies. Except for just a few days and nights when the boat seemed to roll out of control and toss the voyagers around, her own trip passed without much incident.

The worst part about it actually was the unnerving boredom felt by the passengers. Every other day they were allowed up on the top deck in small groups to stretch their legs and get fresh air. On the days they were confined below in the ship's hold, Anne thought she might go crazy staring at those walls all the while trying not to be pressed close to the strangers all around her.

When she wasn't thinking about her Granny, Anne spent her days trying to untangle her hair picking apart the matted mess with her small fingers. She missed having a comb. Auntie Margo had sent her on this long voyage with absolutely nothing but the clothes she was wearing. It wasn't that she had many possessions to begin with. But Granny had taught her to be neat and clean, so Anne was very aware of her increasingly soiled condition.

The travelers were given sea water to wash up with in the privy. Anne was grateful to get that. Unfortunately, it did not take long before she felt like she had a salty crust all over her body. Washing up felt good but it did little to lessen the terrible odor of her clothes. The smell would have been unbearable if she hadn't gradually gotten used to it.

On the 54th day, one of the sailors above began yelling "Land ho!" He kept repeating it until a chorus of the other sailors joined him. This was the first time that smiles appeared on the faces of the weary group. They had arrived at their destination: Virginia Colony. It took another two days before the human cargo was unloaded on the wharf in James City to meet the men who had bought their bonds.

As they were led off the boat Anne's legs were weak, and she felt dizzy. She was not the only one who had to get used to being back on land again. She and the other passengers looked silly, swaying and stumbling like drunkards. Once again, there were gulls circling above them making a racket. Anne wondered if maybe they were the same birds from home who had followed them there.

She and the others were told to sit on the ground and to stay quiet while waiting to hear their names, as the ship's captain and the harbormaster got organized. A soldier set up a chair and a table with a book, an ink bottle, and a quill. A man wearing a curly white magistrate's wig sat down and waited while the harbormaster called the crowd to attention.

"The honorable Squire Owen Tomkin will now certify these indenture contracts. When your name is called, come forward and claim your servants. Squire Tomkin reading from the Cavaliers and Pioneers Patent Book, will call each servant forward for you to take possession of. The patents for your land have been written and recorded and will be given to you on completion of the transaction."

Cavalier was the military title used to describe Virginia's plantation owners who also served as officers in the colonial militia. These men took great pride in their ceremonial uniforms. They had not all earned the right to take credit for soldierly prowess. Just the same, they strutted about as if they were conquering heroes. Anne marveled at the assortment of preening men in their thigh high boots, brightly embroidered doublets, and wide brimmed feathered hats.

Squire Tomkin was the man in the wig. He was a tall slender man about thirty years old with a long nose and small brown goatee. He began reading from the ledger in a high reedy voice.

"William Basely... Come forward sir. Be it known that on October 15, in the year of our Lord 1653, that Mister William Basely takes possession of the following people into his service for a term of no less than seven years: James Turner, Robert Cole, Jonathan Yates, Henry Biggs, Robert Dent, Mary Williams, Susan Hunt..."

Each person called was brought forth and inspected by the landowners. They looked at the condition of their new servants' feet and hands. They even made them open their mouths to show their teeth. They asked what skills the servants had and where they came from. This seemed to go on forever. Pretty soon Anne stopped paying attention to the proceedings and began looking around.

The wharf was like the one in Robin Hood's Bay with its ships and docks. That is where the similarity ended. Back at home the streets were cobbled, steep hills. Here the land was flat. The streets were dirt and sand. The houses at home were made of stone or brick. Here, few buildings were brick. Most were wooden clapboard. And, here, of course, there were no towering bluffs lining the inland horizon.

It was a warm day. Soon Anne was busy swatting at biting flies. She was so preoccupied with them that she did not hear her name called.

"Anne Toft. Where is Anne Toft? Did anyone die on the voyage?"

"You there, girl, let's see your tag. Aren't you called by the name Anne?" asked one of the ship's guards who pushed Anne forward toward the table without waiting for an answer. "Here she is."

"Yes, sir." Anne said timidly, showing him the tag still hanging around her neck. She still had the other tag in the pocket of her now filthy smock. It was a sort of miracle that the string and paper had not been lost on the long journey. Without thinking much about it, she then presented the second tag to the man behind the desk.

"Oh dear." Squire Tomkin said looking through his ledger, "We do have a problem now. It seems you are on two of our lists."

Suddenly two men began talking all at once. "I paid for her." "So did I. She's mine." They began calling each other names and shouting louder and louder. Then they started shoving each other.

"Enough!!" Squire Tomkin began pounding the table and motioned to a couple of soldiers to pull the men apart.

"Here's what we will do. The two of you will still split the acreage for the girl's headrights. But since we cannot split her in half, I will take possession of her and reimburse you each half of what you paid for her passage. Captain, you will have to reimburse me for the passage fee since you are short one indenture. You gentlemen will have to take up any other complaints with your agents back in Scarborough since this is their fault. And you girl, Anne is it? You sit here behind me. Keep quiet while I complete today's business."

Anne could not tell if this turn of events was good or bad. Only time would reveal that. She spent the rest of the day sitting on the ground behind Squire Tomkin, swatting flies and picking at her tangled hair. Her next stop was Squire Tomkin's lodging in James City. He took her up to a room above a tavern and locked her in.

Anne waited to see what would happen next. She had nothing to do until the Squire returned at the end of each day when he provided dinner, usually a bowl of some sort of stew. She was given a small wool blanket and told to sleep on the floor on the other side of the room. After their nightly meal, Owen Tomkin snuffed out the candle and went to sleep on his cot without any conversation at all. His snoring and Anne's fear of what might happen next kept her awake most of those nights.

Each morning Anne was given a piece of bread and a small cup of ale. She spent her time dozing and trying to plat her hair, so it would not become a knotted mess. This continued for a few days and nights. Finally Squire Tomkin told Anne what plans he had for her.

"Tomorrow we'll leave for Northampton Shire on the other side of the bay. You'll live with my wife and become her housemaid. You will call her Mistress Bella. She is a sweet woman, but she misses her home in Yorkshire. You're from that same region, so I am hoping your accent will ease her sadness. If you are good and work hard, at the end of your indenture we will arrange for you a good position with one of the respectable families of the colony. You will be safe and may even have a life much better than that which you might have had back in Yorkshire. Do you understand what I am telling you child?"

Anne really did not understand what he was saying. Some of his words repeated themselves in her mind: "housemaid," "Mistress Bella," "safe." The rest of his short speech did not really register. But his tone was kind and soothing, so Anne nodded and tried to smile.

"Yes sir. I think so. Where is it we be goin', sir?"

"To Northampton Shire, to my plantation. It's called Chiconessex. That is the name given the place by the tribe of naturals who live nearby. The word Chiconessex means "where bluebirds gather." Have you ever seen a blue bird, girl?"

"No sir."

"Well, they are quite lovely, and they are a sign of good luck. There is a whole flock of them living at Chiconessex. You'll see."

Squire Tomkin smiled for the first time since Anne met him, as he turned and began packing up his things. He seemed to get even happier as he began telling her more about his wife.

"Bella is a most beautiful woman. She has golden curls and blue eyes. She's going to have a baby, so she will really need your help. I can't wait for her to meet you."

Even while carrying his trunk, Squire Tomkin practically skipped on the way to the sloop that would carry them across the great inland bay known as the Chesapeake. As they sailed out of the harbor and out of sight of land Anne wondered if this would take as long as the voyage from Scarborough Fair. Because she was given a place to sit up on deck, her thoughts did not linger on that possibility.

It was a sunny, cool day with a steady breeze which brought them to the far shore of the bay within a few hours. The sloop sailed a good distance further, into the mouth of a creek where the water became shallow and impassable. Squire Owens and Anne were lowered into the water into a dory with a sailor who rowed them to a small dock. Carrying his trunk on his shoulder with one hand and holding Anne's hand with the other, they walked down a path a couple of miles through some woods.

When the pair arrived at Chiconessex, it was late afternoon. The sun was just starting to set. Everything looked golden. They walked by a fenced kitchen garden near the house. Before they went inside, Squire Tomkin spun Anne around.

"Look, look over there. What did I tell you? Do you see the blue birds?"

He pointed to the garden fence where several blue birds took turns landing and then diving into the garden. It was like looking at one of Granny's fantastic stories in real life. Anne was sure that those pretty little birds were actually fairies in disguise. Maybe Granny was looking out for her from heaven. For the first time since leaving Robin Hood's Bay, Anne felt hopeful.

Where Bluebirds Gather

Mistress Bella was petite and plump with rosy cheeks and the golden curls her husband Owen was so proud of. She struggled to lift her belly full of child out of her chair and greeted her husband tenderly. Owen kissed his wife on the cheek as she smiled up at him.

"I've brought you a new housemaid to help with the baby. This is Anne. Anne Toft. A couple of reprobates were fighting over her. I feared for her safety if she went with one of them."

"Oh, Owen, she is so young! My goodness, why do they never let them bathe on ship? Maude do we have anything small enough that she can wear?"

Maude stepped forward looking quizzically at Anne. She was an older woman, much thinner and taller than her mistress. She tucked a stray wisp of grey hair into her crisp white cap. "We'll find something to make do for tonight. Come, little girl. We'll get you cleaned up and fed."

Before Anne knew it, she was taken outside, stripped of her clothes, and dowsed several times with cold water. After a good scrubbing with lye soap and a couple more rinses, Maude gave her a shift to wear. She rolled up the sleeves which hung several inches past the end of Anne's hands. The dress was so big that she could not hike it up enough to walk safely. Maude picked Anne up, carrying her back into the house where she was given a plate with a piece of pan-fried fish and some bread. She ate her meal quickly. It was better than anything she had eaten in a long time. By the time she finished it was dark outside and the lamps had been lit. Anne did not even notice. She laid her head on the table and fell fast asleep.

When she awoke Anne thought she had dreamed the events of the last few months. She found herself sleeping under a sheet on a straw stuffed palette like the one she had back in Granny's room. She looked around and saw sunlight streaming in through a leaded glass window. "Squire Owen must be very rich to have glass windows." she thought.

The house was fairly typical of other plantations in the colony. There was a center hall where meals were served and guests were entertained. It had a large fireplace. Maude explained that in the winter this was used for cooking and for warmth. In hot weather, meals were cooked in a separate small building called the summer kitchen. The main house had two wings on either side of the center hall. The south wing was where the Tomkins' had a parlor. Upstairs were three bedrooms which each had a small fireplace. The north wing was the servants' quarters. Its second story was a loft where Maude and Anne slept. Downstairs was a small gathering room dominated by a large table and benches, and the one fireplace that was used to heat the whole wing. Several male servants slept together in the barracks on the same floor which was accessed from a door outside.

Anne jumped up to go look out the window of the loft and promptly tripped on the long shift. She wriggled around trying to find an opening for her feet then tried again to stand up. When she got to the window, she could just see Mistress Bella and Maude at the south end of the house in the garden, pulling up plants. Bundling most of the oversized dress into a ball in one arm, Anne cautiously made her way out of the room through the house and out into the sunlight, following the sound of the women chatting in the garden.

"Well, look who is finally awake Maude!"

"Poor child, what you must have been through to sleep straight through two days and nights."

"Take her into the house and let's see if that dress you cut down will fit her."

And, so began Anne's life at Chiconessex. For the first week Bella and Maude treated her like a new doll they could dress up. They made her one set of clothes for doing daily chores and one for special occasions. They braided her hair and tied it with white cotton ribbons. At first, they did not talk to her so much as they talked to each other about her. This soon gave way to teaching her. They taught her how to weed the garden and how to harvest its fruits and vegetables for cooking.

Bella and Maude knew how to make these and other chores fun. Even washing dishes and floor scrubbing was done with singing and jokes. Anne was given several jobs to do every day to earn her keep: helping with the cooking, dusting and sweeping, and gathering eggs from the chicken coop.

Besides Maude, who was the cook and housemaid, there was an older manservant William. He was mostly bald, and his back was curved. He took care of the horses and cattle, and he drove the wagon, checking on the plantation tenants and making deliveries. He also was a skilled hunter who taught other indentures how to shoot and trap game. He never complained. In fact, he did not speak much at all. He was quiet and dependable.

At the time that Anne arrived at Chiconessex, Jack and Horace were two young men who worked in the fields and helped William to look after the livestock. They, and other men like them usually only lasted a year or so on the plantation before they were given other jobs and replaced by new servants. There was not much time to get to know them. They were given hard work to do which kept them out of the house most of the day.

The Tomkins' household was a busy, congenial place. During the daytime, Anne was so busy learning new things and doing chores that, for the most part, she seemed to settle easily into the new routine. During the evenings Owen and Bella would take turns reading stories to the servants. William would play his fiddle. After she had lived there a while Maude taught Anne to dance a reel. This was Anne's favorite time of day, especially when the stories were being read. She thought Owen's books must be magic to hold so many stories. They sometimes helped her to fall asleep forgetting all she had been through.

But Anne was regularly plagued with nightmares about Granny. Sometimes she relived the day the soldiers arrested her Granny. Other times she dreamed of a ghoulish figure in flowing grey robes, who she presumed to be the evil Lord Strickland, throwing a still defiant Granny off the cliffs above Robin Hood's Bay into a raging stormy sea, while Auntie Margo and the others from the tavern laughed. Anne would bolt up screaming, crying for her Granny.

Maude tried to comfort her, but after many nights of having her sleep disturbed, she asked her mistress what they should do. The two women sat Anne down and talked to her about her nightly troubles.

"Frightening dreams usually come when we are sad about something. Are you sad about something Anne?" Bella knew, of course, that the girl had been traumatized. Getting her to talk about the dreams was the only way she could think of to try and help her.

Tearfully Anne spoke about missing her grandmother, "My Granny was taken away by bad'uns. They said she was dead, but we did not have a funeral for her. How will she find her way to God without a funeral? And now, All Saints Day has passed, and we did not even bless a ribbon for her!" Anne began to weep uncontrollably.

Bella put her arms around the girl and kissed the top of her head.

"Sh, sh. There, there. Calm down now. There, there. That's a girl. Take a deep breath. That's better. Now tell me about blessing a ribbon. What is that?"

Bella gently pulled back from Anne, so she could hear her talk.

"Every year on All Saints Day, Granny and I made ribbons for Mother and Father, one for each of them. We tied dried flowers to them and set them in the waves of an outgoing tide with a prayer. Granny said this is our way of blessing them, so they would sail to Lord Jesus and Mother Mary who would tell Mother and Father how much we love them. They must think I don't love them anymore. Granny must be so sad that I did not bless a ribbon for her!"

Again, Anne was crying with deep despair. Bella and Maude took turns trying to comfort her until she finally quieted.

"Maybe," Bella said; "We could give your Granny a funeral. We could bless a ribbon for her and your mother and you father too."

Anne nodded her head between sobs. The women opened up a basket with cloth scraps to look for something they could make ribbons with. Bella found a piece of pale blue linen holding it up for Anne to see. Her eyes brightened. She nodded again. Maude went to the herb cupboard and returned with three dried sprigs of lavender. Bella cut three strips from the material. She gave one to Anne. Maude handed her one piece of the lavender. Anne tied them together into a small bow with two long tails. She repeated this twice more while Bella and Maude watched.

"Maude go ask William when the next outgoing tide is and where would be the best place to set our ribbons adrift." Bella instructed.

Maude did as she was told. When she returned, she brought William with her.

"The tide turns a little while after four bells, mum. The best place to toss the ribbons would be out in the channel. The seas are pretty calm today. I could row ye out in the dory if ye'd like."

"That will be fine William." Bella replied. "Maude, when I was a girl Anne's age, I had a rag doll. Why don't you and Anne make a doll? You can use the rest of this blue linen for its dress."

"That's a wonderful idea. Isn't it, Anne?" Maude replied.

She and Anne spent the rest of the afternoon sewing a raw cotton body with an embroidered face and hair, and made it a blue linen dress as Bella had suggested. In what seemed like no time at all the parlor clock chimed four bells. Small dried bouquets tied with ribbons in hand, Anne, the two women, and William walked through the woods, then along the marsh to the creek and the dock where the dory was tied up.

William helped them each into the boat. He let loose the lines then climbed in with them and began rowing westward toward the bay. The smell of marsh mud was thick and heavy. As they rowed along the creek, they could hear a great chorus of wildfowl honking. As they approached a bend in the stream the noise got louder. Soon they could see thousands of birds in the water ahead of them. Suddenly the birds became aware of their presence. Anne was amazed as she watched them fill the air and fly a short distance away. She had never seen so many birds in one place before.

As the flock landed on the edge of the marsh north of them, the boat reached the open bay. The sun was sinking quickly toward the now open horizon. The sky was pink with purple clouds tinged with flashes of gold. Anne's mind was back in Robin Hood's Bay where she had seen a hundred other sunsets just like this one from the bluffs above of her village. Once out in the channel, William turned the boat southward, back paddling to stay in place. He nodded to Bella and Maude signaling that they had reached a good spot for their funeral rites.

"Let's begin with the 23rd Psalm." said Bella, as she opened her small Bible to begin reading.

"The Lord is my shepherd; I shall not want. He maketh me to lie down in green pastures: he leadeth me beside the still waters. He restoreth my soul: he leadeth me in the paths of righteousness for his name's sake. Yea, though I walk through the valley of the shadow of death, I will fear no evil: for thou art with me; thy rod and thy staff they comfort me. Thou preparest a table before me in the presence of mine enemies: thou anointest my head with oil; my cup runneth over. Surely goodness and mercy shall follow me all the days of my life: and I will dwell in the house of the Lord forever."

"Dear Lord," Bella continued, "we commend our dear departed Granny to your loving care. In the name of the Father, the Son, and the Holy Ghost. Now, Anne, how does the ribbon blessing go?"

Anne had been trying to remember just what Granny had said last year. Quietly she spoke all the words she could remember.

"To our guardian angels we plead, carry our love on soft sea breezes to our Lord Jesus and the Blessed Virgin Mary, Mother of God that they might wrap our beloved Mother, Father, and Granny in their holy embrace, that they might be with us always, that them and the angels might guide us and watch over us. We bless these ribbons and send them on their way. Amen."

One by one Anne set the ribbons overboard and watched as the current carried them away. It was not long before they were out of sight. With the sunlight fading away, William rowed the dory back to shore. Anne held Bella's hand as they quickly walked back home just before darkness fell.

That night Anne dreamed again of her Granny. For the first time in a long while she could see her face. She smiled and waved to her as she sailed away in a small boat. Anne was never completely cured of her nightmares. They tormented her throughout her life, particularly in times of great anxiety. For now, though, she felt better. She awoke from her dream clutching her new rag doll. This time she did not awaken Maude. She remembered better times with Granny until she dozed off again.

Maude gave Bella a good report of their night's sleep at breakfast. She was happy to hear this news but warned the others not to tell her husband, who was away, about their improvised ritual.

"We probably should not mention the ribbon blessing to the Squire. He does not approve of the old ways. It might offend his Puritan sensibilities to hear that we had been offering prayers to the Virgin Mary. Let's us just keep this as our secret."

From the beginning of her time at Chiconessex, Owen and Bella took Anne to church along with the other servants. Other than her long ago visit to the ruins of Whitby Abbey with Granny, Anne had never been to worship services before. Even though their chapels were mostly destroyed, Granny was privately loyal to the Holy Roman Church, like many in England's north country. Since Robin Hood's Bay was fairly isolated, the people there were less regulated by the official Anglican church, yet another example of how the entire region was greatly neglected by the crown and therefore was mostly left to its own vices.

Things were not much different when it came to religion in Virginia. Largely ignored by the church hierarchy back in England, the colony did not attract enough clergy to fully service the growing population of settlers. Though they were legally bound to attend church and pay tithes, a less than strict adherence to church customs developed there. There was a widespread contradiction among the colonists when it came to piety. The otherwise recalcitrant faithful maintained a strong conviction that God had brought them to the New World to spread Christianity in the form of their own Church of England. This missionary zeal provided a sense of order and justification for any hardship they had to endure as settlers even if it did not make them strict adherents of church rules.

"It's the law. Anyone who does not faithfully go to church risks God's displeasure with our colony and therefore is heavily fined."

Owen explained. Once a month the entire Tomkin household got into a wagon and rode to St. George's Chapel in Pungoteague. The Anglican church rector there was Reverend Thomas Teackle. He served the four chapels in the area, traveling to a different one each week. He was a strange looking man with dark bulging eyes and thin stringy black hair. His voice cracked when he became excited or angry.

During the first service she attended, Anne sat with Maude and the other servants on simple benches without backs in the rear of the church hall, while Owen and Bella sat up front with the other gentry in their own boxes. At first Anne was fascinated with the pageantry of the service though it did not really mean much to her. Her seat was on the center isle where she could watch everything going on.

Soon she began to focus on the finery of the people sitting up front. Anne had been so proud of her new tan bodice and skirt which Maude had embroidered with blue borders. She had never owned anything so fine. She had also been very impressed by Owen and Bella's Sunday attire. Owen wore a deep russet colored doublet trimmed with white lace. Bella's dress was made from the same velvet and was equally ornate, at least by Anne's limited experience. When Anne saw some of the other people sitting in front of the Tomkins, she completely forgot her promise to listen respectfully to Reverend Teackle.

These people wore bright colored satins which were trimmed not only with lace but embroidered with silver and gold. One couple looked especially grand with their jewels and ornate walking sticks. As they entered the church the woman looked pained, rolling her eyes and looking at the ceiling impatiently. The man seemed to be bored. He looked around the room at the other parishioners as if to make note of who was and was not there. Anne was watching them so closely that Maude had to nudge her to pay attention when it came time to kneel or stand.

At the end of the service Reverend Teackle walked down the center aisle out the door followed by the congregation which was led by the couple Anne had been focused on. As they came towards the back of the church, she asked Maude, "Is that the King and Queen?"

"No, but they're as close as we'll get to nobility here in Northampton. That's Colonel Edmund Scarborough and his wife Mary." Maude responded.

Scarborough heard this exchange. He smiled and winked at Maude and Anne as he walked out of St. George's Chapel. Mesmerized, Anne would never forget what happened next.

She and the servants, who were the last to leave the chapel, could hear a disturbance outside as they stepped into the light of the crisp fall day. Two soldiers were attempting to detain the man Anne mistook for being a king.

"Colonel Edmund Scarborough, you are under arrest for treason, for selling arms to natives, and for continuing to engage in commerce with the Dutch in violation of the Navigation Act of 1651. By order of the Governor of Virginia Colony, Richard Bennett, you are ordered to report to James City to answer these charges."

As one man held him by the arm and the other announced the warrant, Lord Edmund started to shake his head and laugh. "Surely as a member of the House of Burgesses, you do not expect me to be taken into your custody? Surely you know that when summoned by my Governor, as a gentleman Cavalier I will certainly respond with my presence and would not need to be conducted there by an armed guard?"

The two soldiers looked at each other, as if trying to decide whether this would be alright. Taking advantage of their hesitance,

Edmund slipped their grasp, and jumped onto the closest horse. As he rode off, he shouted, "I'll see you in James City."

The dumbfounded soldiers began to debate what they should do. They had thought that by arresting Edmund when leaving church, he would be too embarrassed to resist. By the time they decided to pursue him, their quarry was long gone.

Owen Tomkin gathered his household back into the wagon and they headed home to Chiconessex. The servants kept quiet while their mistress began reacting to the unfortunate display, though her husband tried to discourage her.

"Well! I guess no one was surprised by that. What did he think would happen? He is such a fool."

"My dear," Owen cautioned her, "He is our burger and a lord of this county. We must not speak ill of him in the presence of servants."

"I suppose…"

"Bella, I insist you drop this now."

Once back at the plantation Anne could hear the adults speaking about the incident in whispers for the next few weeks. Though their numbers were growing, the colonial community was still relatively small. And, with little entertainment, it thrived on gossip. So, the attempt to arrest Colonel Scarborough was regaled over and over.

Speculation about his whereabouts became fantastical. A few of the more superstitious folks thought he had used black magic to hide in the nearby swamps where he used to play as a boy. Most thought he had found passage on a ship away from the colony possibly south to the Caribbean. Some believed he was simply hiding out in a nearby tavern, while still others thought he had ridden north and taken refuge with the Dutch in New Amsterdam. It would be a full year until he was heard from again.

In the meantime, Owen had to return to James City to attend to his duties working for the Governor of Virginia managing the colony's indenture or headright system. It seemed like he was away for half of every month. While he was gone Bella was like a different person. Her mood darkened. There was no meanness, just deep sadness. She was miserable without her husband whom she loved and depended on. She also really did miss her family and life back in England. The further along in her pregnancy, the more depressed she became. Maude explained privately to Anne that she needed to be extra kind to Bella.

"Our mistress has lost two other babes near the end of her term. She is deathly afraid of losing this one too. So, we must take very good care of her. Do you think you can help me with that Anne?"

"Oh yes. I love Mistress Bella. I would do anything for her."

It was true. Anne, in a very short time, had come to love everyone at Chiconessex. They had been so kind to her after the ordeal of losing her grandmother and the sudden voyage to the colony. Anne was happy to fetch and carry anything Mistress Bella needed without any complaint.

As the weather got cooler, Bella was confined to her bed. In order to keep her mind off the impending danger of childbirth she began giving Anne lessons in her bedchamber. After Anne completed her daily chores Bella tutored her in reading, writing, and simple arithmetic. She also taught her sewing and embroidery. This, she told her young servant, was a reward for doing her chores.

Anne loved all her lessons and would do nothing to jeopardize them. She was diligent in all that she attempted. She loved pleasing both Maude and Bella, not just because she depended on them for everything. They seemed to genuinely like her. Anne knew that she was being treated well.

As Bella's delivery time drew near, she became more and more emotional. She seemed to cry all the time. Owen had not been back in several weeks and had not answered her most recent letters. One afternoon as Anne was gathering firewood to bring in for the evening, a strange looking woman walked up the path to the house. Anne realized this was one of the "naturals" she had heard Maude talk about. She was intrigued by her long black hair, and the leather cloak she wore which had a strange design painted on the hem. She carried a basket with dried herbs and leather pouches.

"Tell your mistress that Nandua is here."

Anne dropped the firewood and ran into the house to tell Maude. This was the first time she had met one of the Kickotank tribe in person. Anne had heard the others say that they had mostly been peaceful neighbors. She had also heard them tell stories of bloody strife with natives in other regions of the colony, so she tensed as the strange woman entered the house.

"It's alright Anne. I sent for Nandua. She is here to help Mistress Bella. Bring her in and then go get the firewood. We will need extra tonight."

Anne did as she was told. Maude and Nandua disappeared into Bella's room while she went back outside to bring in the wood she had dropped. She then went to the kitchen and stoked the cooking fire. That night Anne ran and fetched for the two women. She listened to Bella screaming and crying from outside the bedroom door. It was almost midnight when it was all over. Bella had given birth to a fine young son.

Everyone was relieved once the ordeal was over, including Anne. She was not really sure what Nandua had brought in that basket. But after what she had heard about Bella's previously tragic attempts to bring a child into the world, Anne thought that Nandua must have had special magic potions.

Maude sent William to get word to Squire Owen that he was now a father. It took three days till they returned home to an ecstatic Bella. The boy was christened Henry Owen Bartholomew Tomkin during the same church service that the community celebrated Christmas that year. The holiday was celebrated at the plantation with a great feast, singing, and dancing. Bella recovered well from her labor. For a time Chiconessex was a very happy place.

As winter progressed Anne continued her lessons and helped Bella with young Henry. Now that she could read on her own, Owen began lending Anne books from his collection. This was another reward for doing her chores. Bella had begun to teach Anne to do some of her own work which included bookkeeping. She had large ledgers which she instructed Anne to write numbers and words or names in certain places on their pages.

Bella told her "These are the household records. Every good wife helps her husband by accounting for what money is spent, and what is kept in the larder. This is good practice for you, for when you will become mistress of your own house."

In one volume Anne wrote down expenses and farm yields: the amount of tobacco, cotton, and corn that had been harvested. In another she recorded just numbers next to the names of some of their neighbors. In a third book she wrote different numbers next to those same names. It was not until a few years later that Anne learned that Owen and Bella were keeping two sets of books. They were working the headrights system in a manner that was not intended.

The way it was supposed to work was that investor landowners contracted indentured servants back in England, paid for their passage to the colony where they were bound to work for terms of usually seven years. Some of these poor souls had to work fifteen to twenty years because they were convicted criminals who were given the choice of a long contract or a longer term in jail. Not all of these folks had committed serious crimes. Most of them had simply been unable to pay their debts. A few contracts included giving the servants land to live on once their service was completed. In return for taking on the indentured servants and settling the colony in the name of their homeland, colonial landowners were given a certain number of acres for each person they took on.

Owen and Bella did just that and then worked separate deals with the servants they contracted with. After a short time working on the Tomkin plantation, servants who displayed initiative were given small plots of land to rent and farm. They paid their rent usually in the form of tobacco. This the Tomkins used in turn to pay their own church tithes and colonial taxes. That other ledger that Anne was instructed to enter information in, contained records of the bribes they took from the servants to let them out of their bond early. The Tomkins were paid a small stipend by those servants for every year they did not have to spend in servitude. When they were done, they were free to do as they pleased. Bella called this the "Friends and Neighbors" ledger because for the most part the indentures became just that - their friends and neighbors.

It seemed to be a happy situation all around. The crown got their colony settled, the servants had their freedom, and the Tomkins were flourishing without the headaches of a large plantation operation. It was one of the many ways that landowners were bending the headrights system to suit their own needs. Back in England, neither the King, nor Parliament, nor the church had any idea how much wealth was being subverted. It was not until a few years later that Anne realized the extent of the corruption she was a part of. She was, after all, only eleven by this time.

Friends and Neighbors

The next few years passed quickly. Bella brought another son into the world with the help of Maude, Nandua, and Anne. His name was Malcom Charles Tomkin. The Tomkins' prosperity continued to increase at a modest yet steady pace. Anne became accomplished at needlework and bookkeeping. She was quick witted and often entertained the household with her Granny's stories. She also eventually took over the privilege of reading Owen's books aloud to the servants. She had a dramatic flair and she often included her own little jokes which delighted her audience.

By now Bella had decided that at the end of her servitude Anne should try to make a good marriage rather than look for another position in service. To prepare her charge, she felt that it was important to teach Anne social graces. She wanted her to know how to behave in so called "polite society" so that she would know what was expected of her as a planter's wife. Bella taught her to speak in a more refined manner, using less of a Yorkshire accent. By the time Anne was fourteen she joined the Tomkin family not just in daily prayers, but at meals in their parlor as well.

Anne sometimes found opportunities to sneak off to one of her own special hiding places in the woods or the barn with one of Owen's books. She loved any story that had romance or magic, or both. Anne also liked to walk along the creek out to the marsh where the sky opened up, washing everything in a bright light.

When her nightmares gave her insomnia, Anne began a lifelong habit of sitting up while the rest of the household slept. She often took to the front porch, wrapped in a blanket, listening to the sounds of the forest. She made use of that time, planning the coming day, or fantasizing about finding her one true love.

On her recent name's day Owen and Bella had given her, her own copy of the *Book of Common Prayer*. She had memorized many of the prayers in it, and said them regularly. Words like, "The mercy of the Lord is everlasting..." comforted Anne when she was worried or afraid. Prayer became her primary defense against uncertainty.

Anne had come to believe that Lord Jesus and Mother Mary had brought her to this new land for some grand destiny. She thought they wanted to make up for the hardships of her early life. Bella and Maude had taught her how to dress, how to organize the household, and how to carry herself with dignity.

The servant William was also her teacher. From him, Anne learned about the land, the waters, and all that lived there. Two summers ago, he showed her how to row the dory and to catch fish with a handline and to harvest them from a weir. Anne often went along when he took new indentures out in the dory to learn about digging clams and tonging oysters.

Anne loved being on the water, feeling the wind on her face. It was there that she felt connected to Granny and all those in her family before her. The sea was like a beautiful blue ribbon that tied them together. Sometimes Anne closed her eyes and imagined that if she could just grab ahold of it, she could pull herself all the way back to Robin Hood's Bay where everyone was waiting on top of the cliffs, guiding her back home with bonfires.

One of William's primary tasks was to hunt game and fish. Many years prior to Anne's arrival, William and Owen had worked out an agreement with the local Indians that was somewhat contrary to the colonial treaty which laid out strict hunting boundaries between the settlers and the tribes. The law really did not make practical sense for either group because of the way their prey traveled through the forest. The men working at Chiconessex had long hunted in packs with the Indians and shared in their catch.

William taught Anne many things about the local tribes, the way they lived, their superstitions and customs. There were almost twenty tribes or bands whose small villages were nestled in the most remote enclaves of Virginia's lower Eastern Shore. The Chesconnessex had lived on what was now Chiconessex Plantation. They had joined the Kicotanks to the north. To the south were the Onancocks and the Nuswattocks. The Machapungoes, the Chincoteague and the Assateagues lived eastward near the seaside. Further north, the Pocomokes, the Annamessex, and the Manokin lived across the border in Maryland.

William considered the men of the Kickotank tribe to be his friends. Their village was not too far from Chiconessex. He tried to pass on to Anne some of what they taught him about the trees, plants, and the animals that lived there.

He told her many times, "The earth belongs to the Lord, for he made it. He has given us this land to share with these tribes and the animals of the forest. The land does not belong to us. The Lord lets us borrow it as long as we take good care of it and share it peacefully among us."

Anne respected William and came to think of him as a sort of uncle. He likewise became very fond and protective of her. While the other servants usually went to bed early, William would continue to play his fiddle softly while Anne sat by the fire doing needlework. By now, she had progressed from simple embroidery to impressive tapestries. Anne was growing into an accomplished young lady who was bound to attract a respectable husband.

Anne's greatest talent turned out to be that she was a born negotiator. Anne could easily read people, and accurately assess their character. Without realizing it she had inherited her Granny's crafty intellect. Bella and Maude often found themselves at the mercy of her negotiating tactics when she wanted to get out of doing drudgework. Her ability to talk them out of chores was sweet and guileless. She rarely made them cross in the process. Meanwhile she learned from her masters, observing them deftly as they employed the arts of commerce.

Both Owen and Bella would meet in the parlor with other settlers or travelers. They helped people set up barter arrangements or partnerships, and witnessed sales. They, and now Anne, helped their neighbors, who were mostly illiterate, by reading and writing everything from family correspondences, to invoices and receipts. Anne learned from the Tomkins how to negotiate fair prices and how to write binding contracts.

During this time period she came to understand the value of being part of a community. Neighbor helped neighbor especially as they endured violent storms that plagued coastal Virginia at various times of the year. The Tomkins and other plantation owners regularly banded together to help each other out when unpredictable tempests or fire destroyed barns or farmhouses. Lost crops were the hardest blow to overcome.

Anne frequently helped Bella and Maude collect and deliver food for people who lost their harvest. She traveled with Owen to nearby farms to help him write up loan extensions which helped prevent simple calamities from turning into catastrophe for struggling settlers.

As she matured, Anne began serving as Owen's secretary. She knew how to be discreet about matters that clients wanted held confidential. Anne also had a prolific memory. There was little that she saw that she did not remember. All that information would be very useful someday.

One traveler who regularly visited Chiconessex during those years, was a sea captain named Alistair Minshull. Owen and Bella always enjoyed his visits. Once their business had concluded he usually stayed on for a few days, sharing gossip from around the colonies and back in England. The captain was well known and liked among colonists up and down the coast as much for his honest dealings as for his willingness to carry contraband. He often took on passengers who were escaping some injustice or another.

Minshull was a short, stocky, middle-aged man. Usually he was clean shaven. His strawberry blond hair was already streaked with white. He was quick to laugh and friendly. Anne loved his stories. Like the rest of the household, she came to see him as one of the family. Everyone who knew him called him Uncle Star, a derivation of Alistair. Uncle Star visited two or three times a year and often brought the Tomkins, Maude, and William small trinkets from his travels.

Uncle Star took a shine to Anne as well. He called her his "little blue bird." He began bringing her spools of silk thread in rich bright colors for her needle work. To almost everyone, Uncle Star was a beloved rascal. He was not bad enough for folks to turn him into the authorities, but just ornery and amusing enough to be admired by the average independent minded settler.

Not all the Tomkins' visitors were so well thought of. It was about this time that Colonel Edmund Scarborough began to slowly become a regular part of the Tomkins' life and therefore Anne's. In 1655 Edmund had returned on his own from his year of self-imposed exile. His whereabouts during that time was still a mystery.

Owen told the household how Scarborough had turned himself in to stand trial in James City having already secured the forgiveness of the Governor. He was quickly cleared of all charges. There were rumors that Edmund's brother Charles back in England, who served as physician to the royal family, had arranged for his clemency. Then there was the announcement of the arranged marriage between Edmund's son, Charles, to the Governor's daughter, Elizabeth. The wedding contract must have been very lucrative for the Bennett family. The Governor followed Edmund's acquittal by appointing him to be Surveyor General of the entire colony. Scarborough now lorded his new found favor over his Northampton neighbors like he was actual royalty, without question or opposition.

Feeling above the law, Scarborough began to plot against his enemies in earnest. His ultimate goal was to control all of Northampton Shire and to expand his holdings into the Maryland colony to the north. He set his sights Chiconessex, making plans to rest the plantation away from Owen Tomkin. It had grown over the years and had created a big gaping hole practically in the middle of Edmund's property. Owen also owned small pockets of land here and there all around the county where his tenants lived and farmed. Edmund became angry every time he looked at a map of his realm which was riddled with Owen's properties.

One morning while Owen was away at work in James City, Edmund arrived at Chiconessex with his aide Jasper Darby. Darby was neither tall nor short. He was lean and muscular. His face was leathery tan, almost the same color as his hair which was tied in a short knot at the back of his neck. When she first saw him, Anne thought to herself that his large blue eyes and wide mouth made him look like a snake. He grinned at her in a way that made her feel uncomfortable. He was known as Edmund's enforcer. Settlers suspected him of all sorts of dirty deeds carried out at the behest of his master.

When they arrived at the farm, Anne and Maude were working in the garden. It was late afternoon. The light of the sun bathed the scene in golden hues. Anne was gathering beans in a basket when Darby told Maude to run and fetch her mistress. While she was gone, the two men began looking Anne over without any pretense of hiding their lecherous imaginations. Edmund was a handsome man with reddish-brown hair. Though he had begun to take on a rich man's paunch, he was still an impressive figure in his gold trimmed red velvet doublet and breeches with thigh high black boots. His grey eyes seemed to twinkle. He could be both charming and bombastic, often at the same time.

Bella came out on the porch with Maude to greet the unexpected guests, interrupting their ogling.

"Greetings Mistress Bella. I am here to inspect your indenture ledgers. As Surveyor General, I need to confirm your land holdings and who is working what land for a report to the Governor."

"Good morning Colonel Scarborough. Won't you and Mister Darby come in? You must be thirsty from your travels. Anne, come help Maude with the children."

Once inside, Mistress Bella began a little performance. She began gushing about the latest county gossip. She was clearly avoiding the topic of the ledger that the Colonel had requested. Finally, Edmund insisted that she produce the book.

"I am so sorry, sir," Bella purred. "I wish I could provide it to you, but Owen handles all those matters. And he keeps the ledgers with him in James City."

Anne was a little surprised by Bella's boldfaced lie. The ledgers were in the cabinet right behind her. But Anne's early training as a liar kicked in. When you know that someone is spinning a fiction never contradict or let your face give away the truth. Anne began quietly rocking baby Malcom as if nothing in the world was wrong.

Edmund and Darby seemed to accept this and got up to leave without finishing the bread and tea that Maude had placed in front of them.

"I suppose I will just have to take this up with your husband when I see him next in James City."

"It was so nice to have you visit. We missed you and Mistress Mary in church last month. Please give her my regards. We do not see near enough of each other."

Edmund grumbled something under his breath as he made his way out the door. Once he and Jasper had disappeared down the lane, Bella went into action. She instructed William to sail to James City to warn Owen and take him the "public" account books. For two days she waited and worried until Owen and William returned. Squire Tomkin reassured his wife that everything would be alright. He had allowed Edmund to inspect his bookkeeping. The Colonel had been unable to find any impropriety. Scarborough seemed satisfied, so the Tomkins had avoided a potential disaster, for now.

Because Anne had been helping Bella with the accounting for some time, the Tomkins felt that they would have to enlist her help in keeping up the deception.

"Now, Anne" Owen began, "I hope you will come to see that what we are doing is God's work. Yes, we are rewarded, but this is really about righting wrongs and helping others less fortunate than ourselves."

"You mean like Robin Hood or Uncle Star?"

Owen blushed and began to laugh. Bella smiled. "Yes, dear, that is exactly right."

Owen continued, "There are many people who help us with this. Some of the people in our *Friends and Neighbors* ledger are listed as the people who have bought indenture contracts from us. The bills of sale are not real. We just want to be able to say they are so we can set people free who have been forced into indenture through no fault of their own. We don't want any of them to get into any trouble. There is no shame if we have need of something from them later and they are happy to give it. Do you understand?"

"I think so." Anne replied.

"You just keep doing your chores as Mistress Bella instructs you, and keep this little secret to yourself."

Anne nodded in agreement. She was a little impressed. Owen seemed to be good at this. The mild God-fearing clerk had a larcenous side.

He continued: "We have to be especially careful about Colonel Scarborough. I have seen him inflict cruel attacks on any who he suspects might cross him. He would be a treacherous enemy. When he visits, always let one of us grownups do the talking."

Anne thought back to the scene at St. George's Chapel, when the soldiers tried to arrest Colonel Scarborough. She remembered the large fluffy white feather in his black wide brimmed Cavalier's hat, and the way his gold trimmed cape fluttered as he rode away. Anne wondered about this dangerous yet dazzling man. Was he evil or merely a charming rascal like Uncle Star? She kept these thoughts to herself and promised to follow her master's commands.

The Tomkins were expecting three new indentures to arrive at Chiconessex that summer. The paper work was mostly completed back in James City, but landowners also had to register their new charges with the local council of magistrates which included Colonel Scarborough. When Owen returned home after attending to this, he was full of news about Edmund's latest scuffle with the law.

It seems that he had grown more and more unhappy with his wife Mary, and had hatched a scheme to divorce her. She was well known for her bitter disposition which had gotten worse since some of her children were now grown and moved away. Edmund was frequently gone from home, making her lonely and unhappy. She had begun to rely heavily on Reverend Teackle, complaining to him about being neglected by her family.

One day, Scarborough had found his wife and the pastor talking together. He intentionally misconstrued what he saw and claimed that the two were engaged in a sexual dalliance. He even made up a lie that they had conspired to poison him. He spread these completely ridiculous stories far and wide in hopes of coercing his wife into a false confession which would release him from his marriage bonds.

The furious Rev. Teackle had showed up in court unannounced to charge Edmund with slander. He was intent on defending his own reputation and that of Mary Scarborough. Another local planter and attorney, Colonel John Custis, accompanied the maligned pastor and served as his defender. It was he that stood between the two red faced men, who in a complete breach of courtly decorum, nearly came to blows trying to shout each other down.

"You despicable thieving beast! How dare you try to steal the affections of my wife."

"You know full well that you defame me and Mistress Mary with this vicious accusation. You are a black hearted liar."

"How dare you pretend piety? You're no more than a sniveling prig trying to cuckold me. I'll have you horsewhipped!"

"You are outrageous, sir! I'll have you charged…" Teackle began to sputter in fury, turning toward the magistrates. "I demand that Colonel Scarborough be charged with slander!"

Custis along with Squire Owen and several others pulled the men apart and tried to defuse the situation. Custis demanded satisfaction for his client. The other two judges did not want to contend with the spiteful Colonel Scarborough. They also did not want to lose the only pastor they had. It was almost impossible to get ministers to serve in the colonies because of the low pay and challenging living conditions.

The council decided to try and have it both ways. Edmund was ordered to cease spreading the accusations about his wife and Thomas Teackle. The Reverend was ordered to keep away from Edmund's wife. No one was fined. All charges were dropped. Mistress Mary was never consulted. This was in part because summoning her to appear would have meant the controversy would have carried on for days, even weeks. And of course, such was the lot in life of women in those days. The magistrates did not really care what she had to say. They could not imagine she was attracted to the strange looking preacher even if her husband was a known philanderer.

Owen had great fun regaling Bella with the highlights of the proceedings, breaking with his own taboo about speaking ill of one's betters in front of the servants. He said everyone had roared with laughter at Scarborough and Teackle. This kind of nonsense at court was actually not unusual in those days. Just about all business transactions and most disputes ended up there. Some settlers liked to attend these sessions for their own amusement. They were the closest thing that they had to entertainment.

Owen spoke in passing that Edmund might hold a grudge against the onlookers who had laughed at him. As they left the court session the Colonel had cursed them fiercely. Owen tried to downplay to his wife the growing enmity the nobleman had for him. He tried to dismiss him as a fool who did not know how to manage his own affairs.

The Colonel was known for not paying his debts. He had been accused many times of cheating people in one way or another. One neighbor, Mrs. Jane Eltonhead complained to the court that Edmund had directed his servants to steal six of her oxen to feed his own household. Anthony Johnson, a free African, once claimed that Edmund had forged documents creating a debt agreement between them taking advantage of his illiteracy. Johnson was forced to relinquish 100 acres of his land in payment to the Colonel.

Scarborough had avoided responsibility in all these affairs in part because of his high station, and partly because he was the commander of the local militia that defended the county against Indian attacks. People were either afraid of him, or afraid of what would happen if he were gone. Few trusted him to conduct his business with integrity. Edmund had already tried twice to convince Owen to take out risky loans that if unpaid would mean forfeiting Chiconessex.

That night after Owen finished his account of the spectacle at court, as she left them to go to bed Anne could hear Bella worrying aloud.

"That devil may be the end of us yet. I wish you had not been there. I wish you had not crossed him. It is no secret that he covets our land and every other plantation in this shire. He cares not how he might get it. You and all those others there today stand in his way. What if he discovers the true nature of all our dealings? He could easily put us in jail without thinking twice. It would certainly suit his purpose to do so…"

Anne heard Owen interrupt, speaking in comforting tones as she walked out of earshot. She thought back to the day her Granny was arrested and taken away, never to be seen again. She lay awake most of the night wondering what would become of her if the Tomkins were arrested. It then occurred to her that she might also be considered guilty for helping them. She shuddered and tried to push from her mind the thought of whippings at the public dock, or worse yet: prison.

By the spring of 1657, Anne was old enough that Bella had given her the responsibility of running errands at nearby plantations. She was also allowed to venture into the forest to the Kickotank tribal village to trade with their friend Nandua. William always drove her in the wagon and acted as chaperone.

Anne and Nandua became friends sharing stories about the Tomkins' offspring and Nandua's own children and grandchildren. They also traded the legends and fairy tales taught them by their elders as little children. Nandua spoke English fluently having traveled between her tribe and the settlers since she was a small girl. Anne learned to speak enough of the language of the local tribes to make herself understood. Though she rarely talked to the men in the tribe, Anne thought of Nandua and the other Kickotank women as her friends.

One day Anne and William arrived in the Kickotank village to trade for herb seeds and found everyone in a somber mood. Their king, Okiawampe, had passed away. The colonists saw him as the king of kings among the natives in that region, as most of the other tribes were his allies. Among his own people he was a well-loved leader. Now that he had died his daughter Nandua would become the Queen.

Anne was allowed to enter the newly anointed monarch's lodge without really knowing what was going on.

"Come sit here. There are things I want to tell you."

Anne's eyes grew large as Nandua explained what had transpired. Then Nandua gravely conveyed some very specific instructions.

"I need you to take a message to your mistress and master. Our clan has benefited from good relations with settlers like the Tomkins. But we have not forgotten that our tribes have often been tricked into battle by evil men like the Great Conjurer Scarborough. Many have been killed. Though our clans were paid settlements for these vicious attacks, we have not forgotten them, nor the way settlers have denied us the right to hunt in places that we were promised would always be ours. We need assurance that we will not be provoked further.

"This is important," Nandua continued. "You must tell your master to give the Governor in James City this message. Now that Okiawampe is dead, I am Queen. We want good relations. We will continue to have them so long as our treaties are honored. If the Great Conjurer and other men like him think we are weak because I, a woman, a Queen, am now the leader, he will be very sorry. Tell the Governor if he wants to guarantee the safety of the settlers, he must keep troublemakers in check. Do you understand what I am saying?"

"Yes, Nand…, your majesty, yes…" Anne gulped. She had never heard Nandua speak this way. It frightened her a little.

Nandua smiled at the girl for respecting her new station. "Thank you, Anne. You are a good friend. One of these women will provide you with the seeds you came for today."

As Nandua stood to leave Anne spoke earnestly "Nandua, I am sorry about your father."

"Thank you, Anne."

Anne handed one of the other women a basket containing several yards of unbleached muslin she had brought to trade for medicinal herb seeds: chamomile and hyssop. She and William made a quick exit and returned to the plantation.

Upon hearing Nandua's message, Owen made plans to first notify the local militia and then to travel to James City to take the message to the Governor. The Chiconessex household spent a worrisome few weeks waiting to hear the outcome of his trip. Would Nandua's threat lead to war between the settlers and the Kickotanks?

When Owen arrived home, he reassured everyone that there would be no war. He was charged with meeting with Nandua to offer her those same assurances, which he did immediately. Without knowing it, this was just one more act that would fuel Edmund Scarborough's grudge against him. Scarborough hated any settler who did not share his desire to see the full destruction of the Indians. Things would never be the same between the Tomkin household and theses diametrically opposed neighbors.

Plans Go Awry

By August of her sixteenth year, Anne had grown from a child into womanhood. She was lucky enough to possess natural gifts considered rare in those days. Just about no one reached adulthood with a full mouth of teeth. She had all of hers. Her skin was fair and clear when almost everyone else had pock marks or scars of some sort. Anne spent just enough time outside to have a rosy glow in her cheeks, but she did not carry the leather brown skin of a field worker. She was blessed with cornflower blue eyes, full red lips, and thick wavy light brown hair. She had curves in all the right places.

By any standard she was a lovely young woman and she was starting to attract masculine attention. Men who visited the plantation to see Owen often looked her up and down lasciviously and made suggestive comments. She learned how to deflect with a joke or simply pretend she had not heard what they said. Anne was amused by the attention. The Tomkins were not. An inexperienced girl was at great risk in this uncivilized frontier until they had been settled into the protection of marriage.

Bella and Owen decided that it was time to begin looking for a husband for Anne. Her term of indenture had less than two years left. Bella was hoping that she could secure a good match for Anne before some lout stole her innocence. The first step was to take her to the annual harvest fair. This was where local landowners gathered to sell livestock and bring their cash crops to market. It was also an important social event where young people in particular, could meet prospective mates.

This year Bella and Owen would make sure to introduce Anne to the well-placed parents of young bachelors. If any of them indicated a favorable impression of the girl and the dowry that Owen offered, the next step was to introduce her to the young man at church. If the two found each other likeable, then the Tomkins and the young man's parents would strike a bargain. As a servant Anne did not technically have her own dowry. The Tomkins, who had come to love her as their own, had put aside some land and a small amount of money to use for this purpose.

On the day of the fair, Maude and the children stayed back at Chiconessex while William drove Anne, the Tomkins, and the field hands to the event in Pungoteague. Anne wore a light blue linen dress that she had made herself. It had small white ruffles on the neckline and sleeves. She had embroidered the bodice with bluebirds and daisies. She wore her hair in a knot under a crisp white cotton cap. She looked both prim and lovely. Bella beamed with pride, showing off her protégé as if she were her very own.

The Tomkins introduced Anne to several sets of parents. Though everyone was pleasant enough, as the day wore on the meetings soon became tedious. Anne was bored. She was distracted, with so much to look at, particularly the other young people dressed up in their Sunday best. While Bella chatted with other planters' wives, Owen took pity on Anne and suggested they take a walk over to the corral to see the horses and cattle for sale.

When they got there, a small crowd had already assembled around the auctioneer who was taking bids on a dappled grey stallion. Anne wandered past them to the fence to watch the other horses. A fine bay mare walked up to her and let her pet her on the nose.

"She likes you." A voice from behind her purred.

Anne turned to see that the infamous Colonel Edmund Scarborough was speaking to her. She replied, "She's beautiful."

"She would be even more beautiful with you astride her."

"I've never ridden a horse."

"Oh, it is great fun Miss Anne. You would love it."

"You know my name?"

"Of course. How could I forget the golden girl in the garden at Chiconessex?"

"The what?"

"You heard me. The golden girl."

Anne was blushing now. "Why do you call me that?"

Edmund moved in closer touching her shoulder gently and whispered "I'll never forget the first time I saw you working in the garden at Chiconessex. The sun was low in the sky behind you. You appeared to have a golden glow all around you. I've dreamed of you every night since then."

Ann could not think what to say. She was surprised at how thrilled she was by Edmund's attention. Before she could think of a coy retort, she heard Owen Tomkin behind her clearing his throat. "Good afternoon Colonel Scarborough. How are you today?"

"Just fine Squire Tomkin. Just fine. And how are you and Mistress Bella this fine afternoon?"

He stepped back and turned toward Owen and the now approaching Bella, who looked dismayed at the flirtation she had just witnessed. Through a pained smile she said, "We are quite well Colonel Scarborough. Is Mistress Mary with you?"

"No, she rarely leaves Hedra Cottage and her needlework. The fair is too much commotion for her."

"Come Anne, we'd like to introduce you to Mr. and Mrs. Billingham and their son Samuel." Owen guided Anne away and called over his shoulder "Enjoy the fair, Colonel. And give our best to your lovely wife."

Anne looked back to see Edmund smiling and tipping his hat to her. For the rest of the day she could not stop thinking of her encounter with the notorious nobleman. Each time, she felt hot all over.

"We had better take Anne home, Owen. I think she's had too much excitement. Look how flushed she is." Bella knew exactly what was going on and it made her very upset. If Edmund Scarborough let it be known that he was interested in Anne for himself, she would have no chance of finding a respectable husband for the girl.

When they reached the plantation, dinner was waiting for them. Maude anxiously asked how the day went.

"It was wonderful." Anne said dreamily not noticing the concerned look on Bella's face.

Mistress Tomkin and Maude began fretting over how they could possibly keep Edmund or some other randy buck from swooping in and seducing her. They had underestimated the effect of her beauty. They now feared that it would bring her more danger than luck. Maude kept shaking her head with worry.

Bella was becoming distraught. "He could lead her into to a life of dissolution, of certain damnation, Owen. We may as well send her to the back room of Fowkes Tavern right now. If we can't get her married, we must find her a place in a widow's service. Better to be an old maid doing honest labor in the fields or a scullery maid than to be given to some uncouth rutting beast…"

These comments shocked Anne out of her juvenile fantasies. She stared at Bella as fear began to creep across her brain. Owen patted her on the shoulder and tried to calm his frantic wife.

"Now, now. Calm yourself. You're frightening the lass. I leave tomorrow for James City with Joseph Billingham. You leave it to me. I'll make the betrothal firm with him before I get back and Samuel and Anne will be married by All Saints Day. She will be safe from the evil clutches of anyone who might violate her chastity." He laughed a little at his wife for fretting that that would not be soon enough.

That night Anne lay in bed playing over in her mind all the introductions that day and her intriguing conversation with Colonel Scarborough. His open desire for her was more than flattering. She enjoyed the naughty feeling of reliving it until the thought of Bella's prophesy of doom dampened her sense of adventure.

The worst fate she could imagine was to live out her life in service to some old widow, weeding her vegetable garden and scrubbing her floors until she was old and dried up. She thought it would be preferable to make her living on her back at Fowkes Tavern, even dying young of some cursed disease as a result. At least she would have some fun. This prospect made her feel ashamed. Bella had taught her to set her sights much higher.

Just the same Anne's thoughts turned to faint memories of the women in the tavern on Robin Hood's Bay. They were mostly a happy lot despite the occasional grumbling about one brutish client or another. Anne drifted off to sleep imagining how Granny would have taken charge and helped her arrange her future. Granny would never have let her be sentenced to a life she had not herself chosen.

The next day Owen left for James City. He was gone almost a month when Colonel Scarborough and Jasper Darby arrived again unannounced at Chiconessex. It was a busy time at the plantation. The harvest season was coming to a close. Maude and Anne were busy cutting the last of the corn, while Bella played with Henry and Malcom on the porch. When the men rode up, Edmund dismounted and walked up the steps with a serious look on his face. After a few words from him, the two in the garden heard Bella start to scream. "No. NO. NO!"

The children started to cry. Maude and Anne ran from the garden to help their mistress and to hear Edmund coldly repeat his bad news.

"Squire Tomkin has had an accident on his way home from James City yesterday. A sudden gust of wind caused the ship to heel hard to the starboard side. Squire Tomkin fell overboard into the bay. We were only halfway across the channel. The current is very swift there and I am afraid that Squire Tomkin disappeared into the waters far from any shore. We looked for him and called for him a good long time, but he is now gone. We must accept that he is most certainly dead.

"I am sorry to bear these bad tidings Mistress Bella. I will have the parson notified so he can visit with you and help you make funeral arrangements. I will be back soon to help you settle your husband's affairs. You girls take good care of Mistress Bella."

With that, he walked back down the steps, got on his horse and left with Jasper. They did not look back. Maude and Bella held each other and cried. Anne held back her own tears scooping up the boys to take them inside. There she comforted them as best she could until the others joined them in the parlor.

"Maude you had better start dinner. Anne go get the rest of the servants and bring them to the gathering hall so that I can tell them." Bella shook as she spoke.

Anne did as she was told and listened numbly as her mistress relayed the tragic news to the others. Everyone was sad for the loss of their kind and generous master. At the same time, they felt a sudden sense of insecurity about their immediate future. Anne had company on the porch that night. She and Bella cried and prayed together until the early hours of the next morning.

A few hours later Reverend Teackle called on the new widow and helped her set a date for Owen's funeral. The days and weeks that followed were a blur for the entire household. They had never seen Bella so depressed. She took to her bed for several days until Colonel Scarborough returned to discuss her husband's estate.

"I am sorry to tell you that your husband was deeply in debt to me, Mistress Bella. He signed over Chiconessex to me this time last year as collateral for a loan which he has only half-finished repaying. I will have to take possession of the plantation, your livestock, and all your indenture contracts. My advice to you is to take your children and return to your family in England."

"How could I manage that all alone? At least let me have Maude and Anne." Bella quietly responded.

For Bella the prospect of finally being able to go back to her beloved home in England was bitter consolation.

"You can have Maude, but not Anne."

"I couldn't leave Anne. She would not be safe. Let me have both…"

Anne watched Bella's face go from ashen white to deep red as she clutched the top of her skirt. The Colonel responded without taking notice of the woman's distress. "That is no longer your concern. She still has a year left on her indenture. I mean to keep her to it. According to the patent records, Maude's indenture has run its course. You can arrange to pay her yourself to serve you on your journey. I will pay ship's passage for you two and the boys and give you some silver to use on your journey.

"For the balance left after the satisfaction of the debt, I will provide you with tobacco certificates which you can redeem in London. I'll write you a letter of introduction to my brother Charles who will assist you in returning to Yorkshire. That is the best I can do for you. Sign here."

If she had not been so distraught, Bella might have demanded to see the loan agreement. It had to be a lie. Her beloved Owen would never have entered into such an arrangement with Edmund Scarborough without telling her. But Bella's only thoughts now were about taking her children safely to the home she had missed for so long. Scarborough gave her no chance to argue further, pushing papers and a quill into her hands. She signed without even asking to read them.

Before she knew what was happening, Anne's fate was forever sealed. Bella, Maude, and the boys were set to leave within two weeks in order to take advantage of favorable weather before the winter storm season. The morning of their departure, in mid-September, the three women cried and hugged each other. They knew they would miss one another. Bella worried aloud about what would become of Anne living on her own without the protection of a husband or father. Northampton County was on the eastern frontier of a colony that could barely be called civilized. Despite the relative safety of the plantation, it was nonetheless a dangerous place.

"My darling Anne," Bella tried to hold back her emotions as she embraced the girl. "I can't afford to take more than a few of the books with me to begin my boys' education. I know how much you loved Owen's library. I know you will take good care of it and make good use of the contents. There is much you can learn from my sweet Owen's books. He would want me to make them a gift to you. Anyway, this book... This old Bible belonged to my grandmother. Think of me when you read it. Cherish it as I have cherished you. Look to God to guide you in this wretched wilderness. Maude and I will pray for you every day."

She stepped closer and embraced Anne again, whispering in her ear. "The *Friends and Neighbors* ledger is hidden under the coverlets in the chest in my room. Look to it for those who might help you hold on to your virtue and keep you safe."

"Don't worry." Anne said bravely as she accepted the book from Bella. "I traveled across the ocean at the age of ten. Lord Jesus and Mother Mary looked out for me then. They and William will look out for me now."

Anne was young enough to think she could still conquer anything and just old enough to know that she had to keep a cool head. She could not show any fear or these two women who had treated her like a daughter might fall apart. And then, so would she.

When Maude hugged Anne, she too whispered in her ear. "Don't let any man take what you don't want to give 'em. You move into the master's bedroom and sleep with the carving knife by yer side."

Her last words were given out loud as they pulled away from each other. "Take care of William and he'll take care of ye. We'll pray every day fer ye. Pray for us darlin' Anne!"

Now, all loaded in a wagon with Jasper Darby at the reigns, Bella, Maude, and the little boys set off for the dock in Onancock where a dory would carry them on the first leg of their journey across the ocean to England. Once the wagon was out of sight, they were forever out of her life but never forgotten. Anne gathered the servants.

"William, come into the house and play us a tune for friends who are now gone far away."

Listening to the sweet sad song coming from William's fiddle, Anne wanted to cry. She wondered if maybe she was cursed. What was the destiny that Lord Jesus and Mother Mary had in store for her? What sinful thing had she done to be punished this way? Anne did not speak of these things. It took every bit of inner strength she had not to cry in front of the others. She was in charge now. They must never see any sign of weakness in her if she was to survive.

Anne saved her tears until that night when she perched on the front porch step with a kitchen knife hidden under her skirts. There she sought comfort in the company of the crescent moon and the music of the night: the owls cooing to gentle breezes rustling the trees. In the darkness she rested her head on her knees until the sun began to rise, letting her know it was time to get on with her chores and face the unknown.

A Dangerous Scheme

With Bella gone, Anne worked hard, taking charge of the plantation. She knew exactly what needed to be done this time of year and she kept things going right on schedule as they had always been done since she arrived all those years ago. She slept only a few hours each night. Instead, she camped on the porch praying and trying to plan how to survive the coming winter. Within two weeks, Colonel Scarborough's man Jasper Darby came and took all of the servants except for William to his master's other properties.

Anne and William were left alone to fend for themselves. On All Saints Day, it was just she and William who took the dory out into the to channel to say the ribbon blessing. Anne added their dearly departed master to her list of lost loved ones.

As winter fell on the plantation, they were lucky to have enough food stored for a household of ten or more. William continued to hunt with the Indians as he always had, so there was plenty of fresh meat. Anne took up residence in the Tomkins' bed chamber as Maude had suggested. She told William that for propriety's sake he should continue to sleep in the servants' barracks. There was enough cordwood chopped and stacked for each of them to keep their own fires at either end of the house. They shared their meals and evenings together in the master's parlor. Afterward, Anne would read aloud, and William would play his fiddle.

That year there was more snow than usual. Anne and William missed Christmas services at St. George's Chapel because the weather made travel impossible. There was little for them to do but wait for spring. Anne took advantage of her free time to read many of the books left behind by Bella and Owen. Some she enjoyed so much she them read twice. She read Plutarch, Voltaire, Shakespeare, and Marlowe. She learned about such diverse topics as biology and mythology. She even read a book on business accounting: *A briefe instruction and manner how to keepe bookes of Accounts after the order of Debitor and Creditor* by John Mellis.

This unexpected leisure also gave Anne a lot of time to think about her future. It was rare for a single woman in the colonies to try and succeed on their own. Widows were afforded some agency, but maids who as yet had not been married had no legal rights. Finding a husband or a position in a reputable household were the best possible outcomes most unmarried females could hope for.

With her indenture contract now belonging to Colonel Scarborough, Anne really had little choice in the matter. She knew it was only a matter of time before he returned with some sort of plan to put her to work somewhere. She imagined that her talent for needle work would make her an attractive prospect for Scarborough's own household. Perhaps he would let her finish her indenture sewing garments for his family. He could make her a scullery maid or sell her indenture to some other harsh master. If he discovered the Tomkins' illicit dealings and her complicity in them, her fate could be much worse.

Vacillating between fear and ambition, Anne knew she could not leave things up to chance. What she really wanted was the life Bella had trained her for: to be the mistress of a plantation. Anne decided that that is what she would become, starting with Chiconessex. By the end of January, Anne was hard at work on a scheme to attain the destiny she had chosen for herself.

This began with the *Friends and Neighbors* ledger. Anne poured over it again and again. How could she use the information in it? Soon the seed of an idea formed. Many of these people still would have had many years left on their indenture if it weren't for the Tomkins' generous subversion of the headrights system. Anne had met most of them through their dealings with Owen.

Anne wondered, "How can I get something from these people and still keep them as friends? I will need friends not enemies. If I blackmail them, they could turn on me later."

Anne remembered what Owen had said to her about profiting by doing bad for a good reason – just like Robin Hood or Uncle Star. If only Captain Minshull would visit now and give her some advice on what to do. With no hope of that happening until at least spring, Anne began making decisions. She would not ask the people in the *Friends and Neighbors* ledger for anything at all. There was not much hope of collecting any illicit obligation they might have owed Owen. So, she decided to give them the papers that documented their release from indenture in order to earn their favor. She would tell them it was Bella's parting wish that their debt be wiped out and their freedom secured.

This would be a fact-finding mission as much as anything else. Anne wanted to know how many people were left and who she might be able to count on now that Colonel Scarborough had seized the Tomkins' property. Anne visited with several of the people listed in the ledger when she went to church once the weather finally cleared. In early February she had William hitch up the wagon to begin taking her to see those she had not seen at St. George's Chapel. It actually took ten days to find out what had happened to everyone on the list, or to visit them in person.

Many of Owen's tenants had already been put off their farms. Those still left were grateful to get their papers. They all warned Anne that the Colonel was a ruthless man who she should be afraid of. They believed that Edmund had only allowed them to stay because they were good producers whom he expected to provide him with a steady income.

Edmund had consolidated some of the smaller farms. Quite a few of the former indentures were simply told they were no longer needed. Some of those who now had no work and no place to live had been pressed into militia service under Colonel Scarborough's command, just like the fishermen of Robin Hood's Bay had so often been forced to serve the Royal Navy.

Edmund did not care about the fate of those servants. He had no plans to buy more indenture contracts. He had found a better solution for his labor needs. For several years Edmund had been importing African slaves. Unlike indentures, they were bound to serve him and his family forever.

Meanwhile that winter, Scarborough's cavalry had been on a campaign against the Assateague tribe who lived north and east of Chiconessex closer to the ocean. When Edmund's troops were not attacking them directly, they were destroying the Indians' fields and winter food stores and cutting them off from any hunting in the forests there. This drove the Assateagues north into Maryland and enabled Scarborough to claim all their territory as part of Northampton County and his own plantation.

Closer to home, Anne heard that Nandua and the Kicotanks, were under threat as well. Their communication with the other tribes had been cut off. This made it impossible for a coordinated response by the Indian allies to Scarborough's unrelenting assault.

Anne returned home to Chiconessex from her visiting, feeling discouraged about finding her own allies. William did not seem to care, though Anne was not surprised by his apathy. He was an old man who had never known anything but poverty and servitude. He only knew how to mind his own business and do what was asked of him. William may as well have been a slave. Frustrated, Anne believed that he had no ambitions of freedom because he had no idea how to survive on his own if he had been let go. One master was the same as any other to him. He did not even seem to mind Anne telling him what to do.

Anne had to find some sort of benefactor or protector. Clearly William would be of little help. Most of the neighbors could not or would not do anything. They were too worried about their own security. She needed a bold plan. What would Granny do? Just now, none of her fairy tales seemed to offer any help.

She could try to find out if the Billinghams were still amenable to her match with Samuel. But they would require a dowry, which she now did not have. Besides, if they wanted to take pity on her, they would have called on her by now to make her an offer in light of Owen Tomkin's passing. She wondered if all the respectable neighbors had already gotten word that she was property of Edmund Scarborough and therefore off limits.

Anne thought about how great women had succeeded in her favorite stories from Owen's books. She thought about Cleopatra and Queen Elizabeth. What would they do? Elizabeth never married and ran her kingdom as well as any man might have. According to Owen's copy of Plutarch's Lives, Cleopatra had herself rolled up in a carpet and delivered to her enemy Julius Caesar whom she then seduced.

Anne looked for consolation in the old Bible Bella had given her. It was the King James translation that she had taught Anne with. The teenager looked through its pages for wisdom in the familiar proverbs and psalms. When she got to the section known as the Apocrypha, she came upon the story of the beautiful widow Judith.

Judith and her fellow Israelites were afraid of an imminent attack by Assyrian invaders. After praying for courage, the Biblical heroine devised a plan to help her people. She took one of her slaves to the enemy camp and gave herself to the general in charge. She seduced him with rich food and wine. While he was in a drunken stupor, Judith killed the general and cut off his head. His frightened troops retreated and Judith triumphantly returned to the village she had saved. There she lived out her days in honor and comfort.

Anne wondered if she had the courage to be so brutal. It was Judith's prayer to God for courage that convicted Anne to her cause: *"Give me constancy in my mind, that I may despise him: and fortitude that I may overthrow him. For this will be a glorious monument for thy name, when he shall fall by the hand of a woman."*

Anne decided that this passage was a sign from God through his servant Bella. It was her righteous duty to defeat Colonel Edmund Scarborough and avenge her master's death. She must find her enemy's weakness and use it against him just the way Judith had.

Scarborough had sons. Maybe she could marry one of them and frustrate his desires to have her himself. Anne dismissed this idea. The eldest Scarborough children were already married. Everyone in the parish knew that Charles would soon be wed to the Governor's daughter and the other boys were younger than Anne. It would be a few years before they would be allowed to be married. She could not wait that long if she was to take charge of her own destiny.

Anne thought about how many men had made eyes at her or uttered indecent remarks in her presence. Surely some field hand could be talked into a marriage proposal. But, what kind of life would that be? They would live in a primitive cabin and do hard physical labor, day in and day out. There would be many children and few pretty dresses. More importantly, there would be no more books. No. That was not what she wanted.

Anne wondered how long she would be pretty, and the danger it was putting her in now. She remembered the day that Edmund and Jasper Darby had leered at her. Then she thought about how the Colonel had flirted with her so shamelessly at the fair. Her mind drifted back to the stories she had read of women whose lives were marked by more tragedy than triumph because fabled kings took what they wanted by asserting their Divine rights. People were calling Scarborough the King of Northampton. He certainly acted like he did not have to answer to anyone but God.

Anne wondered how many women Edmund had. She searched her memory of Bella's gossip about Scarborough. People said that a long time ago he had a wife before Mary and that he was notorious for his patronage of the whores at Fowkes Tavern.

How horrible it must have been for Mistress Scarborough to be humiliated in front of the whole county by her wayward husband, accusing her of attempted murder and adultery with the strange looking Parson Thomas Teackle. Mary must despise his treachery. That must be a terrible household to live in. Then again, maybe Mary was a shrew who screamed and threw things. Anne chuckled at the idea of Edmund having to buy affection in the arms of a sneering insolent tart because his wife had rejected him.

Despite the good influence of the Tomkins, prostitution was something Anne had previously been raised with a tolerant attitude for. When she was about eight, Anne had witnessed Auntie Margo having sex with one of her impatient customers on the back stairway of Toft's Tavern. When she asked her about it, Granny explained it this way.

"Men are beasts who need to have their urges satisfied. One woman's rarely enough for 'em. They'd wear out their wives if they could not pay other women to give 'em pleasure. Tis how girls like Auntie Margo, who have no husbands, survive. Someday I hope ye'll have a husband who'll take care of ye so's you do not have to do this. But always have pity in yer heart for the tarts of dis world. They're just trying to get by as best they can, like anybody else. Now go do yer chores and stay off the stairs, lest one of those beasts decides to have his way with ye. Go on now."

This, countered with Bella Tomkin's teachings about the duty of wives, led Anne to believe that sex was the necessary work of all women. Though Bella had tried to teach her good Puritan morals, Anne's earlier upbringing won out. She decided to follow the examples of Cleopatra, Judith, and the like. She would seduce her enemy. Their stories made her think that this would be a game of cat and mouse, one in which the mouse must always think they are the cat. She would have to make Edmund Scarborough think that he had conquered her.

Anne fantasized about creating the kind of home a man would want when he was unhappy with his wife. It should be the envy of every other miserable husband. It should appear to be respectable and yet be fun and exciting. Edmund should come to think of being with her as better than being at home.

Anne wondered if she could pull this off. Was she pretty enough, clever enough? Could she stomach tying herself to this notorious man? Could she share a bed with Edmund – even have children with him – all without benefit of marriage? What if she could not force him to support an illegitimate child? Would she be ostracized from decent society?

Anne didn't mind that too much. Until the age of ten she had never heard one good thing about so-called decent society. Her subsequent life on the plantation had taught her to endure to long periods of time without much outside contact. Maybe it would not be so bad.

What other plan could she make? She could demand her freedom, or simply run away to James City to seek work as a seamstress. What if she got there and found no position? She could be whipped on the public dock for running away. If she was not careful, she might end up right back here in Northampton County being pressed into service as a prostitute. She would have no say in her own life. Bella would be so disappointed in Anne if she wasted all that she had taught her.

One night while staring into the parlor fire, she pondered her options should the church come out against her. Despite a somewhat libertine attitude about sex, the idea of being disowned by the church made her feel strangely frightened. Would she be cutting herself off from God? These thoughts made Anne feel hot then cold all over. The muscles in her neck and back tensed involuntarily. She was considering a life of sin. It made her feel physically ill. She walked quickly outside into the frigid winter air and threw up.

When she came back into the house, Anne washed her face. She prayed "Lord Jesus help me to be faithful. Mother Mary please, please guide me."

She put another log on the fire. She sat there watching the flames until dawn. She had told Bella and Maude not to worry, that Jesus and Mary would watch over her. Was that just a lie she made up to make them feel better? Could she really leave everything up to her faith in Jesus and Mary? She waited and hoped for some kind of sign.

For the next week it rained every day. It was bitterly cold, but it did not snow. A damp chill pervaded everything. Anne kept up her routine of daily prayers, mending, and cooking meals for herself and William. In between chores, she tried to stay warm restlessly rearranging the furniture in the parlor, then in her bedroom. She tried to read by the fire but could not concentrate. Finally, one Sunday morning, the sun came out. Anne took a walk out to the kitchen garden to survey its condition and to begin planning for the spring planting.

The ground was still frozen, but the air was unusually warm for that time of year. As she turned to go back into the house Anne noticed a pair of blue birds on the garden fence. One was a bright azure male with a russet and white chest. The other, a female, was grey and brown with just a little blue in the tail. They were there only a few seconds before they jumped into the air, circled each other, and flew off. Anne thought of the day that Owen had first told her about Chiconessex. She marveled at how these fragile little creatures successfully persisted throughout the harsh winter.

"That is the name given the place by the Indian tribe that lives nearby. The word Chiconessex means "where bluebirds gather." Have you ever seen a blue bird?... Well, they are quite lovely, and they are a sign of good luck."

The memory of Owen's words and all his kindness brought tears to her eyes. It was then that she began to think about something that one of the neighbors had mumbled about him. What was it they had said? "...his death being so suspicious and all..." Anne began to think about the possibility that Edmund may have actually been responsible for Owen's death. He had profited greatly by it. He was, after all, on the ship when Owen "accidentally" fell overboard.

The thought that he might have actually had a hand in this tragedy made Anne furious. The guilt she had been fighting against suddenly disappeared. She now had an even better reason than self-preservation for tricking Edmund. She wanted revenge for Owen's death and all the pain it had caused Bella. She did not want to teach him a lesson. She wanted to ruin him. Judith's prayer reverberated in her thoughts: *"Give me constancy in my mind, that I may despise him: and fortitude that I may overthrow him. For this will be a glorious monument for thy name, when he shall fall by the hand of a woman."*

Anne returned to her scheming in earnest. She tried to think of everything she knew about Edmund. Owen and Bella had said that he was dishonest and arrogant yet some settlers admired the Colonel. To them he was a hero who had kept them all safe from savage Indian attacks. Anne realized that all things considered, Edmund

Scarborough was a complicated man to be reckoned with. He had enemies and supporters in equal measure.

She would have to be very careful about who she got help from. It was unlikely most of the highborn plantation owners would turn on one of their own. Anne went through the *Friends and Neighbors* ledger and put two dots next to each name she thought would be most likely to curry favor with Edmund, those who she thought would be too afraid to cross him. She then looked for those people she thought were the most likely to secretly help her. There were only three. Robert Brotherton, Giles Ishim, and Richard Metcalfe. She memorized their names.

"These people will be my smuggler allies." Anne whispered. Auntie Margo had been right all those years ago. She would always be a smuggler from Robin Hood's Bay. Then Anne thought of another person who might be an important ally. Nandua.

The native queen certainly would have no care for the leader of the militia who so brutally oppressed her people. Right now, Anne knew she was powerless to help Nandua's tribe fight off Edmund's army. Anne surmised that if the Kickotanks decided to attack the settlers she wanted them to know that she was still their friend. She decided she would visit Nandua right away, even though she risked an accusation of treason. Soon the ground would thaw. Planting time would bring Edmund and new field hands to Chiconessex.

Anne had worked out how she would move ahead and who might help her. Before she could set things in motion there was first one person who she had to commit to her cause. That was William. After dinner one night she explained her plan to him in such a way that she did not solicit his opinion. She also withheld as many details as possible in hopes that would make it easier to get him to back her up.

"I am doing this so that neither you nor I will be put out, or worse. You will be able to keep hunting and fishing here, and play your fiddle every night."

"Mistress Anne, yer very dear to me. I do want ta help ye. But I don't know that this'll work. I don't know if I'm a good enough liar. If tis all the same to ye, I'll just keep me yap shut and say nothin'. If it helps ye can say that I've gone simple 'cause I'm old."

Anne smiled and replied, "Then shut up William and play your fiddle for me."

William picked up the instrument. He did not play any of the jaunty reels Anne, Bella, and Maude used to dance to. He played sweet sad songs well into the night.

The next day Anne had William hitch the horse to the wagon and take her through the forest to the Kickotank village. When they got there, the people looked at her with great hostility. Anne was not sure that Nandua would even receive her. She was led to the lodge where the Queen was holding court with several mostly older tribal leaders. They too looked suspiciously at the young woman and her driver.

"Nandua, your majesty, thank you so much for agreeing to see me. It is most important that I speak with you. May we be alone?"

Nandua pursed her lips and squinted at Anne. "Send your man outside. I will dismiss everyone except my daughter. She and I have no secrets. She will guarantee my safety."

The idea that either she or William might try to harm Nandua hurt Anne. It left her feeling sad and worried that her mission that day was already hopeless. Anne told William to wait by the wagon. He left the women and did as he was told. Nandua waved her hand and everyone but her daughter exited.

Now it was just the three women. Anne slowly walked closer to the native empress. "May I sit down?"

Nandua motioned to a place on the wicker platform next to her. Anne's story and plan came pouring out of her so quickly that Nandua twice told her to slow down.

"I want you to know that I am your friend, your ally. If you hear that I have taken up with the Great Conjurer Scarborough, it is because I plan to avenge my master Owen. I don't know how we might help each other. But, if we can stay friends, I am sure that we will."

Nandua shook her head. "I believe that you are sincere. But this is a foolish and dangerous plan. I do not see how it will succeed."

"It may not, but my only other choice is to runaway to James City or north to Maryland. I don't think anyone will help me in Maryland, and in James City the Great Conjurer has many friends who would just send me back to a worse fate than what I have now."

"I do not approve of this, but I see I cannot change your mind. If we find we can help each other, let us hope that works out well for us. I warn you – do not send for me if you become with child. I will not be your midwife and neither will any woman from any of the tribes. Those days are over."

Anne had tried not to think too much about the possibility of having children with the Colonel. She nodded and bowed her head to thank the Queen. "I understand. Thank you, your majesty."

Anne quickly departed after curtsying to Nandua and her daughter. She rejoined a nervous William in the wagon and they headed for home.

"I thought you were never coming out, Mistress Anne."

"Everything is all right. Now, don't forget. This visit will be our little secret, alright William?"

"But…"

"The less you know, the less you have to lie about. Just remember that I'm going to make sure that you and I are safe, and we have good positions."

"How…"

"Don't you worry about how. You just leave it to me. Tomorrow, if the weather holds, we are going visiting again. We are going to see Robert Brotherton, Giles Ishim, and Richard Metcalfe."

"Wha…"

"That's enough William. I need you to be quiet, so I can think." Anne began to mull over ideas for her next moves, while William muttered quizzically to himself.

The next day, Anne made the rounds visiting the three people she hoped would become her allies. She had picked these men, because she had heard Owen speak of them as trusted friends. Their names were at the beginning of the *Friends and Neighbors* ledger. Their debt to Owen was fully paid. They had hired on other indentures given an early release by Owen and had profited from the Tomkins' scheme. Anne told them a slightly different story than the one she told Nandua.

"Mistress Bella trained me to help her run Chiconessex. I helped her with all aspects of the plantation. She and Owen had no secrets from me. I know about their arrangements with you. I am here to honor those arrangements.

"My beloved master and mistress showed me great kindness. What has happened to them is terrible. They wanted me to make a good marriage but now that they are gone, I have no dowry. I will not let them down by doing anything less than what Mistress Bella trained me for. I plan to stay on and keep running Chiconessex. I think you – we – can help each other as all good neighbors should.

"I fear that Colonel Scarborough may have other plans for me. I may have to accommodate him in some way that is not pleasant, in order that I do not end up working someplace like Fowkes Tavern or worse.

"None of my choices are good ones. But if I am successful, I will be in a position to continue to help you in other ways. I do not need anything from you now, but I may call on you at some other time. Can I count on your help?"

Without much questioning, Robert Brotherton and Richard Metcalfe both agreed at least grudgingly to try to help if they could. They thought Anne's plan was doomed to fail. They had no intention of putting themselves at risk. But they felt sorry for the pretty girl, and did not want to dash her hopes. So, without any sincerity, they pledged their allegiance to her.

Giles Ishim could not contain his doubts nor his hate for Edmund Scarborough. Ishim owned a farm on the other side of the forest north of Chiconessex. He was not quite fifty years of age with greying black hair and dark eyes. He spoke to Anne on his porch, just out of earshot of his wife and two children inside their cabin.

"Have ye lost yer mind girl? Scarborough's a devil. He'll ruin you! I've run afoul of him a few times and barely kept what property I have because of it. He won't be happy until he owns all the land this side of the Chesapeake and has kicked out all his countrymen leaving just his Africans to bring in his harvest. He's not right in the head. He wants us to go back to calling this Accomack Shire, instead of Northampton County.

"He thinks he should be the damned king here abouts. Half the colony thinks he murdered Owen Tomkin. The other half don't know whether to curse him for riling up the naturals or thank 'im for murderin 'em. Think about the disgraceful way he's treated his wife."

Ishim finished, "Girl, he'll ruin ye."

"What would you have me do Mr. Ishim? I know every word you say is true. I have no good prospects for my future. And, the only way I might get justice is to take back Owen's land from him. The only way I can do that, is to do this terrible thing."

"It won't be one terrible thing, girl. It'll be many."

"I know. I know. I am not asking you to do anything now. I am promising to help you later, if I can, to stop things Scarborough might do to harm you and yours. Can you make me that same promise?"

The two went back and forth like this for some time until Ishim's wife appeared at the cabin door to invite Anne and William to stay for a meal.

"Thank you, no Mrs. Ishim. That is very kind, but I don't know how long the clear weather will last. The sky is looking very grey. We should be going. Do I have your promise, Mr. Ishim?"

Giles sighed. Anne had worn him down. And any enemy of Scarborough was a friend of his. He nodded his head to indicate that yes, she could count on him.

Anne suddenly kissed him on the cheek and whispered in his ear the same thing she had told her other conspirators. "If ever we send a message to each other always mention bluebirds. Then we will know that we can trust the messenger."

Ishim chuckled. "I get it. Because you are the lass from Chiconessex – where the bluebirds gather."

Anne went home and for the first time in weeks got a good night's sleep. She had some semblance of a plan, and a handful of potential allies. The next morning, she thought through everything and realized that she still had to figure out how to find a way not to be cut off from the church.

Ever the pragmatist, she recognized that she would not be able to do plantation business if proper people were worried about the church frowning on them for associating with her. Also, the church had people fined when caught fornicating outside of marriage. That would cause a lot of unwanted scrutiny and expense that might interfere with her plans.

Anne decided to make up a dead husband making her a widow with all the rights that implied. But, how could a girl who had not left Northampton County in almost seven years explain that she had met and married someone no one had ever met? She would never get Rev. Teackle to go along with her lie. All her books and stories came in handy at this moment and inspired her very own melodramatic plot to deceive Teackle and her neighbors.

The fiction was simple: She would tell people that the son of her father's cousin, a seaman named Henry Toft, was serving on a Royal Navy ship that patrolled the Chesapeake Bay in Maryland. When he heard that she had lost her dowry and any prospects of marriage, he had offered to marry her to give her security. They had been wed by the ship's captain when Henry's vessel was nearby at the mouth of the Pocomoke River.

This tall tale would allow her to remain Anne Toft. She had grown fond of the name given her by Auntie Margo. The whole story was preposterous, of course. Hopefully it would be just preposterous enough to be believed.

Anne forged a letter from the captain of a vessel that Owen Tomkin had mentioned seeing when he had traveled to St. Mary's

City. She then wrote a letter to the parson, asking that he visit her when his circuit next brought him near her in Chiconessex. She would ask him to pray for her and accept the letter as proof that she was now Mrs. Henry Toft. She gave her note to William to take to the parsonage.

All that Anne could do now was wait and see what happened next. She decided that if her plans failed, she would run away to St. Mary's City in Maryland where the Catholics there might give her sanctuary from Virginia's Anglican authorities. Hopefully that would take her far enough away from the clutches of the Great Conjurer.

1660

Shaky Alliances

March of 1660 arrived with warmer weather bringing on an early thaw. Still there had been no word from the new owner of Chiconessex. Anne was never good at waiting. She decided that she would venture south to the Scarborough homestead, Hedra Cottage, to see if she could find out what was going on and force a confrontation with Edmund Scarborough. She concocted a not entirely false pretext of needing tools repaired and additional farm hands to start preparing the fields for spring planting. This would also be a good excuse to assess Mistress Mary Scarborough. Knowing what made Edmund unhappy at home with his wife might help Anne in her attempt to seduce him.

Once again William was called upon to hitch up the wagon. Off they went on their mission, east through the forest and then south on the post road to Pungoteague and west again to Hedra Cottage. They left not long after sunrise arriving at their destination just before midday. There had been no rain for more than a week, so the dirt road was still packed dry and hard. If there had been any rain at all the wagon ride would have taken twice as long and William might not have even attempted it.

Anne had on her best dress under a heavy winter cloak. When she knocked on the door of Hedra Cottage she held her breath in anticipation. An old woman answered the door. Her back was curved, and she had to turn her head upward to look directly at Anne's face.

Anne held her chin up high feigning confidence. "Good morning. I am here to call on Colonel and Mrs. Scarborough."

"The Colonel aint here. What's yer name? I'll see if Mistress Scarborough will receive ye." was the reply.

"Please tell your Mistress that I am Mrs. Henry Toft. I am mistress at Chiconessex and I need to make arrangements for assistance with spring planting there."

The elderly servant mumbled, "Wait there." as she toddled inside closing the door behind her.

A few minutes later the door reopened, and Anne was led inside while William waited with the wagon. Anne had never been inside such a well-appointed home. The paneled walls were hung with expensive looking tapestries. The old lady took Anne into the parlor where there was more of the same, along with several paintings of people who were probably members of the Scarborough clan. Even though it was the middle of the day, there where candles lit all around the room. There was a large blaze in the fireplace. Right next to the hearth sat Mary Scarborough.

Anne recognized her from seeing her in church. She was in her forties, but she looked older. She was thin with angular features. Her dull grey eyes had large circles under them. Her once-blond hair was nearly white and very thin. She wore an ill-fitting dark grey dress with a high white collar which was embroidered on its edge with silver and green thread. The dress looked like it belonged to a much larger woman.

Anne was studying her so intently that she did not immediately notice three of the five Scarborough children were also seated around the room. Charles and the twins, Matilda and Edmund III, were all around Anne's age. The boys each had a book in their lap while their mother and sister were working on hooped embroidery. The teenagers had their mother's looks. All three were blond with blue grey eyes. All were lanky and tall.

"Well? What's this about Chiconessex?" Mary snarled, as she stabbed at her needlework.

"Thank you for receiving…"

"Go on. Get on with it! You don't want to keep your man sitting in the wagon in the cold all day, do you?"

The room was incredibly hot, so Anne untied her scarf and opened her cloak just enough so that Mary could see her pretty dress which showed just enough décolletage to be provocative. Anne pretended not to let the woman's aristocratic arrogance unnerve her.

"I've come to get field hands for spring planting. I also need a letter of instruction to the blacksmith in Pungoteague promising to pay for repairs on some of our tools. There are just a few, but now that they belong to Colonel Scarborough, he will have to pay the blacksmith."

"What are you planting?"

"Wheat, mum."

"Wheat? No tobacco?"

"The soil at Chiconessex is not suited to it, mum. We grow wheat to mill for flour, and for hay to feed our livestock. And, we have a kitchen garden to serve our own needs."

"Sounds like a wholly unprofitable plantation. It's no wonder Owen Tomkin failed so miserably."

Again, Anne did her best to contain any reaction to the haughty woman. "Chiconessex is rich in game, Mum. This winter, all by himself, my man William killed beaver, raccoon, and deer. Their pelts are drying now. When Colonel Scarborough visits, he will take home a harvest in fur and leather as valuable as one in tobacco."

"Did I hear that you are *Mrs.* Toft?"

"Yes, Mum. Mrs. Henry Toft."

"When did you get married? And who is this Henry Toft?"

"On All Saints Day, this past fall, Mum."

"And why isn't this Henry Toft visiting me this morning? Did you marry a lazy wastrel?"

"No Mum. He is a seaman on the HMS Bristol on patrol on Chesapeake Bay. Mistress Tomkin trained me well in the running of the plantation. That is why Colonel Scarborough left me charge of it, Mum." Anne was not going to let Mary insult her husband even if he was a figment of her imagination.

"You three brats - get out." Mistress Scarborough motioned to her children and snarled, "Go on you stupid mongrels. I'm sick of the sight of ya."

The eldest, Charles, blushing red, started to respond to the insulting dismissal, but his mother shot him an angry look that made him think again. He and his siblings retreated into the hall, closing the door behind them without a word.

"What are you really after? I'll bet you're one of my husband's whores. I dare you to produce this husband of yours. Don't just stand there; you stupid wench. Tell me what you want."

Once more Anne, kept her anger in check. "I've come for just what I've asked for, Mum, nothing more."

"The blacksmith bill, and some field hands? Well, I don't believe it. You're just another indentured whore, here to see if my bastard husband will pay their bills."

"It seems Mistress Mary, that I've come on a bad day. May I call again when you are feeling better?"

"*What?!* Get out!" Mary was on her feet and shouting. "Get out you whore! You stupid ugly whore!" Her eyes became wide with fury. Her pallid face turned deep red.

Anne backed away from the crazed woman. "Good day, Mistress Mary. I hope you are feeling better soon." she said quietly.

Anne, making a quick exit into hallway, heard something hit the door just as she closed it. Charles was waiting alone there. Still blushing, he did not apologize for his mother's outrageous behavior.

"My father is in James City. I don't know how much you have heard about affairs in England, but there has been a revolution. Lord Cromwell has been tossed out and King Charles II will be restored to the throne. Just last week, my father joined the rest of the House of Burgesses pledging their allegiance to the King. After being at war here all winter with the savages, he has not had much time to tend to regular plantation business. With mother being ill, it is enough for me to simply help her manage things here at Hedra."

"I understand." Anne replied. The teenagers both tried to sound mature beyond their years.

"I'll send someone up to you with the letter, and some slaves to help you until my father returns. It will probably be a week or so from now. That'll have to do."

Anne started to thank him as more shouting and crashing was heard from the next room. Before she knew it, Charles had ushered her back outside.

"So," she thought, "that was why Mary Scarborough rarely left Hedra Cottage and why Edmund wanted to be rid of her. She's as mad as a tree full of squirrels."

As Anne and William made their way down the lane from Hedra Cottage, they met a finely appointed carriage traveling toward the Scarborough plantation. It was an open-air rig, painted black with red trim. In it was an older couple. They both had grey hair and the ruddy complexion common to many Europeans. The man was dressed in black velvet with a high white collar trimmed with lace.

His female companion had a similar collar and doublet peeking out from her dark green cloak.

The travelers stopped briefly to exchange greetings. Settlers lived such isolated lives that every chance for socializing was taken advantage of.

"Good day. How do you do? I'm Dr. George Hack and this is my wife Anna." The man spoke with a thick Dutch accent.

Anne responded, "Good day to you as well, sir. I am Mrs. Anne Toft and this is my manservant William. We have just been to call at Hedra Cottage."

"With the fine weather we're having, we decided it would be nice to get out and come see how our neighbor is fairing. How did you find Mrs. Scarborough today?" said Mrs. Hack.

"I am sorry to say that the confinement of winter has seems to have had an ill effect on m' lady's disposition. But I am sure that the company of her good friends and neighbors will lift her spirits."

Mrs. Hack looked suspiciously at the girl. Mary Scarborough's disposition was somewhat notorious. The doctor's mission that morning was to visit his patient, the mistress of Hedra Cottage, whose health seemed to be in constant jeopardy. Anna Hack doubted their visit would lift the spirits of anyone but the Scarborough children, who were the real object of her own concern that morning. She was, however, intrigued by young Mrs. Toft.

Anna Varlet Hack and her husband were successful planter-traders from the Netherlands. They had become citizens of Virginia not long after their arrival in the early 1650s. This allowed them to prosper greatly even when trade between the English and their fellow countrymen had been outlawed during the war. Dr. Hack was one of the few physicians in the colony. His services were in great demand, which left commercial concerns under the care of his wife. Anna

Varlet Hack was gaining a reputation in the mid-Atlantic colonies as a creative and skilled merchant who had greatly increased her family's fortunes.

"Where do you live my dear?"

Anne proudly announced that she lived at and managed the Tomkins' plantation at Chiconessex.

Now Anna knew who she was talking to. This is the young indenture that Owen Tomkin had been trying to find a proper suitor for, before his untimely death.

"Oh yes, now I remember who you are. I was so sorry to hear about your master's passing. Did I hear that Mistress Bella has returned to England? She was such a sweet woman. We shall all miss her."

Anne only vaguely recalled Dr. and Mrs. Hack. They were not in the *Friends and Neighbors* ledger.

"Yes, it has been a time of great grief for us. First to lose our beloved master and then his gentle wife and their darling children. We miss them terribly. I am only glad that they have been returned to the bosom of Mistress Bella's family."

"I quite agree." Anna replied. "So, tell me my dear, you say you are now Mrs. Toft. Your marriage must have been quite recent."

Anne blushed. For just a moment she had forgotten all about the grand deception she was trying to weave. She repeated the lie she had told Mary Scarborough and then tried to make an excuse to leave before this nosy neighbor questioned her any further.

"Well, it's been delightful meeting you. I am afraid we have to be getting back to Chiconessex. The weather is so unpredictable this time of year. We don't want to be caught on the road…"

"Quite right, Mrs. Toft." Dr. Hack tipped his hat and began to pick up the carriage reins.

Anna Hack touched his hand to prevent him from signaling the horses to start, so she could say one more thing to her new acquaintance.

"Mrs. Toft, I hope you will rely on me if you find you are in need of counsel, or anything else. I greatly admired Bella Tomkin and I know she would want me to look out for her protégé."

Anne blushed again. "Thank you, Mistress Hack. I am glad we met today."

The two parties took off in opposite directions and were quickly out of sight of each other.

"Have you ever met them before, William?"

"Yes, Mum. I don't know much about 'em. I never heard nothin' bad about 'em, just that they're Dutch and they's very rich."

Anne decided to save that nugget of information for later and then put the encounter out her mind. The Hacks' friendship might be useful to cultivate, but there were more pressing matters at hand.

The next day, back at Chiconessex, Reverend Thomas Teackle arrived in response to Anne's letter. He was a strange, nervous man. As he rode up, Anne thought how uncomfortable he looked on his horse, like he might slide right off. She invited him to take tea with her in the parlor.

"I received your note. I wish I could say that I approve of your marriage Mrs. Toft, but it seems so sudden. The banns were not properly read."

"I know, Pastor. I was in fear of my good name. With the Tomkins gone, and only William to protect me, there were many indecent proposals but none of marriage. I wanted a proper marriage in the sight of God. My cousin wanted me to have a good name. It all happened so quickly. Will you pray for me?"

"Of course, my child. Who made those indecent advances? Are you sure you are quite alright?"

Anne evaded his questions and spent the next hour charming the gullible cleric. He left fully convinced of Anne's story. She did not even have to show him the forged letter from her fictional husband's captain.

As he left Reverend Teackle said, "I will announce your marriage Sunday next, so the word will spread that you are no longer alone and vulnerable. When I meet your husband, we will enter the nuptials in the church records."

This was all Anne needed. She could appear to be married for as long as she needed to be. And as long as she avoided an official church record, she could more easily become unencumbered if that suited her purpose.

It was another three weeks before Jasper Darby arrived at Chiconessex late one afternoon with a wagon carrying three slaves and two new hoes. Anne wished he had brought the letter to the blacksmith, so she could have the tools fixed she really needed. She was disappointed that Edmund had not come himself. She did not complain. Instead, she was politely appreciative.

Jasper introduced the African slaves, men first: Michael and Bobby, then, a young woman named Fannie. They and about thirty-five others had come to Virginia by way of Brazil and a stopover at a Dutch settlement a few hundred miles northward, before they were sold to Edmund.

Jasper led the shackled slaves out of the wagon saying, "Fannie has picked up English just fine, but Michael and Bobby not so much.

They're just a couple of dumb mules but they be strong and should do fine in the fields. Fannie can translate for ye."

Following his master's specific instructions, Jasper did not remain long enough to answer any questions. He handed Anne a large key for the slaves' chains. Then he jumped back in the wagon and disappeared down the lane as suddenly as he had arrived.

It seems that Edmund Scarborough had devious plans of his own for Anne. He had left her alone all winter expecting her to be frightened by the isolation. Now, he was sending three slaves knowing they had been difficult to control. He thought they were rebellious, stupid, or both. They had not shown any tendency toward violence, but they had not yet been productive due to their stubbornness. Edmund expected them to lay about and refuse to work, or maybe to run away. He was setting Anne up to fail, so that when he finally arrived to solve all her problems, she would think of him as her hero or at least beholden to him.

Edmund had been smitten with Anne for a long time. He was actually being truthful at the fair when he told her that he had been dreaming of the "golden girl." Life with his wife was so miserable he had gotten into a habit of only returning to Hedra Cottage for Advent season unless he absolutely could not avoid it. That was all the time he could stand.

The annual visit merely helped to maintain the appearance of being a faithful husband. When back on the Eastern Shore he stayed with his sister's family or at the inn in Fowkes Tavern in Pungoteague. Now he had tired of finding satisfaction in the mercenary arms of prostitutes. What he wanted was to sleep in his own bed with an adoring young mistress who could take care of all his needs. He thought the way to get what he wanted was to trick Anne into wanting him more than he wanted her.

He hadn't counted on Anne successfully meeting every one of his challenges. After the initial surprise of having the slaves dropped in her lap without any instruction or assistance, Anne quickly realized that her new master did not really want them to be helpful. She was not exactly sure what he did want, but it wasn't hard to figure out that he was trying to intimidate her. She was determined to handle the situation.

"Welcome to Chiconessex. I am Mistress Anne, and this is William. Come into the servants gathering hall. Come, tell them to come along…"

Anne motioned to the girl and led the group inside where she directed the slaves to sit down on a bench. William stood by the door as his mistress began a speech that he would hear her give over and over again in the years to come. He had heard Bella give the same speech countless times before. He felt proud of Anne for having learned it so well, but worried that things would be very different with the Africans. Indentures hearing this speech had the hope of being free someday. These slaves did not.

"Fannie you translate for me, please." Anne began slowly, pausing between each sentence. Fannie echoed her using an African dialect from their homeland Akan.

"Here at Chiconessex we work as a family… During the day we each have a job to do… At the end of each day, after our evening meal, we share our stories and music… The men sleep downstairs and the women upstairs in the loft… I stay in the masters' quarters. In this household, we look out for each other… Everyone is fed… Everyone is needed… We are a family.

"Now, William will show you where you will sleep and where you will work... Fannie…"

"My name is not Fannie. It is Fanta. That is Malike. And, that is Botwe."

Anne knew what it was like to have a new name assigned to her without being consulted. Her instinct was to show the unhappy slaves some respect by calling them by their given African names. Building trust was going to be important.

Anne had heard gossip about the challenges of keeping slaves: language barriers, homesickness, and most importantly their natural anger. Some slaves had to be beaten because they refused to follow orders. Some were so miserable they starved themselves. Others became sick from the climate, disease, or just simple despondency. Many died.

Throughout the colony, indentured servants were being replaced more and more with African slaves. Enterprising landowners began buying indenture contracts for skilled tradesmen rather than raw laborers. They continued reaping the reward of colonial acreage and began to enjoy the refined services of artisans who could help the raw frontier feel more like home. As with the Tomkins' scheme, planters freed the tradesmen, then leased them land to live and work on. They used their profits to buy slave labor for their plantations.

Things were changing constantly and rapidly in Virginia. Anne was better equipped than most to adapt. She had the perverse advantage of having known little stability in her life. She also had the rare pragmatic quality of a quick open mind. So, she thought instinctively that treating servants and slaves alike with respect would ultimately benefit her. It was an easy though small gesture to recognize the Africans by their given names.

"I see. Mister Darby must have misunderstood when he learned your names. Fanta, Malike, and Botwe, again, welcome to Chiconessex. Now, you three, go with William to see your quarters.

Fanta, you translate for him. When you all come back to the gathering hall, I will have dinner ready for you."

Anne went to the larder and found the ingredients to make a simple stew and johnny-cake for five people. That night they all ate dinner together in the gathering hall. The men sat quietly while Anne told Fanta how she wanted the meal cleaned up and then supervised that work. When they were done Anne told everyone to sit by the fire for the evening entertainment.

"Tonight, we will tell our own stories. William and I will tell you how we came to this place. Then I want each of you to tell us how you came here. I will go first. Fanta please translate for Malike and Botwe."

Anne told her story while Fanta translated.

"I am Ann Toft. I come from across the sea, from a place called Robin Hood's Bay. When I was a baby both my father and my mother died, so my grandmother took care of me. When I was still very small, soldiers took her away for helping some outlaws. I was sold into servitude and put on a ship with many strangers. My master, Owen Tomkin, bought me from two men who were fighting over me, and he brought me here to serve him and his wife Bella. This was their plantation, Chiconessex. The native tribes here gave it that name, which in their language means: where bluebirds gather.

"Master Owen died last year. Our new master, Colonel Scarborough, sent Mistress Bella back to the place where she lived as a child. Master Owen and Mistress Bella were good masters. They taught me many things. William and I miss them."

Anne paused to let Fanta finish with her translation. She turned to William realizing that she had no idea what he would say. She had never before thought to ask him where he came from.

"William, how did you come to live in this place?"

William looked at the ground and did not say anything for a few uncomfortable moments. Anne was just about to ask him again when he began to speak.

"I'm William of Bradfield Heath in Essex. My people there've always worked at Grimston Manor. My father and his father before him were huntsmen in their forests. So, I was raised to be one too. When I was just a young man we fell on hard times. I helped feed my family by hunting in the Grimston's forest – without permission. When my master the Baron found out, he punished me for stealing. He had me beaten. Then he took me to the magistrate who sentenced me to 20 years of indenture. I was put on a ship and brought to James City. I was sold to Master Owen's father and it was he who brought me here. He had an old servant named Bert who had a fiddle. He taught me how to play. That was many, many years ago. I do not know how long I've been here. Tis the only life I know."

The three African slaves looked confused and suspicious of what they had just heard. It was similar to what they had been through, but by no means the same.

"Fanta, please tell Botwe to tell his story."

Fanta did as she was asked. Botwe shook his head and spoke briefly.

"He says his story belongs to him. He will not share…"

Malike interrupted her with a few curt words then sat up straight with his head turned defiantly away from the group.

"Malike says the same. Mistress Anne, our stories are like yours and William's. We were taken for no good reason from our homeland and our families. We were packed tight into ships and carried across the great waters chained to each other. Some we were chained to died and we had to lay next to their rotting corpses for days or longer. We have been beaten and mistreated by many hands and delivered to strange places where we do not know the language, where we are beaten and forced to work in chains. We are given strange food that makes us sick. We are not permitted to pray in our way, to drum, to dance.

"The winter here is cold and bitter like everything else here. You have been treated with kindness here. We have not. Some masters pretend to be kind. They make promises they do not keep just to get another day's work out of us. In the end they beat us. All our masters have been cruel thieves. They steal our lives. Only our breath belongs to us. We will not waste it giving you our own precious stories."

Now it was Fanta's turn to sit up straight and look away with her jaw set tightly shut and her lips pursed. In any other household this would be seen as insolence and result in at least having one's ears boxed.

Anne thought for a moment and said, "Thank you, Fanta. Tell Malike and Botwe that someday I hope we will be able to share the happy memories of our childhood. For now, let us listen to William play his fiddle before we turn in for the night."

Fanta scowled but relayed Anne's message to the men. William began to play. The music was sweet and sad. Anne noticed that Fanta and Botwe had tears in their eyes as they listened. Malike held his stony gaze until William finished playing.

William put up his fiddle and took the men to the barrack where he chained them to their cots and laid down on his own bed there. Anne took Fanta up into the loft where she chained her to the bed where Maude had once slept.

"I will come for you in the morning, Fanta."

No one at Chiconessex slept much that night. The Africans lay awake in misery, wondering at the futility of escaping with nowhere to go and no way to get there. William wondered how long the men would have to stay chained before they accepted their lot in life. Would they ever be able to trust them not to rebel, or not to run away? Never mind would they get any work out of them?

Anne spent the night playing out different scenarios in her head for how she might get the Africans to work for her. She had no way to know if any of these ideas would work. If the slaves continued to refuse her commands no wheat would be planted this spring. That would be a disaster. In her frustration she cursed Jasper Darby for not providing English indentures. Those she could have handled easily.

Anne began pacing the floor of her bedroom. Now she was cursing the real cause of her troubles. "*Damn you* Edmund Scarborough. You damned Conjurer, you! You did this on purpose. You want me to fail. Well, we'll just see about that." This went on for more than an hour until finally Anne lay down on her bed in exhaustion. Again, she tried to think of some way to make all this work. She was still trying to figure it out when the sun started to come up.

That morning Anne accompanied William and the Africans to the wheat field. William unshackled their hands. Anne told Fanta to tell the men to pick up the tools and start working. Their feet were still in shackles with just enough length of chain between their legs that they should have been able to do what they were told. The men crossed their arms and looked away. Then Fanta did the same.

This is what Anne was afraid would happen. She looked at William who just shook his head. They had never had this problem with indentured field hands. But then they did not have to work in chains. On any other plantation such recalcitrant workers would have been beaten soundly until they complied with their orders.

Anne decided not to take this course of action. Instead she led the group back to the house. She directed William to take the men to the barrack, chain them to their beds, and watch over them.

"Fanta, you come with me."

Together the two women entered the master's parlor.

"Fanta, you sit here."

Fanta sat down at the table where Anne had pointed, wondering what she was going to do to her.

"You and I are going to have to figure this out together." Anne started as she sat down opposite to Fanta at the table.

"I have decided that the best thing to do is to tell you exactly what is going on and then we will make a bargain that will help me and William, and you and Malike and Botwe.

"Our master is very powerful. Many people fear him. The Indian tribes here are greatly afraid of him. They call him the Great Conjurer. He knew that you and the other slaves would refuse to work when you got here. He knew that William and I would never beat you or starve you. Why is he doing this? I do not know.

"He has some plan for me and for Chiconessex. I have an idea, but I do not know for sure exactly what that is. He's made sure that my master and mistress would be gone and that I would be left alone here, unprotected. If you and Malike and Botwe refuse to work, he will send Jasper Darby or some other brute to take charge. They will bring other slaves and make an example of you three. You will be beaten until you give in or die."

Fanta interrupted, "Why would he go to so much trouble to take one stupid girl to his bed?"

Fanta's astute and candid observation struck Anne as funny. She laughed out loud. It felt good. She had not laughed in a long time.

"He has made it known to me that he thinks I am pretty, but I am fairly sure that is not the only reason he has done all this. I think he would have changed things here months ago, but his other duties have kept him busy. He spent the winter waging war on the Indian tribes. My friends have told me that he just wants Chiconessex so he can own all the land in this region and become its king.

"The real question you should be asking me," Anne continued, "is why a stupid girl like me would be willing to bed a dangerous man like the Great Conjurer?"

"Why would you?" Fanta replied.

"Because, if I don't my life could be as bad or worse than what you have already been through."

"You don't know what I have been through."

"No, I don't. I can't even imagine how awful it has been for you. But I can guess enough."

Anne paused, "Let's get down to it. I cannot promise you very much now. If my plan works, I will become mistress of Chiconessex and own everything on it, including you. After that happens, I will set you free in five years' time like other indentures. But that is not all I am prepared to offer you. Being free will mean very little if you have nowhere to go, no food nor shelter. I doubt I will have a way to get you back to your village in Africa. But I will do my best to find you a place to live where you can support yourself. If you and Malike and Botwe will help me now, I will make that promise to all of you."

Long before these three had been brought to her, Anne knew she was probably going to have to deal with slaves and treat them differently than indentures. Though her plan seemed to be highly unlikely to succeed, much of her strategy was actually well thought out. She had spent months on it, even if she had not fully anticipated the situation that had unfolded. Overnight she came up with this negotiation to offer to find them something close to the farm of the Johnson family, free Africans living not too far away on Nasswaddox Creek.

"What makes you think you can make any of this happen? Tis just dreaming."

"Perhaps. But, what do you have to lose? If the Great Conjurer's men come and take over, it will be very bad for all of you. If you do as I say, and my plan does not work, you are no worse off and for a few months you'll have much easier lives than you've been having: hard work but good food, and no beatings."

"I am not sure I could talk those two hard headed men into it."

Anne sensed this meant Fanta was at least thinking about her offer. The bargaining had begun.

"What would it take to convince them?"

Fanta sniffed, "I don't know. Would you cut off your hand to show you are sincere?"

This took Anne back, but she surprised Fanta and herself a little with her response – a bold challenge called for an equally bold bluff in return.

She held up her hand and said, "In your presence I will have William cut off the tip of my little finger to show good faith. If I break one of my promises to any of you, you can take the whole hand."

Fanta's eyes opened wide. Then she turned her head a little squinting suspiciously at Anne. "I don't know…"

The two women sat in silence for a few minutes. Anne used the time to think how she could get the haggling going again. She broke the silence saying, "Let me tell you more about what I am offering."

Anne began to explain in more detail how things worked on the plantation, what were the most difficult chores, and about the times when there was little to do. Before she would sweeten the offer any further, she told Fanta to take her offer to Malike and Botwe and ask them if this was not enough, ask them what then would they want?

Anne led Fanta back to the barrack. She called William to come out and sent Fanta inside to talk to the men who were still chained to their beds. Anne and William could hear their voices but could not understand their African language. At one point one of the men began to shout. More discussion could be heard.

Finally, Fanta appeared at the door to say, "They will accept your offer, but they have conditions…"

"Conditions? Those cheeky bastards!" William interjected.

"Hush, William. Go on, Fanta."

"We want our own food. The last place we were at, someone had planted yams and okra. We want you to send for some, so we can plant our own. We want to work and sleep without chains. We want to make drums, so we can sing and dance our prayers. We want time together when we are not being watched over."

Anne spoke calmly. "What are you willing to do for these things?"

"We are willing to hunt and fish, to work in the house and the fields and help with the cattle and chickens."

"And will you promise not to run away or cause any harm to William, me, or any part of the plantation: our tools or the buildings?"

"Yes."

Anne decided she was doing so well she would ask for more. "You will do all these things and attend morning and evening prayers and evening gatherings with the household. Malike and Botwe will learn English. You and I will teach them. I expect them to speak and understand English as well as you do. After five days of good faith work, I will allow some time unchained and William will give you the materials to make your drums. If all that goes well, you will have more time unchained. Then I will give you all time together alone once a week to drum and dance your prayers. If you agree to do all these things, I will send for the seeds to grow your food today. Go back in and ask them if they agree to these terms. If they do, I will come inside, and I want to see them nod their heads yes when I ask them to agree as well."

"And if your plans work, you will make us indentures instead of slaves, giving us our freedom after five years' time?"

"Yes, I will."

Fanta went back in to talk with Malike and Botwe for a few minutes and then returned to the doorway. "We are ready." she said.

Anne went inside. With Fanta translating, the agreement was struck. No further mention was made of cutting off fingers or hands. This bargain between Anne and the slaves would not be looked on kindly by other slave owners. Anne had no plans to tell anyone about it.

For the next few weeks, the household fell into a new routine. Every midday Anne gave the slaves English lessons, beginning with simple vocabulary and easy sentences. Gradually the Africans were chained less and less until they could be trusted not to run away. Anne had traded some beaver pelts for yam and okra seeds to Anthony Johnson the free African who lived a few miles away. William gave one of the deer-hides he was curing to the men to make their drums. It would take time to find and carve the right wood and then stretch the skins properly so that the drums would not break when played.

Anne tried to win Fanta's trust. She offered to teach her how to read and write even though she knew this was a dangerous idea that could get both of them in trouble. Fanta declined. She was still traumatized by the experience of her village being brutally attacked and forced into slavery. She did not know where she belonged in this cruel world. She did know that every custom of the whites that she took up made her less and less one of her tribe from Akan.

First the whites forced her to live in this strange country, then to eat strange food, then to put on strange costumes. She believed that all this was a way for the masters to eat her soul one bite at a time. She was deeply afraid of her soul disappearing. She did not tell her new mistress this for fear of being punished for figuring out the evil plan. Though Fanta refused to warm up to her, Anne nonetheless tried to treat her as well as she knew how.

Life at Chiconessex for a time became uneasy but predictable. Everyone worked hard. Everyone bided their time expecting any day to have their weird arrangement ripped up by Colonel Scarborough or his aide Jasper Darby. No one slept well, especially Anne.

The Courtship

At the end of the following March, the legal master of Chiconessex finally came to check on conditions there following the end of winter. He expected to find a confused and frightened girl waiting to be rescued from the hardships of running a plantation in a savage land. That is not what Edmund Scarborough found when he arrived with Jasper Darby late one afternoon.

Evening prayers had just been read. Anne was setting the table for her dinner in the master's parlor. In a show of authority over the household, she had begun eating dinner alone and then later joining the rest of the household for entertainment in the great hall. She heard the approaching horses and recognized the men as she peeked out the window.

She did not go out onto the porch to greet them, waiting instead for them to come through the door. Looking prim and proper in her modest dress and apron, she spoke to her master as if he were merely a neighbor paying a call.

"Welcome back to Chiconessex, Colonel Scarborough, Mister Darby. You are in time for supper. Won't you come in and sit down? I'll let Fanta know we have two more joining us."

Anne walked casually out of the room as Edmund and Jasper looked at each other curiously. She left the door open, so they could hear her announce that "Colonel Scarborough and Mister Darby are here and will join me for dinner. Bring in enough for three, Fanta."

It was what the entire household had been waiting for, what they all had worried about. What would Colonel Scarborough do with Chiconessex now? Could Anne pull off her scheme?

Anne started to set two more places at the round table, when Edmund stopped her.

"Just set one other place Mistress Anne. Darby will have dinner with his old friend William."

"As you wish." Anne purred.

Now, for the first time, they were alone. They could hear the clatter of dishes down the hall where there was little talking. Anne was not sure how to start the conversation. Coy silence, no matter how awkward, seemed a good strategy. Fanta arrived with a tray of food, their usual stew with johnny-cake and a pitcher of ale.

"Thank you, Fanta. That will be all." Anne said.

Fanta left without speaking, closing the door behind her.

"I thought her name was Fannie."

"No. It's Fanta. Shall I say grace?" Anne did not give him time to reply. "Bless us, O Lord, and these Thy gifts which we are about to receive, through Thy bounty, through Christ our Savior we pray. Amen."

"Amen. What do you mean it's Fanta?"

"It's Fanta. Always was and is now."

"Funny, the bill of sale says Fannie."

"Well, someone got it wrong. Besides, I like Fanta better, so that's what I am calling her. You have arrived at a very good time Colonel Scarborough. The men have just finished planting our wheat fields. Oh, and we have two new calves born just last week. I'll have William show them to you before you leave if you like."

"Looks like you survived the winter quite well." Edmund said cautiously, as he studied the girl. She was different than he remembered. Her bearing was more mature then when he last saw her at the harvest fair. Still, she looked lovely in her simple everyday dress.

"Of course. It was a very productive time. The winter hunting has been good. William will have to show you all the pelts drying in the barn. I did a lot of mending and needle work. I even had time to read a few books. Mistress Bella made a gift to me of Squire Owen's collection when she left. I read stories to the household from them for entertainment each evening. I would invite you and Mister Darby to stay to hear tonight's selection, but the sun will set soon and if you are to get to Hedra Cottage tonight you will need to leave soon."

With his dinner finished, Edmund stood up and walked to the window. He did not know what to do. This girl acted as if she owned Chiconessex and he was just a passing guest. Who did she think she was talking to?

Turning back toward Anne he tried to contain his annoyance. "And what if I want to stay the night here? This is my plantation after all."

"If we'd been given some notice, you would be most welcome. I would have had Fanta prepare rooms for you and Mr. Darby. Come back tomorrow and we will make things ready for you."

This infuriated Edmund. "Tomorrow? You want me to come back tomorrow?" he bellowed.

Anne was afraid she may have gone too far but decided to push her luck. "Yes. We will make things ready so that you and Mr. Darby will be comfortable for as long as you want to stay."

Then Anne called out, "Fanta, come get these dishes. Mr. Darby, Colonel Scarborough is ready to leave."

Jasper and Fanta arrived from the gathering hall, both wide eyed. Anne handed Edmund his hat, directing him toward the front door. He took a deep breath and stomped outside with Jasper following close behind him. He did not want his man to see that this girl had unnerved him and tricked him into leaving his own property. So, off they rode to find lodging elsewhere.

Once they were out of earshot, William, who had followed the others into the parlor, murmured, "I hope ye know what yer doin'."

The next day, Anne made the master's bedchamber ready for Edmund, clearing out anything that belonged to her. She instructed Fanta to set up two beds in the nursery for the two of them, and to clear the loft for Mister Darby. By midmorning they were done just as the sound of horses riding up the lane could be heard.

Edmund and Jasper dismounted. "You there, William, unsaddle the horses and put them in your paddock. Mistress Toft." The Cavalier tipped his hat to Anne and walked purposefully past her into the house.

"Welcome, Colonel Scarborough. Won't you come in?"

Once inside the master took charge. "Everybody out but Mistress Anne." he growled. "Sit down at the table, girl."

"Can I get you anything Colonel? A cup of tea perhaps?"

"Just sit down. I want to talk to you."

Anne sat down where she had been directed. She held her head high and looked past the man who was doing his best to command her full attention.

Pacing, he began the speech he had prepared for her. "Now that the Indians have been defeated, I will have more time to attend to plantation business. I will personally take an interest in Chiconessex."

"And what are your plans for Chiconessex?" Anne interrupted.

"My plans are to clear more forest and plant tobacco." He replied.

"You could do that, but it'll fail. The soil here is not suited to tobacco. I understand that tobacco does better in places with more warm days than we have here."

"Now see here, I will not have you or any other woman tell me how to conduct my business." Edmund started to turn red in frustration.

"Colonel, why don't we be plain with one another? What are your intentions toward me?"

"My intentions? I uh… I, well, I don't know what you mean."

"Come, please sit, Colonel, and let's talk this through." Anne held out her open hand toward the empty seat across the table from her. She thought if she could make him sit down that she would be able to get him to negotiate with her. Perhaps, not as an equal, but with less bluster.

Edmund looked at the young woman with more confusion than surprise. Anne tilted her head and smiled just a little. "Come, sit here sir. Please?"

The man sat down. This was not going the way he had planned.

"Colonel Scarborough, why don't you tell me what it is you really want to do with me and Chiconessex?"

"I told you. We are going to plant tobacco…"

"You don't really care what we plant here, do you? That's not why you have gone to all this trouble, is it?" Anne teased.

"I don't know what you are talking about…"

Anne could tell that she was getting under Edmund's skin. He was not used inferiors being so direct with him. The bolder she was with him, the more disoriented he became. Anne was gaining an advantage. It was time to make the first offer.

"Why don't you let me continue to run Chiconessex the way it has been for many years? Our greatest profits come from beaver and deer pelts, not from tobacco. Why not let us continue with what has proven successful?"

Edmund started to get angry. "Now see here. You have no say in this. I'll do as I please with this plantation. And you'll do as I tell you. Do you hear?"

"Of course, Colonel Scarborough, of course. But why worry yourself with the day to day workings here? You're an important man with many obligations that keep you away from Northampton. When you're here, what you need most is a place to live that is comfortable, where your servants take good care of you and make you happy. I've been to Hedra Cottage. It is beautiful, but it is not a happy home. Mistress Mary is not well and may never be again. Your children are all just about grown and soon will be gone from you to make their own families. Make your home here. I, and the rest of this household, will make you happy."

Edmund was dumbfounded. His indignation at a servant remarking on the state of his personal life left his mind quickly upon hearing what seemed to be a shocking proposition. "What are you suggesting?"

"I am saying that you are an important man. You should not be bothered with such domestic affairs as the running of a plantation. You should be free to attend to the many duties of your offices. You need someone who can take care of you as a wife should. One who will make sure that you have everything you need and want, so you can be free to attend to more important things."

Edmund clearly understood that this girl was offering herself to him; but he could barely believe his ears. His anger was completely gone, having been replaced by lust. He was glad that he was seated at the table, so Anne could not see that he now had an erection which could not be hidden. He did not want her to see that she had struck him at his libidinous core. This had turned into a very different game than he had anticipated.

"What makes you think that you can give me what I need?"

"I am not sure I can my lord, but I do want to try. You see, I know that I need protection. I am at risk every day that I am living alone without my master. This is a dangerous colony. The savages may be under control, thanks to your military success, my lord. But there are more and more criminals being dumped here as indentures and slaves. A maid is not safe unless she is married or…"

"Or under someone's protection…"

"Yes, sir." Anne whispered as she lowered her head looking demurely at the floor.

"Didn't I hear that you are now married?"

Anne had a difficult choice. She had wrestled whether to come clean with him about Henry Toft. What would be the best way to win his trust? Now that the moment and the question were at hand, and he had asked her directly, she chose an answer that split the difference.

"My marriage is one of convenience, meant to discourage improper advances by opportunists. The fines for fornication with a married woman are higher than those with an unmarried one. I hoped that my being wed would keep unscrupulous men at bay, and buy me time until something more proper could be arranged."

Anne left out the part about Henry not being real. She hoped that she had told enough of the truth to be believable, and enough of the lie to still manipulate Edmund.

"I hoped, Colonel Scarborough," Anne continued, "that when I did secure a proper marriage that it would be simple to annul this one on the grounds that this one had not been consummated. Alas, I have become discouraged. There seems little chance of finding someone here in Northampton County. I have visited many of my neighbors and no family wants to take on a daughter in-law with no dowry. So, what I am proposing to you seems to be the only alternative I can conceive of at this time." Anne added this last part just in case Edmund's informants had gotten wind of her visits to the people listed in the *Friends and Neighbors* ledger.

"And what have I to gain from this proposal, besides a comfortable place to stay? What makes you think you could make me happy?"

Again, Anne was bold. She looked Edmund right in the eye. "You can teach me, my lord. I have not given my maidenhead to anyone yet. You could teach me how to please you."

Edmund tried not to gulp. The thought of deflowering an eager young virgin was very appealing, as opposed to being serviced by a wife who hated him or a bored, worn out whore. He felt like he would come in his pants at just the thought of teaching this pretty young thing "how to please" him. Anne snapped him back to reality with her next remark.

"Before I agree to serve you in this way, you and I will need to strike a bargain. I will be making a great sacrifice. I want you to reward me with more than just the honor of living here and working for you."

This was another twist Edmund had not anticipated. The girl was now going to negotiate a deal with him? "What exactly did you have in mind?"

"First, I want to be properly courted, giving us time to get used to each other before I give myself to you. By the fall equinox if I have not made you happy, my indenture will be complete, and I will leave to find work in another colony. You'll never see me again. But, if I have made you happy, you will sell me this plantation and everything on it including the servants and slaves for one pound, sterling. I will become your mistress and you can make your home here whenever you like and for as long as you like. I will promise to serve you and to keep making you happy. But know this, I will not stand for rough treatment. If you want this to work, you will treat me like a lady. I will not be treated like a common tart. I will be the mistress of this plantation and run it as I see fit. Is that clear?"

Edmund sat and stared at Anne. He was shocked by the provocative offer he had just heard and the audacity of her presumption that he would allow her to run the plantation. Instead of a simpering little maid that he might enjoy for a fortnight then relegate to his cooking and cleaning, he was sitting across the table from a formidable young woman.

She was trying to meet him head on. She was someone he might enjoy matching wits with. This could be fun. And, if it turned out to be too troublesome, he could always send her packing. He had easily gotten out of more binding contracts than this would be. There was very little risk that he could see at that particular moment. It did not take Edmund long to make up his mind to play the game with Anne.

He started to laugh a little and finally spoke, "How would this work, pray tell?"

"Most of my tasks can be accomplished by midday. While you are here, you and I can spend our afternoons and evenings together. You will court me as you would a lady. I will entertain you the way a lady would entertain a gentleman with literature and conversation. We will take walks and carriage rides together. At night, you and I will eat our dinner together. Then we will gather with the household for the evening entertainment.

"Afterward, you will sleep in the master's quarters. I will sleep in what used to be the nursery, with Fanta as my chaperone. The rest of the household will sleep in the servants' quarters. Over the course of the summer we will get to know each other and find out if we are compatible. If we are, those sleeping arrangements can change."

Knowing that nothing was going to happen right away, Edmund lost his erection. He thought about other noblemen who had these kinds of arrangements with courtesans. This privilege enjoyed by others of high station, appealed to his growing desire to be treated like royalty. Though he was impressed by Anne's attempt to draw him into such a brazen bargain, he did not intend to negotiate with a servant girl. The less he said, the less he was committed to. Edmund decided he would dangle the ownership of Chiconessex in front of Anne and begin an unrelentingly campaign to seduce her. He planned to chase her for as long as it amused him. Once he had gotten what he wanted, he had no intention of making her the mistress of Chiconessex or anything else.

So began their life together. Edmund and Jasper took up residence at the plantation with things arranged as Anne had suggested. What followed was not exactly the refined courtship she had proposed. Edmund looked for every opportunity to brush up against her, touching her buttocks and breasts. He made crude remarks and stared at her. He quietly approached her from behind and once close began blowing on her neck or stroking her hair. He was unrelenting in his pursuit of her and enjoyed making her squirm. Anne put him off with a variety of rebuffs.

"You do not have my permission yet to do that, sir!" or "Sir! Please, do not touch me that way." And finally, "Stop that!"

At first Anne felt a bit flattered by the attention. She struggled to keep her resolve from being betrayed by the natural urges of a young body blossoming into fertile womanhood. Part of her wanted to let him kiss her, to respond to her own arousal.

At night she lay awake waiting until she heard Fanta nearby in her bed, snoring softly. Then Anne rubbed her breasts and explored her clitoris and the lips of her vagina. She was tempted to probe between them with her fingers, but she dared not. Despite her inexperience she understood the basic biology of sex. She knew how children were created. She also knew that her hymen must be intact for her to be considered a virgin. It was a prize she would only be able to bestow once. No temporary self-gratification was worth losing it.

Anne satisfied herself as she dreamed of holding sexual power over a man. It was a delicious thought. She had read enough to know that the more she frustrated his efforts the more intense his longing for her would be – up to a point. She wanted to succeed like the Biblical Judith and Plutarch's Cleopatra using her coquettish charms to entice the man. She only hoped Edmund's seduction would not result in her being forced into whoring.

Anne knew she was taking a big risk without any promise of success. At any given moment it might all fall apart. She grew impatient to know if she was making progress. After a while, in her own sexual frustration, she became angry at Edmund's lewd disrespectful behavior.

He had not yet made any sort of promise to her. He seemed determined to have his own way without even suggesting that he might agree to her proposal. Finally, one day when she and Edmund were alone, a discouraged Anne had had enough. He had aggressively pushed her up against a wall and violently groped her. Frightened, then furious, she pushed him away.

"This is no way to court a lady. I would have you treat me with respect. If this is the way you plan to continue, I can pack and be gone by tomorrow."

Anne did not wait for a reply. She started to retreat to her room, but Edmund grabbed her by the arm and pulled her close. He tried to kiss her, but she wriggled free.

"I would have what is owed me. I thought you and I had a deal." he growled.

"We have nothing in writing. You've given me no promises. I have my indenture papers. My bond is complete as of September 20. You may not touch me unless I have a written agreement that you will sell Chiconessex to me.

"I will show you no affection. Nor will I accept any of your advances. And, if you are going to behave like a brute, then we may as well quit this experiment. Even if you offer twice what I have asked, I will sign no such agreement."

"What do you want from me, girl?" Edmund replied slamming his hand on a nearby table, knocking its contents on the floor. He was used to getting his way and he was starting to get tired of this nonsense.

Neither one of them had ever had any instruction on proper courting. Their lives had been very rustic. Though Edmund's family was aristocratic, he had lived in the Virginia colony since he was very young. His marriage to Mary Littleton had been arranged by their parents. Their courtship had consisted of a handful of chaperoned meetings in the parlor of her family home. From the beginning on their wedding night, sex had been quick and perfunctory. He had not asked permission nor cared about how Mary wanted to be treated. Life at Hedra Cottage with her had been of little interest to him. He rarely spent time with her or their children. To him they were merely chattel.

The fact that he and Mary had conceived six children had little to do with love or romance. He had done what he wanted to the woman, when he wanted to. She did not object or even respond to their sexual activity. He did not really care what she felt. As far as Edmund was concerned, Mary was just a brood mare provided to him to assure that there would be quality children to establish the Scarborough dynasty in the New World. Like every other aspect of his life, his only concern was that his own needs were met, preferably at the precise moment he became aware of them.

Edmund had not indulged in the fashion of reading novels of the day as Anne had. He could certainly read, but his education, conducted at home by a tutor, had primarily focused on military history, science, and law. As a young man he had otherwise filled his days with hunting and riding. He actually had very little experience with aristocratic culture. When he was in James City, his focus was on politics and trade. Occasionally, he had been invited into the finer homes there. Though he had socialized with the Governor and other important Burgesses, he had never attempted to master the complicated foppish etiquette practiced in the capital. He was much more comfortable in a tavern than in the stuffy confines of so-called decent society.

Because of her own peasant upbringing, Anne had even less experience than he did in such things. Her knowledge about romance came from what Bella had told her and what she found in the books in Owen's library. She had read about romantic heroes who brought their lady loves gifts, from the very small – a single rose – to the very grand – a palace decorated with gold and silk. And then there were chivalrous gestures like Sir Walter Raleigh laying his cloak in the mud, so his beloved Queen Elizabeth could keep her dainty feet dry and clean.

Anne realized that she had wrongly supposed that an educated person would have the same understanding about the poetic expectations of a genteel lady. All she wanted was some indication that he had even the smallest bit of affection for her. She needed something to allay her fear that he planned to treat her like a sort of sexual meal – to be devoured and immediately forgotten. She was becoming more and more worried that her plan was failing. She would have to explain to him what she was talking about.

"What I want, is for you to be kind to me. I want us to share jokes and stories. I want you to tell me about yourself. I want us to take walks and go riding. Do you only want to rut with me like a pig in the mud?"

Edmund did not respond. He had never had any interest in spending any real time in conversation with a woman – any woman. He had never had to be nice to his wife nor any of the prostitutes he saw frequently. As far as he could tell they had all been focused on pleasing him. That was their sole purpose in life. He had never even thought about pleasing a woman. He was having trouble conceiving of what it would mean to be kind to Anne.

He walked outside and lit his pipe wondering if this was not just a waste of time. Maybe he should just send Anne to another farm to finish out her indenture, so he could simply convert these fields for tobacco. The two did not speak for the rest of the day.

For the next several weeks Edmund remained at Chiconessex. He and Anne remained cool to each other. Anne kept the other servants working efficiently. The wheat field was planted on time. The men plowed the kitchen garden and fertilized it with cow manure. She and Fanta put in corn, carrots, potatoes, collard greens, and a variety of herbs. This year yams and okra were added to satisfy her agreement with the Africans.

The daily schedule followed some, though not all of what Anne had proposed. She kept to her plan to devote time to the needs of her master despite the fact that things had stalled between them. During the afternoons they did not have time for walks and talks. Instead aristocratic Edmund and his servant Jasper spent their time lying about smoking, eating, or holding court with a regular stream of visitors who came to do business.

This is when Anne proved herself to be a proficient secretary and congenial hostess. Edmund's associates began to make comments to him about what a lovely and helpful adornment she was. Slowly Edmund began to appreciate Anne's potential. She made herself useful by writing sales receipts and other documents for Edmund. Her script was far superior to either his or Jasper's, and they were happy to be waited on in any capacity. The access this provided Anne was very enlightening.

Unlike the kindly Owen Tomkin, when Edmund conducted business, he treated most people like peasants visiting nobility. His disdain for them was not masked in anyway. His more prestigious associates were received with only slightly better manners. On those few occasions when Anne was dismissed during such meetings, she listened in from behind the closed door.

From these bits and pieces, Anne began to understand Edmund's character better. She came to the conclusion that Giles Ishim had been right about what Edmund's overall goals were. He really did want to own the entire peninsula and actually establish his own kingdom. Anne learned that Edmund's father had come from a noble family. The senior Scarborough was the third son of his generation, and therefore had been relegated to serve in His Majesty's Cavaliers protecting the newly conquered territory of Virginia. His reward for military service was a sizeable portion of land there on the colony's Eastern Shore.

It was there that he raised his son Edmund to believe that his destiny was to establish a new branch of the English aristocracy with him as its king. He arranged for him to be married to Mary Littleton the daughter of another noble family who had a significant land grant in Virginia but little money to support it. His other son Charles was given in service to an influential physician who saw to his education and his placement within important political circles. Their sister Hannah had been married to James Wise, another son of a land-poor nobleman with a colonial grant. As far as Edmund the younger was concerned, what belonged to his siblings belonged to him. Nothing in his life so far had led him to think differently nor make any secret of his grand desires.

Edmund's trouble with the authorities stemmed from the fact that his actions were clear evidence of his naked ambitions. He had only evaded conviction for his aggressive and illegal tactics by the sheer luck of his family connections. All this came into focus for Anne when James and Hannah Wise came to visit.

Edmund's sister Hannah and her husband lived on a plantation across the creek from Chiconessex. The day they arrived unannounced; it was foggy with a light rain. Anne politely showed them into the parlor.

Hannah looked very much like Edmund. Their nose and jawlines could have been carved by the same sculptor. She and her husband were both well dressed and plump from living a life of leisure. They removed their soggy hats and cloaks to reveal that they both sported the fancy French wigs that had come into fashion back in England. Neither realized that their hairpieces were slightly askew. Hannah proudly patted the pile of horse hair that had been spun into the shape of a beehive with a row of small uniform spirals framing her face from ear to ear.

As Ann took their cloaks, she noticed that both wigs had gotten wet causing the dye in them to run. It was now staining the back of their necks and collars. James' black curls hung on either side of his face like a hound dog's long ears. The hairpieces coincidentally had a wet dog stench. Anne had to hold her breath standing near them. She found it amusing that their attempt at being stylish had failed somewhat comically. They looked ridiculous.

"Well, brother Edmund, I hear you have been staying here practically for months, and yet you have not seen fit to pay us a call. So, here we are on this dreary day, chilled and almost soaked to the bone, just to come see you. Is that anyway to treat your sister?"

Hannah offered her cheek for Edmund to kiss. He brought his face near to hers but did not fully comply with the unspoken request. He grunted something unintelligible and gestured toward chairs by the fire indicating they should sit down.

Now it was brother in-law James' turn to try and engage Edmund. "How are things going here, since you have taken over, Edmund?"

"Fine, just fine." Scarborough replied curtly.

James kept going. "You know, we'd be happy to take this place off your hands. With us being just across the creek it would make a nice addition to our plantation."

Still standing, Edmund ignored his brother in-law. He turned to ask Anne to bring in some hot tea. She had already anticipated the request and was setting up a tray with refreshments.

"Mistress Anne, will you get... oh I see. Here it is. Have some tea."

"Why thank you, Mrs. Toft. It is *Mrs.* Toft, isn't it?" Hannah spoke with the false courtesy every servant recognizes for the patronizing dismissal it really is.

"You are quite welcome. Yes, it is. Mistress *Henry* Toft." Anne smiled a little taking as regal a tone as she could muster.

"And the ever-present Mr. Darby, how are you this day?" Hannah looked past Anne to Jasper standing behind her.

"I am quite fine, Mistress Wise. Thank you for asking."

Edmund did not have much patience for his sister. "So, what did you come here for on this dreary day, Hannah?"

"Brother dear, we merely wanted to congratulate you on your campaign against the savages."

"What do you want, Hannah?"

"I want, uh we want…"

James interrupted his wife, "Hannah, this really is not necessary…"

"Shut up, James. Edmund, we want you to give us some of your Africans for our plantation."

"Give?" Edmund snorted with disdain at his sister's request.

"Most of our indentures are nearly done their contracts. You have wisely seen that slaves are a much better way to go and we want to replace our indentures with slaves."

"I can sell you two or three bucks, but I'm not giving them to you."

Hannah persisted despite her husband's continued protests. "We can't afford that. And why should we? I'm your sister. Why won't you make them a gift to me?"

"Because, you always have your hand out. You mismanage everything. Why can't you make out on your own? Last year my carpenters had to build you a corral for your wayward oxen. I wouldn't have had to do that if your stock had not wandered onto Mrs. Eltonhead's property mixing with her herd."

"Is it my fault the stupid yeoman cannot count and took back more than we lost?"

"Because when I rightfully butchered one of 'em, she sued me for stealing. That wouldn't have happened if your dimwitted husband was the least bit competent."

"I don't care what the silly council says. We had every right to retrieve them. And you took them from *me* without even asking." Hannah interjected at the same time as James began to object.

"See here now…"

"Everything you have belongs to me." Edmund went on, "I was perfectly within my rights to take them. Besides, why did you tell her *I* butchered them?"

"Who says we did? It's not our fault she holds a grudge against you. You're the one who cheated her out of the slaves you promised her dead husband."

The brother and sister were both on their feet and just about nose to nose by now. The disagreeable conversation was deteriorating.

"You don't know that." Edmund pushed Hannah back into her seat and went on, "You always have your hand out. You and everyone else in this damned family."

Hannah began to tear up as her husband tried to come to her defense. "Now, Edmund, we're all in this together. We have to look out for each other."

Edmund's was about to completely lose his temper, "When have you ever looked out for me? You always want something."

James tried to stand his ground saying, "Of course we look out for you! Who was it made sure brother Charles in London got your message during your time of need? It was he who got the Crown to press your case with Governor Bennett. Without his influence you would not have been pardoned. If it weren't for us, you'd be moldering in some dirty tavern somewhere waiting to be allowed back in the colony."

Edmund's face was bright red. Through a clenched jaw he gave in. "*Fine.* But I'm not givin 'em to you ya. It'll be like last time. I'll send a crew over to do the work you need next week."

"That's fine, Edmund, that's fine." James tried to sound soothing as he patted his sulking in-law on the back. "We'll need at least three men to put in the tobacco, and corn. They can fix our roof which began leaking last week too. That's all we need."

"Fine. Is that all?" Edmund snarled, refusing to look James in the eye.

Hannah started to object, "Why won't you just give us the men, so we won't have to ask…"

James interrupted, taking Hannah by the arm. "That's it. That's all we need. Come along, my dear. Let's let Edmund get back to his business."

He led his sputtering wife toward the door where Anne helped them with their cloaks. They quietly said their goodbyes with no response from Edmund.

Anne thought to herself, "So this is how the highborn treat their own. They certainly are a churlish lot."

She kept quiet as she cleared away the dishes. Edmund quickly recovered from the annoying encounter with his sister.

"Jasper, next week you go over there with William and our two boys here and take care of those chores at the Wise plantation. But do not let James or Hannah wheedle anything else out of you. And do not let him keep any of them slaves or add any other work. Ya hear?"

"Yes, m' lord." Jasper's reply was quick and subservient.

The foul aroma of the wet wigs still hung in the air, so Edmund lit his pipe and walked out onto the porch. Jasper did not follow him. He stared longingly at Anne as she opened a window a few inches to let in some fresh air.

Anne had been annoyed by Jasper's leering for some time. She was used to the unwanted attentions of men, but she worried that Jasper's interest in her would be noticed by Edmund. If she showed any sense of tolerating or encouraging Jasper, she could not predict how her master would react. If she gave Jasper any hope of succeeding with her, he would not stop. So, whenever she found herself alone with Jasper, she made an excuse to go somewhere else.

Anne opened the door to the servant's hall and called out "Fanta, there'll be…"

As she tried to make her exit. Jasper quickly crossed the room and grabbed her arm. Pulling her close to him he whispered in her ear, "Surely you can see that he comes from a wicked, corrupt breed. They are weak and stupid. Know this - I am the better man for you, Mistress Anne."

Anne pulled away from him. She did not reply except to give him an angry horrified look. Anne thought that the next time he tried to touch her she would give him a good crack in the head. That night Anne decided to try to send him a direct message and hopefully prevent the need for such an altercation. She chose the myth of Acteon and Diana from Ovid's Metamorphoses which seem to speak directly to their situation.

As she usually did, Anne embellished the story to make it even more dramatic than the book. She naively hoped this not so subtle warning to Jasper would get him to leave her alone. She could not have guessed how the telling of this tale would so infect the rest of her life.

"There once was a magical valley with an enchanted cypress grove known as Gargaphia. This was the sacred lair of the chaste goddess of the hunt, Diana. Local villagers had been warned to stay out of its mysterious dangerous woods. Tall trees blocked the sun there, and all that grew on the forest floor was a barbed thicket. Lost travelers could become ensnared in its thorns, leaving them to starve to death. One day a hunter named Acteon and his dogs became separated from their hunting party when they wandered into this frightful place in pursuit of a great stag. The further into its dark lush shadows Acteon chased his prey, the more lost he became.

"Soon, Acteon came upon a beautiful stone grotto. Though it was made by Mother Nature herself, it had a perfect arched opening more magnificent than anything produced by the most skillful stonemasons. Acteon looked inside to behold an even more wondrous site. There he saw the enchanting huntress queen, Diana.

"He immediately recognized this goddess, who was known for her beauty and her chastity. She had refused all suitors, choosing instead to remain a virgin living at Gargaphia, hunting in its forest with the nymphs who served her. There in her grotto, Acteon saw her standing next to a spring that bubbled from the stones, golden in the light of one hundred blazing candles all around the sacred chamber.

"Acteon bade his dogs lay down behind some bushes by the entry to the cave. There, thinking he was hidden from their sight, he watched Diana's nymphs attend to their queen at her bath. First, they took her bow and quiver of arrows and her helmet and laid them aside. Then they removed her sandals and her belt. They disrobed the goddess and when she stepped naked into the spring, they began to bathe her in its magical waters.

"Acteon was transfixed by what he saw, for nothing in his imagination had ever suggested such an incredible site. He became overwhelmed by passion and could not contain his moans of ardor for Diana.

"Suddenly, Diana and her nymphs heard Acteon. She cast a spell on the trespassing mortal. Acteon could not look away and was now powerless to move. Diana stepped out of the waters and bade her nymphs to dry her and anoint her with her sacred oils. While they did so Diana looked straight into the eyes of the smitten hunter.

"Now he was completely bewitched. That is when Diana turned her most dangerous powers upon him. She pointed at him and with her eyes glowing she said strange magical words that transformed him into a stag.

"Acteon's dogs seeing the creature, jumped up and started to bay ferociously. The startled deer tried to run away. But the dogs ran him to ground and savagely tore at his limbs. In horrific pain, he turned back into a human. As he lay dying, he was found by the other members of his hunting party. With his last breath, he told them what had happened and warned them not to go any further into the woods, lest they meet the same fate.

"The nymphs had by now finished clothing their queen. She appeared before the hunters saying, "Let this be a lesson to any man who would lust after the goddess Diana or trespass upon her sacred hunting grounds." The hunters were sorely afraid. They turned and ran all the way home to their village and vowed never to return to Gargaphia, the sacred grotto of the goddess Diana."

The household was mesmerized by Anne's performance. Both Edmund and Jasper began to fidget in their seats. The story had aroused them. They each thought it was a message to them. For many nights to follow their dreams were haunted by visions of their own erotically hypnotic death at the hands of their quarry: the goddess Anne.

It was now the end of May, and the annual General Assembly of the Virginia House of Burgesses was to be held in James City. Edmund was required to attend. He and Jasper were glad to leave their sexual frustrations behind them. They gathered their things to make the journey while Anne and Fanta packed a rucksack with a wine bladder, bread, and smoked deer jerky for them to take with them.

As they rode away, the men looked back at the lovely young woman standing on the porch. Their minds were not on the legislature. Jasper was wondering if there was any way to get his master to lose interest in this young woman, so he could have her for himself. Edmund was thinking about finding a whore in James City who would let him do all the things he wanted to do to Anne.

A Wedding of Sorts

While in James City, Edmund and the other burgesses received official word that not only were Cromwell's Roundheads out of power, but Parliament was finally meeting again. That previous April, Charles II had been recognized as the rightful Stuart King. He granted a general amnesty to the opposition, paid off the army, and settled many other disputes with his Declaration of Breda. The Virginia assembly was optimistic that stability and prosperity were in their futures as a result.

Edmund was not as enthusiastic about all those glad tidings. Years of political strife had served as a convenient cover for him to get away with violating English trade embargos. He had illegally traded with certain Dutch captains, and under the guise of privateering had his own small fleet raid the ships of others. If sanctions were lifted, black market profits would drop.

Edmund did not let his concerns show. Instead, the Colonel threw his support behind returning Governor William Berkley, who tended to overlook the excesses of his fellow nobles. Like Edmund, he was less sympathetic to the new class of low born landowners who had worked off their indentures. Berkley and Scarborough shared a distinctly old-fashioned prejudice that these people would never be their equals, and that they were still owed feudal loyalty from them.

Feudalism had officially been abolished almost 300 years prior, following the Peasant's Revolt. It was ironically in Scarborough's ancestral home of Walsham, back in England, that the serfs won the right to demand wages for their labor, and were no longer tied like livestock to the estates of their lords. Since then, the aristocracy did everything they could to get around this. Noble born children were still taught that they were entitled to take any measure they saw fit to keep the serfs under their boots.

Edmund was no exception. His family carried a hereditary sense of bitterness for having historically lived at the center of the battle where the English nobles lost these rights. Feeling no pangs of conscience, Edmund rarely thought twice about mistreating people he considered beneath him.

During most of Edmund's nights in James City he could be found in a comfortable bed at his favorite brothel where he attempted to satisfy his carnal appetites. Edmund only grudgingly attended the obligatory social events given by the Governor. He perversely found spending time with his genteel equals to be tedious. He much preferred the company of rough soldiers whose bidding he could command when it pleased him. At the Governor's parties he had to behave within the confining limits of courtly propriety.

During this stay in the capital, he found himself the subject of a kindness campaign by former Governor Richard Bennett who had previously been a legal burr under his saddle. Bennett hoped to get Edmund to move forward on an arrangement they had struck a few years back: the betrothal of his daughter Elizabeth to young Charles Scarborough.

Bennett desperately wanted a political alliance with Scarborough. This was not just because he was looking out for his own prospects — which he was. He was a well-known Puritan reformer and a political opportunist. Having been a supporter of Oliver Cromwell's now ousted Roundheads, he was looking for ways to defend his family now that new factions were forming among Virginia's burgesses following the restoration of the Stuart monarchy. There was much discussion about protecting the Crown and the Church of England from anyone who might try to take power as Cromwell had.

Politics is always a complex game of strategic sometimes strange alliances. Arranged marriages were one way to accomplish such relationships. Edmund may have had his peccadillos, but he had a long-standing record of being a staunch supporter of the Church. Bennett believed Edmund could be counted on to defend the status quo with his militia, just as he had against insurgent natives on the Eastern Shore. By ending the old animosity between them he hoped to feather his own nest and gain an ally in case there was a purge against Puritans.

Bennett began by complimenting Edmund on his recent victories over the Indian tribes. Then he sweetened the pot. "Colonel Scarborough, you would be perfect to serve as our High Sheriff for Northampton County. I'd like to bring your name forward to the Governor."

"I'm honored by your faith in me." Edmund replied cautiously trying to feign modesty.

Scarborough did not need to ask what his duties would be. He knew the post of High Sheriff involved enforcing the law: arresting people who committed crimes, and collecting taxes, court levied fines, debts, even church tithes. It was an open secret that the Sheriff was entitled to skim off a reasonable cut of any money collected. The most common form of currency was tobacco certificates that represented tobacco harvested and sold at auction. Otherwise people had to pay with livestock or forfeiture of their land. Edmund's mind did the quick and mercenary math. No matter what form it took, as Sheriff he could acquire a great deal more wealth, power, and most importantly acreage.

So, he let Bennett curry his favor. When the suggestion was finally broached that they formalize the betrothal between their children, Edmund pretended that he thought they were too young. He would only agree to move ahead if the youngsters could have a long engagement. Scarborough suspected that things in Parliament could be unstable for some time. If he could secure the appointment of High Sheriff now, he could build up his resources regardless of how things worked out politically. He struck a deal with Bennett never fully intending to see it through unless when the time came, it suited his needs.

The two gentlemen drank a toast to their friendship, and then a few more to their new king, their children, and the colony until they ran out of people to toast. Soon Bennett was in his cups. Edmund decided maybe this old fool might be able to help him with his problem with Anne. Under the guise of seeking advice for his son, he began picking Bennett's brain for ideas.

"Children are much more demanding than you and I were brought up to be. Especially the girls. When I was betrothed, my dear wife and I did as we were told. There was no question. I hear tell many young women require they be courted. My Charles may need to woo your sweet Elizabeth. I never had to debase myself in that way, so I have no advice to give the boy. What would you advise I tell him?"

By now Bennett was happily slurring his words. "So drue, so drue. Iz aall come down to a zearies of giffs. He sould start smaaall. Posey's, books – hic – of poetry. My girl loooves poetry. As they get clozer to za wedding – bigger gifts. Jewelry. A horse and carriage!!"

Bennett's eyes were bulging, and he swung his arms spilling some of his drink.

Edmund thanked his new comrade, "This conversation has been most illuminating. I fear the hour is getting late and I must retire. Thank you, Richard. I see many better days ahead of us."

He signaled to Bennett's man servant to help his master to his carriage. Edmund followed them out into the cool night air which made his mind a little less bleary from drink. As he walked to his lodging, he made a plan to follow Bennett's advice. If he had not been so smitten with Anne, he never would have considered it. The truth was the tarts he paid to service him could not satisfy him. He had to close his eyes and think of Anne just to reach an orgasm. He wanted her now more than ever. If buying her gifts, was the price he had to pay to have her, so be it.

In the days that followed Edmund went on what can only be called a shopping spree. He began at the stationer buying 50 sheets of vellum and 75 of parchment. He bought a supply of ink and several quills. While there, he saw a very special large white swan plume. It was lovely and feminine, perfect for Anne's work. Next Edmund visited the bookseller. He said he was looking for gifts for his wife: poetry and romance.

"You are a Cavalier sire, so of course you will want to give her the latest Cavalier poetry. This one by Robert Herrick, Hesperides, is perfect for you. It has mythic odes and poetry perfect for lovers."

The shopkeeper then directed him to classics like The Whole Works of Homer by George Chapman, and a translation of the Spaniard Cervantes' Don Quixote. His final recommendation was a play by Ben Johnson called Cynthia's Revels. Edmund was sold when he heard it described as a virtuous retelling of the tale of the goddess Diana and the hunter Acteon in honor of her majesty Queen Elizabeth.

"I'll take all four."

His final stop was at a tavern which Edmund knew to be frequented by thieves and pirates. He had sent Jasper ahead to make a connection with a smuggler who was well known for dealing in fine jewelry. The three men huddled at a table under the only window in the dark pub.

The anonymous jewel purveyor sat just in the shadows, with his hat pulled low so his face would be hard to see. He showed Edmund several pieces. The one that caught his eye was a gold necklace with a large brilliant blue sapphire. He held it up to the light to see the stone's clarity much to the chagrin of the outlaw. Edmund tested the clasp which held firm as he began haggling. Edmund was just about to walk away when the price was lowered just enough so he could feel like he had made a good deal.

At the conclusion of the General Assembly, Edmund prepared to return to Chiconessex with plans for an all-out romantic assault on Anne. He sent Jasper ahead to find him a bay mare and a saddle. This was the final weapon he needed for his amorous war chest. He planned to have it delivered at just the right moment. Just as he had defeated the Indian tribes, he intended to systematically defeat Anne's defenses against him. He tried in vain to contain his high spirits when he arrived at the plantation the day of the summer solstice.

Edmund bellowed for William to come for his horse after dismounting. Anne and Fanta were out of earshot in the summer kitchen so no one had come out to greet him. Edmund was disappointed but took the time alone to carry small trunk upstairs to his bedchamber. There he unpacked the writing materials and took them down stairs. Just as he entered the parlor, so did Anne.

"My lord! When did you arrive?"

"Just this moment, Mistress Anne. Where is William? I need him to attend to my mount."

Anne explained the men were fishing and offered to take care of the horse. She quickly left to do this without waiting for Edmund to respond. Once she had taken the stallion to the corral, and removed his saddle, she led him on a cool down walk around the enclosure. When she returned to the parlor, Edmund like his horse, was pacing the room trying to stay cool.

"I bought some supplies while I was in James City. Unpack them and put them away."

Anne did as she was told without even looking at Edmund. She opened his leather satchel pulling out the sheathes of parchment and vellum. She took them over to the sideboard and put them in the drawer with the remaining supply of paper there.

"There's more. Don't forget to put away the rest."

Rolling her eyes Ann removed the rest of the contents, first three bottles of ink, and then the quills.

"That, uh, um, that big one, that quill is for you. It looked like the kind a woman should use. So, um, er, you may have it."

Anne was thrilled. "He is giving in." she thought.

Out loud she demurred politely, "Why thank you my lord. That was very thoughtful of you."

She slowly touched her face and neck provocatively with the large feather as she continued, "I shall make good use of it. You have had a long journey. Would you like some refreshment?"

"Good. I mean, um, no. I'm not hungry. Well, uh, bring me some ale. Yes, that, um, yes, that will be fine." Edmund was practically sputtering.

Anne went to the barrel to pour him a drink. With her back turned she smiled feeling confident that the battle of lust was finally being won. She curtsied prettily as she presented him with his ale. That is when Jasper Darby arrived.

Edmund immediately started giving him orders. "Darby, tomorrow I want you to go pick up those things I had you store and deliver them here tomorrow, first thing."

"Tomorrow, but…"

"I changed my mind. Tomorrow. Just do it."

"Yes, my lord."

Edmund had decided, upon seeing Anne, to speed up his plan. He was not patient by nature and just the sight of her playing with the feather quill had stirred up his libidinous frustrations again. Though he was tired of waiting, he resisted the urge to get down on his knees and beg her to accept him. He did not want to spook her. He thought of her like a pony that needed to be saddle broken. He would have a much better ride if she learned to take the bit willingly.

That night when the household gathered, instead of hearing the story Anne had planned, Edmund presented her with the four books he had bought in James City.

"Mistress Anne, these books are a gift for you."

"Why, Colonel Scarborough! I am deeply flattered and most grateful. You have found my weakness, for there is little that I love more than books such as these." Anne pretended to be surprised by his sudden generosity, but after receiving the quill earlier in the day, her confidence had swelled in anticipation of more to come.

"Why don't you read us the first chapter of Don Quixote?" Edmund suggested, "The bookseller describes it as a great story of chivalry."

Anne opened the book and began to read, *"Somewhere in La Mancha, in a place whose name I do not care to remember, a gentleman lived not long ago, one of those who has a lance and ancient shield on a shelf and keeps a skinny nag and a greyhound for racing…"*

After Anne had finished the chapter, she asked William to play a tune on his fiddle. Edmund, who had never taken an active part in the entertainments, interrupted, announcing he had something to finish the evening with. He picked up Hesperides and read aloud the poem *"To the Virgins, to Make Much of Time."*

"Gather ye rosebuds while ye may,
Old Time is still a-flying;
And this same flower that smiles today
To-morrow will be dying.

The glorious lamp of heaven, the sun,
The higher he's a-getting,
The sooner will his race be run,
And nearer he's to setting.

That age is best which is the first,
When youth and blood are warmer;
But being spent, the worse, and worst
Times still succeed the former.

Then be not coy, but use your time,
And, while ye may, go marry:
For having lost but once your prime,
You may forever tarry."

Everyone understood this was a not so subtle message meant for Anne. When everyone retired that night, Malike and Botwe were the only ones who slept soundly. The full implication of what was happening was not completely lost on them. They just thought that it was unlikely that any of it was going to change their lives. Fanta lay awake thinking that Anne was still a long way from achieving her goal and even if she did, Fanta did not trust her to keep her word. She was sure that she would be betrayed.

William tossed and turned, feeling like a father whose daughter was about to marry an evil man; knowing full well that a cur like Edmund had gone to his chamber to masturbate and dream of the pleasures he would have with Anne.

Jasper, knowing this too, quietly stared at his ceiling in despair. He thought he had pledged his loyalty to a great ruler with a God-given royal destiny. Jasper was deeply disappointed to realize that Edmund was just another ordinary man with human weaknesses that could be his undoing. Jasper had accepted his vices of gluttony and bullying as the inherent foibles of privilege. Nobility were entitled to sinful liberties as their reward for the heavy burdens of leadership.

What made the impending union of Anne and Edmund break Jasper's heart was that he wanted her for himself. Jasper's undeserving master would have his way, while he would have to watch, powerless to stop it.

The only person who was truly happy that night was Anne. Her thoughts darted from one anticipation to another. She thought of how much fun the ultimate seduction might be. As she drifted off to sleep, her mind turned to changes she would make once Chiconessex belonged to her, how she would make it more profitable.

The next day began as most other days on the plantation. Anne and the other servants went about their usual tasks. Just before the noonday meal Jasper arrived, having left early on an errand for his master. He was walking both his horse and another when Edmund called Anne out to the porch.

"I have bought you this fine bay mare as gift, Mistress Anne. Do you remember the one we saw at the fair last year?"

"I, I do. Yes, I do. She is beautiful. Colonel Scarborough, you have been so generous since your return from James City…"

Edmund interrupted taking her by the hand. "Jasper you tend to the horses and stay outside. Come inside, Anne, and let us talk there."

Once back in the parlor, Edmund dismissed Fanta who was setting the table for their lunch. "Go on Fanta, that will be all for now. Go on, get out and shut the door."

"What is it, Colonel?" Anne said quietly.

"Mistress Anne, Anne, that is, I mean…" Edmund struggled to get out the words. "Anne, I have decided to sell this horse to you. I want you to own it, you yourself. I want you to write up a bill of sale. Get some ink, and paper, and, um, your new quill."

Anne did as she was asked. She moved the dishes aside and sat down at the table. Edmund dictated the document and they both signed it.

"We'll get Jasper to come in and witness it in a few moments. Now, um, uh, we have, uh, another piece of business to attend to." Edmund went to the cabinet where his papers were kept and brought a document to the table. As he unfolded it before her, Anne saw that it was the deed to Chiconessex.

"I have decided to agree to your terms. If you will become my mistress for the rest of your natural life, I - I will sell you Chiconessex."

Anne looked intently at Edmund for a moment. She then turned to read the document, taking her time to thoroughly examine it. "The terms were Chiconessex and everything on it, the crops, the hunting and fishing rights, the livestock, slaves, and any indenture contracts associated with the land. All mine to do with as any other landowner would. Write that out plainly at the end of this document. Once we have both signed it with Jasper and William as our witnesses, then and only then, will I be yours."

Edmund walked over to the door and yelled for Jasper. His voice screeched as he called for his servant. "Jasper! Jasper, get William and get in here now!"

While they waited for the men, Edmund came back to the table. Anne handed him the large white quill. He was still writing when the men entered the room. Both looked worried.

"You two are our witnesses to this document. This document makes Mistress Toft the owner of Chiconessex and everything on it. I have signed it. Mistress Anne…" Edmund was shaking a little as handed the quill back to her.

Anne read Edmund's additions to the deed. Satisfied, she signed her name. She handed the pen to Jasper who signed his name. William could not read. He did not know whether the agreement said what Edmund said it did. He really did not know how to write anything except his name. Owen Tomkin had taught him to do so many years before for just this sort of service. He could not help but think how dismayed his former master would be if he were alive to see this.

"That will do. That is all. That will do. Go on now. Take everyone somewhere. Get out. Go on."

Anne and Edmund were now alone. He pulled her from her seat and kissed her full on the mouth, then her cheeks and her neck. When he began to paw at her breasts, she pulled away. Things were happening very quickly.

"My lord, won't you allow me to give myself to you in the privacy of your bed chamber?" Anne took his hand and pulled him toward the stairway and they quickly went up the steps.

Once in his room he told Anne to disrobe as he removed his doublet and his breeches. Anne could see his erect penis as she removed her bodice, her skirt, and then lifted her shift over her head.

Edmund took hardly a second to enjoy the view then pushed her onto the bed and climbed on top of her. At exactly the moment that his cock touched her bare thigh, he climaxed spilling his seed on her leg.

In complete humiliation and angry frustration, Edmund rolled away. His face was red. His jaw was clenched and his lips pursed. He punched the bed next to Anne and yelled. "Aargh! God damn it! Damn it!"

Anne was not really sure what had happened. At just that moment he reminded her of the Tomkin boys when they were having a tantrum. Nothing like this was described in any of the books she had read. She only knew he was angry and that if he left that room unhappy all her plans could fall apart. She leaned over timidly to stroke his head.

Edmund pushed her hand away angrily then began to gruffly suckle her breasts. He became aroused again. Anne tried to think of what she could say that would make things go better. The only words that she could muster were "My lord…"

Edmund did not want his concentration disturbed. "Shut up. Don't talk." He put his hand over her mouth with one hand and used the other to guide his engorged cock between her legs.

The pain of penetration for the first time made Anne wince and cry out. Edmund quickly reached orgasm with the realization that Anne's maidenhead had been given to him and him alone. He rolled off of Anne with tears in his eyes, laughing.

Anne had not really known what to expect from sexual relations. She had not anticipated nor experienced the pleasure possible for a woman. Even with the embarrassing false start, it was not horrible. As for the pain, Anne thought that a splinter she once gotten on her finger using an old broom had felt worse than this. All those months of expectation had been building towards an act that was over in just a few moments.

Anne thought, "If this is all that it takes to satisfy the man, life as his mistress at least will not break my back."

Edmund was now feeling very proud of himself. He had achieved his heart's desire. "My beautiful Anne! I have never felt such bliss. You are my queen, my goddess. I will worship you forever." Edmund suddenly bolted out of bed. "I have something else I want to give you. Up, up. Get up. Come stand in the light where I can behold your loveliness."

Edmund took her hands and pulled her out of bed and over to the window where the midday sunshine streamed in, bathing the young woman in a golden beam. Anne felt awkward after the haste of their erotic skirmish. Her hair had come untied and now hung about her shoulders in a tangled mess. Though she looked beautiful, almost magical standing in the light, she felt exposed, wishing she could cover herself.

Edmund turned and began rummaging through one of his trunks. He pulled out a brown velvet bag from which he produced the gold necklace with the sapphire pendant. He put it around her neck and stood back to admire his new possession. Then, he abruptly returned to the chest and brought back a signet ring.

Edmund kneeled in front of Anne as he spoke, "This was my father's ring. I give it to you as my pledge to always be your champion, your very own cavalier. Swear that you will wear it always as a sign that you belong to me, in the name of Christ Jesus."

He tried to put the ring on the ring finger on her left hand. It was a bit too large, so he moved it to the first finger.

"Swear it."

"I swear…" Anne murmured, suddenly feeling a hot painful flush of guilt for making a false promise before God.

Edmund began kissing her hand which she held out in front of her pubis. He inhaled deeply the peppery aroma of her musk mixed with his semen. His lips suddenly found her clitoris which he kissed, then licked, and then sucked as she began to moan quietly. He became aroused once again.

"My golden girl… finally my dreams have come true. My golden girl is mine, all mine."

Edmund rose, then picked Anne up and carried her the few steps to the bed. There he spread her legs and climbed atop her again. This time things took a little longer.

Between moans Edmund declared "Oh, my cock is finally happy inside my golden girl."

Breathing heavily, he rolled off Anne again. He was smiling.

Anne was keenly aware that her work was not done. His ego would need to be stroked. "I never dreamed that to serve my lord this way would give me so much pleasure. Did I satisfy you my lord?"

"Oh, yes. Oh yes. You are my every dream come true. You are tight and sweet. You are luscious. Oh yes."

Edmund began kissing her chest and before Anne knew it, he was at her again. His humping and huffing went on for some time. Anne started to feel painfully dry until Edmund finally came. Now, they were both exhausted. He fell asleep still on top and inside her.

As Edmund snored in her ear, Anne looked up at the ceiling thinking "Will it be like this all the time? This is not going to be as easy as I thought."

Anne began to drift off until, though he was still sleeping, Edmund became erect once again. He began grinding his hips. Anne felt raw. Edmund awoke with a snort. Realizing where he was, he almost immediately reached orgasm.

Relieved, Anne pushed him aside. The man quickly fell into a deep slumber. She tried to stand up. Her legs buckled. She was sore and weak, but she made her way to the door. She opened it calling out hoarsely, "Fanta. Fanta"

When there was no reply Anne put her shift on and went to the top of the steps to call again. It was William who came to the bottom of the stairway. "What is it, Mistress Anne? Are you alright?"

"Yes, I'm fine. Tell Fanta to bring fresh bathing water to my room."

Anne slipped quietly into her bedchamber and stood shivering until Fanta arrived carrying a pitcher of water. The slave helped her mistress bathe and put on a nightgown. Anne got into bed, falling asleep almost immediately. Though it felt like just a few moments had passed, she was awoken a few hours later by Edmund bellowing.

"Anne! Get dressed and let us have our supper. Put on your prettiest dress."

Anne could hear Edmund bounding down the stairs calling back to her, "Come, come. I am in need of a meal. Fanta! Get in here with food!"

Anne put on the dress with bluebirds embroidered on the bodice, the one she wore to the harvest fair last summer. She brushed her hair then pinned it into a bun at the nape of her neck. She touched the sapphire pendant still hanging just above her breasts. She looked down at the signet ring, a heavy weight on her left hand.

That night the couple toasted each other with glasses of port at what could best be described as their nuptial supper. Their unconventional erotic wedding rites were not something that would be considered legal in the eyes of the law or the church. Though this sort of arrangement was by no means unusual among the ruling class, to the rest of society, theirs was an immoral unholy union. At that particular moment neither cared, because they were both busy calculating how to best take advantage of their new partnership.

"You should dress like this every day. My mistress must only ever be seen in the very finest. I will send for the dressmaker in James City to fit you for a new wardrobe. Sunday you will accompany me to church and you will sit in my box by my side, so I can show you off."

"Won't that be a little crowded with your wife?"

"I may not be able to divorce her, but no longer must I suffer her wretched company, except when absolutely necessary. I will see her and the children tomorrow and tell them how I want them to conduct themselves now. According to other nobles, this is how these things are done in the finest houses of England. I will arrange for them to attend church elsewhere. They will be well provided for. I suppose I will still have to agree to keep spending some portion of the year at Hedra Cottage in order to maintain the legal proprieties. A month at Yuletide, like I have done in the past..."

Edmund rambled on for some time, thinking out loud about how to bring his affairs into the new order.

"My darling," Anne purred. "If you would like I would be happy to put all this in writing. It might be advisable to have Mary and the children sign something so that they are bound to follow your wishes on these matters. You wouldn't want them to retaliate by selling anything that belonged to you but which has perhaps been put in their name."

Edmund looked at her intently, trying to decide whether Anne was trying to manipulate him. "Oh, damn! This could get complicated."

"It'll be alright. We can work on a long-term solution later. For now, we'll include a clause that prohibits Mary or the children from selling anything without your written approval."

Anne got up from the table, walked around to him and began massaging his neck and upper back. He turned, looking up at her lovely face then pulled her close putting his face between her breasts. He began to fondle her bottom.

Anne tried to pull away saying "Now, my darling, we have plenty of time for that. Let me write this all down for you while it is still fresh in your mind and then we can make love."

"Oh God, I just want to fuck you right here and now."

"Be patient my darling." Anne whispered and twisted free of his grasp. She walked over to the writing cabinet. Out came paper, ink, blotter, and her special quill. Knowing how it aroused him, she again playfully whisked it across her face and neck.

"Fanta, come clear the dishes." she called out.

Fanta came quickly into the room and gathered the plates and utensils. Anne instructed her to leave tankards and some ale. "Tell the others there will be no story tonight. Tell William to play sweet lullabies on his fiddle. Now leave us for the night. We will be retiring early."

Edmund grinned at her like a love-sick teenager as she began to write the document that he would take to his family the next day. Anne read aloud the first phrases: "This is to certify that we the undersigned members of the family of Colonel Edmund Scarborough do solemnly swear to... You dictate, and I will write..."

Edmund sputtered, "Yes um, well let's see, aahh... Alright, here it is. ...do solemnly swear to sell no property – comma – real or personal – comma – without the express permission of our Lord

Colonel Edmund Scarborough. Written permission. Make sure it says written permission."

He continued, "We – comma – the undersigned children of Edmund Scarborough – comma – agree to see to the care of Mistress Mary Scarborough our mother – period. What else?"

"We should include your promise to provide for them financially and to spend Yuletide with them though you will reside elsewhere. That way they will have confidence that you will keep your word."

"I don't care if they have confidence or not. I'm the head of this family and by God they damn well better sign for no other reason than I've asked it of them." Edmund huffed.

"Do you want to spend your whole day arguing with a madwoman? Make sure the children agree first. Once they have signed it, she'll have no choice. The sooner it's done the sooner you can come back here, my dear."

Anne gently rubbed her pendant with the two middle fingers of her left hand as if to direct Edmund's attention to the signet ring and her breasts. Resisting her flirtations was now pointless. He stared and nodded his head. As she wrote out the necessary additions to the document, they could hear William's fiddle playing down the hall.

Once her task was complete, she put the pen down and said; "We'll read it again tomorrow, and then I will make a copy, so that you and the family both have one."

Edmund nodded again as she walked over, lifted her skirts and sat on his lap saying "What was it you said you wanted to do, my darling?"

His erection was immediate. Anne unlaced her bodice giving him access to her nipples which he grabbed and took into his mouth like a greedy infant. Controlling Edmund, bending him to her will turned out to be a sort of aphrodisiac. Now Anne was fully aroused as he shifted her into position so he could enter her and show her how he wanted her to ride him. As soon as he climaxed, she experienced her first real orgasm. Waves of intense pleasure spread across her body as she relished the satisfaction of her success that day.

Anne went to bed knowing that it would take a lot more work to accomplish all that she had set out to do, even though the first and perhaps most important part of her plan had been achieved. It gave her the confidence to move on to the next part. Though physically exhausted she lay awake listening to Edmund snore and plotting how next to proceed.

Edmund and Jasper left the next morning as soon as Anne finished the duplicate of the contract. As soon as they were out of sight, she found the deed for Chiconessex and hid it in the back of the *Friends and Neighbors* ledger. Then she gathered William and the Africans together to let them know what was happening. She had a little speech prepared.

"I have made great progress on my plans. Chiconessex is now mine. Within five years' time I will deliver on all the promises I made to you. I will need your loyalty, your obedience, and most of all your faith in my promises. You must trust me. Do you understand?"

If they had any misgivings, her servants kept them to themselves and nodded in the affirmative. So began Anne's life with the Great Conjurer, with sexual manipulation and dangerous secrets.

The Colonel's Mistress

In the days that followed their illicit wedding, Anne swiftly took control of Edmund's daily life. She arranged for things she thought he would be pleased by. Keeping all of his appetites satisfied was the key to manipulating him. The daily routine of chores and accommodating guests was now augmented by sexual games to keep the master amused.

Edmund was also eager to please his mistress. He asked what kind of gifts he could buy for her. Anne did not want to appear to be too greedy by asking for more jewelry or clothes, which he had already promised.

"If you will ask the bookseller to regularly send the latest volumes, then you and I can be entertained just like the royal court in London." she said.

Anne truly cherished her books. Reading was the one pleasure she indulged in just for herself. Her request pleased him because it fed his aspiration to live like a noble. This became another of Anne's more clever talents: to make Edmund think that something she wanted was actually his own great desire.

Having sex with Edmund quickly became a chore. He did not respond to her needs. He did not really care if she felt any pleasure or if he left her frustrated just short of reaching an orgasm. Once he was satisfied, he moved on to whatever he wanted next: sleep, food, or drink. The only way Anne could get past the drudgery of it was to imagine that she was experiencing the romantic situations she had read about in her books.

Sometimes she outright invited Edmund to pretend along with her, suggesting that they act out some scene so she could say the name of a character out loud without making him jealous. Again, she had figured out how to present such a provocative idea in a way that fed Edmund's enormous ego rather than challenging it. Edmund was so happy with the arrangement it never occurred to him that the young woman was deceiving him in anyway.

As the weeks went by, the besotted Edmund began to trust Anne more and more. She quietly made suggestions that served to his advantage on almost every business deal that transpired with visiting tradesmen and merchants. Soon he sought her advice not only on his legitimate transactions, but on his more surreptitious business.

Anne took her time before trying to take any overt benefit from her influence over him. She knew that if he became suspicious, her life could quickly become endangered or at least very unpleasant. She had to carefully learn what all his vulnerabilities were before she could systematically destroy him.

Her first tentative attempt to influence Edmund began whenever he mused about whether to hire more indentured servants or import more slaves. He already owned almost one hundred Africans who did the harder labor on his other farms. Anne demurely suggested that the available land was limited. She reminded him that it was more important right now to buy as much acreage as possible and that the headrights system was still the best way to do that and have the help needed to run the plantation. It had worked in the past so he acquiesced to her judgement.

It helped that Anne actually believed this advice. She thought of slavery the way the people back in Robin Hood's Bay did. They resented being enslaved in all but name by the Lord of their Manor.

Meanwhile Anne's nights were still plagued by dreams of Granny being arrested by that corrupt aristocrat. Now when they woke her in the middle of the night, she used the prayer of Judith to bolster her resolve: *"Give me constancy in my mind, that I may despise him: and fortitude that I may overthrow him. For this will be a glorious monument for thy name, when he shall fall by the hand of a woman."*

Though she was motivated by this mission, it did not cloud her vision. Anne had the foresight to see beyond it. She recognized that the headrights system could not last forever. Every day there was less and less land on the peninsula that needed settling just as the number of indentured servants who had completed their contracts multiplied. Ultimately, the headrights system was leading to freedom for many people just like her. Once their contracts were up, newly unencumbered indentures had more autonomy in the colonies than they ever would have had back in England. It was their pathway to becoming landowners in their own right. However, there was a limit on the acreage available. Anne could see a clash coming between unemployed indentures and slave owners.

Anne dared not openly try to prick Edmund's tiny conscience by suggesting it was better for humanity to give people a path to freedom. Those were revolutionary ideas. For now, the most she could do was try and talk him into keeping his focus on increasing the size of his growing kingdom.

Her greatest obstacle to controlling things was not Edmund himself, but his lieutenant Jasper Darby. He was not happy about Anne supplanting him as Edmund's most valued advisor. As much as he lusted after her, he did not trust her. The Colonel had brought a small company of soldiers to live in the bunkhouse at Chiconessex. Jasper was put in charge of them and enjoyed a greater rank than they did. This kept him busy supervising them or running errands. He was rarely invited to participate in his master's business as he had been in the past. To be demoted this way, in favor of this lowborn woman, was humiliating.

Though he was careful not to let Edmund see it, Jasper continued to leer at Anne and make suggestive remarks. He could not bear to listen to her evening entertainments without letting his desires show on his face. So, he made excuses to leave the servants' hall quickly after dinner each night to drink and quietly pleasure himself while thinking of her. Of course, this merely added to his frustration. Jasper became increasingly surly, especially toward Anne and Fanta. His pent-up desire became an evil boiling brew that would eventually consume the unhappy man.

Summer soon faded into fall at Chiconessex. One crisp morning Edmund decided that he wanted to take Anne on what he called an "adventure."

"Fanta, pack us some food and a blanket for your mistress. We'll be gone all day. Come, darling Anne, I have a special place I want to show you. William, hitch up the carriage with Mistress Anne's mare. You drive us. Jasper, bring three men to follow along as our guard."

Edmund never traveled anywhere without protection. His past military actions against the natives made him a target. He also liked to travel with a well turned out entourage to rub his high station in the noses of his lowly neighbors. On this outing, Edmund would not have the opportunity to show off his handsomely dressed guards or his lovely young mistress.

The Colonel's intended destination was a piece of property north and east of Chiconessex where there were few settlements. It took the travelers more than three hours through woods and meadows over what barely passed for a trail let alone a road. It was a rough ride. Anne was nearly jostled right out of the open carriage bruising her rear end. Edmund had refused to reveal where they were going. Anne had a sick feeling in the pit of her stomach. She worried that she had misread Edmund and that he was planning something terrible for her.

When they finally stopped in what appeared to be a recently cleared field, Edmund hopped out of the carriage. He held out his hand to assist Anne.

"This is where we will build our castle. This is where we will hold court." Edmund declared spreading both arms wide. He pulled Anne close and whispered, "This will be your very own Gargaphia, my goddess."

Edmund then continued in full volume, "This will be the finest house in all the colonies. I have ordered the best building materials: English oak, French furnishings, and more! What do you think, my darling?"

"I, well, I, I am overwhelmed with the possibilities, my lord." Anne did not quite know what to say. She had almost forgotten reading Ovid in an attempt to discourage Jasper through the story of Diana and Acteon. It had made an even greater impression on Edmund than she could have imagined.

"Our plantation will be the envy of every land holder in all the colonies. We will build a dynasty here to rival any in the world."

Edmund began prancing around the field explaining where things would go and how they would use only the best carpenters and artisans.

"…And the house will have a great tower so we can see approaching ships on the ocean. That creek over there leads to a lovely little lagoon where smaller ships can moor. It is a perfect place for them to wait for the outgoing tide to return to the high seas. Do you see? This is where I will build my kingdom. Right here! From here the world will be ours. It is going to be spectacular!"

Edmund was grinning. His eyes were wide open, glistening. He looked slightly insane perhaps because he had transitioned from grand ambition into manic delusional fantasy.

"That's wonderful, my lord. I can almost see all of it happening right before our very eyes. Come let's sit in the carriage. We can eat what Fanta packed for us and you can tell me all about what will happen here at our very own Gargaphia."

Anne served Edmund bread and apples. They shared a bladder of wine. While they ate the Colonel babbled on more about his plans. The other men sat down and pulled out food and drink from their own rucksacks. William kept his eyes on the surrounding woods. Jasper shook his head and grumbled disgustedly to himself.

Soon Edmund calmed a bit and turned to Anne, "Now we'll go see the ocean. I have a skiff on the creek to take us there. Jasper and William will row for us. You men," he said to the others, "you stay here until we return." he barked.

The four of them walked over to the creek to the boat which was pulled up part way onto the bank and tied to a stake. Edmund climbed in. William picked up Ann so she would not get her skirt wet in the shallow water getting into it. Then he and Jasper untied the skiff's ropes and pushed the skiff into the water, jumping in afterward.

The winding stream carried them through the forest around to the open marsh. The smell of creek mud faded as fragrant salt air breezed over them. The sound of the pounding surf got louder and louder as they approached the opposite shore. It was slack tide, so the current was not too strong. A small flock of sea ducks squawked and flew away just about the time that they found themselves in the lagoon. They landed the boat on a clear place at the far side. After everyone had disembarked William drove a stake into the ground. He and Jasper pulled the vessel close and tied it off.

"Alright, boys, you cross the dunes and look for savages." Edmund turned to Anne and continued; "Indians come over here to fish when the weather is calm. They'd like nothing better than to take their shot at the King of Accomack." He laughed and looked around nervously.

This was the first time Anne had heard Edmund refer to himself this way. Before she could respond, William appeared at the top of the dune and motioned to the couple to proceed. So, off they went. When they reached the seaside, Edmund gave each man a hearty swat on the chest then told them both with a knowing smile to "stay here."

The couple made their way down to the waterline and began walking south. The smell of saltwater and seaweed suddenly took Anne home to Robin Hood's Bay and the last time she went beachcombing with Granny. Before she could really enjoy the memory, Edmund had grabbed her hand and started running toward the dunes. They were quickly out of the site line of William and Jasper. Edmund sat down. Still holding on to her, he pulled Anne down to him on the ground and began undoing her bodice.

Anne didn't even have time to object. Edmund began licking her breasts and pulling up her skirts. Before she knew it, they were having sex. He had been fantasizing about this beach assignation for some time so he quickly climaxed at its realization. He rolled off her and began to laugh.

"You are a wonder. How do you like your domain, my queen?"

Not waiting for an answer, he tickled Anne's belly then lay back in the sand. "I have never been so happy." he said. "You wear me out, my dear. Come, let's take a little nap."

Anne complied. She laid her head on his chest and closed her eyes. Edmund fell asleep almost immediately. Anne, on the other hand, was wide awake. Once she was sure that he was in a deep slumber, she slowly moved away from him. She sat for a minute then she took her shoes and stockings off.

Anne walked down to the water stepping in up to her ankles as she held up her skirts. It was cold. Anne stood it for as long as she could until she began to shiver, then ran from the waves. Noticing that her bodice was still wide open, she re-laced it. Looking around at the empty beach, she realized it was the first time since Edmund had moved in that she felt completely alone and free. She suddenly felt exhilarated.

It was a little past midday so the sun had not yet begun to set. Even with the cool ocean breezes it was very warm. Anne looked around. She could see William and Jasper far in the distance standing at the top of a dune. Edmund was out of sight in the tall grass still sleeping.

Anne began walking southward toward the endless horizon. For a moment she contemplated running as hard as she could and escaping everyone and everything. Then, she stepped on something hard. It hurt. She almost tripped. Looking down she could see a wide debris field of shells, pebbles, and sticks. It stretched up and down the beach in all directions.

"Well, if I can't run away, I may as well come home with some trinkets." she said to herself.

Anne tied a knot in her top skirt and began picking up shells as she walked north back towards the men. She had almost reached the spot where she left Edmund, when she saw something shimmering in the wet sand. She picked it up and saw that it was a gold coin marked with words that were either Spanish or Dutch. Anne only knew that it was not English. As far as she could tell this coin was the only one on the beach. Looking up in hopes that no one could tell exactly what she was doing, she tucked the coin inside her bodice. "Please don't let it fall out." she prayed.

She made her way towards Edmund. She sat down next to him and woke him up to see her collection of shells. She did not tell him about the coin.

Groggy, Edmund was not impressed with her treasures. He petted her on the head patronizingly. "Aren't you a lucky girl?"

"When I was very young my Granny took me shelling on Robin Hood's Bay. I used to dream about finding jewels there."

"All I have ever dreamed about was becoming king of this new land. By God I will do it too."

"And what sort of king will you be, Edmund? How will you rule?" Anne asked quietly.

Edmund stood up shaking the sand out of his breeches. "With an iron hand, that is how I will rule." he said firmly. "I won't let anyone defy me. We'll go back to the feudal system. Serfs will be part of the land again, none of this foolishness where the peasants get paid and make decisions for themselves. They're just dumb animals no better than those Africans or any ox or goat. Their lords'll manage 'em and pay tribute to me."

Anne didn't know whether to laugh at him or be horrified. She held back her own feelings and played along. "You'll command the respect of all in Accomack then…"

"By God, I will! And we will abolish any notion of other religions. We'll have but one Christian church and everyone else in this bloody kingdom better just get in line on that. The Papists can all bloody well hang and so can the Puritans. That damnable Puritan Obedience Robbins did more damage to this colony… I was never so glad to hear of someone's passing. He made a complete nuisance of himself. If he had not died a few months ago, I would have had to do something about him."

Robbins was a pious conservative who had been a longtime political foe of Edmund's. He had led the charge to have Scarborough arrested in light of his dealings with the Dutch during the trade embargo. More importantly, he had squabbled with Edmund over property lines.

Anne thought of Owen Tomkin who had described himself as a Puritan. She had heard Owen try to explain the reforms they hoped would help the Anglican Church. Anne kept quiet about her opinion of those reforms knowing Edmund would not take it kindly.

On a roll, the King of Accomack continued: "Ha! And if the Puritan's weren't bad enough, now we have more ranting heretics. These idiots, the Quakers, they think settlers can be friends with the damned savages! They refuse to fight them. They don't go to church or pay tithes. They won't even remove their hats in front of their betters."

The sun had moved into the western sky by now. Edmund finally noticed the dropping temperature and that Anne had been shivering for some time.

"Put your shoes and stockings back on. It's time to leave. If we don't get going the tide'll be against us and it'll take us all night to get home."

Anne did what she was told. Once more fully dressed she gathered up her seashells and followed Edmund towards William and Jasper waiting further up the beach. The western setting sun now bathed the clouds in the eastern sky in pink and lavender hues. The sea was a deep azure except for along the shoreline where the puddles were pale blue. Anne gazed out at the beautiful scene wishing she did not have to leave.

The evening light was rapidly retreating behind the trees by the time they were loaded back into the carriage. Anne wondered how they would find their way back to Chiconessex in the dark. She hoped that none of the local tribesmen were out hunting. Anne had never been afraid of them before, but now she was traveling in league with their mortal enemy and his soldiers. She shuddered at the thought of being ambushed.

Edmund responded by putting his arm around her. Anne was grateful Edmund had asked Fanta to pack a blanket, until he pulled it over them leaving most of her back exposed to the cold autumn air. With his free hand under the blanket he grabbed her hand and shoved it between his legs forcing her to rub the hard mass there. Anne tried to pull back but he held tight.

"Don't worry. They can't see what you are doing. Go on – make me come. Go on. Do it." he whispered in her ear.

Anne gave in to his demand and began massaging him, though it infuriated her. She thought to herself, "He is such a pig." Suddenly the carriage hit a large rut knocking Anne free of Edmund's hold. The couple almost fell out of their seats.

"Good God, man! Must you hit every hole and log in the way?!" Edmund barked at William.

He forced Anne's hand to try to revive his fallen erection. After several minutes without success he gave up saying out loud, "Never mind!"

William turned around. "Did you need something, my Lord?"

"Turn around and just watch where you are going." Edmund growled.

Anne turned her head to smile, wondering if William had hit the bump on purpose. The rest of the ride home was unremarkable except for the dark mood of the King of Accomack. Anne herself was tired and grumpy. She was starting to feel the effects of the sun. Her face and chest began to itch and radiate heat. Once home she hoped that Edmund would not insist on having sex.

"Fanta, after we have eaten, prepare a bath for the master. I will have one too when he is finished. And, can you find me a bowl for these until I decide what to do with them?" Anne unloaded her shell collection onto the sideboard. As she had hoped, a full belly and a clean bed quickly put the Colonel to sleep. While everyone else was preparing to turn in, she slipped into her room and took the coin from her bodice, grateful that the rough ride home had not shaken it loose.

"You are a sign from Mother Mary that the sea will reward me for all my trials." she whispered and kissed the gold disk before slipping it deep into the pages of the *Friends and Neighbors* ledger which she kept hidden in plain sight with a stack of other books.

After she had finished taking her turn bathing, Anne told Fanta she was done for the night. By the time she went to bed Edmund was sprawled out and snoring loudly. There appeared to be no room for her. Even after the bath her sunburn was bothering her, making sleep impossible, so she took a blanket and retreated to quiet of the porch where she could hear herself think. The moon peeked through the trees. Listening to the comforting sounds of frogs, crickets, and cooing owls, Anne felt a sort of placid confidence.

Soon Edmund would leave for James City. He told her the plan was to be there a few weeks and return to the Eastern Shore in time for Yuletide. That was when he had to fulfill his family obligation of staying at Hedra Cottage for a month. Anne could not wait for the beast to leave so she could get a decent night's sleep.

Anne worried that Edmund might leave Jasper or one of the other soldiers to watch over Chiconessex while he was away. That did not happen. The fact that no one had run away the year before when they had ample opportunity, gave him confidence that Anne would honor her commitment. Besides, he was a man in love. Despite his paranoia about just about everyone else, he wanted to believe that he could trust her. So, despite protests from Jasper, he took all his men with him when he departed for James City.

Fall was a busy season at the plantation. There was not much time for anyone in the household to misbehave. Finishing up the harvest and getting the house ready for winter were their primary concerns. Anne did, however, find time to prepare for her annual All Saints Day ritual.

Anne knew that like Owen, Edmund would disapprove of the ribbon blessing. This was another reason to be glad he was temporarily out her hair. Last year only she and William had gone out. This year Anne invited the Africans to take part and send prayers on the outgoing tide for their lost loved ones. She made dried herb bouquets for each person to cast upon the waves.

At first Fanta was nervous about getting in the dory. She was afraid of the water, which she associated with her violent capture and transport to New World enslavement. Malike and Botwe, however, had proved to be accomplished fishermen, having spent a lot of time on the water as boys in Africa. Malike sat with Fanta to reassure her, while Botwe and William rowed the boat.

Anne by now had memorized the 23rd Psalm so she recited it along with her own prayer when the dory came to a stop at the appointed place in the stream.

"The Lord is my shepherd; I shall not want. He maketh me to lie down in green pastures: he leadeth me beside the still waters. He restoreth my soul: he leadeth me in the paths of righteousness for his name's sake. Yea, though I walk through the valley of the shadow of death, I will fear no evil: for thou art with me; thy rod and thy staff they comfort me. Thou preparest a table before me in the presence of mine enemies: thou anointest my head with oil; my cup runneth over. Surely goodness and mercy shall follow me all the days of my life: and I will dwell in the house of the Lord forever."

She continued with her own portion of the ritual.

"To our guardian angels we plead: carry our love on soft sea breezes to our Lord Jesus and the Blessed Virgin Mary, Mother of God, that they might wrap in their holy embrace my beloved Mother, Father, and Granny, and our dear departed Owen, and also the loving families of Fanta, Malike, Botwe, and William, that they might be with us always, that they and the angels might guide us and watch over us. We bless these ribbons and send them on their way with all our love and devotion. Amen."

William replied "Amen" and the others followed his lead. The sky was overcast so though the sun was setting they could not see it. The light was fading quickly as they tossed their ritual herbs into the water. The men began rowing back to the safety of the creek just as a stiff wind began to pick up, pushing a wet mist off the bay onto their backs. Once the boat had been secured everyone ran as fast as they could back to the house as a steady rain began to fall. Anne and the others laughed as they bounded up the porch steps in anticipation of a hearty dinner that Fanta had left simmering in a pot over the fire.

Though Anne was conscious that a landowner sharing alcohol with her servants, particularly the Africans, was simply not done, they passed around a jug of rum. It was not only contrary to class divisions. It could be dangerous to allow a slave to get drunk, removing their inhibitions, emboldening them to act out or attempt an escape. Anne may have wanted the power of owning the land but she still felt like just another member of the household. Her humble roots fueled a naïve belief that she could be both the mistress of the plantation and enjoy comradery with her servants.

That night they skipped the storytelling and went straight to the music. William played a reel. Botwe ran out to the bunk room and returned with his small drum. He picked up the beat of the tune William was playing. Malike began clapping. Anne was feeling so good she grabbed Fanta by the hand pulling her up to join her in the dance. She showed her the steps. When the song was over the women collapsed laughing, to their seats.

William was getting ready to play another song, when the front door suddenly swung open and in walked Uncle Star and another man. The Africans froze in fear. Anne jumped to her feet and gave her friend a big hug.

"Why, Captain Minshull! Uncle Star! I am so happy to see you. We missed you last year. Where have you been?" Anne was slightly tipsy and flushed from dancing. "We are celebrating All Saints Day. Come sit down and have something to eat. Introduce me to your friend."

"Well, well, Mistress Anne. I heard you were all grown up, but you are indeed very different than the last time we met. This is John Vassall, he is my passenger and a merchant conducting trade between these colonies and those in the West Indies. John, this is Mistress Anne Toft."

"How do you, madam?" Vassall said removing his hat and bowing. He was not a tall man. His manner was courtly, his hair and apparel were gray and otherwise unremarkable.

"How do you do, sir? Welcome to Chiconessex. Fanta, get trenches with stew for our guests and bring them to the parlor." Anne dismissed William, Malike, and Botwe for the evening and led the visitors to the other side of the house. After they had been served, she instructed Fanta to go and prepare the guest room for her guests.

Anne sat down at the table with the men. Her head was clearing now. She was happy to see Uncle Star but she did not relish the idea of telling him what happened to the Tomkins and how she came to be in her present situation.

As he finished his meal and lay down his fork, the Captain got right to the point. "I heard that you were married, and you are now the mistress of Colonel Scarborough. How could both these things be true?"

Anne blushed and began to explain, "Owen Tomkin's death was a terrible blow to us all. Bella and Maude were gone and I was…" She stopped mid-sentence looking down at the floor frowning. Knowing that Uncle Star and others would disapprove of what she did, should have made her feel ashamed. But Anne, had gotten past all that. She raised her head proudly and continued.

"Uncle Star, I have no husband. That was a ruse to discourage those who might rob me of my virtue. I have entered into this unholy arrangement with the Colonel for my own private reasons. Under better circumstances it is not what I would have wanted, but I have few choices due to my station in life. I am sure I don't have to explain… I hope you won't condemn me or withdraw your friendship because of it."

She was angry about having to justify herself. At the same time, she had hoped that she could count on Uncle Star in some way. Now she feared she was making a mess of things.

The Captain motioned toward the stairs to his friend who rose from his seat, saying, "We've had a long journey and I am tired. I'd like to rest my head if your servant will direct me where to go."

"Fanta!" Anne called out. "Fanta, will you show Mister Vassall to his bedchamber please? Then you can go to bed yourself."

Fanta appeared at the top of the stairs. Vassall climbed the steps and followed her down the hall. Anne heard one door then another close.

"Uncle Star, I hope you are not too disappointed in me. I value your friendship and I could use your guidance."

"My dear, before I came here, I stopped to see Giles Ishim. He confided in me about your plan. I was so dismayed about the stories I'd heard. I couldn't believe that you would take up with the very devil who is likely responsible for the death of the one person in the world who has cared for you more than any other. I will, of course, help you in any way I can. But revenge is a risky game, my dear. The natives call Scarborough the Great Conjurer for a reason. He's a dangerous foe."

"I know how dangerous he is. But in these last months, I have also begun to learn his weaknesses. Everyone knows of his lust for power. Everyone knows that he is greedy and dishonest. He is actually in many ways just a foolish child. When I give him what he wants he trusts me completely."

Uncle Star shook his head. "How will this end? How long must you live this lie? What will be your life afterward?"

Anne sighed. "The woman who sold me into servitude told me that I would always be just another smuggler from Robin Hood's Bay. I'm starting to believe that. Most of the people who are supposed to be my "betters" are sinful rogues. They steal from those who have the least to spare. They keep common folk in bondage. Why should I submit to their rule - follow their laws? Why shouldn't I try to beat them at their own game?"

The Captain took Anne's hand and laughed a little. "Well, my dear, I believe those same things myself. Nobles and their minions have long stood on the necks of the rest of us. Just don't forget that not everyone is going to believe that's what you are doing. Most people will think you've happily joined the ranks with the blaggards for your own profit."

"I know. I'll have to earn my neighbors' trust. Maybe you can help me. Maybe between us we can think of ways that I can help them that will not make Edmund suspicious."

Uncle Star winked replying, "And while we're at it, maybe you can help me a bit too."

Anne and Uncle Star stayed up late into the night. They went through the *Friends and Neighbors* ledger, name by name. Minshull suggested a favor here and there that would benefit their friends and improve her position. He advised her to spread the word of her services as a scribe. There was great demand for forged identification and references. People tended to accept such documents on face value as they had no immediate way to refute them. In fact, most people were illiterate and relied on people like Anne to read and write for them.

"You'll find both saints and sinners for customers. If you become known for your discretion your work will be most lucrative. Always tell the Colonel the truth of who you serve and what they have you do. His larcenous nature will enjoy the profits. When possible, ask to be paid in coin or wampum beads. They can't be traced the way tobacco certificates can. But – and this is most important – unless he's present when you are paid, always save some for yourself. Make a show of giving him earnings but be sure to hide your portion away. Do this and you'll easily hide your activities in plain sight. When the time comes that you need a quick escape, you'll have money to aid you."

Then Uncle Star asked her for his own favor. He wanted Anne to help him alter his ship's manifest with false names and cargo entries, so he would have something to show if he was boarded by the Royal Navy. It seems that Owen Tomkin had been helping him with similar subterfuge for many years.

It was a matter of gently scraping the ink off the vellum manuscript with a sharp knife in order to replace certain incriminating entries. The surface was then burnished with another piece of paper and a spoon before the new information was written in. Anne had already provided this service to some of Owen's other clients. She was glad to help Uncle Star with the deception. It was evidence that they trusted each other. Over the years to come she would become a master in the art of forgery. She would learn to match ink color and handwriting so skillfully almost no one could spot the difference.

All the time they were talking that night, the weather outside was deteriorating. The gentle rain had become a fully-fledged gale. Storms like this were not uncommon in the colony and pretty typical for that time of year. They usually lasted three days with strong northeasterly winds and heavy rain.

The captain's ship, *The Zephyr Queen*, was moored in a cove on the east side of the Chesapeake near Pungoteague where Minshull had rented a wagon in order to see his customers. The creek overflowed its banks making the trail back from Chiconessex impassable. The Captain and his friend had to bide their time there for almost a week after the skies cleared, waiting for the waters to recede. During that time Uncle Star and Anne caught up on all that had happened in their lives since they had last seen each other.

It was later in the season than his usual visit. Star had had his own troubles in the previous year. He had been laid low by a bout of malaria. It took him months to recover and now he was behind schedule. The captain's primary trade was in rum and spices. He also carried brightly colored lightweight fabrics from Italy which were prized among the colonists who often arrived in this more temperate climate only with drab wool clothing better suited for their English origins.

Captain Minshull's most lucrative commerce was in illicit human transportation. He had helped many a fugitive escape justice in various European countries. It was, in fact, he who had given Colonel Scarborough a berth on his ship and delivered him to the

Albermarle Settlement in the Province of Carolina in 1653. This outpost on Virginia's southern frontier, which had become known as Rogue's Harbor, was where Edmund actually spent his year in exile.

Anyone who could earn or steal their fare could book passage on *The Zephyr Queen*. A new name, and a new life could be procured. No questions were asked. No trail was left behind. John Vassall was one of those passengers. He was eluding a quarrelsome wife and angry in-laws in Italy. He had absconded with a great deal of their money, setting out to make his fortune in the Spice Islands. Uncle Star had Anne erase the name Gianni Vespuci from his ship's passenger list and replaced it with the name John Vassall. He then dictated letters of reference for the errant merchant, which she produced to his specifications. He paid her with several gold coins. She followed Star's advice, saving half to give to Edmund and secreting away half for herself.

In the week the men spent at Chiconessex, Anne's guests entertained the household with tales of their adventures on the high seas. Between the two of them they had come across amazing sea creatures, befriended colorful rascals, and braved treacherous seas. When it came time for them to go, Anne and everyone else at Chiconessex was sad to see them and their tall tales leave.

The night before their departure, Anne had her usual insomnia. Wrapped up in a woolen blanket, she took her place on the porch where she now kept a rocking chair. The waning moon cast a magical light on the garden. The deer were rutting. Anne could hear them crashing about in the nearby forest. A large buck with a full head of antlers chased his beloved, a slender doe, right past the house. By now Anne was used to such nocturnal antics by the wild creatures. She smiled to herself thinking, "Poor girl."

When the night air became quiet again, she thought about all the gifts Uncle Star had given her over the years. She wished she had something she could give him in return. Anne's thoughts were coming together with an idea just about the time that the sun and the rest of the household began to rise.

After she and Fanta had given the men breakfast and packed them some travel provisions, the travelers began to say their goodbyes. They thanked Anne for their hospitality.

"I am grateful for all that you have taught me." she replied. "Before you go, I'd like to take your measurements. When you come back, I will have a new doublet for you embroidered with stags to remind you of our beautiful Virginia colony."

"Oh! That reminds me!" the Captain replied. "I have something that I have been saving just for you."

Star went to his rucksack and pulled out a brown oilcloth package which he handed to Anne. When she opened it, she saw that it contained several hanks of silk embroidery thread. Their colors were brilliant blues, greens, and purples. Anne was delighted. She could use these on several projects and still have some left over. She hugged him in gratitude. Anne became tearful as she kissed the men goodbye.

Ann spent a good part of the next weeks checking on neighbors in the aftermath of the storm. Late one day in early December Anne had just finished writing a sales receipt for two of her neighbors when, as she watched them riding way, she felt a sharp stab low in her gut. It was so painful she doubled over and cried out. Fanta helped her across the room. A trail of blood followed them. Anne knew that this was not her ordinary courses. Something was wrong.

The trouble seemed to fade but Anne felt weak so she decided to take to her bed even though she had not yet had her dinner. Once there, she felt another wave of pain, worse than the first one. Her screams brought Fanta running.

"Fanta, send William for Nandua. I think I am losing a child."

Fanta left the room, returning a few minutes later with William.

"Mum, are you alright?"

"I don't know. Go for Nandua. She will know how to treat this."

William looked at the floor, his brow furrowed with worry. "Mistress Anne, Nandua and her people have moved north to join the other tribes and get away from the Colonel's attacks."

"Damn him." Anne muttered through clenched jaws. "Argh. Go for Mrs. Ishim. Maybe she can help."

It was late into the night before William returned with Giles Ishim's wife. Anne was feverish and barely knew she was there. Mrs. Ishim surveyed the situation looking under the covers between Anne's legs.

"She's not quite finished. It'll take another few hours. You girl, bring me more hot water and a fresh cloth so we can clean her up again."

Fanta took away the linens she had been using to soak up the blood to be washed. The two women worked well into the next morning helping Anne through the miscarriage. Once the worst of it was over Mrs. Ishim gave Fanta instructions for her mistress' care. She told her to have William bury the tiny fetus far from the house. She then left for her home promising to come back in a few days. Anne mostly slept until then. When Rebecca Ishim returned, she was sitting up and drinking broth.

"How are you feeling, my dear?"

"I'm still weak, but I think I am improving."

"Was this your first?"

"My first? Yes, I suppose it was." Anne's eyes filled with tears. She hadn't even known she was pregnant, but the thought of her child dying was devastating.

Mrs. Ishim took her hand, patting it. "We are lucky if any of the children we bear see their elder years. There will be more, don't worry, my dear." There was kindness in her voice, though she would not look Anne in the eye.

The woman got up to leave, saying, "I will tell your girl what to do. Within a fortnight you should be your old self. It would be best if no one hears of my presence here. If you are found out and brought forth on charges of bastardy my dear, I would have to testify against you. Midwives are required to ask unmarried mothers who fathered their bastards. I could not lie under oath. Don't put me in the position of crossing the King of Accomack. I have my own children to raise." With that Mrs. Ishim was gone.

As cold as this sounded, she was not trying to be cruel. Anne knew that a respectable Godly woman like her neighbor would not want to be associated with such a scandal. Of course, she would not want it known that she assisted the mistress of the most notorious landowner in the colony. Anne's thoughts drifted from grief to resentment and back again.

She was lonely for the motherly nurture of Bella and Maude. She wondered if they would have understood. Though Fanta did her best to help with her mistress' physical needs, her manner too was chilly. The slave woman never allowed herself to be drawn into long conversations with Anne. Her distrust and resentment made it impossible for theirs to be an intimate relationship. How could she feel friendship for anyone who believed that they owned her?

So, Anne filled her recovery time with books and needlework, trying to block out her sadness. She had not even been aware that she was pregnant. It made no sense to grieve someone she did not even know had existed. And yet she felt a strange emptiness where an infant should have been. It had not occurred to her that she would love any offspring of Edmund's. Anne had not even considered any such possibility. Those consequences of this plan which she had imagined were all things she thought she could contend with. She could not fix these feelings of despair, so she tried to cover them up with busyness.

Soon the household celebrated Yule tide. There was little fanfare that year. An ice storm had confined them to the house for over a week. Other than cooking for the men who spent their days hunting, Anne and Fanta spent their time at mending clothes, fishing nets, and anything else that needed repairs. When they ran out of such projects Anne taught Fanta needlework the way Bella and Maude had taught her.

They were sitting together quietly concentrating on their embroidery the January afternoon that Edmund and his contingent returned. He burst through the door, and with hardly a greeting between them, he grabbed her hand, taking her upstairs to bed. Unleashing his fully erect manhood he threw up Anne's skirts found his target inside her, and quickly reached his satisfaction.

Edmund quickly stood up and laughed, "Oh my girl, I don't think I have ever missed anyone so much! That was delicious. I've waited weeks for that."

He cleaned himself off with a corner of the bed covers, closed his drawers, and headed for the door. "Get yourself together my dear! I have things for you downstairs."

Anne was furious. "That selfish pig! What is wrong with a man who thinks this is the way to treat anyone?" she thought to herself.

When she got down to the parlor, Jasper and another man were carrying in a sizeable trunk. Edmund handed Anne the key with a flourish and a bow. "Merry Christmas, my angel."

Anne's anger gave way to curiosity. She unlocked the trunk and opened it to find several large bolts of fabric. One was a lush gold damask. Another was a bright blue silk. There was velvet in maroon and in black. And, there were cottons and linens in white as well as several other colors. As she looked through the material, Anne found a silver tea set: a pot and a sugar bowl with matching lids, cups, and spoons. Each had the same flower etched on them. At the bottom of this luxurious trove, were several books and a carved wooden box.

"I thought you could use it to keep your baubles in. Open it up. Look inside!" Edmund was ebullient.

"The box is large enough to hold quite a few baubles." Anne thought. She lifted the lid to see a pair of gold earrings each with a brilliant blue sapphire the size of her thumbnail.

"Put them on. Put them on. I can't wait to see how they look! You can wear them with your necklace."

Anne complied, turning her head and smiling prettily. Edmund laughed and sat down pulling Anne onto his lap. He began to kiss her neck.

"Mmmm. That's my girl. I could just eat you up. Mmmm. Fannie, I'm starved. Get me something to eat."

"Fanta" Anne reminded him.

"Fannie, Fanta. Who cares? Get up and sit over there while I eat. I have lots of news to tell you. Jasper, you and Billy can go now. Show him where to bunk. Fanta will bring you two something to eat later in the gathering hall. Anne, this is Captain William Thorn, Billy. He is my new aide de camp. He's come straight from merry old

London with a commission to assist us in eradicating the meddlesome naturals."

As he shoveled mouthfuls of stew Edmund relayed all his news. His time in James City had been very worthwhile. The Governor had, as he hoped, appointed him to be High Sheriff of Northampton County, in charge of law enforcement and tax collecting. With these new duties he would need Billy to command patrols. Furthermore, his son Charles would soon be spending time at Chiconessex to learn accounting from Anne so he could become a "proper landowning gentleman." Edmund had had a scribe in James City who had kept his books but had caught a fever and died last fall. He wanted his son to take over those duties in preparation for becoming a planter in his own right.

Edmund went on to say that twenty-four indentures would be delivered to them as soon as the seas were safe enough for transport from England. He was expecting a cobbler and a blacksmith. The rest would be carpenters and brickmakers who would help with the construction of Gargaphia.

"By the end of summer, we will move there and Charles will take up residence here at Chiconessex in preparation for his marriage."

"Chiconessex is mine, Edmund."

"Wha... well that's alright you can sell it to him. Gargaphia is going to be the grandest plantation in all Virginia, maybe all the colonies. You'll be living like a queen. What difference does it make who lives here?" Edmund put his fork down and looked up at Anne who was now on her feet looking like she was about to take a punch at him.

"I have it in writing. Chiconessex belongs to me. I decide its fate, who lives here, who works here - not you or anyone else! Did you intended to cheat me all along? How could you?! Did you promise this to Charles already? Well, you'll just have to take it back! If that's not the case, tell me now. I'll leave in the morning to find my fortune elsewhere."

Edmund was completely surprised by Anne's outburst. "No, I haven't told him yet, but..."

"But nothing! That is final!"

"What's final?"

Anne was so furious she was starting to not make any sense. She began babbling about him betraying her and taking advantage of her. Between shouts she pounded the table. Then she began to clean up the dishes. Each thing she picked up she put down with a violent slam.

The Colonel was flabbergasted. He had just given her a chest full of treasure. What more did she want? It took him a few minutes to realize that he should have proposed the sale to her in a way that she would not think he was stealing it from her. When she suggested she would pack up and leave, a feeling of terror like he had never experienced hit him hard. It left him almost breathless. His feelings were in total chaos. He was angry, hurt, afraid, and confused all at once.

When Anne finally ran out of words and breath, the Great Conjurer did something he had never done before – for anyone. He apologized.

"I'm sorry. It's alright. We'll give Charles my sister's place. I promise. No one is going to take anything away from you. I promise. I'll do anything you want, just don't leave me."

He timidly approached her then he hugged her and began to beg.

"Please don't leave. Come upstairs with me. Be my Diana. Let me be your Acteon. Let me worship you. I'll give you anything you want. Please, my darling, please."

Again, he took her by the hand up the stairs. This time he slowly undressed her, then himself. He led her to the bed where she laid on top of the covers, completely still, staring at the ceiling. Edmund began kissing her all over. He spread her legs kissing between them and then worked his way up her belly to her breasts continuing to gently rub her pubis.

She refused to voluntarily respond to the pleasure of his caresses but her body betrayed her with a moist invitation that spilled into his hand. Encouraged and aroused, Edmund made love to her. She kept still for as long as she could responding only when finally, her animal weakness took over. After they had finished Edmund happily kissed her, promising that she had nothing to be afraid of, that he would always take care of her.

Anne responded with a fearful grief she had not intended to let him see. "God has punished me for what we have done. He took away our child this December last. And now you want to take from me the only real home I have ever known. God is punishing me for being sinful."

"What? What child?"

"I was pregnant when you left and did not yet know it. God decided I was not worthy to carry an innocent child. So, he took it away. He made me miscarry our babe."

"Why didn't you send me a message?"

"What do you care? You've gotten what you wanted and now you're giving away my home!" Anne's lower lip began to tremble as she fought back her tears.

"What's this? Don't cry. Everything will be just fine." Edmund held Anne for what seemed to him like a long time. He really didn't know what else to say. Weary from his travels, he soon dozed off. It was late and the rest of the household had gone to bed. Anne got up, dressed, and found her nocturnal sanctuary on the front porch.

There she quietly wept for the child she had lost and the loneliness she felt. She had no one she could commiserate with. Though William cared in his way, he was not one to talk much or share deep feelings. He certainly could not help her with this problem.

Sad thoughts gave way to shame as the night wore on. Anne was humiliated that even in her rage about Edmund's plan to sell Chiconessex, she had still let him have his way with her. Why hadn't she fought him off? Why hadn't she banished him from their bedroom?

Though she did not realize it at the time, Anne actually had Edmund right where she wanted. Her remorseful suspicion had grown into resentment for having to live this lie. Maybe she had made a terrible mistake. Maybe the next time he was away she should take her jewels, and what little money she had, and run away. Anne toyed with the idea of murdering Edmund and Jasper in their sleep like the ancient story of Judith. Maybe she could catch up with Captain Minshull and escape the colony on his ship with every valuable she could carry.

Uncle Star's words weighed heavily on her: "How will this end?"

By the arrival of dawn, Anne had run out of tears and self-doubt. She had not figured out exactly how to finish this awful scheme, but she had come to the conclusion that her best defense was legal ownership of her land, duly recorded in court. If she was going to be forced to live there, she resolved to demand ownership of Gargaphia. She would not stop there. She would insist that any other land associated with the headrights of any new indentures be put in her name, starting with the two-dozen people arriving that spring.

She went inside, where Fanta was preparing breakfast. Edmund arrived at the table still groggy. Anne told him she would be happy to host Charles and teach him about bookkeeping by helping set up his new ledgers for his own plantation.

"You leave me to manage our books, and I'll teach him to manage his." she said.

Anne did not give him time to disagree, instead launching into a report of all that had happened on the plantation while he was gone. She finished by telling him about the visit of Captain Minshull and John Vassall. She presented him with the bag of coins Uncle Star had paid her for her services, less of course her secret portion.

Edmund was pleased with all she had told him and especially that she had earned him some pocket change. "What a lucky man I am to have a treasure like you, Anne. Any other woman wouldn't even have told me about that transaction. She'd have kept the money for herself. You must really love me." The Great Conjurer believed every word.

Staking Out Territory

Getting Edmund to give her the deed to Gargaphia was not going to be a simple matter, despite Anne's determination. He had purchased the property many years prior, and as had been his practice, he had put it in his wife's name to avoid incurring a tax bill. He had tried, during his Yuletide visit, to convince Mary to sign the deed over to him without success. After several shouting matches Edmund threatened not to provide her with a regular income. He even threatened her with legal action. They had finally compromised with a written agreement allowing Anne to serve as mistress of Gargaphia as long as Edmund was alive.

Anne did not take the news kindly. She was expected to live at Gargaphia rather than her beloved Chiconessex, yet it would not belong to her. She would always be under the threat of eviction by Edmund's wife. This was unacceptable.

To appease Anne, Scarborough agreed to assign to her the headrights for the two dozen indentures arriving that spring and any such future contracts. These along with any new property associated with them would be in her name. He then turned the whole enterprise of running his plantations over to her, the woman who he considered to be his new wife. She was cunning and bold. And, he believed, she was committed to him. He would teach Anne to manage the properties so that they would provide him with a steady income, thereby freeing him of boring domestic encumbrances.

The Colonel's mind was on bigger things. He wanted to concentrate on his dreams of conquest on the battlefield and in the House of Burgesses. It was his intention to one day be Governor of Virginia and then somehow get King Charles to make him lord proprietor in the same manner he had in Maryland for Lord Baltimore. He would settle for nothing less than ownership of the entire peninsula east of the Chesapeake for him and his heirs.

Anne decided that the best strategy was to relinquish any objections about Gargaphia and accept these new terms. As long as she owned Chiconessex, the other properties were merely investments. Her hope was to amass enough of a fortune to live out the rest of her life comfortably in her beloved home once she and Edmund were inevitably through.

Charles Scarborough soon arrived at Chiconessex where he stayed for several weeks while his aunt and uncle were moved to Hedra Cottage. Edmund had told his wife that she was taking in her ne'er do well in-laws, who could not manage their own affairs alone. James and Hannah Wise were told their sister in-law was too mentally incompetent to care for the younger children or to run the plantation. Though both these explanations were intended to deceive, they each contained elements of truth.

Mary's mental state was mercurial at best and the daily running of the home was now beyond her capability. Hedra Cottage was, at the time one of the most luxurious homes on Virginia's Eastern Shore. The mercenary Hannah Wise was happy to live there and let her nephew take over her own backwater estate which she had come to hate. It was never going to be a happy arrangement, but she and her husband were determined to make the best of it. Mary Scarborough had no choice but to go along with the changes happening around her.

Young Charles was about the same age as Anne. He was a good-looking young man. He was tall, well-built, and had his mother's fair complexion. Charles was bookish and serious. He had developed a steady temperament in direct opposition to the erratic nature of both his parents. For a long time, he had been the only member of the Scarborough household who kept his head while his parents were losing theirs. He was the one who looked after his frightened siblings, helping them to find cover from the frequent tirades.

Charles was relieved to get away from his mother's chaotic orbit even if it meant living briefly in the disreputable household of his father's mistress. He had decided to accept Anne as a necessary evil in his father's life. For her part, Anne maintained a polite yet cool demeanor towards Charles. She instructed him on the system of accounting she had learned from Bella Tomkin and lent him the John Mellis book on the subject from Owen's library. During that time the two established a respectful relationship that was cordial, even businesslike. Once his tutelage had run its course, Charles took up residence across the creek in his new home.

About two weeks later, Anne was visited by Dr. Hack's wife Anna who she had met the year before on the lane to Hedra Cottage. Mistress Hack had written Anne a note saying that she would like to come see her. Anne had replied with an invitation to come once the distraction of Charles' presence in the house had been eliminated.

On a day when Edmund was off checking on his militia, Anna Hack arrived in her fancy black and red carriage, driven by a servant. She was dressed in a fine green velvet cloak, which when removed revealed a dark blue dress also made of velvet, trimmed with gold braid on the shoulders and a simple white linen collar. Her clothing was not ostentatious but it was clearly of high quality.

Fanta prepared tea and biscuits which Anne offered to her guest using her new silver tea service. Once the niceties had been conveyed between the two women, Anna Hack got right to the point.

"My dear, you are going to need my friendship. This arrangement you have with Colonel Scarborough is… shall we say, not unprecedented, but perhaps not what our friend Bella Tomkin would have wanted for you."

Anne started to defend herself, but as she opened her mouth the older woman stopped her, raising her left forefinger in the air as she spoke.

"Let me finish. I am not here to condemn you. I am here to give you some advice and offer my friendship. I have known others who have pursued the same path you have chosen, to be the consort of a wealthy man rather than making a more respectable marriage. Some have done so successfully while others, well, let us say that their lives have been marked by disappointment. You will need allies who can help you protect yourself."

"Forgive me, Mistress Hack, but how can I know your intent? I don't recall you and Mistress Bella discussing my future. Aren't you Mary Scarborough's friend? How do I know that you're not here on her behalf on some mission of sabotage?"

"You are right to ask questions." Anna replied. "Mistress Bella and I liked each other but we did not regularly socialize. The last time I spoke with her was at the harvest fair while her husband was showing you the sights. She spoke highly of your intelligence and bright spirit. Even without notable parentage or a sizeable dowry, she expected you to make a good marriage. I remember we both marveled how here in the colonies, women of low birth had better prospects than they ever did in our home countries. Here in Virginia, any woman with a bit of intelligence can assure her own future. And, women have more opportunities to help each other here. When one of us succeeds, so do we all. When we help each other; we achieve even greater success."

Now Anne was intrigued. Her visitor referred to her as Mistress Toft rather than Mrs. Toft. This was a sign of respect, as the custom was to only use that appellation for people of stature. This could have been mere flattery. But the remarks Anna Hack had attributed to Bella were similar to many Anne had heard herself.

"What are you proposing, Mistress Hack?"

"As you begin to manage your plantation, I hope you will consider me for your shipping needs. The Colonel has shipped his goods with my fleet in the past without complaint, so I know he won't mind. I'll give you a good price. After we have done business together to our mutual satisfaction, I would like to bring you other opportunities from time to time which may be of benefit to both of us."

Anne wondered if this was too good to be true. "I'll certainly think about this. But, Mistress Hack, I hope you don't mind if I do not make any promises today."

"Not at all, my dear. I am impressed that you are not too eager for your own good. You may want to speak to Giles Ishim about me. He and I've made a nice profit on several ventures together. I understand he's a friend of yours. We also have a mutual acquaintance with Captain Alistair Minshull. Squire Ishim can confirm that, too."

The mention of Giles Ishim and Uncle Star, helped Anne to relax a little. "Yes. Yes, I will, thank you." she said. "May I ask you something? Aren't you friends with Mary Scarborough? How would she feel about all this?"

"Mistress Scarborough is my neighbor. But mostly, she is my husband's patient. As you know, she is not a well woman. It is hard to tell whether her husband's neglect caused her condition or her condition caused him to neglect her. In the years that we have lived near them, I've never seen her in a happy state of mind. Her bitter tongue is well known. I'm afraid she trusts no one to be her friend and so she has few."

"Would you like another biscuit, Mistress Hack?"

"Thank you, no. Tell your cook they are delicious. No, I have given you a great deal to think about, so I'll be on my way. Do let me know. This year looks to be a profitable one."

"Thank you, Mistress Hack, I will."

The women rose to their feet and walked out onto the porch.

"I hope you will call me Anna and that you will allow me to call you Anne."

"Of course. We're friends now."

"Good." Anna stepped closer and spoke quietly so no one else might hear. "Let me give you some friendly advice. When negotiating, never let anyone know how smart you really are or reveal all the information you have. Let others think they have the advantage. This will protect you and will help you to have the upper hand in getting the best deal.

"Your Colonel is a dangerous man. I have no doubt you already know this. Do not trust anything he says and do your best not to keep secrets from him. Secrets can be used against you. Hide any deception in plain sight. Never let him get that kind of advantage over you. And, if you ever fear for your safety, come find me."

Anne was taken aback by her new friend's frankness. The women hugged as if they had known each other a long time before Anna Hack left for home. The whole visit unnerved Anne a little, so the next day she went to visit Giles Ishim. He confirmed everything Mistress Hack had said, emphasizing her trustworthiness. Anne was impressed, hearing of the woman's decades long reputation as a successful merchant.

The Hacks' plantation and shipping interests had been financed by Anna's family in the Netherlands and New Amsterdam. It was well known that George Hack was a better doctor than he was a merchant. As a result, many years ago, Anna had taken charge of their business interests. Anne admired all Giles told her. It gave her hope that she might follow in her new friend's footsteps.

Anne's domestic plans seemed to be going her way. She had no idea how her plan to undo Edmund Scarborough would finally unfold, though she felt that she had successfully arranged the chess pieces of this match to her own advantage. She congratulated herself on how much she had won so far. That was good enough for now.

Headrights and Harlotry

The rest of that winter, the Colonel and his troops continued their raids on the Indian tribes, driving all but a few families from the region. It was a bloody campaign which Edmund conducted from the safety of Anne's Chiconessex parlor. While most of the men camped not too far away, Billy, Jasper, and a few other officers came to the plantation to make battlefield reports. One night as they regaled their commander with their vicious exploits, Anne was forced to face the reality of her paramour's barbarity.

"I swear Private Smithson split that savage's skull in two." said one soldier.

Another chimed in, "We must have slaughtered a good three dozen of em' this week alone, my Lord."

Billy confined his remarks to the overall military objectives while his comrades crudely bragged about their accomplishments.

"We've routed the lot of 'em, sir. Any that's still alive have moved north beyond the border. That land now belongs to the colony and can be made ready for sale."

Edmund called for food and wine for his men. Fanta was obliged to comply while her mistress sat next to him as his pretty accessory. Anne listened in horror hoping that Nandua's tribe was still safely out of reach, across the border in Maryland. Looking down at the floor to try and hide her dismay, she was distracted by the heavy mud on the soldiers' boots. It smelled foul and was an odd color. It was a deep brown, almost black.

"I say, Mistress Anne, you're not listening to me. They kicked the Kickotanks' arses. It's funny! Ha-ha-ha." The Colonel chortled drunkenly.

"What?"

"I say, what shall we serve these brave men for dinner, my dear?"

"Fanta has begun a nice squirrel stew, my lord." she replied distractedly.

"Surely we can do better than that. Fanta, get in here! Fanta, go see if William has fresh venison hanging in the spring house." said Edmund.

Anne was still preoccupied by their visitors' feet. Filthy clods were falling all over the floor now revealing bright red streaks on their wet side. It finally dawned on her that she was looking at mud mixed with human blood. Anne felt ill. She got up to turn away and started to help Fanta with the meal.

"Come back, my darling. I want you by my side as I hear about our great triumphs. Let Fanta make dinner."

The color drained from Anne's face as she sat down. For the rest of the evening she endured the horrific escapades of the militia's eradication of the Indians. The more the men drank the more they exaggerated their grotesque exploits. Finally, Anne could take no more.

"My lord, I hope you do not mind if I leave you men to your stories. It's late and I am not feeling myself just now."

Edmund was happily drunk, laughing at one of the soldier's jokes. "Goodnight, my dear. Ha ha ha ha…" He barely noticed as Anne whispered instructions to Fanta to put out a few jugs for the men and then to go to bed. She went upstairs and lay in bed staring at the ceiling praying that Scarborough would be too drunk to be interested in sex that night. She felt sick to her stomach listening to the roars of laughter from downstairs.

Anne drifted off until she awakened to the sound of the roosters just before dawn. Once dressed, she quietly descended the stairs to see all the men sprawled out in various places on the floor, passed out snoring. The acrid smell of ale and sweat filled the room. Anne started to gag as she tiptoed around the sleeping bodies to the front door and outside. She quickly walked over to the kitchen garden, throwing up just before getting to its gate.

"Are you alright, mum?"

It was Jasper. He had suddenly appeared almost from out of nowhere, his hand on her forearm trying to help her. Anne quickly recoiled at his touch.

"Go help your master to bed, then get those men up and send them back to the encampment." she ordered.

"Can't I help you?"

"I'm fine. I told you what I need. Now, do as I tell you, man."

Jasper slinked away grumbling under his breath. "You don't appreciate all I have done for you. If you did, you'd not order me about so. You'd thank me."

Anne wondered for just a moment what he was going on about. There were more important matters at hand than Jasper's snide remarks. She made her way around to the summer kitchen where Fanta was awake and stoking the fire. Even though it was still too cold to need the summer kitchen, when the Colonel was entertaining his men he did not like to be disturbed by the clatter of dishes. So, cook fires were kept going there instead of in the main house. Anne sat down for some tea while waiting for the grubby brutes in her parlor to vacate the premises.

Once Edmund was in his own bed, he stayed there sleeping for the rest of the day, nursing a hangover. He came downstairs for dinner unprepared for his mistress to browbeat him about the behavior of his men.

"They did not even clean their boots! How dare they enter their lord's house in such a disrespectful manner. They were coarse in every aspect. They told the most disgusting tales. They killed defenseless people. These were human beings they've butchered after all."

"That, madam, is enough. The Indians are animals. Killing them is no different than killing vermin infesting the corn crib."

"A lady's parlor is no place for talk like that. How dare you let them behave in front of me in that way? You can't expect me to keep a respectable home where fine people want to come and do business and have such things going on. And the mess they made!! It took Fanta and me all day to be clear of it!!"

Anne's hectoring continued for some time until Edmund, head pounding, retreated back to his bed. The two did not speak of it or anything else for the next few days. Ending the war on the natives was not something he would have even considered. Domestic warfare was, however, something he could not endure. He'd had enough of that with his wife. Soon, Edmund's lust began to take precedence over winning the fight with Anne. He tried to express contrition, offering to meet his men elsewhere, worrying she might refuse him in the bedroom until he did so.

It was about then that Anne realized she had become pregnant again. This time she understood better the signals her body sent her. She relied more heavily on Fanta to lift and carry things. When the new indentures arrived, she was grateful to see that among the laborers, there were three women who she hoped would further relieve her of taxing household chores. After her usual welcome speech to the new members of the household, she took the ladies aside to learn what brought them there.

Brigid Nolan, was a tall muscular woman in her late thirties with brown hair which was turning grey. She wore the expression of one who had been beaten down by life. She was not a bitter sort, just weary from all that life had handed her. Brigid had been convicted of assaulting a lesser nobleman who had drunkenly attacked her. She was a cook in his household and had long suffered his mistreatment despite being a hard worker. Because this terrible incident happened in front of witnesses who all declared it self-defense, the judge sentenced her to colonial servitude instead of prison or -- worse yet -- hanging. This helped the nobleman's family to quickly recover from the notoriety of the incident and helped Brigid escape further reprisals.

Anne was happy to have someone who could help with household chores so she quickly put Brigid to work with Fanta. She was less pleased with Daisy and Delia Sheffield. These twin sisters had also been sentenced to servitude in order to soothe the embarrassment of an aristocratic family. They were prostitutes who had unfortunately been found together in bed with the husband of one of the King's cousins who had demanded their banishment. The King himself was known to be a hedonist. He would have simply let the girls off with a warning, but his cousin's parents were very influential particularly with the clergy. He needed their collective political support. So, he agreed to the banishment to keep them happy.

The Sheffield girls were not your typical bawdy house trollops. Barely twenty-three years of age, Daisy and Delia were lovely petite blue-eyed blonds who were used to the finer things: nice dresses, fine food and drink, and an exclusive clientele. Though their coloring was the same, they were not identical. Daisy was slender, with thinner lips and a longer nose. Delia's features were generally rounder and fuller all over.

The two women had no skills that could be considered practical on a rustic colonial plantation. They were entertainers. They could sing and dance. They were by no means stupid. Both women could read and had a talent for clever conversation. Their most celebrated asset was their training in the ways of carnal pleasure. Among their elite customers they were infamous for their erotic "sisters" act. Anne wasn't quite sure what to do with them.

When she assigned them to menial household work, they rolled their eyes. By the end of the first week of their indenture they put in such a lackluster effort at their chores, Anne knew she would have to make a different arrangement for them. It wasn't just that their talents were being wasted in this primitive outpost. They were a distraction to the male laborers, who made every excuse to be in their presence. Daisy and Delia thoroughly enjoyed the lusty attention. They flirted shamelessly with the men. This teasing was their defense against boredom since they were in no hurry to grant any sexual favors to these ruffians. The sisters were mercenaries after all. They saw no profit in giving away their particular talents for free to paupers.

As Anne watched the interplay between the new servants and Edmund, she quickly realized that it was no accident that he had brought the Sheffield girls to Chiconessex. One evening after the rest of the household had gone to bed, she confronted him with her suspicions.

"You knew why the Sheffield sisters were bonded when you accepted their contracts, didn't you, Edmund?"

"Well, I…"

"Don't pretend otherwise. I know what work they are good at. And I know what they are meant to do here. My only question is, are they here for your pleasure or your profit?"

"Both?" Edmund shrugged. "White women, particularly as fine as these are in short supply. They should attract quite a bit of business."

Most women would have been angry. Respectable women would have been appalled. Anne was simply annoyed. As usual, she was pragmatic about her own needs. Edmund's propensity for debauchery had presented itself as a way to relieve her of her own sexual duties, at least until the baby was born. This was a substantial relief to her. She had no envy for the girls because she did not love Edmund. And in light of her liberal attitude about prostitution learned at her grandmother's knee, it was actually well within Anne's character to indulge the Colonel's illicit plans.

"Edmund," she sighed, "I do not mind if they give you pleasure while I am in my confinement. As for making my home into a bawdy house, that is not something I want. If you expect me to accept these women, you will have to let the builders know they need to construct the guest wing at Gargaphia in such a way that their services can be conducted behind closed doors, well away from the ears of me and my child.

"For now, we have another problem. We will have to move most of the men permanently to the building site at Gargaphia. They already hover around the sisters like rutting bucks. I fear they'll not be able to hold back for long. I don't want the girls hurt, or fights to break out over them. And besides, we want them to attract landowners with money, not crude tradesman who can pay only in pennies or flattery. If we let them lie with the field hands and carpenters, they'll be good for nothing else."

Edmund was shocked and slightly disappointed by Anne's remarks. He thought he had been cleverly circumspect when showing her the architect's drawings of that wing of the new plantation where a public house would accommodate such things. Once again, he had underestimated her. He was not too surprised that she would figure out his plans on her own. But he had hoped she would be at least a little jealous. Part of the fun of his dalliance with the twins was going to be doing it behind her back. In fact, he had already taken advantage of their dubious talents.

"Umm, that is true, I guess…"

"Once the men have been moved, the sisters can move from the maids' room into the loft room above the bunk house. They will need proper bedding built and a more substantial door. Once all that is done, they can begin entertaining you. It is time that I begin my confinement anyway – at least in terms of our lovemaking. I'll take no chances of losing this baby. Do you understand?"

Getting him out of her bed was well worth tolerating Edmund's fowl temper during an albeit temporary period of forced abstinence. Anne knew this would motivate Edmund to quickly make the arrangements she had suggested. It was just another facet of their strange relationship that Edmund actually admired Anne for putting both his needs and that of her innocent unborn child above her own. He congratulated himself for picking such a woman to be his mistress.

Things once again settled into a routine at Chiconessex. Anne insisted that Daisy and Delia do some share of work around the house while they were not producing any income. It would not do for them to be waited on by Brigid and Fanta as if they had some sort of superior status. They were given the job of sewing baby clothes and assisting with the preparation and cleanup of meals. They were also charged with taking an active part in the evening entertainments much to the delight of the menfolk.

Anne focused her attention on her scrivener business and supervising construction plans. Edmund brought slaves up from Hedra Cottage to improve the roadway to Gargaphia. This enabled

Anne to safely make a weekly visit to inspect the progress without endangering her pregnancy traveling the rough terrain.

During this time Edmund was busy with his new duties as High Sheriff. He made his rounds to all the local landowners to collect taxes, and to investigate legal complaints and all sorts of petty crimes. Edmund quickly came to see this work as extremely tedious. He liked collecting the tax monies which he was entitled to take a cut of. But he was still Surveyor General for the colony, and all this added work felt like a waste of his time. He vowed to find a way out of it.

When the Colonel returned to James City for the fall assembly of the House of Burgesses he was in his element. His now contented, even boast worthy, domestic situation further inflated his already brash attitude. Not only did he find someone else to deal with the pesky High Sheriff position, he had what he considered one of his more successful legislative sessions.

Edmund and other slaveholders pushed through a law making any offspring of slaves or indentured women (regardless of who the fathers were) the property of their owners. He actually saw this as rebuilding feudal structures. It excited his morally deficient imagination to think he might act as both stud and master for a growing herd of slaves.

Another accomplishment during that session, was the Colonel's effort to redraw the county boundary lines on the Eastern Shore of the colony. Years ago, at the beginning of the English settlement, there had only been one Virginia county on the east side of the Chesapeake. It was called Accomac after the largest native tribe living there. Landowners at the southern end of the peninsula had subsequently seen to its division into two counties. With little thought to the name's contradiction they established Northampton in the south, and Accomack in the north.

Scarborough had long tried to undo this division in his quest to have dominion over the whole peninsula. He was now one step closer, having bamboozled one of his neighbors, William Waters, into casting the deciding vote to enlarge Accomack County and thereby reduce the size of Northampton. When Waters realized the trickery and its impact on his holdings, he was furious. For several years after that he would fight to restore the previous boundary lines. Yet another neighbor had joined the growing list of Edmund's enemies. Nonplussed by Waters' reaction, he was quite pleased with his own successes.

Meanwhile, nothing compared to the drama that played out at the same time across the Chesapeake at Chiconessex. Anne's pregnancy had so far progressed in a fairly healthy way. Not long before her expected delivery time, she followed the practice of her mentor Bella and took to her bed to help guarantee a safe successful birth, relying on the other women of the household to keep things running smoothly.

While Edmund was away in James City, the only men left at Chiconessex were William and Jasper. Malik and Botwe had been sent with the other laborers to work on the construction of Gargaphia. Edmund's new aide de camp, Billy, had essentially supplanted Jasper as the Colonel's right-hand man. Darby was left behind to serve as a messenger between the plantation and James City.

This latest demotion resulted in a serious decline in Jasper's attitude. He had become more and more slovenly and churlish. He resented Anne and the other women who wanted nothing to do with him. He was not good company for anyone. Edmund had come to see him as a nuisance, despite his sycophantic groveling. He left him behind making the excuse that he needed him to look out for Anne and notify him once the baby arrived. With his commander away,

Jasper spent his days sleeping and drinking. The entire household avoided him because of his foul humor.

One night, Daisy and Delia were taking turns reading to entertain Anne, Brigid, and William in Anne's bedroom. Fanta was still in the summer kitchen finishing dinner cleanup when Jasper appeared demanding the meal he had earlier slept through.

Fanta expressed annoyance that he was making more work for her to do and that she was missing the stories upstairs. "Why didn't you come to dinner when everyone else did?"

"Ya damn cow! Don't give me any back talk. Do as I tell ye!" Jasper barked.

Just as she was about to comply with his wishes, Fanta scowled at the man. Enraged at her display of insolence, Jasper slapped her so hard that she fell back onto the kitchen table. The fear in her eyes excited him, so he hit her again, and again. With each blow he became more and more aroused. Her screams only added to his exhilaration. He threw up her skirts and forced his now engorged penis between her legs as she screamed.

By this time, sounds of the commotion in the summer kitchen reached the rest of the household. William bounded out of the room followed by the women, including Anne. When they all got there, Jasper was laughing like a madman as he raped Fanta, who was wailing and trying to beat him off with clenched fists. Anne, moving slower than the rest, arrived in time to see William pull Jasper off of Fanta and throw him to the ground.

She could see that Fanta's face was swollen and bloody. Infuriated, Anne pushed past the others and began throwing any piece of crockery she could lay her hands on, at the man now cowering in a corner. His bloodshot eyes were open wide. He looked like a crazed demon.

"You black hearted beast from Hell! You bastard! I'll kill you! God damn you… God damn you!"

"Maybe if you had not denied me, this would not have happened. I had to fuck somebody. Why shouldn't I fuck her? She's just a goddamned black cow - nothing more! She had no right to refuse me. She's a worthless good for nothing cow. Next time we're alone - I'll fuck her again! I'm in charge here while the Colonel's away. I'll do what I please."

Jasper then drunkenly vomited on the floor in front of him before continuing his rant, bile dripping from his mouth.

"You don't know the evil you have tied yourself to. They don't call him the Great Conjurer for nothin'. His evil's catchin'. I should know. I thought he was a glorious prince, called by God on high to build His kingdom here on earth. But he breaks God's commandments. And those he doesn't break himself he gets others to do for him."

Jasper wiped his mouth and chin on his sleeve. By now he was crying, but this did not stop his angry screed. His audience was paralyzed, rapt with horror.

"The Great Conjurer, he don't even have to ask. His evil seeps into everyone around him like a fever. Before we know it, we just know what'll please him and we'll do anything to please him. What do you think happened to Owen Tomkin? The Colonel said if they married you off you couldn't have all he wanted to give you. Do you really think our Lord Scarborough would dirty his own hands with murder? Nooo! That was me. That's right. It was so easy, just a sharp elbow at the right moment, and that was it. The man went overboard. That's all it took. He's gone forever. No one ever challenged my story – that he fell on his own. Even if they suspected, we all knew it was what our master wanted. We all went along with it. Just so he could have Tomkin's land. Just so he could have you in his bed 'n' on his arm! And here you are acting like a queen in her castle. You may as well have pushed Tomkin inta the drink yourself."

Anne could take no more. She grabbed the poker from fireplace and screamed with a fury she had never felt before. She raised the weapon overhead and would have driven it right through his skull if William had not restrained her. Jasper took this chance to make a run for it, scrambling to his feet and out the door. As they all tried to collect themselves, Anne and the others could hear the sound of hooves hitting the ground as the crazed man made his escape.

Brigid tried to calm her mistress who had begun to scream epithets at Jasper again. "Madam! Stop! – Stop! You'll hurt yourself. Think of the baby."

She and the others stood by stunned as Anne dropped the poker and turned to Fanta who had by now rolled off the table onto the floor sobbing. Anne tried to comfort her. "Fanta, oh Fanta. Dear Fanta. Brigid find something to help me clean her up."

William exchanged worried looks with Brigid. "Mum, let Daisy and Delia take you upstairs, me and Brigid'll take care of Fanta. Brigid's right. You think of that babe you're carryin'. Come now Mistress Anne. Let us help you."

He gently lifted Anne up and turned her over to the twins who conducted her back to her room where they washed Fanta's blood from her hands. They tried to console the distraught woman who began to weep uncontrollably.

"It's alright. Everything will be alright now."

"It's all over now. Daisy's right. Everything will be alright. Don't cry so hard, Mum."

William and Brigid carried Fanta upstairs to the maids' quarter. Brigid went downstairs to get water and cloth to clean her wounds.

When she returned William left to check on his mistress down the hall who had begun to regain her senses.

"Is Fanta alright, William?"

"I'm not sure, Mum. Brigid is tending to her now."

"You need to go for Mr. Ishim and some men to go after Jasper. He needs to be arrested."

"Mistress Anne!! He can't leave! What if Jasper comes back? We'll all be…" Delia exclaimed.

"Alright, alright. In the morning. He can go in the morning. Girls, you and William, you take turns keeping watch. William, go and get your gun."

The rest of the night passed slowly. No one slept through the tense quiet. When the sun began to peek through the trees, Anne got out of bed and went to see what condition her slave was in.

Every part of Fanta's face was puffed and purple. She peered out from swollen eyelids at Anne. Through missing teeth with a bruised tongue, she managed to say: "Thith ith *your* fault. All *your* fault. I would not be here except for you. I'll hate you forever!" She then began to talk in her native language getting louder and angrier until she began screaming. "Go way! Go way! *Go way!*"

"You'd better let her rest, Mum."

Brigid put her arm around a shaken Anne and led her back to her room. Just then Anne felt a sharp twinge in her belly. Her water had broken. She left a wet trail behind her but she said nothing.

"Oh no." she thought. "Not now. Please not *now*."

"Alright, Mistress Anne, it looks like things is gettin' started. This whole mess has surely woken up your baby. They wants to come out and see what all the nasty commotion's about. Daisy, you go stay with Fanta. Delia you'd better go down and tell William to get going to the Ishim's for help from the militia."

"Tell him to go to Gargaphia and bring back a couple of men to help him stand watch here too. Tell him to bring Malike and Botwe." Anne added.

Over the course of that day, Anne slept lightly between bouts of labor pains. It was the fall; weather was still quite warm. Anne was beginning to feel feverish when Giles Ishim and a stranger appeared at the foot of her bed.

"Hello, Mistress Toft. I hear you ladies have been through a rough time of things. I've sent some men to alert the militia and Colonel Scarborough. William should be along any time now with boys from the new plantation."

Giles continued, "This is a visitor who happened to be at my home when William came to get me. His name is Alexandre Lorentz. He's a physician, and he knows our friend Captain Minshull. I asked him to come with me and check on you ladies. Dr. Lorentz this is Mistress Anne."

"How are you feeling, my dear?"

"Right now, I am just fine. Please, go look in on Fanta. I fear her injuries are very bad. Please, go make sure she is alright. Brigid, show him where to go."

Brigid led the doctor to where Fanta lay, alive but now unconscious. Though the women had attempted to clean and bind up her wounds, she was slowly bleeding to death. Dr. Lorentz set about his work quickly. He methodically surveyed Fanta for every possible wound before deciding on a prognosis. When he finished his examination, he asked Brigid to assemble the other ladies in their mistress' room.

"Madam, I am sorry to tell you that your servant is dying. I have examined all her wounds and, though I could stitch some of them up, she has wounds inside her head that I cannot reach. These are indicated by bleeding from her nose and ears. I have never seen anyone survive such injuries. The only other place I have seen anything like this, was in battle. I'm afraid she may hang on for another day or so, but that is all. There is nothing more to be done but try to keep her comfortable."

Tears filled Anne's eyes. On any other day the other women would have cried too, but they were all in a state of shock and exhaustion. Anne's labor pains were starting up again, though she tried not to show it.

"Giles, why don't I stay here with Mistress Toft and these fine ladies while you go meet with the militia? They could use some rest and I'd be happy to help here for a few days."

Dr. Alexandre Lorentz was a Dutchman with golden brown hair, striking blue eyes, and a flashing smile. At age 30, he was just average height and build, but his bearing was dashing and romantic. Like Captain Minshull's friend John Vassall, he had left a wife and children at home. His were in Amsterdam where, for reasons he preferred not to dwell on, he was no longer welcome. Whatever mysterious troubles his past may have contained, his visit to Virginia was merely a stopover on his way to further adventures in the Spice Islands.

Even in light of the traumatic events, every woman in the room could not help thinking how attractive he was. Alexandre Lorentz was not a scoundrel, just a handsome and incurable flirt. Most women, and a few men, could not help but fall in love with him at least just a little. He had the gift of charisma, of making every person he met feel as if they were special in his eyes. At this particular moment, Anne was too preoccupied with the unfolding events to notice his charms.

"Can't you try to save her, Doctor?" Anne asked wincing.

"I could, Mum." Lorentz patiently explained, "But, even if she were to survive, I am afraid she would never walk or lift her arms again. Surgery and its after effects would be very painful. At best she might live a few weeks. It would be a kindness to let her die peacefully now. Does she have any family?"

"None that I know of, but she came here with two other Africans, Malike and Botwe. They are her friends. Where are they? Brigid, did they come back from Gargaphia with William?"

"William's not back yet, Mum."

Anne's labor pains were starting to increase in frequency and intensity. She closed her eyes and began to mumble nonsensically. Now, no matter how hard she tried, she could not focus her thoughts.

"Are any of you a midwife?" Dr. Lorentz asked.

Brigid stepped forward. "I am not a midwife sire, but I have assisted in several births back in Lancashire."

By now Giles Ishim was ready to take his leave, not wanting to be put to work helping a woman give birth.

"I'll be off then. Mistress Anne, I'll see if we can't get Fanta's friends to come. At least they can help with her burial once she is gone. It looks like you all have things in hand here."

With that Giles was gone. Alexandre sent one twin to sit with Fanta and the other with Brigid to the kitchen to collect what he needed for the baby's delivery. He sat on the edge of the bed and held Anne's hand as the latest contractions began to subside. It was by now late afternoon and the sun streamed in the window, casting the room in a golden light which caught the edge of a crescent shaped scar on Alexandre's forehead. This looked to Anne like the moon.

"How is it that the moon is shining on your brow sir?"

"What?" Lorentz felt the scar. "Oh that. When I was a child a playmate threw a stick or something at me. I tried and failed to catch it and instead it clipped me in the head leaving a mark I am afraid."

"In the light, it looks like the moon is shining from your brow. It's funny you see, Giles said you are friends with Uncle Star. Uncle Star and Dr. Moon."

Anne's exhaustion was finally catching up with her. As her rambling became a whisper, she fell asleep for a little while. Her labor lasted into the early hours of the next day. The doctor and the women took turns caring for Anne and Fanta. William, Malike, Botwe, and one of the new indentures arrived sometime during the night to stand guard. As daylight broke again, Anne's daughter entered the world with shrieking exuberance just as Fanta was quietly slipping out of it.

In the days that followed the horrible melee at Chiconessex, William and the Africans buried Fanta in the forest clearing where William had previously laid to rest the miscarried children of Bella and Anne. Anne insisted that the whole household attend the burial and made the men carry her there, across the bumpy path in a wheelbarrow. She read from the *Book of Common Prayer*. All the others, except Malike and Botwe who stood silently, joined in on the refrain.

"We sinners beseech you to hear us, Lord Christ: That it may please you to deliver the soul of your servant Fanta from the power of evil, and from eternal death,

We beseech you to hear us, good Lord.

That it may please you mercifully to pardon all her sins,

We beseech you to hear us, good Lord.

That it may please you to grant her a place of refreshment and everlasting blessedness,

We beseech you to hear us, good Lord.

That it may please you to give her joy and gladness in your kingdom, with your saints in light,

We beseech you to hear us, good Lord."

Anne had no doubt that the Reverend Teackle would never perform funeral rites for Fanta because she was not a Christian, so she had not sent for him. Other slaves in the colony were buried unceremoniously because at that time, even if they professed a Christian faith, to consider them Christians would have made them ineligible for slavery. This hypocrisy made no sense to Anne. She did her best to invoke God's blessing for Fanta by reading from the requiem mass herself.

This did little to assuage her guilt. Jasper's vicious exit speech echoed in her brain over and over again. Was she really responsible for Owen's death? Fanta's own words were seared on her heart. Anne believed the slave was at least partly right because she had not fulfilled her promise to free Fanta in time to avoid this terrible fate. Anne's remorse was real and deep over this failing.

In the days that followed, Anne's Granny began to haunt her nights again with a recurring dream. Granny denounced her because she had not resisted the tyranny of the Lord of the Manor. She accused Anne of betraying her own kind, of becoming an evil temptress and a dirty slaver. Once again, they were on the bluff overlooking the North Sea. Just as her Granny's ghost cursed her and pushed her over the cliff, Anne would awaken, shaking in a cold sweat.

Anne's only relief came when she held her newborn baby and nursed her. The moment she saw her child, she felt the overwhelming power of a mother's love. She vowed to do everything humanly possible to protect and nurture her beautiful daughter. It was only through this little girl that she believed that she could be redeemed for her own dreadful sins.

Within a few days Edmund arrived, having received word of Anne's delivery and Jasper's crime. He brought with him news that Jasper had eluded capture and was reported to be hiding out in Rogues Harbor, southward in Carolina Province.

The Colonel was annoyed by what he considered to merely be Jasper's misadventures. No one dared share with him Jasper's treacherous allegations about him and the nature of Owen Tomkin's death. As for Fanta, her murder did not even register on him except as a loss of property. Anne was well acquainted with Edmund's lack of humanity when it came to his slaves. What surprised her was his casual attitude about Jasper. She would have challenged him about this if they had had a moment alone.

Edmund avoided any discussion of the events and only visited her when others were present in order to prevent a confrontation. He preferred to just forget about Jasper. The Colonel was too busy bragging to their guest Dr. Lorentz about his position and his latest accomplishments in James City. It did not occur to him to feel bad about Fanta's fate or even to be happy about his new daughter.

Edmund had already sired a healthy brood of legitimate children and probably more who were illegitimate. His rush to return to Chiconessex and any expressions of joy about the baby were performed only to make his mistress happy. Though Edmund was passionate about most things, his obsession to possess Anne paled in comparison to all else. He believed that this required a minimum of fuss over the birth but, in reality, it had little meaning for him.

"Well, my dear, what should we name her?"

"Annabella, for my mistress Bella, who took me in and taught me so much."

"That's fine my dear, that's fine. What do think, Dr. Lorentz? Mistress Anne made a lovely little girl, didn't she?"

Alexandre smiled and nodded. The Colonel had immediately taken a liking to the charming Dutchman. Dr. Lorentz was invited to stay on at Chiconessex while he was waiting for the *Zephyr Queen* to return to the area. Lorentz planned to book passage with Captain Minshull for the Caribbean. He accepted the invitation not because he liked the company of his insufferable host, but because he was intrigued by Scarborough's enchanting mistress. He wondered about this beautiful young woman who was supposedly married to one man and mistress of another. Lorentz was puzzled how someone of her obvious talents came to be in such an uncivilized environment.

It was rare to encounter a woman anywhere who was so well read and who could intellectually hold their own in conversation. She also seemed to be immune to his charms, which he always found attractive in any female. He loved a challenge, wondering if she had not just given birth if her seduction might have been more likely. During his visit Lorentz genuinely began to like Anne, so much so that he surprised himself by turning down his host's offer to enjoy the services of one of the twins.

The Colonel, himself, was completely taken in by the amiable doctor. He and Billy drank and swapped stories with Lorentz, who had seen much more of the world than they had. He regaled them with his escapades in places like Paris, Rome, Constantinople, and West Africa. During the evening entertainments he was the center of attention with his exciting tales of exotic cultures, strange jungle creatures, and audacious pirates.

Anne wondered how everyone could so quickly forget recent events enough to enjoy Lorentz's stories as if nothing had happened. She listened politely to him, trying to resist being beguiled by him like the rest of the household who found him to be a good distraction from thoughts of Fanta's traumatic death.

One morning, the entertaining guest found an opportunity to visit with Anne alone. She only indulged his conversation because she was grateful that he had been there to help that terrible night not so long ago. As their talk progressed, she could not help but warm to him a little.

"Mistress Anne, the Colonel tells me that you have a great love of books. Tell me what book are you reading now?"

"A few weeks ago, I finished *The Countess of Montgomery's Urania*. Once we settle into a new routine, I hope to begin *The Countess of Pembroke's Arcadia*. I have a bookseller in James City who regularly sends me new books. I think he chose these two titles because he presumed that they were written just for women. I wonder if it is now a requirement for countesses to write stories." Anne replied.

"I do not know. I think you will find *Arcadia* very amusing. It is every bit as provocative as *Urania*. Which of the sonnets in *Urania* did you like best?"

It somehow did not surprise Anne that this cultured nonconformist would have read either volume or even be aware of Lady Mary Worth's fairytale which was a thinly veiled defense of the rights of women.

"I found most fascinating the sonnet *Pamphilia to Amphilanthus*... Lady Mary most accurately describes the female condition as shrouded behind the mask of obedience."

"Mmm. Now that women have begun to write I suppose we men are destined to finally come to understand the way they think.

Of course, menfolk would have to be convinced to read their words. I am afraid that is generally unlikely."

"Well, Dr. Lorentz, maybe Lady Mary's real purpose was to incite women to speak their mind more so as to influence their men first hand."

Lorentz smiled slyly at his hostess. "I suspect you're right. My friends call me Alexandre. Won't you call me Alexandre?"

Anne recognized this familiarity for the flirtation that it was. It was at that moment that baby Annabella began to fuss in her cradle.

"Well, Dr. Moon - Alexandre, it looks as if Annabella is already not afraid to openly express her feelings. I am afraid it is time for her to be cleaned and nursed." Anne said returning her new friend's sly smile.

Alexandre was delighted by her nickname for him: "Dr. Moon." This was a signal that she might be open to his advances. But he decided not to take advantage, as he might have done with other women. Though he was usually an unrepentant romantic adventurer, Lorentz had his own "gentleman's" code of conduct which prevented him from taking undue advantage of a woman he considered to be vulnerable. Anne had been through so much already, he decided that he would not make any real attempt at seduction.

This did not stop Alexandre from flirting or making excuses to be alone with Anne. He was, however, careful to be discreet and chaste with his attentions toward her lest the Colonel become suspicious of his motives. What began for Alexandre as an amusing conquest developed into genuine affection, in part because they had in common a deep love of books.

For her part, Anne found his company a welcome reprieve from Edmund's. The Colonel's constant need for flattery was somewhat exhausting. Alexandre was especially enjoyable, because he knew how to make people feel like he was genuinely interested in them. Meanwhile, Anne always welcomed talking with any visitors to Chiconessex who could provide colonial gossip or news of the outside world.

Virginia's Eastern Shore was in fact the crossroads for every huckster and con artist in the colonies. In the last year alone, quite a few of them had made their way to Chiconessex to avail themselves of Anne's scrivener services. This had given her a quick education in how to spot deception. She was starting to become cynical, believing that most people were not to be trusted. Alexandre was no exception, but he was funny and she enjoyed engaging in friendly debate with him.

One evening after the household entertainments, he and Edmund retired to the parlor to share a bottle of rum. After being baited by Anne, Edmund was trying to defend slavery in his usual ham-handed way.

"My darling, I know you have great affection for your Africans, but they are just dumb animals after all. Believe me they are much happier being our slaves than being slaves to other savages in the wretched jungles they come from."

"They are not animals. They are simply people with dark skin, Edmund."

"What do you think, Doctor? Animals or people?"

"Well, Colonel, I think if you treat someone like an animal, they soon behave like one."

Anne found Edmund's remarks infuriating in light of what had happened to Fanta. After all, who was the animal when Jasper raped the poor woman? Deciding to challenge both men, Anne replied trying to hide her anger.

"With that logic, you must think most women are animals, because very few of us are ever given the chance to decide our own future for ourselves, and therefore are fated to work like dogs for our masters."

"Clearly, my dear, you are the exception to the rule." Edmund retorted, taking another swig of rum.

"And aren't you glad of that? Only someone as exceptional as yourself could be smart enough to enjoy my company. Isn't that so, my lord?" Anne teased.

Edmund smiled at that, as Alexandre brought the conversation back to the debate at hand.

"I wonder how would these Africans do if they suddenly found themselves to be freed? How would they survive?"

"Well, in fact, sir," Anne replied, "not far from here lives an African named Anthony Johnson, who owns his own plantation."

"And, his own slaves..." Edmund interrupted.

"Do you think he thinks of his slaves as just animals, as livestock?" Lorentz asked.

"I don't know, but he must treat them like animals. One of them ran away and bound himself to one of his neighbors. He had to take the neighbor to court to get 'em back."

"This Johnson fellow must have some intelligence if he owns property."

"He's a clever enough beast, Doctor, but he can't read nor write."

"You should know, Edmund. Didn't you sue him for a debt on a promissory he could not have actually ever read or signed?" Anne slyly prodded. She knew that Edmund had in fact forged the note.

He routinely pulled such stunts on his illiterate neighbors because he was always short of ready spending money. They rarely made formal complaints because they were either too ignorant to understand the swindle or too intimidated by the Colonel's authority.

"Well, er, he made his mark and agreed to it by voice in front of witnesses. And, yes, the court ruled in my favor." Edmund rubbed the back of his neck and looked at the floor. This conversation was starting to turn sour.

The rum had begun to erode their cleverness. The debate had run its course without a resolution so they decided it was time to find their beds. Edmund, too drunk for lovemaking, quickly fell asleep, snoring loudly. Anne nursed Annabella and put her back in her cradle then lay awake, deep in thought. That night the subject of Anne's insomnia was thoughts of what she was going to do with Malike and Botwe.

Seeing the men everyday was a painful reminder of Fanta. Anne wondered why the two had not reacted with fury at her death. She worried that if she did not fulfil her promise to them sooner than later, that they could become a threat leading to a fate not unlike Fanta's. Because they were woefully inexperienced in the rules of white society, she feared that they would simply end up bound to someone else who would trick them into giving up their freedom again. How could she release them and be assured that they could survive on their own?

It was an unusually warm fall night, so when Annabella began to fuss a few hours later, Anne took her down to the front porch. Late season mosquitoes quickly made that an uncomfortable place, so she moved back inside settling into a chair by the window in the parlor. With the child sleeping in her lap, she was praying quietly for guidance as the sun came up and Brigid arrived downstairs to prepare breakfast. Alexandre soon followed. He, like Anne, had been more conservative in his rum consumption than Edmund. The Great Conjurer would sleep away most of the morning, giving Anne and the doctor another chance to talk without him.

"The Colonel tells me that he has many slaves across his plantation, but I only notice the two who you had brought back from Gargaphia the night I first came here. Should I guess from our conversation last night that you do not like the use of African slaves, Mistress Anne?"

"Having been bound out, myself, I do not think I could bear the idea that my bondage would not eventually end."

"You were an indentured servant?"

"Yes, at the age of ten I was sent to James City and was bound to a man named Owen Tomkin. I was very lucky compared to most. He and his wife were very kind to me. They taught me many things, including how to read and write."

"Where were you from?"

Anne told Lorentz about Robin Hood's Bay, about being a smuggler's granddaughter, and how she came to Virginia.

"How did you come to be the mistress of Colonel Scarborough?"

"Ah, well, if I tell you that, then you will begin to know some of my dark secrets." Anne coyly deflected his question.

Alexandre summoned his all his charms, asking, "Oh come now, surely it would not hurt to share just one of those secrets with me?"

Though she was tempted to take him into her confidence, Anne's guard was now up. "Dr. Moon, I fear you would not think kindly of me if that story were told."

"Oh, I doubt that…"

The clatter of dishes being set out rescued Anne from this questioning. She asked Brigid to retrieve the cradle from the bedroom upstairs so that she could have her breakfast. In the short time the woman was gone Anne playfully brought the flirtation to an end.

"You, sir, could probably pry confessional secrets from a papist priest. But I'll not be telling you mine today."

Anne smiled and gestured toward the table where he sat down just as Brigid returned with the cradle. Anne nestled the baby in it and sat down to join her guest for bread and tea.

Exchanges like this made Dr. Lorentz' time at Chiconessex pass quickly, despite the fact that it was more than a month until Captain Minshull came to pick him up. When Uncle Star arrived, he only stayed a few hours, long enough to hear the latest news and leave his usual trinkets for his favorite hostess. Anne in turn gave him the smartly embroidered doublet she had promised him, which he accepted and wore with great pride.

Edmund had gone to inspect the work being done at Gargaphia, so before Anne said her farewells to the travelers, she took advantage of his absence to do something she knew he would not approve of. Anne had written manumission papers for Malike and Botwe. She turned them over to Captain Minshull with a pouch of silver coins.

"Uncle Star, I would like you to take these men with you. I am giving them what I promised them: their freedom. It is very hard for free Africans to survive here. My fellow countrymen tend to treat them badly. I have heard there is a town in Jamaica where free blacks live peacefully among themselves. I would like to book passage for Malike and Botwe on your ship. I know I can trust you to take them there, without fear of them being diverted in any way. I want you to introduce them to people there who can help them to get safely settled. I've written up papers giving them their freedom."

"Yes, Port Royal. I know it well. Of course, my dear, I'd be happy to do this."

Anne instructed her now former slaves to make ready for the trip. "Malike, Botwe, gather up your belongings. I am sending you with Captain Minshull. He will take you to a safe place where you may live among your own people."

The two slaves looked bewildered as Anne tried to explain to them what was happening. This was yet another wrenching change in their lives. They had gotten used to their life at Chiconessex. It was a better time than any they had since being enslaved. Yet, they had almost lost their will to decide for themselves their own fate. Challenging white people had only brought them trouble and not knowing what else to do, they did as they were told. They gathered their drums and put their clothing in leather sacks Anne provided them.

When they returned with their things, she kissed each man on the cheek and said goodbye. "I hope someday when you're living a better life, you'll find it in your heart to forgive me for what happened to Fanta. I never wanted that."

Anne then expressed her gratitude for all that Alexandre had done for her and bade her new friend farewell.

"Thank you, Dr. Lorentz, for coming to my rescue. I owe my child's life to you. Uncle Star, one night soon when you are sharing a jug, I give you permission to tell the truth of my story to Dr. Moon here. He seems a kindly sort, who might not condemn this orphan girl from Robin Hood's Bay for the choices she's made."

"As I would tell it, there is little to condemn my dear." The captain replied, kissing her gently on the cheek.

Then, without any further fanfare, the four men departed from Chiconessex, off for points southward. Malike, Botwe, Uncle Star, and Dr. Moon would all be well missed.

1662

Queen Anne's Palace

Anne's time was now full with motherhood, serving her customers, overseeing the running of Chiconessex, and the completion of Gargaphia. To say it was a busy time is an understatement. Edmund was not much help. He had returned to James City almost immediately after Dr. Lorentz left. The excuse he made was that he had left some of his business unfinished when he had rushed back to Chiconessex. This was only partly true. He was never able to tolerate a squalling infant and had made a practice of making himself scarce during this period of all his children's lives. He would not return until after the Yuletide season.

Anne did not complain. Servicing the Colonel's appetites was one less chore she had to deal with. His constant need for her attention and flattery was a drain she did not need. Most nights her dreams were overrun with flashbacks to that horrible night of the attack, and the blame that Fanta and Jasper had assigned her. During daylight hours her rational mind was firmly in control. As long as she concentrated on a list of specific tasks, she remained free of those troubling emotions that plagued her few moments of rest.

Gargaphia's completion was now totally under her supervision. Anne asserted her authority over every aspect of its construction. Edmund's original plans for an observation tower, were not to her liking. They called for it to be an open platform accessed by a simple ladder. Anne felt a flimsy rail would be insufficient and insisted they fully enclose the structure. She had them build a more substantial staircase with landings. The mistress of Gargaphia further required the men to add a roof and shutters on all sides so that the interior would remain dry during storms. She had four chairs, a table and a cabinet installed which was to be stocked with candles and writing supplies. This would be a place of work as well as comfort.

Next Anne turned her attention to the rest of the estate. She ordered the finest furnishings, linens, cutlery, china, and other household items. She bought only the best, feeling that it was an added benefit to spend as much of Edmund's money that she could. He wanted to own the finest plantation in the colonies. She was determined that he would have it, even if it bankrupted him. And if it did, so much the better.

That year Anne was sent another group of thirty indentures. Their headrights allowed her to buy more property. There were six couples among the latest arrivals, all who had farm experience. The rest were young men with no training who would need to learn a trade. She put some together with a cobbler who had been in the previous batch of servants. Many of the laborers and slaves had no shoes so she put these recruits to work making footwear. Once they were done outfitting her crews, Anne, ever the entrepreneur, ordered them to produce shoes for sale to other settlers. The rest of the new servants were dispersed throughout her now growing holdings to serve as simple laborers.

Anne assigned the married couples to run various farms whose previous occupants had been dispossessed by the Colonel for one reason or another. She chose one couple who had a baby on the way to live at Chiconessex. William would remain there to guide them once Anne moved to Gargaphia that next fall season.

Anne was not happy about this. William, had uncharacteristically stood up for what he wanted and refused to move to the new plantation. He had insisted he had no desire to leave the place he had called home, now for most of his life. He did not ask for his freedom, even though his indenture contract had long ago run out. He felt rooted to the forests and waterways around Chiconessex. He kept to himself the disgust he felt watching her with the so-called King of Accomack.

"I am too old to learn the woods around Gargaphia. I would be useless there. I suppose Mum, I am of the old ways. I serve the land and all that lives on it. Please don't make me go. I'd be satisfied with just room and board as pay for my work, Mum."

Anne knew she could have forced him to go with her, but her affection for him governed her response. She was not just grateful for his support and loyalty over the years. Her feelings were deeper than that. He was the only person in the colony whom she thought of as family. So, she released him as he asked, and tried not to make him feel any worse about it than he already seemed to.

"I will miss you and your fiddle terribly. We will be here until just after All Saints Day. Will you take me out for one last ribbon blessing, my friend?"

William nodded and left to attend to his daily chores. Tears filled Anne's eyes. She tried to hide them from Brigid who went about her work without comment.

All Saints Day came. Anne and William completed the ribbon blessing one last time. They went out in the boat alone while Brigid looked after Annabella. This year Fanta was included in the prayers. The recent tragic experience had brought on the full mantle of adulthood for Anne, sapping her sweet childhood ritual of some of its healing magic.

In future years Anne never asked anyone else to take part in the ribbon blessing, not even her own children. Wary that its origins could cause her trouble, she knew her Protestant neighbors would be suspicious of this practice. She persisted with it because, though Anne's rational mind recognized it as just a charming old superstition, this small vestige of her past felt like a balm upon her troubled soul. It connected her to lost loved ones. It was a secret that Anne carefully treasured in private.

Though they hardly knew each other, shared trauma would become a silent bond between Anne, Brigid, and the Sheffield sisters. They never spoke of Fanta's horrible rape and murder changed them. Each in their own way was now older, more serious. As twins, Delia and Daisy looked to each other for comfort. Anne and Brigid, by virtue of the amount of time they spent together came to trust each other, even though they rarely crossed the line of mistress and servant into the succor of friendship.

As long as she knew these women, Anne felt a guilt-ridden loyalty to them. They had survived something terrible together. Whenever she could, she tried to protect them and promote what she considered to be their best interests. She could not afford to have them turn on her. They in turn, had no way to endure on their own in this wilderness. They all needed each other.

Anne with her infant daughter, moved into Gargaphia the first week of November along with Brigid and the Sheffield twins. The luxurious new accommodations should have made for a happy time in their lives. Anne's mood, however, was dampened by missing Chiconessex.

Daisy tried to lift her spirits with stories of the Twelve Days of Christmas as celebrated at court in London. These revels were marked by sumptuous meals, music, comic performances, and dancing. Together the four women tried to make their first holiday season as joyous as possible. There were no visitors yet so they made the best of the quiet time in anticipation of the unique festivities that Gargaphia would soon be known for.

The plantation was now Anne's to run, but it would always be filled with people she did not completely know or trust. Though Anne often felt like she was sailing out into the ocean in a boat with no rudder, she was determined not to show it. That is the curse of any leader. They govern only by the good graces of those they have power over. Anne would have to learn as she went along how to inspire the allegiance and hard work of others.

This was no easy task in a society that was making up its own rules as they lived them. Old customs would only survive as long as they were practical. New ones would be accepted only when a prevailing majority was willing to live under them.

There were two driving beliefs among the settlers. The first was the understanding by most of them, that they had come to the colony on a sacred mission. God had sent them to this new land to expand His Christian Kingdom. Even those who were secretly nonbelievers, knew that their fortunes depended on their ability to act accordingly. The second belief was that every person, free or bound in service, lived in the hope that eventually they would have a chance at self-determination. Slaves outwardly accepted the permanency of their bondage. Yet the seeds of freedom were discreetly planted in their hearts as they watched indentures complete their terms of service and set off on their own.

Anne could not keep the Colonel from buying slaves to work in his fields, but she did try to keep them out of the house at Gargaphia. For a long while, she could not bear the presence of any Africans because of her memories of Fanta. Sometime after settling at Gargaphia, Anne received a letter from John Vassall. With only vague references to Captain Minshull, he relayed that her two former slaves had been safely conveyed to Port Royal in Jamaica. Anne's money had assured them a place to settle in the free black village there, where they had been welcomed warmly. This news was a great relief, and a Christmas gift which meant much more than the lavish trinkets Edmund had sent from Hedra Cottage.

Colonel Scarborough did not come to see the completed Gargaphia until the Feast of the Epiphany fulfilling a promise to her to be there on that date. Anne, knowing when to expect his arrival, prepared a lavish homecoming, anticipating his desire to feel like a victorious new king being coronated. His children, his sister, and their respective spouses were invited along with a selection of the wealthiest landowners in the county to attend the grand affair. Everyone came dressed in their finest attire to congratulate the Great Conjurer on the completion of his magnificent new home; and secretly to gather gossip about his now notorious household.

Anne's recent collection of indentures included two musicians. One played the fiddle and the other a penny whistle. She had them rehearse songs to accompany dancing by the Sheffield girls. After a grand feast in the large gathering hall, the four entertained the crowd until late into the night. Several casks of fine Spanish wine were consumed before the visitors were invited to stay in rooms prepared for them in the luxurious guest wing.

After the rest of the household had gone to bed, Anne had planned a special celebration for Edmund in his bedchambers. He was in high spirits when she told him that she had a surprise for him. Anne had concocted a special erotic performance which she hoped would help ensure his continued devotion until she was finished with him.

Anne told him to wait in the dark until she arrived dressed, not in the beautiful gown she had spent the evening in, but a short plain white toga. She carried a candelabra with four lit candles which she set on a small table on the opposite side of the room from where Edmund sat in the shadows on the bed. She was followed into the room by Delia and Daisy also dressed in togas, carrying a basin of water and a bottle of perfumed oil. Their milky white skin seemed to glow in the amber light of the tapers.

Edmund watched feverishly as the blond nymphets disrobed their mistress and slowly washed her body. They slowly danced while making a ritualistic application of the oil to Anne's glistening breasts and thighs. Her hair was piled high on top of her head. The only thing she was wearing now was the sapphire jewelry he had given her. She paused for a moment to let him fully take in the scene.

"Behold! Who spies on us in the shadows? It is a wandering hunter. Catch him and strip him of his clothes!" Anne commanded the sisters.

They obeyed immediately and to Edmund's delight they disrobed him revealing him to be completely aroused and ready for anything they might do. Anne clapped her hands and the Sheffields backed away from the Colonel, closing the door behind them as they left the room. Anne dribbled some of the warm oil on his exposed genitals.

"I command you to worship me and me alone, Edmund Scarborough."

Anne's voice was deep and husky as she climbed on top of the man and took him inside her. They reached orgasm quickly, almost simultaneously.

"While you are at Gargaphia, my lord, I and I alone will have the pleasure of satisfying you. Do you understand?"

This aroused him again and he moaned "Yes, yes, oh yes." as he rolled Anne over and made love to her again. That night Anne conceived another child. In seeming acknowledgement of their erotic ritual, Anne would name her Atalanta for one of the vestal virgins of the goddesses Diana. Ovid in his Metamorphosis, had praised the mythological Atalanta for successfully competing against men as a huntress. Through this tribute Anne expressed the pride she felt for her own accomplishments and her secret hope that her daughters would be brave self-sufficient women in their own right.

After the celebrations were over, the Great Conjurer turned his attention back to his campaigns against the Indians and anyone else who might get in his way. He was particularly focused on settlers belonging to the new religious sect known as the Quakers who were known for their tolerance of the natives. The Colonel coveted their plantations, and cursed their brand of piety which was interfering with his plans.

During the previous session of the House of Burgesses he had pushed through "an act prohibiting the unlawful assembling of Quakers." Once he had returned to the Eastern Shore, this law allowed him to confiscate properties from members of the dissenter sect who were living just to the north of Gargaphia along the border between Virginia and Maryland Province.

As another year quickly passed, Edmund acted more and more with the unfettered swagger of royalty. His arrogant habit of taking what he wanted without paying for it went unchecked. Wherever he went, he demanded to be fed and housed for free. People were openly calling Edmund the "King of Accomack." For a time, Anne and Edmund felt satisfied, each with their own progress.

Gargaphia

Now that it was finished, Gargaphia was not only the most opulent home on Virginia's Eastern Shore. It was the largest. It was constructed of English bond brickwork with oak timbers and a cedar shake roof. Its windows had leaded glass. The trim work was white washed. The interior had walnut paneling throughout except for the servants' quarters which were plaster over lath.

The master suite was comprised of bedrooms for Edmund and Anne each, as well as a sizeable nursery, a guest chamber, and a maids' room. Downstairs was a large parlor, the library, a dining room, and the winter kitchen. Each room in the master wing was spacious, well-appointed with thick tapestries, heavy carpets, and its own fireplace. This wing was on the southern end of the building and had a porch that rimmed the first floor on the south and west sides facing the road leading to the estate.

The guest wing was even larger with a total of twenty bedrooms. Since few overnight visitors were expected in the depths of winter, these rooms did not have their own hearths. Warming pans would be provided for the beds of those guests who felt a chill during their stay. Just the same, these rooms had windows, carpets, and expensive furnishings. At the end of the hall on each floor were living quarters for servants and prostitutes. These were more or less dormitories. The rooms were not as nice as the master quarters, but they did have small fireplaces. These were not just for the servants but to provide coals for the bedpans and hot water when guests need it.

The two wings were each connected by short hallways on the first floor leading to a large single-story gathering hall with enough seating to accommodate more than fifty people. This also had a large porch on its west side. At either end of the hall were two large fireplaces. One was for guests to warm themselves during cold weather. The other served as the winter kitchen for the guests. A door on the east side opened onto a landing with steps down to an herb and rose garden. Just outside the main building was the summer kitchen that served both master and guest quarters.

There were several other separate buildings with laborers' dorms and another kitchen and dining hall for the various men and women servants who otherwise kept the plantation going. There was a large barn for livestock, and drying sheds for corn, wheat, and tobacco.

Another luxury of Gargaphia was its bathhouse. Most British settlers followed the hygienic customs of their homeland where the cleanliness of their clothes was valued over that of their bodies. It was not uncommon for men and women alike to carry sprigs of herbs to mask their usually terrible odor. In the age of the Protestant Reformation bathing had gone completely out of fashion and had been relegated to sin houses as self-indulgent carnal gratification. At Gargaphia there was no such disdain for the pleasures of bathing.

The bathhouse consisted of two rooms, one with just one wooden tub, the other with two. These were lined with white linen to prevent splintered buttocks. The wall between the rooms was a double-sided fireplace with a great cast iron pot for warming water. The room with the single tub was often frequented by customers of the Sheffield sisters. During winter months when the plantation rarely had visitors, clothes washing that was usually done outside was done in the bathhouse. In summer time, the bathhouse was a welcome relief from the oppressive heat. Edmund and Anne each had their own tubs in their rooms. The bathhouse was reserved for their guests, though Anne sometimes allowed servants, as a reward for good work, to use the tubs.

Gargaphia, like most plantations, was a burgeoning community which spread beyond the main compound and farm fields. About a mile and a half away from Gargaphia, a small village was gradually being built. Anne had her carpenters build cabins as needed and rented them to the various bonded tradespeople, or to freemen who had arrived to live in the colony on their own.

Every year more and more people were emigrating to Virginia. Just forty years prior, there were fewer than one hundred Europeans living on the Virginia portion of the peninsula. Now the population had risen to close to twenty thousand. People arrived to Accomack County every day, looking for work and a place to live. More and more skilled tradesmen left their homes in England to take advantage of this new land of opportunity. Farmers came with their most prized livestock. There were coopers, millers, and waggoneers. Their women were seamstresses, candlemakers, weavers, and cooks.

These God-fearing immigrants mostly came with good intentions. There were more upstanding citizens among them than there were criminals. Unfortunately, there is always a certain element with compromised morals who form the edges of society, surviving by taking advantage of others. Occasionally people arrived in the colony with no money and no prospects.

Within a few months of taking up residence at Gargaphia, it became clear that food and wine was being stolen. Anne employed the blacksmith from Pungoteague to create locks for her store rooms. She and Brigid each carried copies of the keys on large rings which they wore tied to a belt around their waists. Another set was made for Edmund. This was largely symbolic, in deference to his role as master.

Anne had three large boxes with locks made to keep valuables in. She made a special show of giving Edmund copies of the keys to one box which would be kept in his bedchamber and to one she called the "ready silver" box for petty cash. This and the third box were kept in Anne's room. She never showed the last chest to Edmund nor provided him with its key. It was a good-sized trunk, too heavy for one person to carry because it was made of iron. Anne had it built to withstand a fire. She covered it with a cloth and stacked other boxes on top of it. In it, Anne kept the *Friends and Neighbors* ledger, deeds to her land, the money she skimmed from the scrivener's business for herself, a stash of wampum beads, and a variety of jewels and other trinkets that people had used as barter for her services.

Despite the new security measures, eggs from the hen house and vegetables from the garden were still going missing. Finally, some of Anne's field hands discovered four teenage boys hiding in the barn. They were orphaned English street urchins who had stowed away on a ship to the colony. These enterprising lads had not only managed to avoid detection on the ocean voyage, but they had come ashore without anyone noticing. They had somehow found their way to Gargaphia and were hiding out there until they could figure out what to do next.

When the boys were brought to Anne's parlor, they were not exactly contrite. They had never seen anything as opulent as Gargaphia, or a woman as beautiful as its mistress. Childhood neglect made their manners unruly. As they stared at the floor sniggering, Anne peppered them with questions.

"Where did you come from? Who told you, you could sleep in my barn? You, boy, what is your name?" Anne said as she lifted the chin of the biggest boy, forcing him to look her in the eye.

"I am Garret, Mum, Garret Supple, Mum."

"And where, pray tell, Garret Supple, did you boys come from?"

"Bristol, Mum."

"Bristol? You're indentures then. Who are you bound to? What plantation did you run off from?"

The smallest boy spoke up answering in a high-pitched voice that cracked with every other word, "We're not bondsmen. We're freemen, m'lady."

Anne had to stifle a laugh. "Oh, you are free men, eh?"

The boys began elbowing each other and telling the younger fellow to "Shut up."

"Alright, that's enough. That's enough. I guess we'll have to throw you lot into jail for stealing. Here in Virginia colony we don't tolerate such things. You'll be put in the dock and whipped every day for a week, I expect. Unless, that is, you can tell me who your master is and they can make this right."

The younger boy spoke up again, much to the consternation of his companions.

"It's true m'lady. We came on our own in the hold of a ship. We're here to make our fortunes. We got no master who can make it right. Please don't throw us in the jail. Please don't have us whipped!"

Anne put her hands on the child's shoulders. "Tell me your name, son."

"Patrick Easton, Mum."

"Alright, Patrick. I required to take you before the magistrate to register you. Unless I speak up for you, they will still want to throw every one of you in jail for being stowaways."

The boys all began talking at once.

"Can't we stay and work for you?"

"We'll be good! We'll work hard!"

"We promise, we won't be any trouble."

Anne wanted to help the boys, but she knew if she brought them before the court without a plan the magistrate could separate them and impose a stiff multi-decade sentence of indenture on them.

"Be quiet. Hush now. Here's what I'll do," she said. "If you will work hard for the next few weeks until court is in session, I will stand your bond and pay your passage. But you will have to sign on for seven-years with me."

"Seven years…" Garret complained.

"The magistrate will start at fifteen. I will offer to keep you each till you are twenty-four. You ask the other servants. This is a good place to work. You're lucky you did not hide out on some other plantation. You'd be laid bare by the lash by now. I want to know each of your names. Come on, let's have 'em."

The last two identified themselves as Owin and John Murfee. They were fifteen-year-old cousins. Patrick was the youngest at age thirteen, and Garret was seventeen. Anne sent them to the laborer's dorm where they were fed a hot meal and given beds together. She instructed the crew captain to keep an eye on them and make sure they were kept busy with useful tasks. Anne referred to them as the Bristol Boys thereafter. They became part of the colorful growing family of Gargaphia.

Anne now had queenly authority over a great plantation. But, hers was not a life of leisure. She had no time to read her books or practice needle work during those days. Nor did Anne have time to think about her grand scheme. Where would it take her, and now her children? How would it end? It was clear she did not have the stomach to enact the Biblical Judith's fierce justice on Edmund, especially now that she had much more to lose if she did.

A myriad of day to day decisions preoccupied her. Where do you want this cabinet put? How much corn should we plant? Which men should work in the fields and which should build more drying sheds? Anne had learned to always answer with confidence even when she simply said the first thing that came into her mind.

The lookout tower that Anne had been so particular about was beyond the large kitchen garden to the east of the main building. The structure was an impressive four stories tall. Most of the year the shutters, which were hinged at the top, were propped open. Its uppermost room was only about ten feet long by twelve feet wide, with a trap door to the stairs.

When its shutters were all open, a person could see for miles in every direction. To the east was the creek and the small bay with an inlet leading to the wide-open ocean which stretched out beyond the dunes. Forests surrounded the property to the north, south, and west where on a clear day the Chesapeake Bay could be seen on the far horizon.

This was by all accounts a spectacular view. As Anne had ordered, there were table, chairs, and a cabinet to keep the tools of her scrivener's trade. She even had a trunk brought up containing quilts for cooler weather.

Anne kept a brass spyglass there to look for ships and storms approaching from afar. She spent hours enjoying the wonderous spectacles afforded by the height of the structure. She watched eagles and great flocks of birds flying above the land. During certain times in the year, she could even see whales making great leaps in the ocean. Travelers on the road to Gargaphia could be seen from a distance of more than a mile.

The tower became Anne's place of work and refuge. On those nights when she could not sleep, she could be found there. She used its quiet solitude to do bookkeeping and write letters. Occasionally she invited guests to climb the winding staircase to enjoy the setting sun. Mostly she used the tower as a place to get away from the constant demands of the plantation. Edmund rarely climbed the staircase. He was too lazy.

During those times when Colonel Scarborough was in residence at Gargaphia, court proceedings were held in the main gathering hall. The Governor had appointed four prominent landowners to serve on magistrates' councils in each county. Edmund was appointed to head the Accomack court, along with his brother in law Nathaniel Littleton, Edmund's son Charles, and his daughter Matilda's husband John West. The royal family of Accomack presided over all matters of importance there.

Until now, the council had held their sessions in various homes and taverns around the county. Because the large gathering hall at Gargaphia could accommodate many more people, the council agreed to hold all their meetings there until a proper courthouse could be built. This was convenient for Edmund and it inflated his already exaggerated sense of importance to literally "hold court" in his home.

Proceedings were usually well attended by the local community. This is where all contracts were recorded and disputes were settled. These assemblies were often followed by meals for the magistrates and their friends who stayed the night as court sessions were usually held over the course of a week to ten days at a time.

Anne became a regular fixture at these proceedings. Her work as a scrivener meant she was frequently consulted about her memory of various contracts and documents that she had written for clients. Anne had already served for several years as a witness to so many of her neighbors' business dealings, she was called often to testify. Naturally proximity to these legal procedures helped her scrivening business to flourish.

Many of the cases heard were boring, but often there were melodramatic outbursts which were quite entertaining. At first Anne was excited by her newfound importance. It did not take long for that sentiment to sour. Anne began to notice the disturbing regularity of women being brought before the court. Usually they were unmarried maid servants who were charged with fornication or bastardy with their masters when they became pregnant. The men were fined and forced to pay maintenance for the resulting children. Indentured women who were convicted of these crimes would have their bonds extended for two years to make up for the time lost to their pregnancy. This was true even for women who claimed they had been raped.

Over the years, Anne sat quietly and watched while men and especially women received punishments, having done little to deserve them. There were times that women successfully brought complaints to the court for issues like theft, or nonpayment of debts; though these instances were rare by comparison. Anne observed these things, realizing with increasing pessimism the risk she and her children faced because she was not legally married.

There also was a disturbing celebratory atmosphere that followed the conclusion of court sessions. Those who lost their cases left to face the unhappy circumstances of jail, public whippings, or further indenture. The winners spent the next few days reveling in the guest house at Gargaphia often committing the very acts that had just been condemned.

Gargaphia became the center of social life in northern Accomack County. On a given evening the landed gentry could be found carousing there with wealthy merchants and sea captains. Not all of the plantation's visitors were from the region nor were they all English. Often there were French, Spanish, and Dutch travelers; despite the various trade embargos on their home countries imposed by the crown of England. Among the guests were often pirates and smugglers who openly consorted with the local planters.

Captain Minshull was a regular, with visits several times a year. Gargaphia was always on the way to somewhere for him. He was Anne's one true confidant. He fussed over her and her children as if he were their grandfather. He was often the life of the party among her other guests.

Anne now rarely stayed up late to hear his ribald jokes and stories. She kept herself out of the sphere of any scandalous behavior by relying on the Sheffield sisters to lead the revelries and report regularly on who did what. Though she was never a direct witness to bad behavior, this knowledge gave Anne a blackmailer's advantage over her guests, should she need it. The longer this went on the more leverage she had over other colonists who indulged themselves at Gargaphia.

She rarely had to use this power. Anne had no interest in extorting her guests. It was reserved as ammunition in case someone tried to turn colonial authorities against her.

Gargaphia was not a place for the pious or the poor. Its gathering hall was a hedonistic playground for anyone with money to spend or lose. Gambling over draughts and dice was common. Entertainment was provided by a growing contingent of storytellers and musicians among the indentured servants who worked for tips. Young women, known as wenches, were employed to serve food and ale, along with more erotic hospitality.

Anne did not directly profit from the sex work performed at the plantation. This was intentional. If it were proved in court that she had accepted any portion of the women's pay she could be convicted of running a bawdy house or promoting fornication. She in fact was, but this gave her some plausible deniability. She saw this business as merely a discrete comfort provided to guests. Allowing it only furthered the profits from other services rendered there. It did not trouble Anne's conscience to let these women ply their trade having been born into a similar establishment. She may not have fully understood what was going on as a child, but she did now and she had experienced enough of life to know morality was often in the eye of the beholder.

So, the prostitutes working at Gargaphia were allowed to keep any money they made, as long as they behaved in a refined manner and helped with household chores when there were no guests. They lived at the plantation free of charge. They were required to dress modestly, avoid coarse language, and confine their sexual activity behind closed doors. The only prohibition they were given was that they were not allowed to gamble with their own customers. It was too easy for foolish gentlemen to lose their money then lay the blame on the wiles of their female companions. That would have been a recipe for assaults or complaints to the authorities.

Anne also made it a practice to release women from indenture to do this work. She wanted only willing uncoerced participants. She did not want anyone to make a claim that she had forced them into immoral behavior. Anne also allowed the girls to leave when they attracted marriage proposals, when they had earned a stake to go elsewhere, or if they got hurt by unruly guests.

There always seemed to be more women waiting to take their place. The Sheffields were the exception to the rule that most of the girls only lasted a year or two at this profession. Daisy and Delia supervised the others and taught newcomers the house rules. They enjoyed a sort of seniority among the other wenches which allowed them to have first pick of the wealthier patrons. They built up an exclusive clientele which almost made up for their exile to the rustic colony. They liked their life as celebrated courtesans.

Anne did not have to worry about the Edmund's fellow magistrates. They were both family and regular customers. This setup was mostly Edmund's idea anyway. He was in a position to protect the running of Gargaphia from unnecessary interference. Anne did have to bribe a succession of Anglican pastors to not bring charges of fornication against her wenches and allow them to attend church.

Gargaphia's substantial annual tithe to the church along with this additional stipend soothed any moral qualms those preachers might have had. Such was the influence of Mistress Toft's money, and perhaps as Jasper had said, the Great Conjurer's not so hidden talent for corrupting everyone around him.

In a relatively short time Edmund's mistress had come to enjoy a level of acceptable notoriety among the Accomack landowners and even some of their wives. Though they did not openly socialize with her, she found ways to ingratiate herself to them with small acts of kindness, gifts, and by lending her servants to them in times of need. Anne was known to be a generous amiable neighbor.

Through her business activities she enjoyed a reputation for honesty and fair dealing. Even her more illicit customers valued her standing in the community because it provided them with an effective cover for her assistance with smuggling and forgery. She had unintentionally fallen right into her Granny's footsteps, except on a much grander scale.

Colonists on Virginia's Eastern Shore had developed their own code of conduct. Not unlike societies everywhere, there were double standards that were deemed tolerable. When the most powerful person around makes up their own rules, others follow their example. Survival in this frontier community took precedence over laws and mores that were sometimes out of touch with their life on the peninsula. And, since authorities from the capital rarely visited, local residents took pleasure in doing things the "Eastern Shore" way.

Before the leaves turned golden that first fall at Gargaphia, Anne gave birth to Atalanta. She was a healthy baby. Her delivery was normal and thankfully much less remarkable than that of her sister. It did not take long for Edmund to leave again in order to avoid dealing with a newborn in the house. As was his practice, he would not return to Gargaphia until after the coming Yuletide season.

Anne was too busy with business to care. A few weeks after Atalanta's arrival, a southern storm blew in as they often did that time of year. For one full day and a night, strong winds and rain pummeled the new house.

The skies cleared around dawn the next day. Anne climbed to the top of the lookout tower to survey the damage done. Things had held up pretty well. She made a list of small repairs to give the servants along with their daily orders. Before descending the stairs, she looked eastward toward the ocean which still boiled in the aftermath of the squall. Looming on the beach she saw the hull of a grounded ship. Its mast was broken in half. Anne could see no movement on her decks.

Anne quickly went into action. She gathered up her skirts and practically flew down the steps. Once outside she began ringing the bell that had been hung on a post near the kitchen garden to call servants to meals.

"Bring everyone to the gathering hall immediately. Everyone. Get everyone up!" Anne called out to every person she saw.

Soon the entire household, including guests, was assembled. Anne stood on a chair to address the bleary-eyed crowd, many who had been pulled from their beds.

"A ship has run aground up on the island. I could see no survivors from the tower. Rights of salvage belong to the household of Gargaphia!" she declared. "That means – each and every one of us – all those here in residence today. We will follow the customs for wrecking as they did in my birthplace on the northern coast of England. This is the law of the sea.

"Everyone will be assigned a duty." Anne continued. "First, we must do our best to rescue any survivors, if there are any, and bring them back to the house to be cared for. The dead must be buried. We will carry back all that is salvageable. I will assess the value of what we have brought back and distribute an even share to each soul. Everyone here today gets a share. That includes guests and servants alike, even the people who have to stay back, to care for the children, cook our meals, or care for the wounded. Everyone, go get any sack or bucket you can find and meet at the dock."

Anne chose who would stay behind. Then she picked the men who would ferry people down the creek and across the lagoon to the dunes where they would walk to the beach. Anne was in the first boat, leaving the girls under the watchful eyes of Brigid back in the master's quarters. As she said in her speech, she doled out jobs as people came off the boat.

A half dozen dead bodies were found in and around the ship. The ship's dories were still tied to the gunnels. This suggested that the rest of the crew had likely been washed overboard or sucked out to sea through the gaping hole in the hull. There were no survivors.

Anne told three men to take the dead down the beach and dig their graves in the dunes. She walked up to the top of the highest dune near the wreck to supervise the salvage operation. She thought of the gold coin that she had found when Edmund had first brought her there for an assignation. It was still carefully locked in her iron trunk. Its seeming promise of riches to be found was not, however, realized with this particular shipwreck.

This vessel had carried a cargo of tobacco which was now drenched with seawater and ruined. The damage to the hull had rendered it unusable as well. Its only value was in its fittings and repurposing a few timbers. Though the servants scoured the beach, little else could be found that would be considered worth anything.

After a few hours Anne sent a man back to the house for her prayer book. When he returned, she gathered everyone and led them to the place where the graves had been dug. She read funeral prayers for the dead sailors then led everyone back to the few baskets and sacks of junk that had been collected.

This had been a disappointing haul after the initial excitement about shipwreck treasure. If anyone had found any small thing of value, Anne decided not to begrudge them keeping it. After having read the requiem, somehow the idea of pricing and dividing the inconsequential personal effects of the dead captain and his crew felt unseemly to Anne. She decided to give everyone a shilling and allow them to keep any worthless trinkets they had found.

She satisfied herself that maritime rights of salvage on Gargaphia's beach had now been established. The household now knew that they were trusted and that their loyalty would be rewarded. The next time she would be better prepared. She would have a barge built to bring large timbers back. And, she would appoint certain servants to help assess the value of what was found and police the operation for thievery. As usual, Anne's foresight was on target. Going forward shipping in the region increased every year with more and more vessels risking travel to the colonies regardless of the season. There would be many more wrecks on Anne's beach bringing yet another source of revenue to her.

Thus, Gargaphia became an enthralling attraction for people near and far. It developed an almost mythic reputation for being a place where anything could happen. An evening's gambling entertainment could change someone's life. Someone else's calamity could be your happy destiny. Gargaphia was a place where bad fortune could transform into good for aristocrat and servant alike.

Rising Tides

Motherhood for women of the planter class in colonial Virginia was very different than that of common women. The elite hired wet nurses to help them care for their offspring through their first three or four years and longer. With her elevated status as mistress to one of the wealthiest men in the county, no one would have thought it strange if Anne had followed that same custom. That was not her way of doing things.

Instead, Anne herself nursed all her children until they were two. She kept them with her most of the time, unless their playing or fussing interfered with her business. Only then did she have her trusted servant Brigid look after them. When Annabella was big enough to climb the tower stairs with her mother, a cot was installed so she could nap there while her mother did her paperwork. A basket of toys was also brought up to occupy the child. It was not long before Atalanta joined them. Anne's greatest joy was now playing with her girls. She told them her Granny's fairy tales and made them rag dolls.

In those years, everything Anne set out to do flourished. Luck was on her side. She turned the work of a few cobblers into a successful tannery and shoe factory. She invested in merchant ships, some legitimate, some not. Through her growing network of associates, she bought land in Carolina, Jamaica, Nevis, and Barbados. She exported tobacco and other crops from Accomack to England. She traded in cotton, indigo, sugar, and rum.

In her prosperity Anne did not forget those who had helped her along the way. She provided business opportunities and loans to people in the *Friends and Neighbors* ledger which continued to grow. Old confidants like Giles Ishim were given inside information whenever possible to protect them from potential problems with the Colonel. Anne paid off some neighbors when Scarborough made deals in bad faith with them. Her aide was given on the condition of secrecy. Anne came to be known affectionately by her friends as Mistress Bluebird in reference to her start at Chiconessex. She sometimes even signed notes to friends with this moniker.

Anne was not without her detractors. Her enemies called her the Great Conjurer's Whore. Certain Puritan neighbors believed that the couple were agents of the Devil himself, intent on corrupting the entire colony. They felt powerless to act against their influence, but this did not stop them from disparaging the Colonel and his mistress, nor pitying his neglected wife Mary.

Anne was too busy to think much about her reputation or even about her original plan to ruin Edmund. But once a scheme like Anne's gets started it cannot be stopped. Avenging Owen's death through Edmund's downfall seemed to take on a life of its own and continue on without any overt effort on her part.

She had not stopped blaming him for what had happened to the Tomkin family. Quite the contrary. She was not sure whether Jasper's drunken confession had been a lie. There was no way to prove it. Regardless, Edmund had profited from Tomkin's death. He had used it to keep her from making a respectable marriage. Despite the high life she was living, these things were unforgiveable to her. What Jasper had said did not exonerate Edmund. It had actually indicted him with the greater crime of being an insidious corruptor.

By some strange coincidence, as Anne's fortunes rose Edmund's slowly began to fall. This was evident when Anne had a large commercial saltworks built near Gargaphia to produce the condiment which was greatly needed by fellow settlers. It brought such a good profit that Edmund decided to take credit for and advantage of her initiative. He successfully petitioned the House of Burgesses for the exclusive rights to produce and sell salt to the entire Virginia colony.

Importation or sale of salt by anyone else was prohibited, giving Anne's saltworks a monopoly in the region.

The whole endeavor failed miserably when, despite their best efforts, Anne's workers could not keep up with demand. Angry settlers, who really needed salt to preserve food for winter storage and who could not legally get it anywhere else, forced the Burgesses to rescind the legislation, much to Edmund's embarrassment. He blamed the "lazy" indentures Anne employed, suggesting slaves could have been forced to produce a higher yield.

Scarborough did not openly hold Anne responsible, though he did chide her for not being willing to directly employ slave labor. He loved his mistress obsessively. He was paranoid about losing her, so he encouraged most of her whims. In truth, he really only did this to make himself feel magnanimous. Edmund liked feeling good about himself. He was self-indulgent to every extreme. He ate rich foods. He smoked a pipe and drank enthusiastically. Any physical labor was done for him by others.

Debauchery was beginning to adversely affect his health. His paunch had progressed into obesity. Minor afflictions, coughs and belly aches, plagued him. His now nightly consumption of rum sometimes had a diminishing effect on his bedroom performance. Those nights, he fell asleep before Anne could satisfy him sexually. No matter. Whenever he was in residence at Gargaphia, Anne would whisper in his ear before retiring to her own bedchamber:

"You were wonderful my Lord."

She did this to keep his tender ego from deflating. Even in his inebriation, he always believed that he was a virile wonder. He liked bragging to comrades about the delights of having a passionate young mistress.

The Colonel was also very proud of the income that came from Anne's management of Gargaphia. One of his great weaknesses, however, was that he never fully understood how to manage his own fortunes. The man built up large debts by living completely beyond his means. Anne paid those bills she knew of. Many were never brought to her attention. Edmund could not get the hang of Anne's accounting system and eventually stopped keeping track of his annual profit and loss. His mind was on his true vocation: maintaining a nobleman's power through the acquisition of land.

Edmund was completely immersed in his delusion of becoming king of his own province. He insisted on royal treatment wherever he went without thought to the cost incurred. As Anne's list of friends grew so did Edmund's list of disgruntled creditors. Those who had the courage to confront him in court were usually rebuffed. The Colonel regularly manufactured some blatant fiction to prevent taking responsibility for his debts. Many neighbors were genuinely afraid to cross him and demand what they were rightfully entitled to. He convinced himself that God had sanctioned his behavior entitling him to all the advantages of royal birth.

Not surprisingly this delusional thinking began to diminish what political influence Edmund had achieved. His plan to become the next Governor and then Lord Proprietor was foundering. Yet he was undaunted. It would take several more years before his intemperate behavior would finally become his undoing. In the meantime, he simply ignored the bad feelings he left in his wake from James City to Gargaphia and beyond. He held onto his remaining alliances through blackmail and other forms of coercion.

Scarborough was not the only landowner to take undue advantage of their privilege. The resentment of selfish aristocrats by the lower class bubbled to the surface in the summer of 1665. While Gargaphia was the center of high society, other smaller public houses scattered around the region served everyone else. One night the denizens of one such establishment, Fowkes Tavern in nearby Pungoteague, were entertained by a small troupe of actors who put on a play called *"The Bear and the Cub."* This was a thinly veiled satire of King Charles II, who apparently enjoyed the so-called sport of bear baiting, where the creatures were taunted then fought by any man crazy enough to risk their lives in the ring with them. The audience roared with laughter at the physical comedy which belittled the foolish sadism of royalty.

This play was a somewhat unusual event. Theater in the colonies had been forbidden under the influence of the Puritans, who felt such displays led to the deterioration of public morals. One such righteous individual, who happened to be in Fowkes Tavern that night, was appalled at what he saw. He brought charges against the actors in the next session of court, citing the play's lewdness and disrespect for authority. The complaint probably would not have gone any further except the man also wrote to the Governor who sent word that a trial was necessary. A large crowd assembled at Gargaphia to see what would happen.

"My lords, how can you render a decision without seeing the play itself?" someone in the throng shouted.

The players were brought forward to recreate their performance, much to everyone's delight. Again, laughter rang out from the audience. The play's allegorical reference to the noble class was lost on Edmund and his fellow council members who chortled along with everyone else at the silly antics. Naturally, the case was dismissed as frivolous. This was not only the first record of a theater production in the colonies. It was evidence of a growing number of rebellious seeds taking root there.

Anne, too, was amused by the incident. It reminded her that she had not kept up with her reading since coming to Gargaphia. She had been so busy that she had not gotten back to it in quite some time. She wrote to the bookseller in James City to order more books. While waiting for their delivery she turned to a few still waiting in her library. She began with *The Countess of Pembroke's Arcadia*. It had been the next book she had planned to read around the time that Annabella was born. As she devoured the story, she felt again that delicious sensation of imagining a world beyond her own.

Arcadia described a utopian society, filled with dashing comedic characters. There was romance, drama, and action. The lives of the high and low born were contrasted, overlapping in tantalizing plot twists. Anticipating what would happen with each turn of the page gave Anne great pleasure. It filled her mind with thoughts of the possibility of living in a utopian society. She remembered that Dr. Moon had said that he liked the book. It had lived up to his recommendation. The only place the book fell short for Anne was its portrayal of slaves and servants who were contented with their station in life.

"Only someone of high birth would think that in a perfect world slaves could be happy while in bondage." Anne thought to herself. This brought Fanta to mind and the fact that even though she had been avoiding the employment of slaves for her personal needs at Gargaphia, she still profited from their labors on her plantation.

Anne pushed those troubling thoughts out of her mind. She refused to let her past sins get in the way of the work in front of her now. She consoled herself thinking: "Someday, when there is less to do, I will make all that right."

The book *Arcadia* was inspired by a legendary wilderness in one of the Greek myths that Anne was very familiar with. She remembered that the Italian explorer Giovanni Verrazano had referred to the very region she was living in as Arcadia. He had done so because the lush forests he saw there reminded him of that same myth.

This revived Anne's memories of time well spent in the woods with William, and those precious years when she first arrived at Chiconessex. As a young girl walking those trails for the first time with him, Anne had experienced the mysterious magic of the woodlands. She marveled at the tall trees and the emerald green canopy above. William taught her that the forest was a dangerous place where wonderful things could happen. Anne wished he could teach her daughters just as he had taught her.

This was not to be. Not long after finishing the book *Arcadia*, Anne got word from Chiconessex that William had died unexpectedly. He was returning from the bay carrying a stringer of fish when he had fallen to the ground in front of the main house. In a single moment, his heart had given out and he was gone. Nothing could be done to revive him. Anne was grief stricken at this news.

William was the closest thing to family that Anne had and vice versa. She took charge, seeing to his burial, and the distribution of his few possessions to the young indentures he had been supervising of late. She gave his fiddle to a young man among them who expressed an interest in learning to play. Not trusting herself to read prayers for William and wanting him to have a truly Christian burial, Anne paid the pastor at St. George's Chapel to preside graveside. Anne chose a place near where Fanta was buried. William would have wanted to spend eternity in is beloved forest.

Anne said her own private goodbye to William later that fall with a ribbon blessing on All Saints Day on the creek leading to the inlet bay near Gargaphia. That night her dreams comforted her. She saw herself with William, and Granny flying over the ocean, all connected by blue ribbons. She believed her beloveds would always be with her.

By the new year in 1666, Edmund's faltering political career was temporarily revived when he was again named to a two-year term as the colony's Surveyor General. He was elevated to the high court of the colony. And, he also was elected to serve a term as Speaker of the House of Burgesses. This kept the Colonel away from home allowing his pretty mistress to profitably run their plantations without interference. This in turn kept him well supplied with spending money.

He had the best of all worlds: complete freedom to pursue his own pleasures, authority over his peers, and work that could mostly be relegated to underlings. He even had a son he could be proud of. Charles's own plantation was thriving and he had earned the respect of his neighbors there by earning a seat in the House of Burgesses by his father's side.

Meanwhile, back at Gargaphia, Anne had found fulfillment through her children and one achievement after another as a merchant planter. This was a testament not only to her intellect and negotiating skills, but to her good luck.

A few years earlier, when Anne heard Anna Varlet Hack's proposal to do business together, she could have no way of knowing what an auspicious opportunity she had just been given. In her parlor at Chiconessex she had met the one person who would guarantee her success. Though Anna and her husband had moved from their Virginia plantation to live on the upper reaches of the Chesapeake Bay, she and Anne maintained a mutually beneficial association that would last more than twenty-five years.

Anna Hack's network of business associates became Anne's network. If the *Friends and Neighbors* ledger held the names of those she could count on nearby, Anna's contacts brought her commercial alliances throughout the hemisphere. One such person was John

Winthrop, Jr., the Governor of the colony of Connecticut. He was an attorney who Anne hired to defend her interests in New England.

Anne had hired a ship known as the *Virginia Bounty* and its captain Robert Risdon to transport a shipment of tobacco to England. He had done so but had absconded with the proceeds of the cargo's sale. Having registered her complaint in Accomack County Court, Winthrop had successfully managed seizure of the ship from its errant captain in Massachusetts and had the boat delivered to the port in Pungoteague.

The ship was renamed the *Providence* and became one of several ships Anne owned or had a stake in. Anna Hack helped Mistress Toft find a new man to helm her, a fellow Dutchman named Simon Jansen. It was years before they would meet in person. Their business was conducted through written messages sent through an early postal system run by harbormasters at ports of call throughout the colonies.

Anne's naming of that first ship was based on her belief that providence favors the quick minded who act before their luck runs out. Anne let no opportunity go unrealized. She did not know when her fortunes might turn. She remembered the way William described stalking a deer in the forest. He said that the hunter had to be swift of mind *and* foot, judging when to take their best shot then run down their prey. Anne often thought of this in her business dealings as she moved in to make a killing.

Dancing with The Moon

For the first five years of her life at Gargaphia, Anne's top priority beyond her business was that Annabella and Atalanta be safe and happy. They were pretty little things with their mother's coloring: light brown curly hair and blue eyes. They had the chubby cheeks of children who wanted for nothing.

Anne had great plans for them. She was raising them to be refined ladies who would attract respectable men of means for husbands. She would teach them as Bella and her friend Anna Hack had taught her: to be successful colonial women of commerce. She was determined to assure that their futures were better than her own past. Her devotion to them was equal only to her genuine affection for them.

One spring morning she and the children were in the tower. Anne was writing a letter to John Vassall in Jamaica, thanking him for assisting her in arranging for transport of a shipment of rum and proposing trade deals for the coming year. Five-year-old Annabella was standing on a stool playing with her mother's spy glass while little sister Atalanta slept on the cot nearby.

"Mummy! Look! Look! There's a ship on the horizon."

"Let's see, Annabella. Good girl! You are quite right. She's still pretty far out. She'll likely take a couple of hours to get here. You lay down with your sister and take a little nap and when they get closer, I'll get you up so you can tell me what flag they're flying."

The winds were light that day so the ship had to tack several times to catch enough air to bring them to within mooring distance. Just as they weighed anchor Anne woke up the girls.

"It's the British flag, Mummy." Annabella proudly announced.

"Let me see the spy glass. That's right, my dear. Well look there. It's the *Zephyr Queen*. Uncle Star is here. Isn't that wonderful?"

"Does he have treasures for us?" Annabella began hopping up and down, clapping her hands.

Atalanta, who was not quite four years old, perked up from her slumbers when she heard the mention of Uncle Star and gifts.

"Ooo, Mummy, what do you think he brought us?"

"I don't know. We will see. How'd you like to go down and tell Brigid that you're ready for lunch and that we have visitors coming?"

Annabella nodded and ran to prop open the trap door. Down she went followed behind by her sister and mother. Brigid greeted them in the dining room with porridge for their lunch.

"It looks like we will have guests for dinner tonight. Captain Minshull's ship will soon weigh anchor. I'll feed the girls. Send someone up to wake the Colonel, then go to the larder and see what we can put together."

"The men brought in rabbits and possum from their hunt this morning that should make a nice stew."

"That would be nice. Do you have dough started for fresh bread today?"

"Aye Mum."

"Well then, we will have a party then, won't we my darlings?"

"Oh goody, fresh bread with butter!" Atalanta squealed.

"Goody, goody!" Annabella chimed in.

"Yes, that's right. But you must behave like proper young ladies for our guests."

"I will Mummy."

"Me too!"

Once they had finished their meal, Anne took the children by the hand and led them outside.

"Alright ladies, let's go greet our visitors. Don't forget to show Uncle Star your very best curtsies."

"Yes Mummy." the girls said sincerely in unison.

When the welcome party arrived at the dock, Captain Minshull and two men were climbing out of a dory. Forgetting their curtsies, Annabella and Atalanta broke free from their mother's grasp running down the dock to Uncle Star who scooped them up into his arms with a big laugh before making introductions.

"Annabella and Atalanta, Mistress Anne Toft, may I present Augustine Hermann who I've brought here to meet with Colonel Scarborough on business matters. And of course, you remember Dr. Lorentz."

Ever the gracious hostess Anne greeted her guests sweetly after giving Uncle Star a warm embrace. The other men bowed and gave her a courtly kiss on the hand. Dr. Moon winked at Anne when it was his turn. He was flirting already and they had barely said hello.

Anne almost did not recognize Alexandre. He was tanned with closely cropped hair and now wore a small but thick gold hoop earring in one ear, having adopted the look of the pirates he had been consorting with. He looked thinner than Anne remembered. He had on a brown leather vest and breeches with black thigh-high boots. His white linen blouse was unbuttoned to the middle of his chest revealing a gold chain and medallion nestled in a thick rug of chest hair. One thing that had not changed was his dashing smile, which lit up at the sight of Anne.

Anne, too, had changed some since they had last seen each other. She was no longer a young girl. She had rounded out into the fullness of her womanhood. Her breasts were larger, the result of nursing two babies. She had a more mature, stately bearing now. Most women her age had not only lost their youth, but had endured the ill effects of disease and a poor diet. Their bad skin and teeth made Anne, by comparison, remarkable. With her clear complexion and exceptional wardrobe, Anne would have been considered a handsome woman by any standard.

Minshull and Lorentz's traveling companion, Augustine Hermann, was a Bohemian trader who had settled farther north in Maryland Province. He was a well-dressed man of property. Herrmann already had a reputation in the region for his success as a trader and privateer. Anne had not yet met him, but she already knew a bit about him through the settlers' gossip network. Edmund had had dealings with him for more than a decade. Hermann had recently married Jannetje Varlet, the sister of his neighbor, Anne's good friend Anna Hack.

"I am happy to finally meet you, Mistress Anne." he said after he had kissed her hand. "My sister in-law speaks highly of you. I bring greetings from her and sad news. Her beloved husband was taken from us last year, a case of ague I am afraid."

"Yes, I had heard that. I'm so sorry. Please come to the house and tell me more of dear Anna."

As they walked off the dock she continued. "Gentlemen, I hope your stay will be most comfortable. You are in luck. We have room enough for each of you to have your own bedchamber. We have a bathhouse for your convenience, and our servants will be happy to see to your every need. Please join myself and the Colonel in the master's quarters for dinner at five bells."

This concluded her standard guest orientation to Gargaphia. All this time the little girls, were tugging at Captain Minshull's coattails. Annabella could finally keep quiet no longer.

"Did you bring us something, Uncle Star?"

Minshull chuckled, tussling her hair. "I did, my dear, but you'll have to wait till after we have settled in to get it. Can you wait till then?"

Both girls shook their heads no.

"All right, ladies," Anne interjected. "Go make yourself useful and see if Brigid needs any help. You'll have your treats later."

Off the girls ran, giggling all the way back to the house. Anne led the men to the guest quarters where three of the wenches saw to their accommodations. She then returned to her own dining room. Anne set the table with clean linens and silver. She put out cut flowers in vases and fresh tapers so that the meal would be well lit. Anne was decanting a bottle of port in the parlor when Edmund came down stairs.

"Those girls are making too much noise. Can't you get them to behave?" he grumbled.

Anne responded, ignoring his question. "We have guests. Captain Minshull has brought Augustine Hermann and our old friend, Dr. Lorentz."

"Hermann has arrived, you say? Good. He's been contracted to do new maps of the entire region. Who'd you say was with him?"

"Dr. Lorentz. You remember him. He visited here about the time when Annabella was born."

"Can't say that I do." Edmund lit a pipe and sat in his favorite chair. "Where's Billy? I need him to do something."

Anne stepped into the kitchen were Brigid and another servant were preparing the dinner. The aromas of fresh bread and a savory stew filled the air.

"Sally, go get Major Billy in the gathering hall. The Colonel wants him." Anne instructed. "Dinner smells wonderful, Brigid."

Anne went upstairs feeling the usual high spirits she always felt when Uncle Star visited. Dr. Lorentz' wit and fantastical stories would be an added attraction at dinner. As she dressed for dinner, she remembered the pleasure of their flirtation.

Anne changed into one of her now-trademark blue gowns. This one had a pale azure silk bodice trimmed in white lace, and an indigo colored damask skirt with a floral print. She brushed her hair and tied it with a blue ribbon in a neat bun on top of her head. She put on a set of simple pearl earrings with a matching pearl necklace. She looked at them in the mirror thinking about Dr. Moon's wink as he kissed her hand. Suddenly, the events that brought about their first meeting flooded her brain.

She remembered that horrible night that Jasper attacked Fanta. She could see the whole awful scene and hear his vile ranting followed by Fanta cursing her through swollen lips saying, "Thith ith your fault!"

Anne began to weep. The prospect of spending the evening with anyone now filled her with dread. Every time she thought she had gotten over those traumatic events, there they were again as if it was just yesterday. Anne did her best to shake off the unexpected wave of grief. Gritting her teeth, she poured a little water into her wash basin, moistened a cloth, wrung it out, and covered her face with it. She held it there for a few moments then used it to blow her nose before rinsing it in the basin again and hanging it on the windowsill to dry.

Anne looked outside to see Brigid and the girls picking herbs in the garden. The late afternoon sun made the scene sparkle. She felt her emotions welling up again, thinking how the beautiful life she was leading was possible in part because of the terrible ugly end of Fanta's. She closed her eyes and tried to push away those dark thoughts. She picked up her prayer book and opened it to read the vespers. This calmed her enough that she could now face her dinner guests. After one more look in the mirror, Anne smoothed her hair, then her bodice, then her skirt. She was ready to go down.

When Gargaphia's celebrated hostess made her entrance in the parlor, her guests were already there. Everyone in the room, except Edmund, rose to his feet as she entered, then kissed her hand. The Colonel puffed his chest out with pride. He loved having such a lovely mistress to show off. He gestured to her to come sit by him and for the guests to return to their seats. His momentary basking ended abruptly when Atalanta and Annabella came running in the room.

"Uncle Star! Tell us where you've been."

Uncle Star and the girls had a set ritual. His gift giving usually came at the end of one of his stories. Annabella knew her mother would not approve of greedy begging, so this is how she got things started. She and Atalanta plopped down at his feet with great anticipation.

"Well, this time I have been to Hispaniola where there are great crimson blossoms bigger than your lovely little faces. They have birds there with feathers every color of the rainbow. And, the natives make the most beautiful carvings."

Captain Minshull opened up the rucksack next to his chair and with a great exaggerated flourish and a playful look of surprise on his face he presented each girl with a small carved ebony box. The girls squealed with delight, when they opened their boxes to find small carved brightly painted birds and pieces of sugarcane candy.

"I think," the Captain continued, "your Mummy will want you to wait till after your supper to eat your sweets."

"Uncle Star is quite right. What do you say, girls?"

The children jumped up and kissed the kindly man on each cheek saying in unison: "Thank you, Uncle Star."

"Alright, alright. That's enough of that. Minshull, you spoil them. Go get your dinner girls." Edmund grumbled. He had had enough of this pablum.

Anne kissed each girl on the head. Then she led them to the door so Brigid could see to their dinner and get them ready for bed. She whispered to them, "Be good girls and eat all your dinner and I will come up and kiss you good night later."

Anne returned to her seat next to Scarborough to hear the latest news from the travelers.

"Hispaniola, is currently under French control, though the Spanish have certainly done their best to rout them out. Lorentz and I met the French governor, Bertrand D'Ogeron. I'd say he is someone we can all do business with. Wouldn't you say so, Alexandre?"

"Star is right. D'Ogeron seems amenable to commercial partnerships without prejudice. He's pragmatic. He's above these foolish squabbles between our respective crowns."

"Good. Good." Edmund responded. "Sugar is fetching a handsome price these days. Anne seems intent on investing in sugar, don't you, my dear?"

"Well as you say, dear, sugar is fetching a handsome price."

Anne smiled coyly at the Colonel. Unbeknownst to him, she had already been trading in sugar with some of the plantations near Santa Domingo on Hispaniola. Captain Minshull's news merely reassured her that future deals there would be unaffected by recent naval skirmishes between the French and Spanish.

She changed the subject. "So, Mr. Hermann, tell us about your plantation up north. I understand you've built near the headwaters of the Chesapeake."

"Please, call me Augustine, my dear lady. Yes, our manor house is not so grand as this one, but I think my wife Jannetje likes it. The plantation of her sister, our mutual friend Mistress Hack, is just across the river. She is doing quite well and will soon remarry, another Dutchman named Nicholas Boote."

Edmund, who was not interested in the family gossip, interrupted. "Tell us about the lay of the land there. What crops will you plant?"

"We live on a river where there are great rolling hills. We also have a lush forest like yours. This year we will plant corn and barley…"

Hermann continued on at length about other crops he was planning to grow there, and the natural flora and fauna of his estate. Anne listened politely until she got tired of waiting to talk to Dr. Moon.

"It sounds lovely. Tell me, Dr. Lorentz, have you been sailing the high seas all this time since we last saw you?"

"I have, madam."

At that moment, Brigid appeared at the door to announce dinner, preventing Alexandre from going into any detail. The group filed into the dining room. Anne and Edmund sat at opposite ends of the table. Uncle Star and Alexandre sat on one side with Augustine on the other. After Edmund recited the grace, Brigid served the meal.

"Anne, Hermann here has been commissioned by Lord Baltimore to map the entire peninsula and Chesapeake Bay." Scarborough began, then turned to his guest. "So, you would like permission to explore Virginia Colony as well then?"

"Yes, sir, I would. I am here to offer you your own set of maps based on my survey."

"And what will that cost me?"

"I am only charging fifty pounds sterling. I think you will find that the costs you will save in disputes about your borders will render my maps invaluable to you, and are therefore well worth the investment."

"I, too, am a surveyor, sir. I can produce my own maps. The value of yours is knowing what Lord Baltimore knows before everyone else. If I pay you half now and half upon completion will you promise to give me all the maps to Virginia exclusively before taking commissions from my fellow Virginians?"

"Well, I had anticipated raising additional funds on the other side of the Chesa…"

"I also want the right to reproduce the map and sell it. I'll up my share of the commission to seventy-five pounds. I will pay you twenty-five now and the rest later. You won't get a better deal. Let's shake on it now and Anne'll write it up for us after dinner."

Hermann agreed. Commissions alone were not expected to be the source of his profits. The mapping expedition was a cover for reconnaissance for a more pressing endeavor. Spanish naval ships had been in the region looking for weaknesses in English fortifications. Lord Baltimore and Governor Berkley had given privateers permission to attack and plunder Spanish interlopers. Hermann owned a frigate called *La Grace* which engaged in just such activities. Ships with the most complete maps would have a distinct advantage over their prey.

Hermann shook hands with Scarborough. His map funding was paltry in light of what he would make in ships and cargo if he was able to beat the Spanish. The wily Bohemian had every intention of making his own reproductions of the map for any paying customer.

After the meal was over Anne wrote up the contract as the men smoked their pipes and drank a few drams of rum. Signatures in place, twenty-five pounds in tobacco certificates were given to Augustine. Anne then excused herself to check on her children and wait for Edmund in his room, as was her usual practice.

The Colonel retired earlier than he usually did when he had guests. He and Anne made love quickly and he was soon asleep.

"You were wonderful, my Lord." she whispered and quietly got up to find her own bed.

Anne lay awake thinking about Dr. Moon now sleeping in the guest wing. She wondered why he had been so quiet at dinner. Maybe he found her too matronly now to flirt with. Anne was not a vain woman. Neither was she easily tempted to indulge in dalliances. She certainly had many flattering opportunities. Her scrivening customers often made advances toward her, sometimes even in front of Edmund. She had turned them all down. He took pride in watching her deflect her suitors. It fed his ego to inspire the envy of his neighbors. Anne made a game of leaving the men disappointed yet complimented.

Gargaphia's mistress was a realist about why the men who came there flattered her. Not all of them saw her merely as a sexual conquest, though some did. They usually wanted something else from her: a good deal, favorable even false testimony, or forged documents. Though she had both chance and reason, Anne had no need of the complications of superfluous love affairs. She had enough to do keeping the Great Conjurer happy along with all the other work she had to do. So, she was never the least bit inclined to act on any temptation. Just the same, Anne was a little bit intrigued by the seemingly reticent Dr. Moon.

"No matter," Anne thought. "He'll be gone in a few days."

The next morning Edmund departed for the General Assembly in James City. Augustine Hermann also left. He and his expedition, who were still on board the *Zephyr Queen*, took a small sloop which they had tethered to the ship and set off to map the region. Captain Minshull and Dr. Lorentz remained at Gargaphia to rest for a few days before continuing their voyage back to the Spice Islands.

For the next two nights, Uncle Star and Dr. Moon joined Anne and the girls for dinner then went next door to the gathering hall to partake in the gambling and entertainment. Anne rarely joined in Gargaphia's revelries. She left hostess duties there to the Sheffield sisters and the other wenches. This kept any of the guests from getting the wrong idea about her role on the plantation.

On the third night of their visit, music and the laughter from the guest house carried through the open windows on the warm evening air. Anne decided to join Uncle Star for a drink after the children went to bed. Her curiosity about Dr. Moon was too much to resist.

Anne did not put on jewelry or change her gown, a simple pale blue-green linen dress. She only intended to stay a short while. The fiddler and a drummer were playing an infectious reel. Most of the wenches were dancing with customers. At one table there were two men Anne recognized as neighbors, playing draughts. The room was hazy from pipe smoke. Anne caught the eye of Uncle Star who jumped to his feet to find her a chair.

"Here you go, my dear. Well, well, I have not seen you at the evening entertainments in a long time."

"Yes, I've been thinking about William. I miss him and his fiddling. When I heard the music through the windows, I couldn't resist."

"What say we drink a toast to our dear departed friend?" Captain Minshull suggested as he motioned to one of the barmaids, to bring over another cup for Anne.

For a while Anne and Uncle Star swapped happy memories of William. They spoke of his steady reliable help and the kindness he showed to Anne when she was a child.

"When I first came to Chiconessex, I was just ten and I remember Maude sent me to get William. I wandered off into the forest and could not find my way back. I was terrified. I was sure that some great beast was going to eat me up. It wasn't long before William came and found me and carried me home. He was my hero."

"He was happiest in the woods, wasn't he?" Uncle Star asked. "When last I saw him, he said you had released him from his indenture. He could have gone anywhere but he chose to stay and work at Chiconessex."

"Yes, he said he was bound to the land and all that lived there. He used to say that such bonds of love do not bind. You know, I think he was the freest man I have ever known. He never had a complaint. If he had a problem, he found a way to fix it. He never laid blame elsewhere."

The fiddler finished one song and began another. Alexandre stood up and took Anne's hand, pulling her out onto the floor to join the other dancers saying, "Come, let's dance a reel for William."

Anne let the music carry her. Round and round they went. It had been a long time since she had danced. Anne found herself laughing. She thought she had reached a certain level of contentment but that night she felt a joy she had rarely experienced. She danced three more reels with Alexandre until she realized she was losing track of time. She excused herself explaining that she had to rise early to see to her children.

"This has been delightful, gentlemen, but it won't be long before my girls will be up and will need their mother's attention. So, I am off to sleep. Please enjoy yourselves."

Anne went to her bedchamber and readied herself for bed. She laid down and tried to sleep, still feeling flushed. That night all her dreams were pleasant ones. In the morning she awoke refreshed, ready to take on the business of the day.

After dinner, Anne invited her two special guests to join her and the girls in the tower to watch the sunset. The moon was full that night and at that time of year it was at perigee, its closest orbit to the earth, causing it to look quite large as it rose above the eastern horizon. Anne had a game that she played with her girls that she thought Uncle Star would enjoy.

Annabella explained the little fantasy they liked to play at. "Mummy says that her Granny told her that if you reach out on the full moon you can almost touch it. And if you do that and make a wish the fairies'll make the water sparkle. That's how they let you know that your wish'll come true. But you have to keep your wish a secret or it won't work."

It was a magical scene. As the sun set behind them the sky looked pink and purple. Through the warm humid haze, the moon rose looking like a great polished copper disk. The wind laid down making the sea close to shore look like pale blue silk. Further out, the deep azure water shimmered with the lunar reflection.

Anne wore a gold damask skirt and a deep blue bodice embroidered with a crescent moon and stars. She wore it whenever she played this game with the girls, knowing it added to the mystique. Anne let the girls stand on two chairs facing east. She held onto their waists as they reached out over the tower rail and tried to touch the moon. The girls squealed with delight.

"We did it, Mummy! We did it!"

"Look, the water's sparkling! That means we'll get our wishes doesn't it?"

"Well, I don't know," Anne teased. "The fairies like to grant wishes to good little girls who go to bed without a fuss. What do you think?"

Atalanta was not ready to think about bed. "Aww. Mummy, can't we stay up just a little longer?"

"Well, not too long. You don't want to keep Brigid waiting, do you?"

After a few moments Anne sent the girls to bed. "Alright, girls. Let's get you down stairs before you need a candle to find your way."

"How bout I carry ye down?" Uncle Star offered. "I'm a might thirsty so I think I will go see what they're serving in the gathering hall."

The Captain lifted a girl in each arm and carried them down to Brigid who was waiting by the back doorstep of the master's wing. He did not return. For the first time since he had arrived, Anne was alone with Alexandre. The celestial magic show was not quite over. For a little while they stood admiring the views in every direction.

Lorentz broke their silence. "Did you ever get around to reading *Arcadia*?"

"I did." Anne replied.

"What did you think of it?"

"Well, I found it amusing and interesting. I decided I needed to reread Moore's *Utopia* and compare them. I also asked my bookseller to recommend other books like it and he suggested *New Atlantis* by Francis Bacon. I think I like it the best of the three."

"Why is that?"

"All three authors explore ideal societies where the rights of the many are protected, not just those of a chosen few. But in Bacon's make-believe land, Bensalem, slavery is abolished and women have the right of self-determination. In my imagination, this is a land in which I would like to live."

"In your imagination is the only place such things will come true, I am afraid. There will always be slaves, and women will always be under the dominion of men. Though they do not know it, women have the real power anyway."

Anne had heard this before from Edmund when she had tried to engage him in a discussion about her books. She wanted to hear Alexandre's logic just the same.

"Really. And tell me, sir, how do you reach this conclusion?"

"Well, first of all, women control the household. They determine what gets done and what is neglected. They can withhold their charms in order to get their way. No husband wants a troublesome wife to make their lives miserable."

"Not all wives are the harridans you describe. And what of those women who are not married or whose husbands have run off? They suffer greatly with no protection. It is true that we do not have the burden of paying taxes for now, and sometimes the courts here have shown us sympathy. The court does recognize women like me as a "feme sole" – a single woman who is solely responsible for their own property. But it is made clear at every turn that we own our property only through the good graces of men who are free to take it anytime it should suit their purposes. I have seen many women abused in court; maids raped by their masters then sentenced to a longer term of indenture to reimburse time lost when that rape produced an infant. Men make decisions about a woman's fate to suit their own purpose..."

"That is because men know what's in their best interest..."

"You mean they know what their own needs are and they decide accordingly..."

"Not all men are like Colonel Scarborough."

"And you, Dr. Lorentz, I suppose you make decisions in the best interest of your wife and children back in Amsterdam?"

"That is none of your business, madam."

"I see. You are free to pass judgement, making commentary on me and Colonel Scarborough, but I shouldn't inquire about your wife. Thus, we see that in a man's view a woman's rights are not reciprocal to their own."

"Well, I..."

"Women must run their home to the best of their abilities while their men are away at their work. When they return their women are expected to relinquish their authority even when their husbands violate the vows of their marriage. And men wonder why their wives withhold their charms. Ha!"

"So, someday you would like the New World to be like Bacon's Bensalem?" Alexandre asked, trying to avoid Anne's personal questions.

"I would, and I think it may be someday, though from what I have seen it may take a long time to get there."

"Well, the world is changing. Commoners have more and more rights being conferred upon them. And more countries have some sort of representative government working for the betterment of their people. Even pirates govern themselves by voting."

Anne responded carefully. "These are indeed advances for human society, but they do not yet address the inequities women must bear. They do not prevent the cruelties of slavery nor the slaughter of innocent natives. The Virginia General Assembly has voted time and again to abuse and destroy the villages of the Indians even those who are peace loving. It is interesting to see how so much destruction can be wrought by an institution meant to build a better world.

"Look at the corruption of our House of Burgesses." Anne continued. "Only nobles and male landowners with large estates can take part. In all likelihood, I own more land now than most of the men in that assembly and yet I have no say in the laws they pass. I cannot even attend their sessions to petition the Governor on the most minute and practical matters.

"Nobles like Colonel Scarborough abuse the trust of their neighbors without restraint. They fear what he can do to them as much as they fear what they would do without his vicious militia. They believe his tall tales about savage naturals plotting to massacre them. The Indians' numbers are so depleted they couldn't mount an attack even if they wanted to. We settlers came here to build God's new kingdom. Instead we are making one in the image of man's old kingdom. It is not much better…"

"Why do you trouble yourself with such things? You appear to be living quite well. Aren't you happy here at Gargaphia?"

Anne thought for a moment before responding. "I am grateful for all that I have. When I am with my children, I can honestly say that I am truly content. But that does not mean that I do not see the struggles of people all around me. One of the tribes that has been driven from Accomack were our neighbors at Chiconessex. Their queen Nandua was a kind wise woman. She was my friend. The Colonel's militia pushed them north into Maryland. I hear that their life is very hard. Their hunting grounds are greatly restricted, so they have little food. Nandua and her people suffer because of Edmund's ambitions, which the General Assembly has encouraged."

Alexandre gently put his hands on Anne's shoulders, turning her so that they were face to face.

"Surely, you have prospered enough to afford leaving him. Minshull told me that this all started as a way to get revenge for the death of Owen Tomkin and assure some sort of future for yourself. You must have thought of a way to avenge Owen Tomkin by now. Why do you stay?" he asked earnestly.

"Captain Minshull told you about my plans then – the reason why I am with the Colonel."

"You gave him permission, didn't you?"

She nodded then spoke quietly, "I have not actually found a way to bring the Colonel down."

"Wouldn't your leaving with all your property humiliate the Colonel? Wouldn't that be punishment enough?"

Anne frowned. "It would not be as easy as you make it sound. Besides, what is sufficient punishment for taking the life of another? That night that Fanta was attacked, when you and I first met, the man who attacked her admitted that he was the one who pushed Owen Tomkin overboard to his death. He said that he did it for the Colonel. He spoke of him as if he was Lucifer himself. He was right.

"At the beginning, I thought that by becoming his mistress I would find a way to ruin him. I don't know, bankrupt him, ruin his reputation – something. The more of his money I spend, the more Gargaphia prospers. His reputation has not been ruined. We are welcomed as a couple to church services. I may not be invited to their homes, but the finest families attend court here acting as if we were fully married. The more I skim and steal from him, the more he trusts me. Uncle Star and others warned me that it would not be so easy to bring him down. They were right. It is not going to be easy or simple.

"And now, my priorities have changed somewhat," Anne sighed. "I feel I must stay with him until I find a better situation, one that guarantees a future for my girls, one that does not include the fear of him coming after me and putting us all in bondage. Every one of our neighbors knows that I am no widow, that my beloved daughters are illegitimate. Somehow, I have to find a way to give them a respectable start in life, assure them husbands from good families. I need to redeem their illegitimate births. I don't want them to be forced into bondage the way I was. I want them to be free to raise children who will help build that more utopian world I've been reading about.

"Until I figure that out, I will remain Edmund's mistress and continue to build up my fortune in hopes that someday I will actually be able to put it to good use. You know, it's funny. I have not spoken of these things to anyone for a long time."

Anne realized she was sharing a dangerous secret with this man she barely knew. "There are few who I can trust with this conversation. I hope I can count on your discretion."

Alexandre carefully lifted Anne's chin with just one finger. He answered her by kissing her on the lips. It was a sweet, gentle kiss. He cupped her face in his hands and spoke quietly.

"You can trust me. You've never given me reason to think that you might have the smallest bit of affection for me. And yet, when I left you all those years ago, the thought of you lingered with me long after. When I knew we were coming here, I could think of nothing else. I think I may be in love with you."

He kissed her tenderly, again. Anne's arms hung limp by her sides. Instinctively she took one step back, still not sure of

Alexandre's motives. His hands dropped and picked up hers. He kissed her finger tips.

Anne felt warm all over. She wanted to respond, and yet, she would not give into his charms without at least some declaration of noble intent.

"Alexandre, you are not the first to try and take me away from Edmund. What do you want from me? What have you to offer me?"

They stood looking at each other for a few moments in silence. Anne frowned again, wondering if there was any way she could tell whether he was sincere or if he was trying to seduce her as some sort of game. Alexandre looked annoyed by her resistance. He thought his profession of love would have made her more pliable.

"I usually don't have to work so hard with women like you. I suppose you give nothing without getting something. You are a merchant after all. What then is the price you demand for a little affection?"

Anne was angry now. She stepped back. "Apparently my price is greater than you can afford. Perhaps you mean to simply take what you want. Is that what this is? Am I a pirate's prize to be stolen?"

Alexandre shook his head. He wasn't going to force himself on the woman, but he wasn't about to give up.

"Madam, I am a gentleman. I am not intent on taking anything unless freely given."

"And you think that calling me a whore will entice me to give in to you?"

Anne sat down by the rail looking out over the placid sea still sparkling in the moonlight. She sighed and shook her head. Looking perplexed, Alexandre sat down in the chair next to her. He covered one hand balled into a fist with the other and rested his chin on them, leaning on the rail. The look on his face was somewhere between angry and weary.

"I apologize. I am not used to having to work so hard for a little feminine attention."

Anne tried to read him the way she had so many other men who sat across her table bargaining with her for one thing or another. She saw a handsome charming man who seemingly wanted to make a deal, yet who was not really sure what he wanted.

"Dr. Lorentz, I think you've been spending too much time in brothels where women make it their business to succumb to any compliment no matter how clumsy."

Alexandre leaned back in the chair and let out a deep breath. "Perhaps you are right."

"You seem troubled to me. The fates have not been kind to you since last we met, have they?"

"No, they have not. Pirates are a vicious selfish lot. I've seen things which I dare not describe and which I would sooner forget, but they plague my dreams."

"What will you do now?"

"I am a ship's surgeon. I have no other skill to offer the world. I will sign on with a Dutch privateer in the Lesser Antilles."

"A privateer is not much different than a pirate. They still profit from the plunder of…"

"The Netherlands are at war with the Spaniards, madam. We privateers will do our part to rout them wherever we find them in service to our homeland. It is no different than serving in the Royal Navy. We merely have a different paymaster."

"So, you are not returning to your family in Amsterdam out of patriotic duty."

Alexandre was not used to explaining himself to a woman. "My wife, if you must know, has no interest in me. Not long after we married, she became pregnant. The boy died during her labors. And, the delivery was an ordeal which rendered her incapable of bearing more children. Belinda blamed me for these things. She locked me out of her heart and her bed. She returned to her family. She had no further need of me and would not see me. I became a husband without a home. I have had no choice but to go out into the world seeking the succor of others. Won't you take pity on me?"

Alexandre tried to see Anne's reaction out of the corner of his eye. She caught him looking sideways and deduced that this story was probably a colossal fiction.

"How many women believe that nonsense, Dr. Moon?"

Alexandre smiled, laughing a little. "Some women respond to a man who takes an interest in their thoughts, some to brutes, and some to pitiful lost souls in need of mothering. What moves you, my dear?"

He turned, taking her hand, he continued. "Perhaps it is complete honestly that will entice you to open your legs for me. Maybe it is curiosity. Don't you want to know how my cock would feel inside of you? I guarantee I can give you more pleasure than that old fool Scarborough. Won't you let me show you?"

For a moment Anne was tempted. This dashing pirate's vast experience with women would likely make him a skilled lover. It might have been fun to play with him in bed.

"Dr. Moon, somehow I know without experiencing your cock that it would – fill me with delight. But, sadly for you, my delight will not be yours. I am a woman of my word. When I give my promise, I aim to keep it."

"Even to someone who deceives you at every turn, one who you have vowed to ruin? You only gave him your promise in pursuit of some sort of vengeance on him. Who's spinning a fiction now?"

"You misunderstand me. The promise I refer to is not some misguided fealty to Edmund. The pledge I made was to myself. I promised that I would not be distracted by love nor pleasure in pursuit of my goal. And though they are not aware of it, I have since promised my children that even in the pursuit of that goal I would do nothing to jeopardize their futures. To be caught in the arms of another man would be dangerous for me and my children. I may dance with you in the company of others, but I will not dance with you in private. I am afraid you and I cannot be more than just friends, Dr. Moon."

Alexandre admitted defeat. "You are a rare woman, Mistress Bluebird. I shall always regret that my quest to enjoy your mysteries was rebuffed."

The sky was dark now and the moon slid behind a bank of clouds. Anne lit a candle and led her disappointed suitor down the stairs. He made his way alone to the gathering hall and engaged the services of the Sheffield sisters to try and satisfy his unrequited lust. Meanwhile, Anne retired to the master's quarters to kiss her now sleeping daughters in the nursery. She went to her room and changed into her nightgown. Once hidden under her own covers, Anne pleasured herself imagining Dr. Moon dancing inside her.

Uncle Star and Dr. Moon's visit lasted only two days more after the full moon encounter in the tower. Alexandre avoided Anne, taking his meals in the gathering hall instead of with her and Captain Minshull in the master's dining room. Anne and her friend conducted business as if nothing had happened. Neither spoke of Alexandre.

They concentrated their conversation on a variety of other pending deals. On the morning of the *Zephyr Queen's* departure, Anne and the girls walked down to the dock to see their guests off.

Dr. Lorentz took off his hat and with a sweeping motion bowed low. He kissed Anne's hand but did not look her in the eye before boarding the waiting dory. Uncle Star hugged and kissed the girls and their mother goodbye, then handed Anne a leather satchel.

"This is one last gift from my friend and I before we go. We give it in gratitude for your generous hospitality, my dear. Be well until I see you next fall."

With that he jumped into the boat. Lorentz and Minshull rowed down the creek and out of sight. Anne looked in the bag and saw that it contained a handwritten manuscript of some sort and a sealed letter with her name on it.

"Shall we go up and watch them sail away?" she asked the girls.

The three of them climbed the tower stairs, then took turns looking through the spyglass, watching the ship get underway and disappear southward along the eastern horizon. Anne settled the girls on the cot for their nap and opened the letter in the satchel.

June twenty-sixth, in the year of our Lord MCLXVII

My dearest Anne,

Please find enclosed an English copy of a book I have written to aid the Dutch Navy in their quest to safeguard new world Christendom from the scourge of piracy. It is a compendium of known pirates and privateers, their associates, hiding places, and methods. My spoken English is sometimes better than what I can write, but I hope you will find this readable nonetheless.

You may find the information herein to be useful. Should any of the scoundrels listed in my book seek hospitality at Gargaphia, you will be forewarned of the dangers they pose. You will notice my dear lady, that neither you nor Captain Minshull are mentioned, so no suspicion will be cast upon you as a result of this work.

Dear Anne, I give this to you only partly in gratitude for your hospitality. When we spoke the other night in the tower, I meant what I said. I am in love with you. You were right to rebuff my advances. I suppose the sin of pride prevented me from telling you that I have little to show for my life and therefore almost nothing to offer you and your beautiful daughters. I acted like a cur because I am ashamed that I am completely unworthy of your love. I have spent almost every penny I have ever earned. I am married to another and therefore cannot make you a proper proposal. All that I can give you is the truth of who I am.

Many years ago, when we were first married, my wife Belinda asked me to choose between my calling to be a healer and the more lucrative work of a merchant working for her father in the Dutch East India Company. I tried to comply with her wishes. When I sailed to New Amsterdam in service to her father, I found that the only thing I loved more than medicine was life on the sea. I also discovered that the work of a merchant was not only distasteful to me, but would have crushed my soul under the weight of duplicitous deals and false friendships.

I wrote to my wife of my unhappiness and of my plan to join the Dutch Navy as a ship's surgeon. The response I got came not from her but from her father. He said if I proceeded in this manner, he would use his influence to have me barred from naval service and ban any loyal Dutch captain from signing me on merchant vessels.

I returned to Amsterdam in hopes of convincing my wife to take my side in dissuading my father in-law from this course of action. She was quite furious with me and would not hear my case. When it was clear that neither of us would compromise, I offered her an annulment. We had no children and this would free her to find a more suitable husband.

Belinda has so far refused this offer several times and has since gone to live with her parents. I tried to open a surgery in Amsterdam, but my father in-law *again used his influence to slander my reputation. He has told me directly that wherever I go he will endeavor to prevent any success I may have unless I come back to the fold, and be the husband and son in-law he expected me to be. I will never do that.*

My life on the sea has, in a way, chosen me. Only pirates and privateers are willing to hire me on to do the work I feel called by God to do. The sea is a mysterious dangerous place where men must show the true measure of their souls. For me, life on the sea is both a fantastic elixir and an overwhelming infection which cannot be cut out. The magical beauty we witnessed from the tower the other night is seen regularly from the decks of ships. Imagine the intoxicating effect of being completely surrounded by water bathed in those fantastical colors.

Not all my experiences have been so beautiful. My life in the last few years has been marked by one battle after another. I have been the witness to the most terrible cruelty one human can inflict upon another. You say there is little difference between pirates and privateers. You are not wrong. They are both a vicious lot who would cut the throat of their own mother for a handful of silver. Privateering is often just an excuse to do evil in the name of a righteous cause.

Strangely, though they are indeed criminals, and rightly condemned by God fearing society, there is a profound honesty among the men I sail with. They are fiercely loyal to each other. They have a code of honor that sets them apart from even the most pious Christians. I have not seen evidence of that same intense integrity anywhere on land, save the devotion you showed me for your daughters. The difference between pirates and privateers is that pirates serve only themselves without allegiance to anyone. Privateers may take the same profits as pirates, but regardless of any personal greed, they still serve the greater good in service to their God and country.

That small difference allows me to hold on to some few threads of conscience. These represent the only remaining bonds I have to decent society. By serving on a Dutch privateer I am doing my small part to build Christendom among the savage lands of the New World. We are protecting our colonies from the evil of papist domination by the Spaniards and heathen corruption. Like you, I dream of building Utopia. This is the only way I know to do that.

So, my dearest Anne, the only thing I have to offer you is my unrequited love from afar and the knowledge contained in my manuscript. I hope you will sometimes think kindly of me and include me in your prayers. Should we ever meet again, I hope that you will allow me to properly show you the respect and affection I have for you.

With love and admiration,

Alexandre Johannes Lorentz

There was a crescent moon drawn next to his signature. Anne folded the letter and placed it in the back of the manuscript. She was at once sad and flattered. She was sorry that they had not consummated their attraction to each other. Alexandre's description of privateers made her think about her own indirect complicity in such things and wondered if they were not all doomed to hell for their sins here on earth.

She gazed over at her innocent sleeping children then looked out over the now empty horizon. Anne pondered whether she and Dr. Moon would ever see each other again, if they would ever dance another reel together. She wished she could keep her children together in their tower forever, magically safe from the evils of the world.

The Dreadful Hurrycane

By the time of Edmund's return to Gargaphia in early August, Anne knew that she was pregnant again. By her calculations she was about four months along. She was beginning to show a full round belly. The Colonel was very excited by this news because it showed that at the advanced age of fifty, he was still a virile man who could sire a child.

Only a few people lived well into old age in the colony. Death stalked even the healthiest person with a host of incurable diseases. The slightest mishap could turn into a gangrenous mortal wound. Edmund was overweight. He suffered from gout and his susceptibility to most minor maladies made him a chronic hypochondriac. Yet, despite frequent bouts of rum-induced impotence, there had been plenty of occasions in the past year that his body had not failed him. So, Anne's latest pregnancy gave him hope that his health was not as bad as he feared.

That did not completely assuage his insecurities and suspicions. Edmund quizzed Daisy and Delia about the possibility that he might not be the father. They reassured him that they knew of no such dalliance by Anne. They even relayed the story of how Dr. Lorentz had complained that their mistress had refused him and he had to seek the solace of their unique talents to relieve his pent-up frustration. They sincerely marveled how Anne could turn down the handsome doctor. If she could turn him down, they told Scarborough, it was unlikely she would take on any other lover.

Edmund naively had counted on the Sheffield sisters over the years to serve as his spies when he was not in residence at Gargaphia. They had in fact played that game without revealing they were in fact more loyal to Anne's interests than his. Beyond the natural bonds of woman kind and shared trauma, they were pragmatists. They knew they would not have enjoyed their current prosperity without her willingness to let them set up their illicit business at Gargaphia. They would certainly have lied to protect Anne. It just so happened that such deception was unnecessary in this case. Edmund believed them and thought no more about it.

He moved on to plans for how he would spend that year's profits. The harvest had been very good that summer. The yields for corn and tobacco were especially high. Edmund wanted Anne to buy more property. Between them they now owned most of the land in Accomack County. The Colonel wanted to turn his sights north, intending to expand the border of the county even further into Maryland's Somerset County where Anne had already bought a few properties.

On the morning of August 27, 1667, Edmund was discussing business with his son Charles in the parlor of Gargaphia when Annabella and Atalanta burst in the room.

"Mummy says there is to be a storm!" Annabella said excitedly.

"What are you two doing in here?" Edmund growled. "Go on with you, now. Can't you see I'm talking to Charles?"

"But," Atalanta insisted, "Mummy said to tell everybody to get ready for the storm."

"Go tell somebody else. Go on. Get out of here," Edmund replied impatiently as Anne now entered the room.

"Thank you, girls. Go tell Brigid that she and the other servants should meet me in the gathering hall so we can get organized. Then come back in here and stay with the Colonel where it's safe. Hello, Charles, how are you this morning?"

"I am well, Mistress Toft. How are you?"

"I'm fine, thank you. There's quite a storm brewing south of here. You may want to continue this at another time. If you leave now you can get home in time to be with your family before it starts to blow."

"Stay right where you are. I want to do this now." Edmund did not like it when Anne took charge in front of his son. "The sun is shining. The storm must be miles away…"

"The sun may be shining now, but from the tower I could see that the sky is completely black not far south of here. Charles, if you want to make it home before the storm hits you need to go now."

"I'd better be on my way, Father. I'll come back as soon as it blows over." Charles pulled a few papers into his valise and headed for the door giving Anne a knowing look.

"Where's everybody going? Anne, don't you do anything that will make my lunch late. I'm already hungry." Edmund shouted yet stayed where he was with one gout swollen foot propped up on a stool.

Anne ignored him and went to the gathering hall to give instructions to the servants.

"Latch all the shutters and doors. Make sure that the gates to the livestock pens are tied firmly. Bring in anything that the wind might carry away. Once you hear the bell, I want everyone to come back here in the gathering hall until the storm passes. We don't want to be out looking for stragglers in a gale."

Daisy and Delia were given the task of counting up everyone and reporting back to Anne that they were all safely accounted for. There were only three guests staying at Gargaphia. They were neighbors who had arrived early for the next session of court which was to begin the next day. After hearing of the dangerous weather, they all departed for their own homes.

Anne went back up into the tower to watch the storm roll in. The ocean looked black. White caps were already visible on the waves from her vantage point. The sky was getting darker and what sunlight there was cast a strange greenish-yellow glow over the landscape. She watched as lightning strikes got closer and closer. Anne loved feeling the warm wet wind on her face. She felt a certain thrill at facing the raging tempest from the tower, standing up to its great forces. At the same time, she had a healthy respect for the power of weather. Having always lived near the sea, she knew what dangers it posed.

Anne watched the sky-borne drama as long as she could until she decided it was no longer safe. After closing the tower hatches, she made her way back downstairs to ring the bell. Anything not secured would now have to be sacrificed or retrieved later.

Anne went into the library which was dark, now that the windows had been shuttered. This room only had two windows on the wall facing south. In a storm it was the safest place to be in the house. Edmund was sulking silently in his chair, his ailing foot still propped up. Brigid was lighting candles. The girls ran to their mother. They were starting to get scared as the sound of thunder got closer and closer.

"Everything is going to be just fine, my little bunnies. You'll see. This isn't our first squall, is it?"

The girls sat down on the floor to play with their rag dolls. They knew the Colonel did not like their chatter so they whispered to each other. Delia Sheffield entered the library announcing that all the guests had left and everyone else in the household was in the gathering hall. Her report finished, she returned to wait out the storm with the other servants.

For the rest of that day, and well into the next, the wind raged. The house shook. Thunder cracks got louder and louder. Lightning struck nearby several times. The brilliance of each bolt was so intense it lit up the library through spaces between the boards of the shutters.

Anne tried to keep the girls occupied by telling them one of her Granny's bucking up stories.

"Once upon a time, in days of old, there was a town called Ravenscar not far from Robin Hood's Bay on top of the towering bluffs which face the Great North Sea. The town was built by an evil wizard prince. He kept the people there as his slaves. He had built the town on the cliff above the raging sea and treacherous rocks below, so that if any of them tried to run away, they would only have one road that they could take.

"The prince had bewitched a huge raven who kept guard over that one road. If the raven spied a runaway, it would swoop down and catch them and deliver them back to the evil prince who beat them soundly and denied them food for days.

"The slaves were very sad. They worked hard for the prince who was very cruel to them. One day, on a day like this when the sea was raging and the sky was storming, the slaves were hiding in their homes, trembling with fear. The evil prince went through the town demanding that the villagers come out and get back to work. One little girl named Bonnie bravely stood up to the prince.

"We will not go out until the storm has passed us by!" she shouted from her doorway. The prince decided to make an example of her. He pulled her from her house and dragged her through town.

"You had better come out and get back to work, or I will surely toss this girl into the sea!" he yelled.

"The towns people came out and got back to work as the wind howled. Thunder and lightning shook the earth. Little Bonnie prayed harder than she had ever prayed before. Mother Mary in Heaven heard her prayers and decided to help because Bonnie had been so brave. She sent her angel fairies on the wind to free the raven from the spell he was under. He swooped down and grabbed the girl up as the fairies whispered in her ears not to be afraid. They gave her these words to say:

"My friends, follow me and this raven who once was cursed but now is blessed. Follow us down the hill and north beyond the moor to safety."

"The townspeople believed Bonnie. They dropped everything and ran behind her and the raven, leaving the evil prince behind them. He yelled and screamed but no one would listen because he was the only one left in the village. Just then a tremendous bolt of lightning struck the ground by the prince. This caused a great crack in the earth. Suddenly the entire town of Ravenscar along with the evil prince fell into the sea and disappeared forever.

"The sun came out. The fairies danced along a great rainbow back out to sea. Bonnie and the townspeople were so happy to be free. They built a new town on the bay where they lived happily ever after."

"Until the pirates attacked them, Mummy. Tell us *that* story now." Atalanta begged.

"I think we have had enough stories for now. I think you two need to be brave girls like little Bonnie, and get some rest. Now be quiet. The Colonel and Brigid are already sleeping."

Anne kissed both girls on the head and tucked them into the bedrolls set up for them in the library storm shelter. She was grateful that Edmund had slept through her fairy tale. He did not like Granny's stories, which he said were corrupt heathen lies.

There was little sleep for anyone else at Gargaphia that night. Just before dawn a thundering boom made everyone jump. The howling wind sounded like a demon from hell. The girls began to scream as they heard the loud creaking and cracking of timbers being torn apart. Anne and Brigid tried to comfort them. Edmund, who was too afraid to move, could not stand the crying of the children.

"That's enough of that caterwauling." he screeched angrily. "Shut up! Everyone just shut up!"

Gradually the maelstrom outside quieted. The rain had stopped. It was just about midday. Edmund got up and walked outside to the front porch to look around.

He came back into the parlor and reported: "It's clear on the west side." As he returned to his seat he continued. "I'm hungry. Brigid, go out to the summer kitchen and rebuild the fire so I can have some lunch."

Just as the words left his mouth a great gust of wind blew open one of the library shutters. The glass in the window shattered all over Edmund who screamed hysterically. Anne and Brigid sprang into action. First, they checked that the girls were not hurt. Next, they ran outside to re-latch the shutters in the once again pouring rain. They returned to the parlor soaked to the skin. Edmund was cursing, pulling broken glass from his hair and clothes and throwing it on the floor.

"Goddamn it. Clean up this bloody mess! Damn it all to hell! Hurry up why don't ye?"

Annabella and Atalanta were whimpering on the other side of the room. Anne and Brigid looked at each other disgustedly for one brief moment, then set about picking shards of glass off of Edmund. Anne brought over a candle to look for any pieces they might have missed. Once satisfied that there was no more debris on the man, she handed him the taper. She and Brigid swept the floor around him until they thought they had gotten everything. They would find slivers of glass around the room for weeks to come, but for now their task was complete.

By this time the wind and rain had become a steady barrage again. The terrifying effects of the squall continued for several more hours. Finally, everyone in the library settled into an uncertain slumber. The next morning, they awoke to just the sound of a steady rain. The wind had died down considerably.

Anne told Brigid to go change her clothes and then light a fire in the winter kitchen of the master's quarters to prepare them a meal. While the girls were still sleeping, she walked down the hall to check on the servants. There were, thankfully, no injuries.

Anne asked for volunteers among the men to go outside and see what damage there was. The Bristol Boys jumped up, anxious to get out of the confinement of the hall. Their mistress went back to her room and changed into something dry. She could hear Edmund in the next room. She went to his door and knocked.

"Brigid is making us something to eat."

"Good tell her to bring it up here. I'll take it in bed. I'm exhausted. And tell Billy to mount a search party for any escaped livestock. There'd better not be one cow missing."

Anne rolled her eyes and went downstairs. She spent the rest of the day supervising the servants' work addressing the storm damage. The horrendous sound of timbers cracking and things crashing about outside had been the roof of the tower being sheared off and thrown about fifty yards away near the trail to the creek. The structure of the enclosed tower remained otherwise sound. There were some missing shingles on the main house, yet most of the plantation's buildings were miraculously still intact.

The raging wind had subsided but the hurricane was not over. The residents of Gargaphia were trapped indoors for another miserable twelve days of nonstop rain. Brigid and the other household servants tried to keep up with their daily chores which included the seemingly unwinnable battle against mold forming on every surface. Its musty odor, and the heat of confinement in the closed-up house made for an oppressive atmosphere which further frayed nerves.

Annabella and Atalanta mostly stayed in the nursery playing and doing their lessons. They kept asking their mother when it was going to stop raining. They were generally good children but boredom naturally led to teasing and bickering. Brigid more than once had to separate the little sisters to stop them from slapping each other.

When Anne was not pacing or looking out the upstairs windows for signs of sun, she was fighting with Edmund about his constant wretched complaining. It was not long before he took refuge with the Sheffield sisters indulging in their particular talents.

Anne was glad to be rid of his unpleasant company, though that did not prevent each day from feeling like an eternity. The baby in her belly was as restless as she was. It shifted and kicked every time she tried to sit at her desk. Her back ached. No amount of fanning relieved her of the humid warm air that hung like a perpetual heavy blanket over her. Her personal discomfort was compounded by a creeping dread about what they would all face when the skies finally cleared.

The colony had lived through bad storms in the past, but nothing like this. Trees that had not been blown over fell when their roots could no longer hold onto the saturated soil. Before the storm was finally over, the creek and marshes overflowed. Their waters rose to the level of Gargaphia's porches. Once the foul weather had finally passed, it took another three days before the water receded enough for people to safely go outside and begin the cleanup.

In assessing the damage, Anne found that they had lost all of that year's corn and tobacco harvest. Much of what had been dried and stored was now covered with mold. A third of their cattle herd, two hogs, and ten chickens died. The kitchen garden had nothing edible left in it. It would need to be plowed under. Even the root vegetables were ruined.

Anne quickly realized the gravity of their situation. The worst part of the storm would hit them months later when they did not have enough food to get through the winter. They were not alone. If Gargaphia suffered badly, she knew that many of their neighbors with less substantial infrastructure would be much worse off.

Anne began making a plan to pull the community together to assure their mutual survival. This was not her own innovation. Anne was merely doing what she had seen Owen and Bella Tomkin do in similar situations. The larger plantations usually took a leadership role because they had the most resources to fall back on. She took her plan to Edmund. His response took her by surprise.

"Do what you feel is best. I am leaving later today to check on Hedra Cottage."

"When will you be back?" Anne asked cautiously.

"I don't know. I'll likely head on from there to James City."

Anne was incredulous. "Don't you think your place is here? Shouldn't you be leading the community through this crisis?"

"What crisis? The storm's over."

"The storm is over but our harvest has been wiped out. We've lost a lot of livestock. This winter is going to be very hard to survive. Those who do may lose their land because they will have no income to show for themselves this year. We can't just…"

"We can't what? Stand by and do nothing for them? That's exactly what we can do. This works to our advantage. We'll buy them all out."

Anne did not think she could hate Edmund as much as she did at that moment. Not only did he show an inhuman lack of compassion, but he had no idea how tenuous his own financial situation was. Anne could no longer pretend to support his foolishness. She could no longer hold back her contempt for the Great Conjurer.

"Buy them out? I don't know what is worse: your stupidity or your selfishness. How could you think to profit from the suffering of your neighbors? Buy them out? You idiot, you barely have enough money of your own to get through till next year's harvest. What are you going to buy them out with? Your good name? Your name isn't worth spit. You certainly can't get credit. Do you even know how many unpaid debts you have? What if *your* creditors come calling? Have you lost your mind? *Buy them out?!*"

Edmund was shocked and infuriated by Anne's rebuke.

"How dare you speak to me this way? I am your lord and benefactor. Without me you'd be scrubbing someone's floor or worse you'd be making your living on your back. Oh wait, that's what you're doing already! How'd you like to be doing it in the filthy back room of some rot gut tavern? I can make it happen it quicker'n you can say yer morning prayers."

Anne was now defiant.

"I'd like to see you try. Who do you think you are? The only place you're the King of Accomack is in your own deluded mind. Don't be such a stupid buffoon. Can't you see what your responsibilities are?"

"My responsibility today is to check on the welfare of *my wife and family*, not to stand here arguing with my tart. Billy! Billy! Get in here. Billy go pack my bags. We're leaving as soon as you have everything together. Leave me in peace, woman. Goddamn it, get out of my sight. I'll not hear another word!"

"Fine. Leave! See if I care. I'll fare better without your wretched interference."

Anne stomped out of the parlor and upstairs to her room and slammed the door shut. She waited there watching through her window until she saw Edmund, Billy, and the Colonel's retinue mounted their horses and left. Once they were gone Anne got out the *Friends and Neighbors* ledger and the official Gargaphia account book. In a third still-blank volume she made a list of all the landowners and tenants she could think of in Accomack. She gave each name its own page with columns labeled to make a record of what was owed, pledged, bartered, and resolved.

Anne then set about writing open ended letters of agreement for each person to pledge goods and services to the community in exchange for forgiveness of rents, debts, and tithes. Anne hoped to assure their mutual survival by getting her neighbors to agree to combine their resources during the harsh winter to come.

Among the indentures at Gargaphia was a young Irishman named Stanley Waln. He was not a convict or a debtor. He was the educated son of the court clerk in Dublin. Waln had accepted indenture so he could come to the New World and make his fortune. Just a little more than twenty years of age, the slender redhead had been a hard worker on the plantation for about a year. Anne needed someone who could sign their name to serve as a messenger and escort on her visits to her neighbors. She chose Stanley because he seemed dependable and ambitious. He was an amiable young man and she hoped that his bearing would not be seen as threatening.

The first step in her plan was to send a message to the current pastor at St. George's Chapel, requesting that he sign a letter forgiving the annual tithes of settlers who had been wiped out by the hurricane and asking those who had not, to pledge their tithes or other goods and services to help their neighbors through the coming year. Anne planned to show this letter to the neighbors as part of her pitch to get them to join in the mutual support of other settlers.

Anne sent Stanley with her note to the parson and waited anxiously for the rest of that day until he returned not long after nightfall. She worried that she should have gone personally to promote her plan. Stanley presented her with a sheath of papers. First was a note agreeing in part to Anne's plan. The Reverend said that the church would never allow him to forgive the tithes, but he could give people the option to spread that year's tithes out over the next five years or defer the debt until each individual settler could repay it, whichever came first. It was not exactly what Anne had hoped for but it still provided some hope for people who would be in sore need of it. It was her intention to offer similar debt relief and forgive her tenants' rents for a full year.

Next was the letter to the settlers laying out the church's terms for deferring that year's tithing. The last document was an extensive list of the settlers in Northampton, Accomack, and Maryland's Somerset. It showed the tithes the parson was expecting from them. It made good sense to include colonists in all three counties. There were several overlapping properties between them, and if they were not included in this arrangement it was likely that at least some of them might ask to be.

Anne's first visit was to her friend Giles Ishim whose plantation had survived relatively well the storm. He agreed to provide the meat of a few steer and several large bags of corn meal that had not been ruined to be distributed to those in need. He also pledged to lend out three of his bondsmen to help with repairs needed on other farms.

Most of the neighbors offered support for Anne's ideas and additional helpful suggestions on how to distribute relief when the need was greatest. There were only a few who opted out of the plan or who offered only the barest minimum of their resources. For some of the people who rented directly from Edmund, Anne offered promissory notes to use instead of their rents should the Colonel try to collect from them. She knew this would infuriate him and leave him without spending cash. She took great pleasure in doing something good for the tenants while at the same time inconveniencing Edmund.

As she traveled around the county, Anne saw the damage and heard news of the storm's widespread carnage. There was a great loss of life both at sea and on the southernmost reaches of the peninsula which took the brunt of the devastating winds. Stagnant flood waters carried diseases that took more settlers and their livestock. Several ships were reported missing and had surely wrecked. A few of the remaining Indian villages were destroyed. Refugees sought shelter with local landowners who took them in, in exchange for indenture contracts. Anne too took in several stragglers.

It took a long time for the colony to fully recover from the damage and the economic impact. The storm's catastrophic ripple effects continued to be felt for years afterward. Investors back in England sustained losses which lowered the amount of taxes raised. That in turn restricted the Crown's ability to respond to foreign aggression. The hurricane may as well have hit all of the English empire.

Back at Gargaphia, Anne dealt with each set-back and moved on to the next without showing any fear. She used all the money in the ready cash box and most of her own savings. She wanted to make sure her plantation gave their fair share to help the other settlers who were willing to accept it.

After making deals with the other local survivors, Anne broke into Edmund's personal strong box for funds to buy food from colonists in the northern provinces which had not been hit as hard. She sent Stanley north to look for planters who could sell them part of their harvest for their winter stores, and seeds to replant next spring. It took him more than a month. He traveled as far as the plantation of Anne's friend Anna Hack Boote. She was a great help connecting her southern neighbor to those who were willing to help the storm torn region.

When Stanley returned, he brought with him the names of those planters along with a list of what they had to sell and their prices. He was accompanied by a Maryland colonist named Captain Daniel Jenifer. He was an Army officer and an attorney who owned a cattle farm.

When Stanley introduced him to Anne, Captain Jenifer bowed low and kissed her hand.

"Madam, your reputation as a great lady is known by many. When I heard you were seeking help for not just yourself but for all your neighbors, I felt it was my duty as a gentleman to do whatever I could to come to your assistance."

Daniel Jenifer, a Catholic, was as well known for his piousness as for his courtly manner. He was tall, broad shouldered with auburn hair and brown eyes. He wore clothes that were well made but not ostentatious. He was neither handsome nor ugly. A relatively young man in his thirties, his manner was serious and curt. He did not seem to smile much.

Just as he had heard of her, Anne had heard that he was a much sought-after widower who was known to be friends with Maryland's proprietor Lord Calvert. He was also counted among Colonel Scarborough's detractors. Maryland settlers were uniformly resentful of Edmund's attempts to expand the Virginia territory northward into their province.

Anne was a little surprised to be visited by someone who had loudly criticized court proceedings which were held in a house of such sinful repute. She was suspicious of the man's motives, but did not feel she could turn down any help offered in this situation. So, she demurely entertained her Maryland neighbor.

"Captain Jenifer, I am delighted to meet you. And, I am so very grateful that you have come here personally to offer your help. Once we have concluded our business together may we offer you a bed for the night in our guest quarters?"

"Um, well, er... I don't think that will be necessary." the Captain blushed. "Let's have a look at the list young Stanley has brought you and see what we can do to make sure we get you what you need."

So, began their negotiations. He made her an offer of livestock and transportation of flour, corn meal, and other foods from several Maryland plantations that had dodged the hurricane. The cost he estimated for all this was much more than she had in available cash or tobacco certificates. She got the price down by offering him some of her future salt production. Still she was short the amount needed.

"Madam, perhaps I could purchase your plantation and take it over, and relieve you of this terrible burden altogether."

"Sir, your offer is most generous, but I don't think it has come to that. Last year I purchased a small farm in Maryland from Garret Revel. It has a tenant who is doing quite well there. The land is valued at just a bit more than what you are asking. Let me write a letter of introduction for you to the tenant so you can look over the property. If it's to your liking, I will sell it to you for the for the price of all you are offering today."

"Does that include the salt production as well?"

"Well, no. That would exceed the price we are discussing. But I will offer you salt at a two percent discount of the regular price for this coming year."

The Captain was impressed by Anne's negotiating skills. He had been intrigued by her reputation. He was fascinated by her refinement and beauty at the same time that he scorned her for clearly being pregnant and unmarried. He wondered how she had evaded the fornication laws. Now that he had met her in person, his interest grew. He was not a man motivated by physical desire. What made him salivate was the fact that she was known to have extensive landholdings.

Daniel Jenifer was not the first person to wonder how they might take advantage of her feminine weakness, hoping to trick her out of her property. For all his reputed papist piety, he clearly had no qualms about taking an un-Christian advantage of storm victims. Anne quickly assessed his mercenary character but played his game. She did not let on what she thought of him in order to get what she needed. With their business concluded for now, the Captain made his exit with as deep a bow as he had entered with.

This deal took care of a significant portion of what would be required to get through the months to come. Anne feared it would not be enough, however. That night she tossed and turned with worry about facing troubles she could not anticipate. When sleep did come to her, she dreamt of the terrible storm. Finally, Anne gave up trying to rest. She dressed and put on shoes.

It was early October. The air was beginning to cool. That night the three-quarter moon was waning but still bright enough to make visibility very good. The roof had not yet been replaced on the tower. When Anne reached the top, a stiff easterly breeze made her hold tight to the rail with one hand while she looked to the beach. She scanned the shoreline from north to south and back again.

Anne looked out toward the horizon. The salt air smelled clean and fresh. It had taken weeks for the odors of dead animals and rotting plants to go away. Even though the missing roof made her feel exposed and unsteady, the bracing wind on her face felt good. Just as the sun started to come up Anne noticed the silhouette of a ship heading towards the coast. Anne lifted her spyglass to get a better look.

The small craft had clearly seen heavy weather. What sails there were on it, were tattered and clearly useless. In the dark, Anne could not see any colors flying to identify it, nor any movement on the top deck. The ocean currents gently brought the vessel through the breakers to rest on the beach. It was high tide. If the ocean did not pull her back out to sea in a few hours, the ship would rest where it lay at least until the next high tide.

Anne watched as the breakers washed up against the hull of the boat and receded again several times. Suddenly as the waves pulled back the pinnace teetered for a moment and then tipped over, its mast pointing southward. The sun had almost fully risen.

Anne walked with purpose down the tower stairs and headed toward the creek. Forgetting the precautions which she had been taking to guard her pregnancy, she untied a row boat and jumped in, heading for the island. After landing, she got out and pulled the boat up onto the beach tying it off to a post that had been put there for just that purpose. She hurriedly made her way through the path in the dunes over to the beach.

The wrecked ship was further down than she expected. Anne was breathing heavily when she arrived at the site. She approached it from behind the hull and peered cautiously around the gunnel of its now vertical deck. What she beheld was horrific. A half dozen sailors lashed to the mast and rails were clearly dead. Anne guessed they must have tied themselves to the rigging during the storm for fear of being washed over.

They had been dead for some time. Their bloated rotting flesh had begun to fall away exposing their bones. Screaming seagulls and other carrion birds had already arrived, circling above. The smell of death was intense. Anne began to retch. She walked further south to get away from the stench trying to figure out whether the wind was still out of the east and what would be the best approach.

She looked at the terrible scene and threw up. Holding her belly, she remembered she was with child. She looked up and saw one of the bodies slip its bonds as gravity pulled it to the ground with hardly a sound. It landed on its side. The scum covered skull seemed to stare at her beseechingly.

"Should I go back over there and risk getting sick?" she thought.

Anne decided to venture nearer to get a quick look. She walked as close as she dared and stood surveying the situation while trying to hold her breath. She saw that the sailor who now laid on the ground had a pouch the size of a horse hoof tied around his neck. When she could stand it no more, she backed off again.

After breathing heavily for a few minutes, she took a deep gasp and ran over to the ship. She tried to grab the pouch with both hands and pulled hard. It did not budge. Again, she backed off to breathe clean air.

"Damn. Why didn't I even bring a knife with me?" she thought. "Once more. I will try once more and then I'll go for help."

When Anne went again for her quarry, she pulled with all her might severing the man's neck. The disgusting head rolled off. Anne fell back retching again. Recovering a little, she took the pouch over to the surf and rinsed off as much of the foul slime that covered it as she could.

She walked upwind toward the dunes and sat down to see what the leather bag contained. It took a few moments for her to get it to open. When it revealed its treasures, Anne began to laugh. There were more than fifty gold coins. There were also a dozen loose gems. They were cut and polished emeralds ranging in size from that of a pea to that of a raspberry. They sparkled in the light of the rising sun.

"Thank you, Mother Mary! Look what I have found! Many blessings on the sea fairies for the bounty of these gifts!"

Anne could not believe her good luck. She put everything back in the bag which still smelled terrible. She headed back over the dune to row the boat back up the creek to Gargaphia. When she got there Brigid was waiting for her.

"Mistress Anne, where have ya been? I was frantic."

Annabella and Atalanta ran up to their mother to give her a hug. They stopped abruptly when the awful smell of the pouch she was carrying hit them head on. They squealed and ran away from her holding their little noses.

Anne laughed. "It's alright my little cabbages. We'll get rid of this nasty thing soon enough. There's been a wreck. Brigid, I'll need bathing water in my chamber and a bowl for the contents of this bag. Girls, you get back to the kitchen and finish your breakfast…"

"We already did, Mummy." Atalanta said.

"What's in the stinky bag, Mummy?" Annabella chimed in.

"Never you mind. Go on now. Go play in the parlor like good little girls while Mummy cleans up."

Anne rushed upstairs, quickly closing the bedroom door behind her. She poured her treasures out onto the top of her dresser. She checked to make sure the bag was completely empty. She counted exactly twelve emeralds of different sizes and fifty-five gold reals –

Portuguese coins. She separated the emeralds and five gold coins from the rest of the money. These she carefully hid away in her iron strong box. Just as she was covering it back up, there was a knock on the door.

"I have your bathing water, Mum"

Anne let Brigid in and began to undress. Brigid noticed the money on the dresser. Before she could ask anything, Anne was giving her another set of tasks to do.

"I need you to wash this dress and burn that pouch. Then tell Delia to bring the household to the gathering hall at – what time is it?"

"It is almost half past nine bells Mum."

"Tell Delia that everyone should meet at ten bells. We have a small ship to salvage. There are dead to bury."

Despite the somber news, Anne was smiling. She had really good news for everyone. She planned to stay quiet about keeping the jewels and five gold coins for herself. The rest of the money would just about cover what was needed for the winter and get the plantation started again next year. She would still need to sell Captain Jenifer the Maryland farm but this bit of luck would assure their survival.

The remaining salvage of the ship was conducted as many others had been. Its log book revealed that the vessel had been a ship tender for a cargo fleet out of Portugal which had been captured by pirates who in turn then set the crew free with no cargo. The last entry by their captain was brief. It described a storm that was approaching too swiftly to outrun. As Anne had guessed, the captain and crew had lashed themselves to whatever they could as their last hope of surviving. She wondered how the man with the pouch had kept his fortune from the pirates.

There was little of value for the household to split. Anne announced to them that rather than dividing the money among them, which was their usual practice, she would use it to buy the remaining food they would need to get through the winter, and starter seed for the spring. When Anne read the requiem prayers over the graves of the crew, she thanked them for their sacrifice which would help the settlers to survive.

Though she had a great hand in it, Anne did not single handedly save the colonists of the Eastern Shore of Virginia that winter. Other landowners showed their ingenuity and generosity as well. It was everyone's mutual efforts to pull together during hard times that made the difference. Edmund's now grown children all joined in to support their community. Unlike their father, they had a more dependable moral center. They also recognized that to take undue advantage of the situation would make their lives more difficult later.

Edmund, languishing in James City, was not heard from during that time. He was not the only one to shirk their duty in a time of crisis. Some indentures took advantage of the chaos following the storm. Anne filed a complaint against one man, Thomas Bell, who took off with several of her sheep on a tether in the rainy days following the worst of the storm. He was caught at Fowkes Tavern three months later. The court did not look kindly on runaways. He was fined, publicly lashed, and his indenture to Anne was extended in order to pay off his time on the run and the loss of the sheep.

Most of the settlers on the Eastern Shore of Virginia made it through that brutal winter alive. There were a few planters, however, who were demoralized by their struggles. They, as Edmund had predicted, gave up their farms and sought the safer environs of more established towns across the Chesapeake. A few even returned to their home countries. For everyone else, the experience did not defeat them. It made them stronger.

Anne was now more determined than ever to get out from under her obligation to Edmund, with or without his ruination. The sacrifices she witnessed being made by landowner, indenture, and slave alike gave her hope. She was sure that she could now thrive on her own, without Edmund's patronage.

On Epiphany during the winter of 1668, Anne gave birth to another daughter. She called her Arcadia in homage to the mythic name given what was now coastal Virginia, by the Italian explorer Giovanni da Verrazzano. For Anne it conjured up visions inspired by Virgil's *Divine Comedy* and Sir Phillip Sidney's *The Countess of Pembroke's Arcadia*. It contained all the promise of this New World, the rich resources to be found there, and the potential of the utopian society that might be built there. The name represented the best aspirations of the community settlers had built there. Choosing the name Arcadia expressed all the hope Anne had for her daughters' bright future.

Brabbling Women

When Edmund Scarborough returned to Gargaphia after his annual Yuletide family visit in 1668, he found that Accomack County had become most inhospitable to him. Even given his predilection for ignoring the opinions of others, he was unprepared to be greeted with nearly universal hostility. Those he owed money to or had cheated in some way, had lost patience with his excuses. He encountered a general attitude of contempt wherever he went because he had left hurricane relief efforts to his mistress and his children. People no longer hid their resentment of the Great Conjurer.

When the fall session of Accomack County Court opened, Edmund had the duty, as head magistrate, of organizing the docket. He noticed a number of people bringing complaints against him. He put them at the end of the list intending to use the delay to try and come up with a way to deny their claims. He could not have known that the case he put first in line would unmask a worse reprobate than him.

Elizabeth Carter was brought before the court on a charge of killing her newborn child. An indentured servant, she claimed the baby's father, her married master, had forced her to take a potion to abort the pregnancy prior to her quickening and this had damaged the infant causing it to be stillborn. She further complained that he beat her and had seduced her with proposals of marriage but instead married the widow, Joanna Matrum.

Carter brought with her corroborating witnesses who were so compelling that a grand jury was impaneled to consider charges against the man in question, Henry Smith, a planter who owned the tract of land known as Oak Hall.

In such cases of infanticide, a few respectable women in the community were recruited to sit on those juries because of their expertise in such feminine matters. They were called on to examine the infant corpse and listen to witness testimony. What followed was a week of stories so searing that the residents of Accomack County would not forget them for generations to come.

Henry Smith had made it a regular practice to rape and brutalize all the women on his plantation. This included servants, slaves, even his wife. Feeling emboldened by Elizabeth's testimony, two other bondswomen testified that they had also given birth to Smith's children. The madman captured one servant who tried to escape and held her for two years at property he owned on Smith Island in the middle of Chesapeake Bay.

At the end of the first day of hearings Joanna Smith, the accused's wife, joined the chorus of complainants. She was so terrified of Henry Smith she had taken her four-year-old daughter from her first marriage to a neighbor for safekeeping. She broke down, weeping with relief, believing that that the court would finally do something about this brute.

"I beg you to take pity on me and my child. Please help us. Please help us." Joanna said, collapsing on the floor.

From the sidelines, Anne and several other women jumped up to comfort the distraught woman and helped her back to her seat. Anne then approached Edmund and the other magistrates presiding over the case.

"My Lords, Mrs. Smith is quite overcome." she whispered. "Let us adjourn so the grand jury can consider the charges. I can take her to the guest quarters so she might recover from this ordeal and await a determination from the court."

"Step back Mistress Toft." Edmund responded. "The grand jury will retire to consider the evidence. Court is adjourned to reconvene tomorrow morning at nine bells."

That night Anne invited Joanna Smith to stay at Gargaphia until the conclusion of the trial. She found her a room in the guest wing that was the farthest from the noise of the gathering hall in hopes of giving the woman some peace and quiet. The trial continued for the rest of the week. Each day Joanna Smith looked paler and more frightened.

The night before the last day of proceedings, Anne went to check on her guest. She knocked on the door and opened it quietly in case Joanna was sleeping only to find Edmund fondling her on the bed. Joanna was mortified and became hysterical.

"I did nothing to encourage him. I swear Mistress Toft. I swear! Please I beg you, do not tell my husband of this."

"Go to bed Mrs. Smith." Anne replied. "Edmund, get out of here, you idiot. Have you no shame? Come with me. I want to talk to you."

Anne grabbed the Colonel by the arm and pulled him down the stairs and through the gathering hall back to their wing. All the while he snickered at her, amused by her indignation. When they arrived back at their own parlor, she slammed the door shut and began to shout at him.

"You depraved pig! How dare you subject that poor woman to your evil desires? What is wrong with…"

Edmund stopped laughing, turned and smacked Anne across the face with the back of his hand. She stumbled backward trying to get away from him. He continued to hit her. Open palm then back of the hand. Open palm then back of the hand. Open palm then back of the hand. Anne froze with her back was against the wall.

"Humph. For once you're silent. Ya damn well better stay that way. Don't you ever tell me what to do - *ever!* Is that clear? You disgusting cow. I'll do as I please and you'll like it. Do you hear me? Get over here and sit down."

Edmund dragged her across the room by the arm, pushing her onto a chair. He opened his pants and pulled out his limp penis and tried to force into her mouth.

"Suck on it, wench. Make it hard. Goddamn, I say suck on it."

Anne resisted, clenching her teeth. She reached up between his legs, grabbing his scrotum, pinching and twisting the skin as hard as she could. Edmund squealed in pain and jumped backwards.

Once he had caught his breath he growled, "You will learn your place! I'm sick of this. Who do you think you are? Don't you know that I can have you bound out at any time to some other horny devil? Your daughters will be next to some brute who likes 'em young. I know a tavern owner who would make a pretty penny renting them out by the hour. In fact, I think that is just what I will do."

Anne was horrified. "You would do that to your own daughters?"

"They're not my daughters. They're the daughters of *Henry Toft*. They are the daughters of a bondswoman. By law, they must be bound out at the age of thirteen."

"I was free when they were born. No one will make them into bondswomen."

"Who is to say? I am head of the magistrates' council for this county. Who would take your word over mine?"

Edmund walked over to the sideboard, pulled out a bottle of rum and took a long swig. Anne stood her ground. The two stared at each other in stony silence for a few moments.

"You won't do that, Edmund."

"Is that so? What makes you so sure?"

"A great majority of your property is in my name. It would take quite a bit of time for you to untangle all of that legally. There are too many witnesses you would need to bribe. And, you have no money. You and I are stuck with each other until we can figure out an equitable separation. Oh, and if you try and take my girls from me, I will kill you in your sleep."

Without waiting for a response Anne walked out of the room leaving Edmund to finish the bottle of rum while he pondered whether his mistress might actually try to murder him that night.

The next day the grand jury indicted Henry Smith on a long list of charges, including fornication, bastardy, and assault on his wife and stepdaughter. It took Edmund and the other magistrates only ten minutes to convict the man of all charges. Despite this victory in the name of justice for those terrified women, the sentences handed down that day were typically misogynistic.

Henry Smith was verbally reprimanded and told to cease his bad behavior. He was ordered to pay fines for his misdeeds and maintenance for the upbringing of his illegitimate children. Their mothers were ordered to endure a two-year extension of their indenture to him to reimburse him for the work time they missed while pregnant and caring for their newborns. Joanna Smith was denied a legal separation. All the women were forced back to her abusive husband's household.

Court records were rife with such heinous injustice. The prevailing belief was that women were inherently immoral. It was they who were responsible for arousing men against their will. Their inherent wickedness infected men, making them incapable of controlling themselves. In the eyes of the law, women were too mentally and ethically inferior to consult for their consent sexually, so none was required. Servants and wives were bound to honor the wishes of their master for this reason, no matter how cruel they were.

The case was concluded for now, though in the years to come Henry Smith would be brought back to court again and again to answer for his cruelties. Anne was deeply unsettled by the outcome. She had seen women mistreated by the courts before, but this was an extreme. The whole affair also marked the end of any hope of peaceful reconciliation between Anne and Edmund. They were officially at war with each other.

For the week following the notorious Smith trial, the master and mistress of Gargaphia kept their distance from each other. The Colonel's discomfort was made complete by the intolerable squalling of his newest daughter Arcadia. He called for an early conclusion of that session of court, citing the exhausting nature of the Smith case. Escaping his creditors once again, he quickly departed to the more pleasant atmosphere of James City.

The capital served as safe harbor for gentlemen like Edmund. The old boys club was so entrenched there, that in light of other cases of complaining women folk, they had actually enacted laws prohibiting "brabbling" females from bringing frivolous and slanderous suits against their husbands or masters. The Cavalier class enjoyed the privilege of being shielded from creditors and meddlesome family obligations while in residence at the capital. Though rumors swirled about Edmund's domestic problems, he still found sympathy and comradery among his peers.

Virginia's Governor Berkley, unphased by what he considered petty squabbles across the Chesapeake Bay, assigned Colonel Scarborough the duty of negotiating an agreement with Maryland's proprietor, Phillip Calvert, to codify the official border line between Virginia and Maryland. Noting his former role as Surveyor General for the colony and his militia leadership, he claimed Scarborough would favorably pursue Virginia's interests.

Edmund was glad for the chance to ingratiate himself to the Governor and the much-needed distraction. He took to the work with great vigor. The northern boundary of Accomack County was settled for the time being as were other property disputes in the western portion of the colonies. He considered the resulting charter a triumph. This agreement would buy him time to continue with his own agenda. He fully intended to violate its terms and continue his push northward in hopes of securing the entire peninsula for Virginia. It was an achievement just the same, and Edmund enjoyed being feted as a result.

Meanwhile Anne was greatly relieved that he was somewhere else bothering somebody else. Once the Colonel left, she went back to her daily work without much thought of him. She was happily preoccupied with the care of infant Arcadia when she received a threatening letter from Edmund who was feeling emboldened by his recent success.

3rd day 4th month, the year of Our Lord MDCLXVIII

My dear Mistress Toft,

Since you have seen fit to interfere with the collection of rents from my tenants by giving them promissory notes, I demand that you make good on those loans and pay me what is owed to me in rents.

Your Lord and Master,

Colonel Edmund Scarborough

Anne returned fire with a letter saying that she now held notes for enough of his other debts to equal double what rents he was owed. She suggested that should he sue her for the promissory notes she would demand redemption of these debts. Further, if he persisted, she would join suit with his other creditors and demand that the Governor force him to repay all that he was in arrears for.

For much of the time they were together, Anne had a pretty good idea what Scarborough had in assets and what the size of his debts were. She had paid his bills when she had direct knowledge of them. The profits she had generated from running the plantation had subsidized his extravagant lifestyle.

Anne knew that if the full extent of his money troubles came to light, he would be ruined. She had a stack of letters from his creditors demanding payment from people as far away as England and Brazil. He owed money for outright loans, for slaves he had purchased, and for shipments of tobacco that had never reached their destinations. He still owed unpaid fees to the Dutch mapmaker, Augustine Herrmann whom he had made a deal with the year before.

The formal nature of Edmund's letter made Anne wary of what would happen next if she did not have something in writing from him that would protect her from any more of his threats. Anne decided it was time to make her break from Edmund. Her first step was to write to her friend Anna in hopes that she would offer her shelter if she had to suddenly flee Virginia.

12th day 6th month, the year of Our Lord MDCLXVIII

Dear Anna,

I hope that you and your family are enjoying good health and that all are prospering well in Cecil County. I send greetings and good wishes from all your friends here in Accomack.

I am happy to report that I have recently welcomed a new daughter Arcadia. She is as lovely as her delightful sisters are. I am sure you will understand a mother's prejudice in these matters.

You may not be surprised to hear that Gargaphia may not remain the best place to raise my precious girls. I wonder if we might visit you after the harvest season to see your lovely plantation and discuss other possibilities?

Your dear friend,

Anne Toft

Anne was puzzled by her friend's response which came within a few weeks.

2nd day 8th month, the year of Our Lord MDCLXVIII

My dear friend,

I am delighted to hear of the arrival of your new daughter Arcadia. You are indeed blessed. I would treasure the chance to have you all enjoy the hospitality of my home.

I have heard much about life in Accomack County these days. You are right to be concerned about where the best place is to raise your precious children. I would, however, recommend that you hold fast for a while longer. The information I have is in your favor. If you leave now, you may forfeit much of your property rights.

As always, keep good records and protect yourself with legal contracts. You have many friends who will stand by you in the days to come. Be of good cheer.

With warm regards,

Anna Varlet Hack Boote

This was not exactly the response that Anne had hoped for. She thought about what contracts could protect her, which friends she could count on. Seeing no other recourse, she drew up papers that would settle things between her and the Colonel, forgiving the debts between them and giving her clear title to Gargaphia which technically still belonged to his wife Mary Scarborough. She included a clause that also bound him to honor her ownership of most of her other properties as payment for her services running his various farms and businesses.

Anything she had come to own without Edmund's help would remain hers while properties he had acquired prior to their association would remain his. She would include a sizeable cargo of sugar and indigo which she was expecting through her shipping interests as an incentive to make the deal. Anne held these documents ready and waiting until Edmund returned for the next session of court to be held in May. It would not be easy to get him to sign them.

When Colonel Scarborough arrived that spring day, he brought with him a larger company of soldiers than usual. He wanted to intimidate anyone who might demand money from him and, in particular, Anne. He had every intention of putting her in her place.

"Billy," he barked at his aide de camp, "Tell the wenches to clear out guests to make room for you and the other officers. Then have the rest of the company set up camp on the north side of the house."

"Welcome back to Gargaphia, my lord." Anne spoke with polite seriousness.

"Madam, I would have you and I come to an understanding. Come into the library and let's get things straight, right now."

Anne followed him and closed the door behind them so they would be alone. It was late afternoon. Brigid had taken the children to feed them their supper.

"Now see here," Edmund began. "You owe me a great deal of money."

"And likewise, you owe me a great deal of money, sir."

"Let's start with you paying me and then we'll see if I pay you anything."

Anne laughed. "I'll pay you nothing. I have here a document that will wipe out what is owed by those promissory notes from your tenants and place the responsibility for repayment of some of your debts with me. Certain properties will be deeded back to you. In exchange, I want the title to Gargaphia. I also want you to renounce any other claim, to this plantation, the servants, slaves, animals, and any goods on this or any of my other rightfully owned properties. Furthermore, in this document you will give up any claim after your natural life that might be assigned to your heirs and your creditors."

"You've lost your mind. I'll do no such thing." Edmund scoffed.

"Well, my dear, I have about twenty letters from other creditors demanding repayment from you that are not included in this document. Should I take my demands and join suit with them, I have no doubt that Gargaphia will be awarded as settlement for what you owe me. If you sign this document, you can continue to hold court here and live indefinitely in your quarters here without incurring any further debt to me. This will allow you to avoid the embarrassment of penury. And, maybe you can recoup your losses enough to redeem your bad reputation with your fellow Cavaliers."

"You wouldn't dare. We have a law against brabbling wives. The court will dock you for making such slanderous accusations."

"First, my lord, I am not your wife. Secondly, I know the law well, my lord. I may not speak against you on my own but many of your creditors are willing to stand with me."

"If you do, I'll counter sue you for the time in pregnancy you owe me."

"I was not your servant when I had your daughters. This is a fact of law based on the documents we signed at the beginning of this..."

"How long have you been planning this, you mercenary bitch?"

"Since the day I heard that Owen Tomkin was murdered." Anne met his anger with equal vehemence.

"Owen Tomkin? What's he got to do with... Murdered?! Christ Jesus. What are you talking about? The man fell overboard. What makes you think that he was murdered?"

Anne tried to contain her anger. They were finally going to speak some semblance of the truth to each other.

"Everyone in Accomack watched you profit from his death. You stole Chiconessex out from under Bella. You had every intention of bonding me to you as your mistress just to satisfy your own sinful lust."

"That doesn't mean I murdered anyone..."

"No, you got that cur Jasper Darby to do it for you. He confessed it to me in front of witnesses the night he attacked Fanta."

"I never told him to do any such..."

Mid-sentence Edmund was struck with the realization that he had just admitted to cheating Bella Tomkin. The full implication of what Anne was saying was dawning on him.

"Just a minute! Why exactly did you agree to be my mistress?" His face flushed. His lower lip began to quiver. In over ten years, his deluded obsession had so saturated his mind with fantasy, he had actually come to believe that Anne cared for him, that their recent rift was mere squabbling, that she thought of him as her heroic Cavalier. Anne's words had ripped him from his perverted world of make-believe into the harsh light of reality.

The anguished look of this awareness on his face was what Anne had been waiting for. She finally saw some small evidence of human pain in this selfish, selfish man. It should have made her triumphant.

Instead she felt sickened. Her stomach began to turn and a hot flash rose up through her spine. She began to defend her actions.

"Why do you think? I did what I had to do to survive. Where would I have gone with no money or prospects? What difference does it make now? You never really loved me. All you wanted was a pretty young whore. You wanted me to serve you in bed and to show me off to other men as your courtesan. Surely you didn't think I felt anything but obligation to you?"

"I've given you everything, a fine home, clothes, jewelry."

"And children Edmund, let's not forget our children. Three beautiful daughters, who have no claim to anything. What's to become of them? You don't care. Apparently, you're planning to have them turned out. They are – I am – nothing more to you than livestock – like any of your other slaves. You have no honor where my children and I are concerned. For more than a decade I've served you…"

"Is it my fault that women are bound to serve men? The Bible requires it just as it requires men to give protection to their inferiors."

"Protection? Is that what you call it? Am I supposed to love you for that protection, which is just an excuse to enslave me? Don't pretend to be hurt to find out I do not love you. After all, how could a dumb cow love you?"

"You're turning everything around. I don't understand…"

"All you need to understand is that if you do not sign this agreement in front of witnesses and have it registered in court this week; you will be disgraced. None of your ambitions will be realized. You will never be Lord Proprietor of Virginia. You will live out your days with only those comforts granted by the good graces of your family and your lunatic wife. Look over the papers. Once we have signed them you are free to stay in your quarters at Gargaphia whenever and for as long as you like. You will not be publicly embarrassed. You can continue to hold court here. But, you and I sir, we will both get on with our lives."

"You once made a promise to me."

"Yes, I did. Even though you took advantage of me when I was a young impressionable girl. Unlike you, I always keep my word. I'll not make love with you but I'll continue to see to your comforts, no matter how distasteful that may be, because I promised that I would. I will not make you look foolish in public so long as you do nothing to hurt my reputation."

"Your reputation, that's a laugh. Everyone in the colony knows you are nothing more than my filthy whore."

Anne laughed a little. "That is true. Isn't it sad then, my lord, that everyone in this county holds your filthy whore in higher regard than they do you, the so-called King of Accomack? The Great Conjurer has lost his magic sway over the people in this colony. You are nothing more than a ridiculous old buffoon, a mere pauper. No one gives a damn about you anymore."

With these caustic remarks Anne had gone too far. Edmund lunged across the table between them, his arms outstretched in an attempt to wring her neck. She was too quick for him. She stepped back and he fell forward then tripped on the table leg as he tried to get around it. He lay on the floor groaning and rubbing the elbow he had landed on.

Edmund's face was red. Waves of anger and humiliation washed over him. He tearfully rose to his feet as Anne made her way to the door speaking with all the authority she could muster.

"If you sign those papers in the morning, I will include 9,000 pounds of Mevis Sugar in cask, and 700 pounds of indigo. That should provide you enough money to live comfortably for at least a year. Think it over carefully, Colonel." she said as she walked out of the room.

Anne went to the kitchen to get a large knife which she took to the nursery, joining Brigid and the children. There behind a locked door, she sat vigil all night for fear that Edmund might try to use force against her. Anne wanted to throw up, but she had not eaten any supper. There was nothing in her stomach. She stifled her retching as best she could so Brigid and the girls would not be more frightened than they already were. As the hours passed and the others fell asleep, Anne prayed that this would not be the end of her.

Despite her fears, the night passed without any further incident. The next morning the couple returned to the library. Anne brought Brigid with her to serve as a witness. Billy accompanied Edmund for the same purpose. Anne had one more card to play. She knew that Edmund was desperate for money so she decided to present him with one more enticement in hopes of resolving their tangled financial conflict.

"I have here a letter that I have written to John Vassall, instructing him to sell my property in Port Royal, Jamaica. It is a sizeable piece on the wharf there, comprised of several businesses and dockage. It is worth a great deal more than Gargaphia is. I will consign, in writing, the proceeds of that sale to you. You can see that the amount expected will solve your present difficulties and allow you to live comfortably while you regain your financial standing. Give me what I want and soon your coffers will be full again and we can move past this..."

Edmund looked over the documents. He knew that when his mistress gave her word, she was good for it. The amount of money in her proposal was too tempting to turn down. He held out hope that he could eventually confiscate the rest of her holdings. He believed that he was entitled to them even though she had built up her fortune mostly on her own. Edmund saw her as his chattel. Whatever was hers by rights belonged to him.

He was, however, strangely conflicted by this proposal which essentially divorced the couple. Edmund had lost Anne in every way it was possible to lose a spouse. He could not help being heartbroken. Fighting back tears, he signed his name. Anne followed suit. Then Brigid and Billy added their names as witnesses. When court convened later that day the agreement was officially registered, though not read aloud.

Anne had won that round because Edmund did not want anyone to know that this lowly woman now controlled most of what he considered to be his land. If she put him out of Gargaphia, he could not hold court there and everyone would find out he was nearly penniless. Edmund knew a scandal of this proportion would not only destroy what was left of his reputation in Accomack County. It could destroy any standing he had with the General Assembly.

Once court proceedings were completed, the Colonel retreated to his own chamber for several days, demanding his meals be brought there. After he had licked the deep wounds to his pride, his thoughts turned to revenge. He resolved to punish Anne any way that he could until he could devise a plan to undo all she had accomplished and claim all her property for himself. He was intent on getting even.

What followed was an unmitigated campaign of harassment. Edmund was more garrulous than usual. He made unreasonable requests from the servants, demanding to be fed at all hours of the night and day. He insisted that someone be with him at all times to fetch things that were only as far away as his arms' reach. He began to regularly invite the most obnoxious guests he could find to drink and gamble with him in the master's parlor, insisting that Anne serve as hostess to a continuing parade of ill-mannered riff raff.

When Anne stoically tolerated this bad behavior, Edmund escalated his boorishness by demanding that the guest house wenches sexually service him and his guests in the master's wing. When the revelers were too drunk to seek the privacy of their bedchambers or even to stand up, the women were forced to perform their erotic tasks on the men sitting by the fire in Mistress Toft's parlor.

Anne was disgusted by this debauchery. She had long protected the innocence of her children by forbidding such behavior in the master's wing. But she was just as stubborn as Edmund, so she refused to let him see her anger. This went on for a month until Edmund, having been drunk for most of that time became seriously ill. He developed a high fever compounded by near constant vomiting and diarrhea. He was unable to keep down any food. For several days he refused to see a doctor and insisted that the only person who could nurse him was Anne.

Finally, Anne sent for Charles Scarborough to bring the doctor and talk some sense into his father. She left them alone hoping that Charles would decide to take the man to Hedra Cottage to die with his family. When the two men emerged from Edmund's bedchamber, there was good news for Edmund and bad news for Anne.

"It seems Father has been overdoing himself." Charles announced. "The doctor will write up a course of treatment. He is to have small amounts of claret or brandy to reduce his trembling – two tablespoons every two hours for the first day, then every four hours for a day, then as needed. You are not to give him any more, no matter how hard he begs. Feed him broth and porridge for a few days and add meat and vegetables as he regains his appetite."

"Charles, shouldn't he be with his family?"

"The doctor says he should be himself by week's end. He says he wants to recover here, right where he is. He insisted."

The doctor finished writing the instructions and handed them to Anne who accepted them grudgingly.

"Don't worry. He'll be fine. You always take such good care of him. I am sure he'll be fit as a fiddle in no time." Charles remarked.

Anne gave the men a small smile with raised eyebrows and bade them goodbye. "Maybe he will die in his sleep." she thought to herself.

For the next two weeks Anne and Brigid nursed Colonel Scarborough through the after effects of his alcoholic binging. He was miserable. He demanded ale and rum. When the women refused to give it to him, he screamed and threatened their lives. He was too weak to stand on his own two feet and find the spirits himself. One night when Anne came to Edmund's chamber to clear his dishes, she found him weeping.

"For all these years I've loved you more than life itself. I thought you loved me. Weren't we happy together once? Can't we return to those happier times? Please, come into my bed and let us forget our hateful words. Please, my darling Anne, please…"

For a moment Anne looked at the pitiful remains of her once insatiable lover. She felt nothing at all for the man. She could not think of anything to say, no insult, not even a rebuke to his pathetic entreaties. She silently put his dishes on a tray and left him crying in his bed.

The next morning Edmund came downstairs for the midday meal and that afternoon was back in the gathering hall looking for guests to join him in another cycle of hedonism. There he found Matthew Moore and his wife Margaret. Moore was a brickmaker who lived in the tradesmen's village near Gargaphia. The couple had come to the plantation in order to ask the Colonel to make good on his debt for work Moore had done on Hedra Cottage.

Edmund tried to distract the man from his mission with flattery and the prestigious invitation for he and his wife to dine in the master's dining room. Anne, tired of the Colonel's shenanigans, made Brigid serve the small party while she attended to the children. The threesome drank and played dice all afternoon. That night Anne and the girls could hear them talking and laughing through the floorboards. Soon they began to hear shouting and furniture crashing.

Anne told the girls to stay in their room and went downstairs to investigate. She found Edmund and Matthew screaming nonsensically at each other while Margaret sat on the floor, red faced and blubbering. It seems that after her husband had passed out from too much rum, Edmund had made aggressive advances toward Mrs. Moore. Her loud protestations awakened Mr. Moore who was intent on defending his wife's honor. Fists began flying between the men. Mrs. Moore, caught in the crossfire had been thrown to the floor.

Anne slammed a pewter trench on the table with a loud bang and yelled, "*What* is going on here?"

Edmund sat down in his chair and began to laugh, enraging the drunken brickmaker who began to rant.

"Your master is a deceitful liar annn cheaterrr. Gargapheeee is a den niquity. A den niquity, I say! I seen what goes on here. Whores and highwaymen consort, consort – consorting! I'm nnn honest man. I do good work. I just wannu be paid wut I'm owed. I come here to ask like a proper tradesman for my money, and wut happens? He gets me drunk and tries to su, su, sully my wife!! I will work no more for ya Scarborough! Nor yer whores and bastards. You hear me?! None of ya. None – ya hear?!"

Moore pulled his distraught wife to her feet and picked up one of the parlor lanterns intending to use it to guide him on his way home in the dark. Once outside, the couple had not even reached the lane when Edmund came barreling out of the house yelling at the top of his lungs.

"Billy! Billy! Where are you? Billy, get your men! Stop that man! Stop him I say! He means to burn us down!"

Despite limping, Edmund quickly caught up with the Moores and began viciously beating Matthew with his cane. The brickmaker responded by smashing the parlor lantern over Edmund's head. The flame was snuffed out, glass and oil flying all over Edmund, who began to wobble and fall over, passing out. Both men were bleeding profusely. Matthew stumbled and fell to the ground. When Billy and the other soldiers finally responded to the ruckus it was already over. Margaret Moore was trying to help her wounded husband to his feet but he was now unable to stand.

The entire household of servants and guests alike were outside now. It was a cool clear May evening with a nearly full moon illuminating the melee. Anne took charge, instructing the crowd to go back inside.

"It's all over. Everyone, go back to the gathering hall. Go back to what you were doing. Billy, you take two men and escort the Moores back to their home. Stanley, you and Brigid get the Colonel up to his room and clean him up. Go on. Everyone, go back inside. There is nothing to see here."

Anne went back to the nursery. Annabella and Atalanta had been watching out the window. Their mother told them to get in bed. Arcadia in her cradle had slept through the entire debacle. Anne waited until she was sure that Edmund had been deposited in his bed before looking in on him. Brigid was picking the last shards of glass out of his bloody head and cleaning his cuts while Stanley held up a candle giving her light. As the woman finished, Edmund began to mumble incoherently.

Anne quietly dismissed the servants. "I'll stay with him to make sure he doesn't bleed to death. There isn't much more we can do. He'll just have to sleep it off."

Edmund required another week of bed rest and pampering. Anne wished she could think of a way to bring Edmund's drunken siege of Gargaphia to an end. Not even her insomniac's ritual of sorting things out in the tower in the wee hours of the morning produced any ideas. Her only hope was that once the money arrived from the sale of her property in Jamaica, she could convince him to take the money and be done with her. That could take months, maybe a year. If that did not work, she considered offering to give up Gargaphia completely and taking the girls to live quietly at Chiconessex.

Once a fortnight had passed, Anne sent Billy to find out how the Moores were and see if they were planning any repercussions. When he returned, he brought bad news for the Colonel. The Gargaphia brawl was the talk of the county. Condemnation of Edmund was almost unanimous. Rumors swirled that Scarborough had tried to murder Moore. He had in fact, maimed the brickmaker's arm so badly, that he would be unable to work for the rest of his life. As a result, Moore and some of Scarborough's other creditors had written a petition to have Edmund charged with attempted murder and a variety of other crimes. A delegation of disgruntled neighbors had already left for James City to present their claims to the Governor.

Matthew Moore, a mere commoner, had allied himself with a group of influential landowners who were already looking for a way to be rid of Edmund Scarborough and his dirty dealing. They had been waiting for this a long time. By the end of the summer, a letter arrived from the capital recalling the Colonel to face the charges against him at the fall General Assembly. In a direct blow to his authority, he was suspended from all his official offices. To further put Scarborough in his place, Accomack County was dissolved to again be reabsorbed as part of Northampton.

The time had finally come for the Great Conjurer to answer for at least some of his misdeeds. For the rest of the summer and into the fall, he spent his time at Gargaphia, trying to come up with a plan to talk his way out of this mess. He had done it before. Why shouldn't he get away with this now? His first tactic was to stall. Claiming ill health, he wrote to the Governor and asked him to delay the proceedings until the following spring. In the meantime, he wrote to his brother at the court of King Charles II in case royal intervention may be needed again.

In late September he decided that he would execute another of his favorite tactics to distract the community from his transgressions. The Colonel sent Billy to invite the Pocomoke Indian tribe living near the northern Accomack border to a feast to celebrate the fall harvest. They were to meet by a large ditch where the Great Conjurer would invite the Great Spirit to speak to them. This, of course, was a ruse. Scarborough planned to provoke the Pocomokes into a confrontation which he would then resolve. The idea was to remind Scarborough's neighbors that he was their heroic Cavalier, protecting them from savage attacks.

On the appointed day the tribe arrived at the agreed upon place along Euwamus Creek near the Maryland border. This was in the middle of a tract of land known as the Pocomoke Hundred, where the tribe of that same name still had villages. Edmund also sent an invitation to Jenkins Price, a nearby landowner. He was well known for trading with the Indians and news of his participation would help convince the tribe to trust in the friendly nature of the gathering.

The men gathered around a campfire sharing a pipe and food prepared for the occasion. Edmund rose to his feet and started to make a speech.

"It is time for Virginia Colony and the Pocomoke Tribe to…"

The word "Pocomoke" was the signal for three soldiers hidden in the woods around the gathering to begin firing their muskets into the treetops. Edmund pretended to be surprised and indignant.

"How dare you shoot at us while we are making peace with you! You heathen dogs!"

With that the rest of Edmund's men began beating the tribesmen who tried in vain to defend themselves. When the fray was over, members of the militia had sustained few injuries, but several of the Pocomoke were dead, the others greatly incapacitated. This massacre came to be known as the "Ditch Murders."

Edmund ordered the surviving Indians taken prisoner and declared: "This was an act of war. These savages must be wiped out for the welfare of all the Godly people of our colony. I will not rest until all our neighbors are safe."

The Colonel used this terrible ambush as an excuse to order his troops to rout out the remaining tribes in the region. Adults who did not escape were brutally murdered. Defenseless children were taken and sold as slaves. Another brutal winter campaign would be conducted while Edmund stayed warm and comfortable at Gargaphia.

Feeling victorious, Scarborough expected to use the easy defeat of the Indians as leverage in his defense. When he finally left for James City in April, the week after Easter, he hoped that his detractors' tempers would have cooled. He would make the case that tradesmen like Moore, unused to the responsibilities of freemen, had misunderstood the situation and caused the disturbance. He counted on the fears of other nobles for the rising power of the burgeoning laborer class.

Edmund believed that his contributions to the colony should far outweigh charges made by such an inferior who did not know his place. The Great Conjurer convinced himself that the accusations against him would be dismissed and life would then get back to normal.

Colonel Scarborough greatly underestimated the ill will his high-handed selfishness had created over the years. Even his closest allies in the General Assembly would not give him cover. They were incensed by his irresponsible act of war against the Pocomoke which had spilled well over the county's northern border and threatened to incite armed conflict with the understandably furious Maryland settlers there.

This time, there was no interceding letter secured by his brother from the Crown, to bail him out. Exasperated, the Governor made the suspension of Edmund's official appointments final, and set a fall sentencing date to give the disgraced Cavalier time to settle his affairs.

Awaiting his fate, Edmund retreated, this time to Hedra Cottage. He was so desperate to look respectable that he decided to avoid Gargaphia. He did not want to further inflame any challenge to his status as a respected scion of the colony. This was, at this point, futile. He was a broken man. His already fragile health had been further compromised while staying at his favorite brothel in James City. His bedding companion there had been exposed to smallpox and had unknowingly passed the disease on to Edmund. By the time he reached his home on the Eastern Shore, he had a high fever and painful blisters began to break out over his entire body.

For several weeks Edmund's condition slowly deteriorated. Neither his wife Mary nor his sister Hannah would nurse him, claiming to fear infection. Those duties were left to servants. Finally, after the doctor said nothing more was to be done, Hannah sent for her nephews and nieces to join their father's death watch. Charles Scarborough, realizing the seriousness of the situation sent word to Gargaphia that the Colonel was dying.

20th day of May, in the year of our Lord MCLXXI

Dear Mistress Toft,

This letter is to inform you that my dearest father, who loves you deeply, is gravely ill with the pox. He is asking that you attend to him at your earliest availability.

Sincerely,

Charles Scarborough

When Anne read the note, she felt a great wave of relief followed by intense guilt for having wished the man dead. Would this unholy partnership finally soon be over? All things considered, the decision not to visit Edmund was easy and her response was swift.

21st day of May, in the year of our Lord MCLXXI

Dear Charles,

I am sorry to hear that your father's condition is so serious. I know you will understand that I cannot possibly visit him at this time. The risk of infection would not only put me in danger, but it would make my darling daughters, your sisters, vulnerable to the dreaded pox.

I shall pray daily for the salvation of your father's soul. May God's mercy shine on him in his final hours.

Sincerely,

Anne Toft

On May 23rd in 1671, Edmund Scarborough passed from this earth, much to the relief of all who knew him.

1672

The Great Conjurer's Debts

Colonel Edmund Scarborough's funeral was sparsely attended. The trails leading to St. George's Chapel had been rendered impassable by spring rains. His immediate family, Billy, and a few other servants or soldiers under his command were the only people who came. Even the few neighbors who admired the old Cavalier for safeguarding them from attacks by savages stayed home. The so-called King of Accomack was buried somewhere on the Hedra Cottage property in an unmarked grave. The hate for him was so great, his family feared it would be desecrated if they erected a proper marker.

The officiant that day was Reverend Samuel Hensley, the latest priest to minister to the Anglican flock on Virginia's Eastern Shore. Hensley was an extremely pious Puritan. He let it be known that Anne Toft and her ilk were not welcome in his church for this ceremony even if the law forced him to tolerate their presence at regular services.

Despite the Colonel's disreputable fall from high station, he was still considered part of the aristocracy. The stratified order of society was conferred by an act of God and this was not to be forgotten even in light of recent events. The pastor would not allow the Scarborough family name to be sullied by the appearance of the infamous Mistress Bluebird. Hensley was well aware of Gargaphia's reputation.

Anne had not really planned to attend. However, the pastor's message reminded her that her troubles were not over yet. Edmund, for all his faults, had actually in his way protected her from the cruel realities of an unmarried woman's position in society. Anne had succeeded with greater autonomy than most women. Just the same, being the mother of three illegitimate children was scandalous. Bastardy was, after all, a criminal offense, one that Anne had avoided prosecution for, because her daughters' father was a privileged magistrate. Anne's standing in the community was further complicated by her role as the notorious mistress of the guest house at Gargaphia and its wicked revels.

Anne was in danger of being charged with crimes of immorality, and unless she acted quickly, she could lose everything. Other women had been imprisoned and bound out for far less. She realized that the message to stay away from Edmund's funeral was just the first strike against her.

Anne thought that if she safely secured her property rights, any moral accusations could be dealt with through acts of contrition. Surely the rest of the council would protect her knowing that she was privy to their own peccadillos. Finding some malleable gentleman to become her husband was the most obvious solution. This was the standard response to widowhood for most women, particularly in the colonies. In a place with many perils, there was no time for sentimentality. Marriable men far outnumbered unencumbered females. Few ladies remained single by the end of the first year after widowhood. Anne knew that eligible bachelors would soon be circling like vultures to pick Edmund's bones, namely her property.

Her first priority was to stave off any of the Scarborough family's demands to relinquish her assets to help settle Edmund's depleted estate. She took the preemptive measure of sending a letter to Charles Scarborough, offering condolences and reminding him of the deal she had struck with his father. He had been in court the day the contract was registered since he himself was one of the sitting magistrates. Anne hoped that when she explained some of the details, this would assure Charles that completion of the land sale in Jamaica would alleviate the pressure creditors would surely impose on his family.

Instead, she was visited the next day by Charles, his sister Tabitha with her husband Devorax Browne, Matilda (another sister) along with her husband John West, the very pious Reverend Hensley, and, surprisingly, Captain Daniel Jenifer of Maryland. Anne greeted them when they arrived at her door and invited them into her parlor where she faced them alone. Looking at this grim looking delegation, all dressed in black, she was grateful that their quarrelsome mother had not shown up that morning.

Devorax Browne, John West, and Captain Jenifer were all attorneys. They informed her that they represented the law and the Scarborough family's interests. The Reverend Hensley claimed to be the moral authority in attendance, as a representative of the church. While he and the extended Scarborough family said little, Captain Jenifer was clearly in charge.

"Madam, we have come here today to inform you of certain of certain matters. First, we are here to take possession of all property belonging to the late Colonel Scarborough. His family desires to have all those things which rightly belong to them as his heirs. This includes personal objects as well as deeds of ownership for this property and all others he may have given you to oversee."

Anne responded quickly, jumping to the subject of her note the day before. "Charles you know full well that your father signed Gargaphia over to me in return for the promise to pay off many of his debts. I have that agreement in writing, a copy of which – as you well know – was duly registered with the court."

"Madam," Captain Jenifer interjected, "You will address your remarks to me. Do you have a copy of this agreement?"

"I do, but as one of the magistrates presiding at that court session, Charles can certainly attest to the truth of what I am saying."

"Mrs. Toft speaks the truth Captain…"

"Charles, do be quiet." Tabitha said glowering at her brother. "Let Captain Jenifer move ahead with what we've come here to do."

Captain Jenifer continued. "Mrs. Toft, you and the late Colonel have created an unfortunate situation. As a "feme sole" you do have the right to own property. However, it is not in the best interest of the colony that a woman of dubious marital status be in control of so much land along the border to Maryland Province. More importantly, there is a legitimate question as to which tracts are truly yours and which were put in your name fraudulently, and in fact should be included in the Colonel's estate, therefore rightfully passing to his heirs now that he has gone on to his great reward. This situation cannot stand. You are not equipped to maintain the border nor see to its defense against savage attack."

Anne stood firm. "My lord, I can produce witnesses to every one of those transactions…"

"Madam, please allow me to inform you in full, so you will have a complete picture of what is about to transpire."

Captain Jenifer opened his leather valise, produced a sheath of papers, and continued.

"Virginia Governor William Berkley has appointed me as High Sheriff to oversee the dissolution of Accomack County. It will return to its former state as part of Northampton County. The Governor has authorized me to see to the execution of that matter and to address the following charges and other matters whereas you are concerned.

"One, in answer to the charge of running an immoral enterprise, the guest house at Gargaphia will be closed. Anyone who is found to be carrying out the corrupt business of fornication on these premises will be jailed and bound out to hard labor for a term of no less than seven years.

"Two, Mrs. Anne Toft, mistress of Gargaphia and mother of three bastard daughters, shall agree to marry, thereby submitting to the moral authority of her husband over her person and that of her daughters.

"Three, said new husband shall take immediate ownership of all of Mrs. Toft's property in order to see to the resolution of the estate and outstanding debts of the late Colonel Edmund Scarborough to the Virginia Colony, and to the Colonel's creditors. Said husband is ordered to do so in cooperation with the Colonel's executors: widow Mary Scarborough, Mr. Charles Scarborough, Mr. John West, and Mr. Devorax Browne.

"The Governor has personally written a letter to you. He asks that your read it carefully before deciding your response to the charges against you."

Anne was dumbfounded. She opened her mouth to object but the Captain did not give her a chance to find her words. He handed her the letter and the legal document she was being asked to sign.

"Finally, Madam, the Governor has appointed me to serve as your husband. You and I shall be wed in one month's time."

"You? I am to marry you? I am being forced to marry and I being forced to marry you? Reverend, surely you do not condone this?" Anne sputtered.

"My dear," Reverend Hensley spoke with disdain veiled as compassion. "I fear that you are a child who may be lost to the fires of purgatory if you do not repent. The Governor has proposed a most elegant solution to end your wicked influence on the settlers hereabouts and bring you into Christ's fold. I not only condone this.

I am determined to conduct the wedding ceremony myself to be sure that your days as the devil's own temptress in this colony are brought to an end. This is the only way you and your daughters can avoid hellfire and damnation, the likes of which will make being bound out pale in comparison."

"My daughters? You can't indenture them!"

Charles stepped forward taking Anne's hand. "If you do not go along with this, you will be bound out to a plantation near Richmond far from your girls. They will be bound out to me. They will be treated well, but they will spend the rest of their lives as servants."

Anne pulled away, angry and incredulous. "You would do that? You would enslave your own sisters?"

"You have no proof they're our *half*-sisters." Tabitha interrupted. "Anyone could be their father. If you've been a widow all this time, where did they come from? What happened to this man Henry Toft?"

Devorax Brown put his hand on his wife's shoulder, signaling her to be quiet. Anne was caught in her own lies. She needed time to figure a way out. She would not get it. Captain Jenifer took control of the conversation once again.

"Mrs. Toft, if you agree to this match all charges will be dropped, and we will guarantee your daughters each a dowry so they might make respectable marriages. You can live quietly in comfort with your girls until they are properly married. If you read the Governor's letter, I think you will come to see that you have been made quite a generous offer."

Anne covered her face trying to blot out the situation. Questions poured into her mind. How could she buy some time to enlist the help of her friends? Why was the Governor involving himself in his matter? Why, Anne thought, does it feel like there is more to this? She broke the seal on the Governor's letter and read it silently.

1st day 6th month, the year of Our Lord MDCLXXI

To Mistress Anne Toft,

It is my great honor to make a proposal to you which will allow you to greatly serve the Crown, your colony, your neighbors, and your children. With the passing of your benefactor Colonel Edmund Scarborough, I have great concern for your wellbeing and that of your plantation and all its inhabitants.

The proximity of your property to the Maryland border and the unruly Indian tribes that dwell nearby, puts you and your neighbors in a precarious state of jeopardy. I am sure you will see that you are gravely in need of the protection which only a husband would afford you.

The bearer of this letter, Captain Daniel Jenifer, is a man of high character. He has not only my confidence but that of Maryland's Lord Proprietor, Cecil Calvert. Captain Jenifer will make you a fine husband and father to your children.

It is my most ardent wish that you accept this proposal as soon as the banns can be read.

Governor William Berkley

On a second page was another letter written in a different hand.

1st day 6th month, the year of Our Lord MDCLXXI

Dear Mistress Anne,

Please allow me to express my condolences on the passing of your benefactor Colonel Edmund Scarborough. I am sure that this is a difficult time and you have many decisions to make to ensure the wellbeing of your daughters.

You are well known to my husband and myself because of your reputation which has oft been carried by your neighbors to the capital, in particular for your great efforts to help them following that devasting storm a few years ago. Our mutual friend, Mistress Anna Hack Boote, also speaks very highly of you. She says that you are a woman of great intelligence and deep Christian faith. It is because of her recommendation and your reputation for honest dealings across the colonies, that my husband makes this proposal of a match between you and Captain Jenifer. This is not only to your credit but of utmost importance to Virginia.

I urge you to consider this as a matter of the highest priority with the greatest possibility of benefit to you and your dear daughters. I believe this marriage will be a profitable arrangement, and very advantageous to the future of you and your children.

If you agree to this union, you will be paving the way to end many years of strife and border disputes between Virginia Colony and the province of Maryland. The Governor and I, indeed the entire colony would be in your debt if you should agree.

I send you my deepest prayers for happy days ahead.

Lady Frances Culpepper Stephens Berkley

The letters surprised Anne. They were less threatening than Captain Jenifer and the pastor had been. It quickly dawned on her that Captain Jenifer had a greater role in this than he was letting on. She wondered aloud why he was chosen for this duty that was so urgent to her Governor.

"My lord, why would Governor Berkley appoint you, a Catholic, and a resident of Maryland, to be High Sheriff in Virginia? There is more to this than you're telling me."

Daniel turned and spoke to the others. "Reverend Hensley, why don't you go with Mr. Scarborough and his sisters to the Colonel's bedchamber and collect his things? Mr. Browne, Mr. West, and I will continue this discussion with Mrs. Toft."

Tabitha started to object but her brother took her by the arm and led her out of the room. Matilda and Reverend Hensley followed.

The sisters' husbands remained behind in silence as the Captain continued the negotiations.

"Mrs. Toft, you have astutely recognized that this is a complicated situation. You know of course that Colonel Scarborough had built up many debts and longstanding animosity in both Virginia and Maryland, and indeed well beyond these shores. There are property owners in Maryland who are threatening to take Scarborough's land forcibly as repayment.

"What is worse, not long ago, the Colonel engaged in a heinous skirmish with the Pocomoke Indian tribe which may yet result in armed conflict between them and our two colonies. Governor Berkley and Lord Calvert want to avoid this at all costs. This agreement will assuage your aggrieved neighbors and create a united front for negotiation with the savages. Property sales will satisfy the debts and keep our border agreement intact."

"You cannot expect me to agree to such a thing until I have had time…"

"Madam, my orders are to not give you one day to consider this. If you do not sign this letter of intent to marry me, I am to take you away in irons and turn your daughters over to Charles Scarborough."

"There is no need for such threats. You've barely given me time to read the Governor's letter!"

"Madam you must sign this today."

"I will not sign anything until I have read it thoroughly."

Anne read the documents again twice. The provisions for her daughters were vague at best. There was no guarantee they would not be bound out.

"I want to add a codicil to this document. I want it in writing that my daughters will have 5,000 acres to be divided among them for their dowries. I want it in writing that you will prepare such a deed to be registered with the court once we have married or I will not submit."

"I don't…"

"It is a small price to pay for avoiding a war." Anne interjected. "The Governor and Lord Baltimore must answer to King Charles. After the financial losses suffered in the Great Hurrycane, the Crown will not tolerate armed conflict which interferes with the taxable revenue of their plantations. They will not abide us making ourselves ripe for takeover by the Spaniards or the Dutch, or worse, by insurgent Indians. Most importantly, the Crown needs the income from colonial profits."

"Mrs. Toft, what makes you think you can dictate terms in these matters?"

"What makes you think that I will stand by and let you steal my children's inheritance."

Now Devorax Browne joined the fray. "What makes you think we won't simply take your daughters and throw you into jail?"

"I don't think so." Anne replied. "The Governor's friends here on the Eastern Shore don't want their own dirty business exposed at trial. And, the Captain apparently needs a wife. Being a Catholic must make it difficult to find one among all these wealthy Protestant families looking for respectable in-laws. It would not do for you to take on a wife with no assets. Isn't that right?"

Daniel began to blush and scowl.

"There's more isn't there? Let's see. You're a captain in the army. You're also an educated man, an attorney. That tells me you come from a well-positioned family.

"I hear that you're a widower with no surviving children. Maybe your father's will, or your late wife's will, stipulates that any inheritance must pass through you on to your children for some reason. Perhaps you're some sort of embarrassment. Whatever the reason, you need a broodmare to wed and sire a child. That's why a gentleman, such as yourself, would deign to marry a woman such as me."

Now the Captain was angry. He grabbed Anne's arm, pulling her close, glaring at her. She stood staring back defiantly. Someone behind them cleared their throat. Daniel released his grip and composed himself.

"Bring me a pen and ink and I'll add the codicil." said Devorax.

"Not just a codicil. I want the deed written now as well. I'll show you which land I have in mind on the plat map. We will register the agreement in court before we marry and the deed afterward. I have also set aside some things that my daughters should have when they begin their homes. I want those added to their dowry as well so there is no dispute later about whether I have the authority to give them these gifts on their wedding. I will write those items in myself."

Devorax did as she requested and handed her the documents saying, "You will need to provide us with an inventory of your real estate holdings and any other valuables so they can be assessed."

Daniel thought for a moment then added, "The girls must be chaste until their marriage, which will take place no sooner than the age of 17. I will agree to this on the condition that the deed for the girls' dowry be submitted to the court after enough time following our marriage for Mistress Anne to have submitted to her wifely duties and made every effort to conceive and bear my child. If she does not comply with all that is required of her, the marriage will be annulled and she and her children will be bound out."

Anne looked grimly at him for a moment. This was not just a terrible dream. The reality of her situation was a nightmare beyond imagination. Nonetheless, she began writing. Despite the heat of summer, she felt a cold chill run down her back.

About that time Charles, Tabitha, and Reverend Hensley returned to the parlor. They carried a variety of Edmund's personal effects: books, boxes, a tapestry, and even the damask bedcovers. The group sat in awkward silence for a few minutes while Anne finished and reread the papers. The deed, written in past tense for a future court proceeding read:

"Daniel Jenifer of Gargaphia, Gentleman, who married Ann Toft, gave her three daughters, Arcadia, Atalanta, and Annabella, 5000 acres including Chincoteague and Mattapenny Neck, to be possessed and enjoyed by each as she attained age 17. Also at that age, each were given 25 cattle, 11 sheep, 6 silver spoons, a silver cup, a feather bed and furniture, two pair of sheets, 12 Holland napkins, 2 Holland table cloths... If any daughter were to marry before age 17 without parental permission, she shall receive nothing."

The men took turns looking over the codicil and the deed. They signed the papers, as did Anne.

Turning to Tabitha, she asked with a polite sneer, "Did you find everything you were looking for?"

"There is one more thing." Tabitha shot back. "I want my grandfather's ring, the one you are wearing on you left forefinger. It should stay in our family. I want it. Make her give it to me, Captain."

Anne, rolling her eyes, took off the ring Edmund had given her on their so called "wedding" night, placing it in Tabitha's hand. She had worn it all these years as a symbol of the authority she held, that which had been conveyed to her as the official consort to the powerful Colonel Edmund Scarborough. It was somehow fitting, now that she was to be deposed as the mistress of Gargaphia, that she would have to give it up. It was a heavy weight that Anne was ready to relinquish despite all the uncertainty this small act symbolized.

To conclude their business Daniel and the Reverend set the dates for three readings of the banns and then the wedding which was set for St. Swithun's feast day, July 15th. They gave her ten days to deal with the closure of the guest house operation. With that the delegation departed leaving Anne to wonder what she had gotten herself into now.

When Brigid brought the girls in to see her, Anne fought back tears telling them she wasn't ready to talk about the events of the day. That night as the rest of the household slept quietly, she took to the tower to ponder her fate.

"Maybe I should just be done with it and throw myself over." she thought to herself. "That won't do. The girls would be bound out for sure. I won't do that to them."

Anne looked out across the ocean. She picked up the spyglass to watch several gulls working a school of fish just beyond the surf. The birds dove into the water catching their prey then flew off to enjoy it somewhere in the dunes. When the commotion died down Anne scanned the now empty horizon wishing she could be rescued like some beleaguered damsel in one of her Granny's fairy tales. Her thoughts turned to her old friend Captain Alistair Minshull.

"Uncle Star, if you are out there why haven't you come back? If you don't get here soon, I'll have tied myself into bondage once again, when I was so close to freedom. Why is it that you never get here until your help can do me no good?" Anne mused out loud.

The *Zephyr Queen* and Captain Minshull had not been back to visit Gargaphia since before the storm the settlers now called "the Great Hurrycane." Anne had guessed that Uncle Star had been on one of the many ships said to have perished four years prior. In any case, he would be of no assistance to her now. Anne's thoughts drifted to Dr. Moon. She imagined him on the deck of some ship about to head into battle.

"Why are men so damned useless?" she thought.

Anne found no way out of her predicament that night. In the bright light of day, she would have to tell Brigid and the girls what was going to happen. She tried to think of ways to soften a blow the children were really too young to understand. She decided it would be better for them if they did not know she was being forced into this arrangement. Things would go far better for them if they did not treat the Captain with fear or hostility.

As the sun began to rise Anne began to think about what she would tell everyone who worked in the guest house. They had little time to make plans before Captain Jenifer and his garrison would be there to enforce the edict to close down the hospitality business at Gargaphia. Anne left her tower refuge to face the heat of the day.

After Brigid served Anne breakfast, she broke the news.

"Girls, Brigid, I have great tidings. The Governor, out of concern for our wellbeing, has arranged for Mummy to be married. Captain Daniel Jenifer and I will be wed on St. Swithun's Day. He is going to take care of us. He will become your father."

Brigid had had a lifetime of withholding her opinion about anything her masters and mistresses decided to do. Her response was automatic and respectful. It showed nothing of what she was thinking inside.

"Congratulations, Mum."

Arcadia simply sucked her thumb, oblivious to any of the implications of this announcement. Annabella and Atalanta had many questions.

"Is he going to live here or are we going to live at his plantation?"

"What does he look like Mummy? Is he nice, or grumpy like the Colonel?"

"He is tall and handsome, and I'm sure he will be nice to you. We will be living here for quite some time, I believe."

The girls began talking all at once until Anne laughed and said, "Alright you two little hens go outside and play for a while. Mummy has work to do. Brigid, would you go and fetch the Sheffields? If they are still sleeping, wake them and tell them I have something important to discuss with them."

Neither Daisy nor Delia were early risers. Ordinarily they would have resented such an intrusion on their beauty sleep but they could see from the serious look on Brigid's face that it was some sort of trouble. So, they dressed and made their way to Anne's parlor. where she had just finished nursing Arcadia. She put the now sleeping infant in her cradle and told the women what was happening.

"Colonel Scarborough's death has created a predicament for me and apparently for the entire colony of Virginia. It seems that Gargaphia's guest house is now seen as a bad influence and the church has called for it to be closed down. And, the Colonel left so many dissatisfied creditors here and across the Maryland border, they are threatening to mount an armed rebellion to get back what they are owed. The Governor has appointed Captain Daniel Jenifer, a Marylander, to serve as High Sheriff and keep peace along the border. Governor Berkley and the Reverend Hensley have ordered that the Captain and I .... that the Captain and I be married so that my property can be dispersed to pay off the Colonel's debts."

"Dear God!" Daisy gasped. "You agreed to this?"

"I was not given much choice. It was that or go to jail and see my girls bound out."

"That's terrible!" Delia chimed in. "You're not going through with it are you?"

"You and Brigid pack up the girls and your things and we'll all go find our fortune somewhere else." said her sister. "Nevis or New Amsterdam – which shall it be north or south?"

"I can't do that. Ever since Annabella was born, everything I have done has been to assure her future and then, that of her sisters. I insisted they put in writing that they provide my girls with dowries so they can make respectable marriages. This is what I want for them more than anything."

Delia put her hands on Anne's shoulders, and spoke with sincere kindness. "Look, I know you think you want respectability, but what has respectable society ever done for you? You're not welcome to eat at their tables. Even when you helped everyone after the great storm, no matter what their station, did they greet you kindly at church? Did they look in on you when Arcadia was born? Of course not."

"I want my children to be free. I don't want them to live their lives in servitude or running from the law." Anne looked across the room to Brigid hoping that she had not hurt her with her remarks. She tried to explain. "There is honor in service when you choose to serve. But when you are forced against your will, that only leads to bitterness."

The usually quiet Brigid responded. "Aye, Mistress Anne, there is truth in what ye say. Yer girls were meant for finer things. It would be a cruelty to make 'em into scullery maids now. I aint ashamed or nothin'. But if I had a daughter, I wouldn't want this life for her."

"Daisy and I are free." Delia responded. "We come and go as we please. We choose what business we want to do. We enjoy life's pleasures. What more could anyone ask for? Come with us. You have the makings of a great courtesan, Mistress Anne. With our help you could be very successful. At the very least, you could make your own choice about a husband. What if this Captain Jenifer is worse than Edmund?"

"Delia is right. You shouldn't be held to any promise made under duress. How do you know what they told you is even true?"

Things had happened so quickly. It had not even occurred to Anne that this might all be some form of trickery. She thought for a moment and then rejected that idea.

"No, I've seen enough official documents and plenty of fakes. I can tell the difference. They even had a letter from the Governor's wife. She made out that this would be a favor to them, to the Crown even. She laid it on pretty thick.

"No. Even if there is some sort of deception going on, those papers were real. No. I'm afraid this is settled. You two need to gather your things and go as soon as you can. There are weekly packet boats leaving Pungoteague for James City, or St. Mary's City, even New Amsterdam. There is no time to waste. The Captain and his garrison will be back to enforce the shutdown in a little more than a week. Please... Go tell the other guest hall servants to come see me. I'll give everyone papers releasing them from their bonds, so they won't be mistaken for runaways."

With that the Sheffields left, leaving Anne and Brigid staring at each other.

"Brigid, you have been a faithful servant. These last years I could not have done without you. I don't know how I will manage if you go, but if you want your freedom, if you want to leave with Daisy and Delia, I'll give you traveling money and my blessing. You are free to choose."

"Mum, I love them little ones as if they were my own. I couldn't bear bein' apart from 'em."

Both women were crying now. They held each other until little Arcadia began to fuss nearby in her cradle.

"I've got her, Mum. Isn't it time for you to do your paperwork?"

Anne smiled, wiping her tears. "Yes, I believe you are right."

She kissed her daughter on the forehead and went into the library to begin making lists of all she would need to do. Over the course of the next three days she met with those servants who needed to leave. All of them were already free to go, but in those days anyone who was not a landowner was not free to roam about the colony without proof of employment. Anne prepared letters that they could present should any of them be stopped.

It took time to create some sort of fiction to keep each person out of bondage at least until they found placement elsewhere. A few people simply went to work in the few nearby taverns. One woman sent word to a favorite customer that she was now ready to accept his marriage proposal. Most of the servants had not saved any money during their time at Gargaphia. Those that did not have the imagination or courage to strike out on their own simply agreed to be bound out to Anne or one of the neighboring plantations as farm labor or household servants. Anne tried to reward all those leaving with a few coins and good wishes.

The Sheffields, on the other hand, had managed to amass an impressive profit over the years, even with what they had spent on their lavish wardrobe and jewelry. They had no intention of being bound out again, but finding a place to land was going to be difficult. They came back to Anne to see if there was any hope of being set up temporarily in a discreet location in the tradesmen's village.

Anne, worried about trouble from Reverend Hensley, discouraged them from this course of action. "You know, if you book passage south to Rogues' Harbor in the Carolina Province you will undoubtedly do well and have less scrutiny than in other more conventional settlements."

"If we go south at least the winters won't be any colder." said Delia.

Daisy was not convinced. "Rogues Harbor is better known for those dregs not welcome anywhere else. If we go north to New Amsterdam, we will have all those wealthy Dutchmen for customers. They can afford to keep our fires going all winter long."

"I believe New Amsterdam is under English control now." Anne warned. "But I have also heard that commerce continues to thrive there."

Ultimately, that is what the Sheffield sisters decided to do. Being astute business women, they invited two of the best-looking guest house wenches to go along. Off they went, armed with the names of some Dutch merchants who had visited Gargaphia and enough jewels concealed in their bodices to buy their own house and more. Eventually Anne would receive a letter from Daisy reporting their almost immediate success as madams in the city now called New York.

The departure of the Sheffields, and the other girls who provided their special brand of hospitality at the Gargaphia guest house, was deeply felt in the community. Not everyone had been anxious to see them go. For years, returning travelers would arrive at the plantation disappointed to find things had changed. More than one fellow begged Anne to give them the address where they could find the ladies. She declined these requests, saying only that they had left the region.

One man, John Stephenson, was made completely heartsick by the loss of Daisy Sheffield. He was a local planter whose farms had failed in the aftermath of the "Great Hurrycane." Penury had forced him to be bound out to Edmund's son Matthew. He returned repeatedly, imploring Anne to contact Daisy on his behalf, claiming that when his indenture was complete, he would marry her. Anne felt bad refusing to help the broken-hearted man. It was, she felt, for his own good.

The immediate next few weeks passed very quickly. There was so much to do. The guest house had to be cleaned out. Edmund's room had to be prepared for the new master. More importantly, Anne had to organize the assets she listed for the Captain when they negotiated the marriage contract.

Her inventory included deeds to all her plantations in Virginia and Maryland, a tract of land in Carolina, as well as her financial interest in three merchant ships. She prepared a stack of tobacco and silver certificates, and a catalogue of the jewelry and household items that Edmund had given her. She had porcelain dishes, a set of crystal wine glasses, a silver tea service, pewter utensils, trenches, and mugs. She also had valuable tapestries, rugs, and a variety of expensive furniture.

Altogether Anne held back about a third of her wealth as insurance in case she decided to make a hasty escape from her impending arranged marriage with Captain Jenifer. She had not disclosed in the list all of her holdings in the Caribbean and points north in New England and New Amsterdam. She also held back some jewelry she had bought for herself and the emeralds found in the shipwreck after the Great Hurrycane, along with a sizeable cache of wampum beads, the preferred currency of colonial commoners. Anne also retrieved that first gold coin she found on the beach. She held it back for luck.

The asset she retained, which she valued the most, was her ownership of the *Providence*. Simon Jansen had proved to be an excellent captain. Though they had still not met in person, he had represented Anne well and she had had a steady reliable income from their shipping activities. It was risky to not include everything in the full inventory of her holdings. She hoped that her inventory was believable expecting her new husband to underestimate her business skills.

Anne's insomnia was worse than ever as her anxiety grew about taking this fateful step. When she did sleep, she dreamt of her Granny standing on the bluff overlooking Robin Hood's Bay with bonfires burning all around her. The old woman was screaming some sort of warning that Anne could not make out over the crashing waves on the beach below.

Once the banns had been read without objection and her wedding day was upon her, Anne found herself walking down the isle of St. George's Chapel in Pungoteague in a haze of worry. It was a small ceremony attended by Brigid and the girls, Mr. and Mrs. Giles Ishim, and Reverend and Mrs. Hensley. Anne wore a pale blue silk gown with white lace trim. She carried a nosegay of daisies and mist flowers. All three little girls wore matching blue dresses. With white ribbons in their hair, they made a pretty picture. The groom, wearing his red and brown Cavalier's uniform with its gold braid and a wide brimmed feathered hat, came unaccompanied by friends or family. After it was over, everyone went home without fanfare.

A Proper Planter's Wife

When the newly wed husband and wife arrived back at Gargaphia following their nuptials, it was already mid-afternoon. The rest of the wedding party had returned to their own homes without joining them for the customary celebrations. The Captain asked Anne to join him in the library to discuss her inventory making clear there would be no pretense of romance. This was strictly a business arrangement.

"Your inventory is quite impressive, Mistress Toft."

"We're married now. Shouldn't you call me Anne, or at least Mistress Jenifer?" Anne purred. She had every intention of making the best of things and wanted to alleviate some of the nervous apprehension she expected that they both were feeling.

"Madam, please do not anticipate any false show of affection from me. This arrangement between us is not…"

"I was just trying to be pleasant, sir. There is no need for hostility between us. We've made a commitment that requires some level of civility between us."

"Let's just get back to the inventory. You have done quite well for yourself. I appreciate the delineation of the Colonel's property from your own. Your accounts are quite meticulous and thorough. I know his family will be glad to get these deeds. What about the property in Jamaica? When do you expect that transaction to be complete?"

"It should be any time now. We usually see several ships from the Spice Islands here before the storm season begins at the end of August. I am sure one of them will carry the silver certificates needed to complete the purchase of Gargaphia."

"I see. That'll be all for now. Tell Brigid I would have my supper served at eight bells."

"Very good, my lord." Anne frowned, but the man paid no attention so she left him studying his papers.

That evening, after the children had already been fed and sent to bed, Anne met Daniel for a lovely wedding dinner that Brigid had prepared. It was more extravagant than most meals. Fried flounder was served for the first course, followed by roasted chicken, wild rice, green beans, and fresh bread. Brigid had even baked a raspberry tart for the couple to share.

Captain Jenifer ate his meal quickly without conversation. When they both had finished, he pushed back from the table and headed for the cool night air of the porch.

"You go on and wait for me in my chamber while I have my pipe." he said quietly on his way out.

Anne went up to her room, disrobed and put on a shift of nearly translucent white silk. It had just a bit of lace about its neck. She still had a fine figure. Her breasts were full and had not yet begun to sag. Her small belly sloped gently toward round fertile hips. The nightgown covered the stretch marks sustained by three births yet revealed enough of her nipples and pubis to be provocative. Anne took the ribbon and pins from her hair, letting it fall about her shoulders.

Barefoot, she went down the hall to her new husband's room carrying a lit candle. She placed it on a small table. It was a warm night so she opened the window then sat down on the edge of the bed. She waited impatiently for at least an hour before she heard her new husband's footsteps on the stairs.

Daniel entered the room, closing the door behind him quickly with a loud thud. With one hand he removed his belt which he dropped on the floor and kicked aside. With the other hand he began to unbutton his trousers.

"Lay back." he said.

There was no emotion in his voice. Anne did as she was told. He walked up to the bed and spread Anne's legs wide apart stepping between them. He lifted her shift up to her waist, inspecting her labia for a moment, satisfying himself that there were no telltale lesions of venereal disease. The smell of tobacco smoke on his clothes filled her nostrils. After he was done unbuttoning his pants, he untucked his shirt and pulled out his limp penis.

"Close your eyes." he said as he began rubbing his shaft with one hand.

After what seemed like several minutes, Anne felt him enter her vagina. Remembering how much Edmund liked her to respond to him, she reached around to caress his buttocks and began to move her hips.

"Stop that. Put your hands down. Just lay still until I am finished." His voice was cold but not angry.

Again, Anne did as she was told. It took several minutes for him to complete the act while she did her best to remain motionless. Three quick grunts indicated he had orgasmed. Then he stood up and walked over to the window, wiping himself off with his shirt tail. He re-buttoned his pants then turned to speak to her.

"Madam, from now on, do not try to introduce your sinful instincts into our duties. Congress between man and wife is not a matter of pleasure. It is a sacred act of obligation for the sole purpose of conceiving God's children. I'll not have you sully it with the dreadful practices of that sybarite you consorted with for so many years. Now go back to your room and leave me in peace."

Anne sat up and opened her eyes. A light breeze cleared the air of the scent of tobacco and now sexual fluids. She looked around at this man who now was her husband, feeling perplexed about what had just transpired between them.

Anne had not given much thought to what their lovemaking would be like. She had only ever been with one man and presumed there would be little difference. She had regarded her own sexual pleasure as God's reward for having to endure the many indignities of womanhood. Now it seemed no tender passions would transpire between her and Daniel. Their carnal knowledge of each other was to be just a perfunctory transaction.

Back in her own bed, Anne stared at the ceiling. Sleep eluded her once more. She heard Daniel go down stairs again. She lay there trying to think of what she would do the next day. He probably would want to confer more about the details of their now joint business affairs. After the girls' studies, what would otherwise fill her time?

Sometime later, she heard the Captain making his way back up the steps and into his room. Anne could just barely make out the door latching shut. One after the other she heard his boots fall to the floor. She waited until the only noise she could hear was the sound outside of nearby crickets and frogs. Anne got up and dressed by the ambient light of a crescent moon glowing in her window. The hot July air felt suffocating.

She carefully closed her door behind her and tiptoed downstairs, out to the tower and up to the coolness of her sanctuary leaving behind the mosquitos who seemed to prefer staying close to the ground. As Anne looked out over the trees and then toward the ocean, she felt relief that the day was finally over. She wondered how long it would be before the Captain invaded this outpost of sanity and imposed some unnecessarily pious rules about it.

The next morning Anne came down for breakfast to find the Captain already up and eating in the dining room.

"Where are you coming from?" he asked.

"I like to get up early and go to the tower to plan my day before the rest of the house is up." Anne replied, sitting down at the table.

Before the interrogation could continue Brigid brought her tea and a small bowl of porridge. She was followed by three sleepy girls who took their place at the table for breakfast.

"Shouldn't they eat in the nursery?"

"I prefer they learn to eat at the table like proper ladies, my lord." Anne spoke tersely.

"Madam, I would prefer they ate…"

Anne slammed her spoon on the table.

"My lord, you have insinuated yourself into this household on the pretext of reforming me and providing me and my children with your moral guidance. Does that mean I can expect you to rearrange everything we have been doing for these last ten years? Do you intend on demonstrating the righteous insufficiency of every aspect of our lives?"

"I am head of this household, madam. If I would like to have my meals in peace and quiet without the prattling of children, then I shall have it."

"You may now own this plantation, sir, but I am still mistress of this household. If you do not want to take your meals with my children, I suggest you eat in the gathering hall or the parlor. After breakfast, the children and I will be in the library for their lessons. After the midday meal, we shall be in the tower where I like to do my paperwork while the girls take their nap."

Anne resumed eating her porridge trying to contain her ire with each deliberate bite. The girls looked wide eyed at the stranger who their mother said was to be their new father. When the Colonel had been grumpy, they had learned to keep quiet. It looked like the Captain was grumpy, too.

Daniel took the napkin from his lap and threw it onto the table. In an instance he was at Anne's side pulling her from her chair by her arm and dragging her with him.

"Come into the parlor with me, madam." he snarled in her ear as they walked. "Now you listen to me. I am your husband. You will not speak that way to me, ever. Do you understand?"

Daniel's tone was menacing. Once they reached the parlor, Anne squirmed free. She stepped back, and unleashed all the authority she could find within her.

"You will not instruct me how to speak. You and I will be civil, one to the other. That is all you can expect from me. You are due my courtesy, but nothing more. Furthermore, you have no right to dictate how this household is run, nor how I raise my children. That is my right as a mother. I'll not allow you or anyone else to bully me on this point. Is that clear?"

Daniel was shocked by Anne's defiance. He raised his hand to slap her face but she defended herself throwing at him the first thing she put her hand on. This turned out to be her copy of the Anglican *Book of Common Prayer*. In all the commotion she had neglected to mention the family's ritual of reading morning prayers. She realized this as she saw the fluttering pages sail through the air and hit him squarely in the forehead.

Not waiting for him to react she shouted "Now see what you've done! You've been so disagreeable that you've made me throw the

"Good Book" at you. Prayers are at eight bells after breakfast and before lessons. You are welcome to join us."

Anne picked up the prayer book as she stomped past a dumbfounded Daniel. She went back to the breakfast table. Everyone continued, eyes agape, petrified that the new master would come barging back into the room to put Anne in her place. Instead they heard him storm outside and down the porch steps. Anne blushed deep red and looked at Brigid incredulously. Daniel saddled a horse and rode away. Anne had won the first round.

When the Captain returned later that afternoon, Anne watched him ride up the lane from the tower. The girls were just waking from their naps. Anne sent them down to have their afternoon tea with Brigid. On the stairs, they passed their new father. Anne was business like in her greeting as he entered the tower loft.

"Good afternoon, my Lord."

"Good afternoon, madam."

The couple stood looking out over the sundrenched vistas in silence for several minutes.

"We did not get off to a very good start this morning." Daniel began.

"No, we did not." Anne replied; thinking that the bad start actually was the night before, though she kept this to herself.

"You are clearly a woman with unusual powers of organization. I too have a strong need for a sense of order. It will not be easy for either of us to have our routines dictated by the other, and I recognize that it is a mother's prerogative to manage her own children. Might I suggest you and I take this time to discuss our needs and see if we cannot come to some sort of understanding?"

A negotiation. That was something Anne could deal with. She sat down at her writing table, motioned to the Captain to have a seat, then pulled out writing materials.

"Shall we begin with meals? Which meals shall we gather as a family, and which do you prefer with just myself without the children?" she asked.

"I see no need to put anything down in writing, madam. It was the custom of my family that children did not join their parents for meals until they were at least sixteen."

"I am used to sharing my meals with my children. They are a delight to me. I would prefer not to sacrifice their company."

"I see." Daniel thought for a moment then continued. "Let us say then, that when I am in residence at Gargaphia, that we will share the midday meal together as a family. I will take my breakfast alone, before the rest of the household; and that you and I will share supper after the children have been fed and put to bed."

Anne recognized that these were easy concessions, and the schedule he proposed was not much different than what she had with Edmund for much of their time together.

"That would be agreeable to me. Except for those times that court was in session, my tendency has been to spend the majority of my mornings with my daughters, seeing to their education and simple chores like gardening and needlework. I use my afternoons to see to plantation business and bookkeeping. When court was in session and my presence was required, Brigid kept the girls occupied."

"That should not change, though now that court will not be held here, you will no longer be needed…"

"I am sorry to interrupt, my lord, but I have served as witness to many contracts and other legal matters over the years. I am often called to give testimony in court. It does not happen at every session, but you should expect that my presence will be required from time to time."

Daniel sighed and looked at the ceiling. "We'll deal with that should we have a need to. That leaves the matter of plantation business. You will no longer need to trouble yourself with the day to day operations. It is my intention to promote young Stanley Waln to serve as overseer. He will be my secretary while I am here. When I am away, he will be in charge of plantation operations overseeing the livestock, and the work of indentures and slaves. Also, I will be bringing a few of my household slaves here from my Maryland plantation. They know how I like my food cooked and my garments washed."

"Captain, I am still mistress of this household. Can I presume that you will instruct Stanley and the new servants to answer to me?"

Daniel stood up and went to look out over the tower rail. "Yes, yes. Of course." He paused and then went on to more consequential matters. "Tomorrow, I will draw up the papers to transfer ownership of all your property to my name. The list you gave me looks quite extensive. Are you sure it is complete?"

Anne looked at the man's back with contempt and then answered with quiet calm. "I looked the list over several times. I don't believe I have forgotten anything. I'll be sure to read the transfer papers very carefully, just in case."

Her response was, of course, a lie of omission. He had not asked if she had forgotten anything nor if she had left anything off intentionally. She had not directly answered his question. The list would in fact be incomplete.

Daniel turned to her speaking in his most courtly manner. "Thank you, madam. I am sure that once all that is completed you will be much happier tending to your children and the household rather than the distasteful chores of commerce. Women should not trouble themselves with such things. They are best managed by men of means."

"I am sure you are right." Anne lied again. "Shall we go down? It is time for me to consult with Brigid about the evening meal."

"I'll need your keys so that I can have duplicates made for Stanley."

Anne put away the paper and ink she had gotten out but had not used. She took her time so that Daniel could see the contents of the writing desk which held no mysteries. Then she handed him the ring of keys she kept tied around her waist. She hoped that he would not think she had given in to him too easily.

Daniel took the keys. "Thank you. One other thing, I expect you to visit my room each night until we are sure that you have conceived a child. It is my intention that I should have an heir within a year's time."

"Of course, my lord." Anne said as they descended the staircase.

The ring Anne gave her husband did not include the key that unlocked that iron trunk in her bedchamber which held her most valuable secrets. That was hung behind the tapestry above it. She would have to think of some way to safely dissuade Daniel from checking its contents. She remembered Anna Hack's advice to her so long ago. Hide the truth in plain sight.

She decided to put on a little show for him. After she tucked the girls in to bed that night, she went to her chamber and took anything out of the trunk that could be easily seen as valuable or incriminating. These she put under her bed making sure that they could not be viewed from anywhere in the room. She put some coverlets, books, and other bric-a-brac in the trunk and left the lid wide open. She opened her jewel case on top of her dresser so its contents would be on full display. Later, after Anne and Daniel finished their dinner, she returned to her room and waited to hear the Captain coming up the stairs.

"Captain, won't you come in?" she called through the open door. "I am not quite ready to join you in your room. I need to take down my hair."

Daniel stepped into around the room and looked around while Anne untied her bun and began to brush her hair. He walked over to the dresser, looked at the jewels and peered into the open trunk. Anne took her time brushing her tresses, making him wait until he became impatient.

"I'll wait for you in my room. Be quick about it. I have a full day tomorrow. I want to get some sleep."

Daniel was still talking as he made his way out the door and down the hall. Anne followed him after a few moments and the fertility ritual from the night before was repeated. She returned to her own bedchamber hoping her act of subterfuge had worked. She quietly moved her stash back into the trunk, putting less risky content on top. After locking it she hid the key behind the tapestry.

In the next few weeks, Daniel's house servants arrived. Though Anne disliked having Africans working in her house, they fit neatly into the day to day life of the plantation. Before long Anne and Daniel coexisted without much conflict. They kept to their own business and spoke only when necessary. Anne did her conjugal duty without complaint. It was just another daily chore as far as she was concerned.

By the end of their third month together, Anne announced to Daniel that she believed that she was pregnant. By the fourth month, quickening had taken place and she began to show. Daniel expressed no signs of being happy, only relieved. There was no need for sentimental displays between them. So far as he was concerned, they were each fulfilling their part of the bargain.

Captain Jenifer remained at Gargaphia until well after April 1672, when Anne gave birth to his son. During that time, he had kept a close eye on his wife to be sure of the expected child's paternity. In that time, he came to trust her to be not only a good mother but a person who honored her word. Her seeming submission to his will convinced him that she had been faithful. So, he named their child Daniel St. Thomas Jenifer with full confidence that he had produced his rightful heir.

Within a month of the child's arrival, Anne and Daniel received the proceeds of the sale of her property in Jamaica. This allowed them to settle any remaining debts with Edmund's family. The couple appeared in court together to make the payment and be officially protected, in writing, from any further claims by the Scarborough clan:

Charles Scarborough, John West and Tabitha Browne, as agent for her husband, also released Daniel And Anne Jenifer from all debts to themselves and the estate of Col. Scarborough from the beginning of the world till the present date.

2 May 1672, Charles Scarborough, John West

Daniel had already sold off some of Anne's smaller tracts of land to pay off the other debts he and the Scarborough's had agreed to. This brought to a close their obligations to Edmund and his creditors. The neighbors and the Indians had all turned their animosity away from Gargaphia for now, so the plantation once again thrived. Stanley Waln had lived up to Anne's earlier assessment of him. He was a capable young man who made a good overseer of farm operations.

There were rarely visitors to the plantation now that court sessions were no longer held there. Occasionally a ship would moor not far from the beach and send officers ashore to buy provisions. But most captains who traveled these waters had heard by now that the plantation's legendary hospitality was no longer being offered to travelers. And since the "Great Hurrycane" the inlet to the creek was more often than not almost completely filled in with sand. This made passage from the ocean by anything larger than a dory impossible. Gargaphia was no longer a reliable place to stop for resupply nor entertainment.

Anne concentrated her attentions on her children, and especially her new son. Though he was named for his father, Anne preferred calling him Tom, from his middle name. Like her daughters, he was a healthy baby with a good appetite. She and his big sisters doted on him as did Brigid. Babies were innocent after all, and easy to love. Anne nursed him herself as she had done with the girls. The Captain was impressed with the care and sincere adoration for his son by the women of his household.

The first year of Anne and Daniel's life passed quickly, with little contention between them. Daniel now felt confident that he could safely leave his wife for weeks at a time to conduct business. By their second Yuletide season as a married couple, Daniel was spending as much time away from home as Edmund had. His Maryland properties and his duties as High Sheriff left Anne to her own devices. She was content with her circumstances for a time, happily ignorant of the way of life playing out around her. She only had concern for her children.

For the next three years, Anne's secret shipping interests prospered. Making use of the compendium of buccaneers and their practices written by her friend Dr. Lorentz, she had her captains reach out to those pirates operating in the same waters as her vessels. She paid them protection money to leave her ships alone. In turn they knew that they could count on her to warn them when she knew of anything that might threaten them particularly in the waters off the Virginia coast. It was a profitable alliance.

Anne took great pleasure deceiving the high and mighty planters who she believed had treated her unfairly. From the safety of her tower, Anne's complicity in pirate crimes was very real, though her personal risk was minimal. It was for her mostly a matter of shuffling paperwork. Anne's attitude was pragmatic. She was trying to recoup her losses and eventually rid herself of the constraints of marriage which had been forced upon her.

Anne adeptly concealed her buccaneering by comingling it with plantation business. She promoted the use of her friend Anna Hack Boote's shipping services to her husband. Anna, who had her own criminal proclivities, in turn hired on Anne's vessels as part of her own fleet which carried Gargaphia produce. It was a neat trick that escaped Daniel's attention because like Colonel Scarborough before him, Captain Jenifer was focused more on his own political ambitions.

He had assigned the mundane duties of managing exports to Stanley Waln, who was malleable and susceptible to Anne's trickery. Waln was used to Anne's supervision. He complied with her desire to inspect any contracts and of course to manage the bookkeeping. The naïve young man did not question her suggestions, following them implicitly. He never once considered that Mistress Jenifer might be capable of betraying her husband.

Everyone was lulled into a false sense of security until not long after her third wedding anniversary, when Anne received a new shipment of literature from her bookseller in James City. She had trusted him to surprise her over the years with selections similar to those that had pleased her in the past. This time he outdid himself. He sent her the complete works of Margaret Cavendish, Duchess of Newcastle-upon-Tyne.

The Duchess had written extensive works including poetry, plays, philosophy, and studies of the natural world. This progressive author decried cruelty to animals and servants. She extolled the talents of womankind. She had even written a work of Anne's favorite genre: utopian fantasy. It was called *The Blazing World*. This was the fascinating story of the queen of a new land of imaginative creatures and mechanical inventions.

The intellectual stimulation of Margaret Cavendish's writing reawakened Anne's sense of curiosity. She did not agree with the author on all topics. The Duchess was a staunch Royalist, whose family had paid dearly for their loyalty; at one point being forced into exile in France and losing all their property. Anne, who publicly expressed fealty to the crown, privately believed that the people should govern themselves following the principles expressed in the *Magna Carta*. Anne looked forward to any moment she could find to read and think of point and counterpoint to the texts.

Anne dove deep into the Duchess' memoir of her glamorous experiences serving as a lady in waiting to England's Queen Henrietta Maria. She read with envy about the Duchess' love match to a considerate supportive husband. Though often romantic, the Duchess did not advocate for an overly idealized amorous love, but for the mutual respect of people who cared for one another. She had a healthy skepticism for the benefits of marriage, calling it the *"tomb of wit."* These ideas infected Anne with a nagging dissatisfaction, reminding her that hers was a union without affection.

Since little Tom's birth Anne had been enjoying a respite from her chronic insomnia. Now her sleepless nights returned. She found herself once again in the tower several times a week to ponder the futility of her unsatisfying domestic arrangement. One night as she considered these things from her perch above the plantation, she heard voices below.

It was Daniel and Stanley Waln. They were leaving the slave barracks. She heard them bid each other good night as Daniel turned to go into the master's quarters, presumably to go to his bedchamber. Stanley then made his way to what used to be the guest wing where he and other indentures now had their rooms.

Anne wondered what they were doing. Sometimes the men were called to the slave quarters to break up fights. Perhaps that is what it was. Anne would not have thought again about the unexplained nighttime visit to the slaves' barracks, except that the next time she could not sleep, she noticed it happened again.

The third night she saw the men returning to their own quarters she was watching for them. There was only one reason she could think of for these nocturnal visits. The pious Captain Jenifer and his servant were fornicating with the African women. That would explain why Daniel had not required her to submit to his conjugal requirements since Tom had been born. At first Anne wondered if she wasn't being overly suspicious. After all those libidinous revels that took place at Gargaphia over the years, maybe she unfairly expected these men would be as corrupt as the clientele of her guest house. She would have to find out.

The next night, Anne listened carefully to hear Daniel's nightly exit. She kept her window open and listened for him and Stanley. They spoke quietly but she clearly heard them enter the barracks and the door closing behind them. It was a clear cool October night. Anne threw a shawl about her shoulders and tiptoed downstairs. She looked around in case anyone else might be outside. She did not want anyone to see her before she discovered what was going on. She prayed no one was looking out a window.

Anne crept around to the west side of the slave barracks where the females were kept. She could see that only one room in the entire building had lamp light shining from it. It was luckily on the first floor and if she could find something to stand on, she might be able to see in. Anne walked quickly to the pig pen where she found a slop bucket and brought it back to the window, turned it over and carefully stepped on to it.

Anne was prepared to see something immoral so the sight she beheld did not shock her. It disgusted and infuriated her, but it did not surprise her. Three slave girls were bent over a table, their arms stretched out in front of them holding on to the far edge with their bottoms bared. They were chained to the table legs. Daniel and Stanley were taking turns performing the sex act on each of them from behind. Anne watched them for a short while then got down. She leaned against the building, closed her eyes, and shook her head suppressing the urge to scream with rage.

After she returned the bucket to its place, she quietly went back to the tower where her anger began to build even more. This behavior was beyond hypocrisy. She knew men were capable of such things. She had heard that it was not unusual for slave owners to feel entitled to carnal rights with their human property. She had even heard Edmund boast of his right to commit such acts. Being forced to face the despicable practice directly, hit her harder than she expected. The more she thought about those men taking depraved advantage of those girls, the sicker she felt.

When the men returned to their own quarters a little while later, she began to hear Fanta's voice again. *"Thith ith your fault!"* That night fifteen years ago came flooding back. Anne began to weep, thinking of it. What could she do to stop this? She had so far avoided confrontations with her husband. Her reward had been a carefree existence in which to raise her children. What would happen if she openly crossed him?

As morning light began to emerge, a cloud bank rolled in, casting a grey pall over the landscape. Anne felt flashes of heat rising from the base of her neck to the top of her head. The cool fall breeze made her shiver as she listened to the rooster crow down below.

She dreaded the day ahead of her. Could she keep this to herself? Should she? Who would help her? Who would care? Finally, Anne went down to see to breakfast with the children. She told Brigid she was not hungry.

"Are ye alright Mum? Ye look flushed." Brigid put the back of her hand to Anne's forehead. "Yer burnin' up Mum. Best ye get to bed and I'll bring ye some hot broth."

Anne went back to her room and changed into a nightgown. She stood by the window watching Tom, Atalanta, and Arcadia who were now out in the yard playing. Nearby she could see slaves working in the fields. They were many shades of brown. Anne stood there awhile, wondering who their fathers were.

"Mother, you should be in bed. Look at you. You're shivering." Annabella had come in carrying a tray with the broth Brigid had made.

Anne climbed under the covers then took a sip from the small bowl.

"I'll be alright. Thank you, dear."

"You were up in the tower without a cloak, I'll wager. Mother, it is a wonder you haven't caught your death up there before this."

"Don't fret. I'm fine."

"Well, finish your broth. Atalanta and I will keep Arcadia and Tom busy so you can get some rest."

Annabella was maturing nicely in many ways. She was quite pretty. But, like many adolescents, she had developed an insolent superior attitude toward her mother. Anne looked worriedly at her teenaged daughter. She and her sisters had generally taken well to the changes at Gargaphia. Though Daniel's attitude toward her children could best described as cool, they seemed to enjoy trying to please him. The idea that he might one day try to take advantage of them crossed Anne's mind. Fornicating with her girls might be seen as no different than being with the slaves. And what better way to cheat them from their dowry, than by stealing their chastity himself? Anne shuddered.

"Tell the Captain I'd like to see him."

She didn't know what she would say to the man, but she could not leave it alone. She had to draw a line with him lest he cross over it with her own children. When Daniel arrived in her room, she did not waste time.

"Close the door, please."

"Annabella says you're not well."

"I may have caught a chill. That is not what's wrong with me."

"What is…"

"I saw you and Stanley in the slave quarters last night – fornicating."

Captain Jenifer blushed deep red and said nothing.

"You can't deny what I saw with my own two eyes. Your purpose in marrying me, among other reasons was to reform me, was it not? It seems the reformer himself needs reforming."

"I beg your pardon. I do not."

"How can you justify…"

"Madam, you have no right to question me."

"Why shouldn't I go straight to Reverend Hensley with charges of fornication?"

"This is not fornication. There is no sinful pleasure enjoyed by anyone. This practice is sanctioned by the church and the Governor for the long-term success of the colony. I'm simply seeing that my slave stock continues to increase, as I would my cattle or pigs or chickens. We're breeding a milder more compliant sort than would be accomplished by using the African bulls. I have Stanley take part to be doubly sure that a seed is planted now so that offspring come during warm weather when a healthy birth is easier. We're done for this season. If last year is any indication, we should have five more healthy slaves born in nine months' time. We'll sell the girls for breeding stock and keep the boys to work in the fields."

Anne felt sick. "That is disgusting. How could you? I cannot believe what I am hearing. You are more indecent than Edmund Scarborough. Get out. I don't want to see you. Get out! Get out! Get! Aggh!"

Daniel shook his head and left the room.

Anne began to cry thinking, "Is there no one of decent character in this Godforsaken world? How will I teach my children to live God fearing lives if all around them there is such wickedness?"

Realizing this had been going on for some time, she began to feel ashamed that once again she had been oblivious to the terrible cruelty being endured by others so that she could live a comfortable life. She wondered if that sybarite Edmund and his sons had really engaged in this atrocity.

She was afraid to close her eyes for fear of seeing Fanta's bloody bruised face again. Suddenly she began to wretch, heaving up the broth she just drank back into the bowl on the tray still in her lap. At just that moment Brigid quietly opened the door. Seeing her mistress in need of care she quickly helped her get cleaned up, then took the dishes downstairs to wash.

Anne spent the rest of the morning in bed. By midday she had recovered physically if not mentally. She dressed and joined the family in the dining room. No one spoke during the meal. When the children finished eating, Anne spoke to the older girls.

"Take Arcadia and Tom up to the nursery to nap. The tower is too cold."

Following their mother's instructions all four children left the adults alone. Anne was about to continue where they had left off earlier, but Daniel did not give her a chance.

"Madam, I do not want to hear another word about what we discussed earlier. These matters are none of your concern."

"And what, pray tell, will you teach our son about such things?"

"He is three."

"He won't always be. At what age will you tell him of this chore he must do? How will you explain…"

"Madam, what I teach my son is none of your business."

"He's my son, too."

"When he reaches the age of majority, I will…"

"What? Show him how? You disgust me."

"By the time he is old enough to understand these things I am sure he will respect my authority on such matters. For your own sake, I hope you do as well."

Daniel neatly placed his napkin on the table, stood up, and walked out of the room. This was his way. He did not suffer questioning by inferiors of any kind. Rather than address his wife's objections, he simply ended the conversation and left.

"Never. Absolutely never." Anne said aloud, though Daniel was already out of earshot.

Despite the chill Anne, spent the rest of the afternoon in the tower. As she watched a few slaves working in the kitchen garden, a large dark moving cloud of birds of began swooping and diving all around her. Hundreds of grackles landed in the fields to eat and then swirled high in the air circling the tower before landing in a new spot nearby. Their shiny iridescent black feathers flashed purple, blue, and green as the sunlight broke through the cloudy sky.

"They're feeding in anticipation of a storm." Anne thought. "They know when foul weather approaches. Perhaps, as Granny used to say, the fairies have sent them to warn me of trouble ahead."

Anne was struck by the irony of her situation. Nothing she had been taught about the sanctity of marriage by Owen and Bella Tomkin, nothing she had learned in the *Book of Common Prayer*, nor in any church sermon, allowed for the sinful practice of breeding with slaves. She, the notorious mistress of the Gargaphia brothel, obeying the authority of the church had properly married the pious Captain Jenifer. Yet, as far as she was concerned, his wicked soul was more damned than hers.

Anne decided she must bring an end to Daniel's evil practice of forced breeding with the slave women of Gargaphia. She convinced herself that this would in turn prevent any immoral coercion of her daughters. She had the same feeling she'd had believing she was taking on a righteous mission so many years ago when she impulsively decided to avenge the death of Owen Tomkin. She was young then and had deluded herself in thinking that she could feather her own nest at the same time she wrecked that of Edmund Scarborough.

This time she vowed things would be different. This time Anne would not be seduced by jewels and silk dresses. She would use every resource she had available, and risk everything.

Building God's Kingdom

For months following the revelation of Daniel's breeding program, Anne kept her distance from Daniel. She spoke to him only when necessary. Their conjugal visits were rare. She had refused him altogether at first, but his veiled threats against her and her daughters had forced her to capitulate. The frosty home environment made staying there less and less appealing. He, like Edmund, therefore spent more and more time away, traveling to James City and his Maryland estate.

Anne became hyper vigilant, observing every aspect of life on Gargaphia. She made mental note of who associated with whom, who worked hard, who was lazy. She paid close attention to the slaves especially those who had come from Daniel's Maryland plantation.

One was an older woman, Milly, who served as his personal cook and laundress. She was an older woman. Anne could not tell if she showed signs of being subjected to forced breeding. Her demeanor was warm and friendly toward her master. Another, Harold, was a strong young man who fetched and carried for his master, and drove his carriage. These two often accompanied Daniel when he traveled. They never formed attachments to their fellow servants at Gargaphia. These two enjoyed the status of being the Captain's favorites. Anne would not be able to trust them with her plans.

Abner, Joseph, and Dutch were three field hands who among the crew of twenty seemed as most likely prospects for Anne's manipulation. She observed in them not only intelligence but leadership. The other workers seem to follow their advice. One in particular stood out. That was Dutch. He was slight of build yet muscular with a deep chestnut skin color.

As a young captive from West Africa, he had learned to speak Dutch quickly, which is how he got his name. He was, in fact, adept at most languages. He was fluent in English and Spanish, and could verbally translate these European languages into many of the African dialects encountered in the colony. Stanley Waln had begun relying on him to make sure that his orders to newer slaves were properly understood. Anne thought if she could earn Dutch's trust, he might help her with the others.

There were only five other women slaves at Gargaphia at that time. Their primary duties were to manage the kitchen gardens, and to cook and do laundry for the other slaves. This was in addition to their now obvious role as breeding stock. Four of the women already had children. They each helped the others in the care of two infants, three two-year old's, and one four-year old child -- all light-skinned boys.

The only one who did not have her own child was the youngest and newest, having been bought only in the last few months. Anne had been told that this girl, Retta, was born in captivity and had therefore been bred and trained to be more docile. She was a pretty young woman with a heart shaped face that easily broke into a smile. She had a full figure, round in all the right places. She was light skinned and had blue eyes. Anne understood now that this last attribute meant her father was probably her mother's master.

Retta caught Anne's attention because she noticed the girl's friendship with Dutch. Watching them from the tower with her spyglass, Anne noticed them finding reasons to be near each other. Occasionally she saw them giving each other knowing looks. Their hands touched whenever they thought no one was looking.

Anne could see that they were in love. She was touched by how beautiful they were together. Each time she watched them she felt a little twinge of jealousy. They were lucky to have the gift of romantic love that she believed she would never experience.

Anne began to request Dutch as her driver when she went to visit the tradesmen's village to look in on the indentured servants' families. This was a monthly practice she had begun after she first became the mistress of Gargaphia. She felt it was her duty to be sure that these families were doing well. She always took a basket of bread and herbs to give away. She listened to the women's complaints, mostly offering commiseration, being careful not to interfere in matters that were not of her own concern. It was also how she kept in touch with people in the *Friends and Neighbors* ledger and learned of local gossip which might be used to her own advantage. Now she would use these trips to get to know Dutch.

As for Retta, Anne assigned her to work as a sort of apprentice to Brigid. Brigid was almost fifty now. Her hands were gnarled with arthritis and she had trouble lifting heavy things. Retta would be taught to cook and sew for the mistress of the house and her children. Anne's instructions all seemed perfectly normal.

Anne was grooming both Dutch and Retta to help her with the scheme she was hatching. She worked at this slowly, methodically over several weeks. She showed them special kindnesses, giving them nicer clothes to wear, special meals. Soon Retta began to show signs of pregnancy. As soon as Daniel left to attend the General Assembly in James City, Anne decided it was time to make her first bold step. She called the couple into the parlor and confronted them with Retta's now obvious condition.

"Retta, my dear, it appears that you are with child. Dutch, are you the father?"

Retta's eyes grew wide and she burst into tears. Dutch looked furiously at the woman he loved and growled. "No Mum, I am not."

"Are you sure?" Anne coyly asked again.

"Yes, I am sure. Retta and I have never lain together." Dutch's face darkened and tears welled up in his eyes.

Retta put her hands over her face and began to weep. Anne felt a little badly for what she was doing, but not enough to stop.

"Now, now Retta. You haven't done anything wrong. Everything is going to be alright. Pull yourself together. Dutch, Retta has not betrayed you. I am sorry to say that your master and Mister Stanley have impregnated all the slave girls. They were not given any choice. Didn't you and the other men know this?"

"We heard something... I thought Retta was too young. I thought, I hoped I could take her as my wife before... well I don't know what I... I know it's not allowed... our being married... Still I... I..."

"Dutch, if you will forgive Retta for that which was no fault of her own, I will help you two to be married. Can you do that?"

Retta's hands dropped from her eyes yet still covered her mouth. She looked at Dutch with heartbroken hope. Unable, at first to meet her gaze, he looked at the floor for a few moments. He was so sad and so angry. He clenched his fists. When he looked up at beautiful, frightened Retta, he could not help but want to comfort her.

"Yes, Mistress Anne. I can try."

"Do you both promise never to raise a hand against each other or your children?"

Retta and Dutch both nodded.

"Alright then," Anne continued. "If you are willing to become Christians, I will see that you are married. Are either of you followers of the old religion?"

Both shook their head no. Anne knew that slaves who were forbidden from practicing the faith of their forbearers, sometimes still did so secretly. The slaves essentially were held in religious limbo. They were denied access to Christianity by law. Yet, the old religion was considered demonic heresy. Conversion to Christianity would mean they were human and should therefore be treated as such, not as mere livestock which also could lead to ideas of freedom. Anne had every intention of using these contradictions to her own advantage.

"Are you willing to convert to Christianity? If you are, I will see that you are married and that Retta is never again violated in this way."

Dutch and Retta looked at each other, both were confused and afraid. They were not really sure what they were agreeing to. They cautiously nodded, not wanting to defy their mistress.

"Dutch, I have one other condition. You must promise to love Retta's child as if it were your own. Babes come into this world completely innocent. Trust me, as soon as we see Retta's little one we will all love it no matter what."

Dutch looked at her suspiciously then replied quietly, "I have not always seen that to be true, Mum."

"Well, we will do our very best here. Won't we, Retta? This baby will need your protection Dutch. Can we count on you?"

Dutch, realizing he could not argue any more than he had already, sighed and nodded in the affirmative.

"Very good. I am proud of you both. Tomorrow, Dutch, you and I will visit Reverend Hensley to enlist his help. For now, the three of us will keep this to ourselves. Do not tell Master Stanley or anyone else."

Anne's next step was to enlist the help of the Anglican parson who had always made clear that he had only disdain for her. If she could make her case, she would ask him to convert all of Gargaphia's slaves, thereby protecting them from the likes of Daniel. Her ultimate scheme was to inflame the evangelist passions of the good Reverend so he would begin a crusade to convert all the slaves to Christianity in Virginia.

The next day Anne told Dutch to hitch up her carriage and off they went to St. George's Chapel. She made him wait outside while she went in to work her wiles on the pastor. Hensley greeted her suspiciously but allowed her to come into the privacy of his office and offered her a seat.

"What can I do for you, Mistress Jenifer?"

"I am here today on a matter of utmost importance. I am here to speak to you about a moral crisis the likes of which only you can address."

"My, my... Whatever could be so terrible, my dear?" he said, sneering at her. His initial instinct was to distrust her.

"My lord, are you aware that many planters, even my very own husband, are breeding with their slaves?"

The Reverend blushed deep red. "Why, uh, well I suppose I had heard…"

"Is it true that this is sanctioned by the church?"

"Well, I am not sure that is exactly how I would characterize it."

"This is an outrage! Reverend, ever since you admonished me to repent, I have seen the great glory of God's benevolence. I have been saved from my past wickedness, and I have you to thank for this. But have you forced me to marry one of the Devil's own minions? How can such a sinner help me to follow God's path? It is my duty to care for my husband in every way including seeing that he is right with God. I fear desperately for Daniel's soul! You are the Lord's representative here in this parish. I beg you to please help me save the soul of my husband. Only you can do it. We must save him from damnation."

"Madam, perhaps if you could think of this like breeding a better line of livestock, it would not distress you so."

"Livestock!!" Anne shrieked. "Does not the Bible call out carnal knowledge with animals as the mortal sin of bestiality?! If slaves are animals then breeding with them is an act of bestiality! If they are human, then have we not been called to bring even the most lowly person to the loving embrace of Christ Jesus?!"

Anne was up out of her chair pacing and pulling at her hair. She grabbed the pastor by the shoulders.

"Are we not here in this, the New World, to build God's Kingdom? You're a man of God. We all look to you for wisdom and grace. Oh, Reverend Hensley, I beg you to help me!"

Blushing, the Reverend began to feel aroused by the lovely Anne whose hands now clasped his cheeks inappropriately. He could not help but notice that her low-cut bodice exposed a substantial portion of her ample heaving breasts. They both took a step back. Anne fell to the floor prostrate, kissing the tops of his shoes.

"My Lord and Savior, please help me to know God's will. Help me to save the souls of my husband and my poor misbegotten slaves. And, my children… my children!! How can I raise good Christians in a household where such evil persists?"

Hensley lifted Anne to her feet. Her hysterics had confused and beguiled him at the same time that his long-held suspicion of her made him furious about this display.

"Alright, my dear, calm down." he growled. "Alright. Alright. I will help you, but I don't know what you want me to do."

"Of course, you are so wise you must tell me. The slaves need our guidance. They want to become God's children. In fact, I have two slaves who have asked to be converted in order that they might be wed. They want so much to give themselves over to Our Savior. Couldn't you oversee their instruction and then marry them? Don't you think that other slaves might then follow in their example? Wouldn't God smile on such a growing flock of his faithful?"

"Yes, but how would that stop, I mean, I am not sure slaves being married would keep the planters from exercising their rights…" Hensley was completely flustered. He had the biggest erection he could ever remember having at the same time he was trying to sort out a sin-free solution to this problem. Anne could see his pants bulging. This gave her the confidence to press her case.

"Oh, yes, how insightful you are to think of that. You will have to preach against it from the pulpit. Oh, my lord, I have found you to be such a brilliant orator. I know that God will speak through you with such fire that no man shall be able to deny the righteousness of your message. Your words will be so powerful! You must absolutely send a copy of your sermon to be read to the General Assembly, and to the Archbishop of Canterbury! You will be made a saint for this. You will be remembered forever for saving the soul of Virginia!"

Anne grabbed Hensley's hand and held it to her bare chest just above her breasts. With lips quivering and eyes looking toward heaven, she delivered the final speech of this performance.

"My Lord God, I am so blessed to be your humble servant. If only I had been made the wife of such a saint. I would have gladly borne the babes of such a holy race of men to begin with such a man as our dear Reverend Hensley. Thank you, dear God, for allowing me to be in his holy presence. Thank you, Reverend, for being my knight in shining armor. I shall love you forever. Think of me each night as I pray for you."

Anne was counting on his masculine lust, counter-balanced with his Puritan shame, to contort his will. She intentionally planted the libidinous fantasy of being his wife in his mind and played on his prideful ambitions. She hoped that she had inspired him to channel his urges into a holy crusade.

Then, Anne decided she had done enough for one day. She knew she could have seduced him on the spot. Making her exit at just that moment, would leave him in the agony of unrequited arousal and spiritual confusion which would guide his actions better than any blackmail attempt. She invited her newly appointed protector to visit Gargaphia before the week's end to minister to a fresh flock of souls awaiting his benevolent ministry. They were both still blushing when Anne waved to him from her carriage.

"A fine piece of piracy," Anne thought triumphantly smoothing her hair after getting into the carriage. "I think I have just hijacked the man's soul."

When Reverend Hensley arrived at Gargaphia a few days later, word had gotten out about Dutch and Retta's planned conversion and the possibility of other slaves taking part. The Africans, thought this would make their lives better, give them time off from their labors, and maybe even lead to freedom. They all wanted in.

The slaves dropped what they were doing and rushed to crowd around Anne and her guest as he tried to make his way onto Gargaphia's front porch. They begged to be converted. Two other couples besides Dutch and Retta came forward asking to be married. Men and women alike began to cry when the Reverend agreed to help them. His suspicion of Ann was displaced by his bursting pride at the idea that he had inspired such religious passion. Anne was thrilled with the chaotic scene.

That day it was agreed upon that on Wednesday afternoons anyone wanting to convert could meet in the gathering hall to hear Reverend Hensley. Stanley Waln, taken aback by this turn of events had no chance to object. Things were moving too quickly for him to respond in any way.

When the pastor met Dutch and Retta, he saw the girl's obvious state of impending motherhood. Then he saw that two other women who had asked to wed were also pregnant. Waving the reading of the banns, he married all three couples on the spot, with the entire household of servants and slaves in attendance.

Anne acted like a silly girl in the preacher's presence clapping and cheering when they were pronounced husbands and wives. She made arrangements for the newlyweds each to make their own quarters in cottages formerly used by indentured couples. Married slaves' place at the top of the slave hierarchy was thus established with the privilege of not having to live in the barracks.

Anne then gave the entire household the night off to sing and dance as they pleased. After Hensley had left for home, Anne even allowed everyone to share a few bottles of rum. Most of the residents of Gargaphia went to bed pleasantly tipsy that night. It had been a long time since there had been any fun there. Anne reveled in her accomplishment.

The next step in her plan was to find a woman to marry Stanley Waln to distract him from breeding duties. Blackmailing him for his complicity in piracy was not out of the question. That, hopefully, would not be necessary if he had a wife to keep him satisfied. The Harvest Fair was on the horizon. That would be a good place to look for likely prospects.

This effort was interrupted by the return of Captain Jenifer, which of course, Anne had anticipated. She had concocted a finely woven tale of half-truths and omissions to inform him of recent happenings at Gargaphia. Anne waited for the moment when she knew that Stanley Waln was about to give his report on plantation operations. She joined her husband and the overseer in the library sitting quietly pretending to read a book.

"It was the most extraordinary thing, my lord. Reverend Hensley came for a visit about three weeks ago and when the slaves heard that he was here they dropped what they were doing and beseeched the pastor convert them to Christianity. He was so overwhelmed that he agreed to come each Wednesday to teach them with a plan to baptize them all next week. I must say, since this began, the crews have never worked better. I have had no reports of insolence or shirking. They willingly work longer hours to make up for the time lost to their catechism. The preacher really has done magnificently, teaching them to mind their masters. It really has been quite amazing."

"Good God! Whatever gave them the idea?"

"I don't know, sir. But that is not all, several of the slaves asked Reverend Hensley to marry them. He saw that the women were with child, so he married them on the spot."

"He what? Which ones?"

"Dutch, the fellow who is so good with languages; and Retta the young one, the one we just bought last fall. And there was Abner, the one who handles the cattle with Paula the tall one, and Joseph who I've had building the new drying shed, he was wed to the quiet one. Sally, I think, yes, that's her name, sir."

Daniel's face turned red. He turned to look at Anne with fury in his eyes. He changed the subject so he could send Stanley on his way.

"Are the pigs and cattle ready for the harvest fair auction next week?"

"Yes, Captain Jenifer." Stanley replied.

"Fine. That's all for now. I have a few matters to discuss with my wife."

Stanley quickly departed, leaving Anne to face an interrogation by her husband.

"I don't suppose you know anything about this miraculous conversion of the slaves?"

"Well, I was as surprised as Mr. Waln. It was truly inspiring, I must say."

"How stupid do you think I am? I know damn well this is some little plot of yours because you disapprove of the way I manage the Africans."

"You must admit, Captain, that there is a flaw in the logic that says they are animals and can be treated as such. If they are animals, what you are doing is bestiality, a mortal sin. But, now that they are to become Christians, well if you continue – it will be considered bastardy. Either way, I am afraid you will be committing a sin if…"

"There will be no baptism. This nonsense will come to a halt, right now." Daniel's voice was getting louder.

"Do you really want to go against the zealous Reverend Hensley? Doesn't he have the ear of the Governor? It might not be such a good idea to cross him."

Daniel pounded the desk with his fist and shouted. "These are my slaves we are talking about. I'll be damned if I am going to let you get away with this."

"Me?" Anne said, feigning innocence. "What have I done?"

"You know damn well…"

"Captain, please calm down. You heard Stanley. This conversion has improved the work of the slaves. Why not let it continue? Why not match up the remaining women to be married and let nature take its course. You could make having a wife a reward for faithful service for the bucks."

"You are not going to let this go, are you?"

Anne stared at him blankly. They sat looking silently at each other for several minutes until Daniel, exasperated, gave up.

"Get out. Leave me be. I have things to attend to."

Anne left the library, trying not to smile wondering how she might subvert any attempt by Daniel to reassert what he believed were his ownership rights over his slaves. She spent the next few days worrying about what would happen when he would eventually confront Reverend Hensley.

The pastor, like all zealots would not easily be dissuaded. He came fully prepared to deal with Captain Jenifer. He had, in fact, long wanted to force Daniel to give up Catholicism. The Reverend found it unseemly that a Catholic High Sheriff was enforcing the tithes in an Anglican shire.

When the Reverend arrived, Daniel did not wait for him to be ushered into his parlor. He strode outside fully intending to stop him before he dismounted from his horse. The entire plantation came out to see what would happen. By now, everyone knew that there was going to be a fight over the slaves' baptism and right to marry.

"Good day, Reverend, you may as well not even get down. There will be no baptism today." Daniel said, taking hold of the bridle of Hensley's horse.

Ignoring Daniel, the parson got down and immediately began ministering to the flustered planter.

"Now, Captain Jenifer, I understand your apprehension but I think you will come to see the wisdom of bringing the Word of God to the Africans. Your brethren papists have been converting heathens all over the world. I'm surprised you've not brought a priest here to do this yourself."

"Sir, you know that I made a promise to Governor Berkley that I would not promote my religion in the colony of Virginia…"

"That's true. That's true. What does your religion say about the practice of breeding with slaves?"

"I… I am not sure…"

"Captain Jenifer," Hensley interrupted, "I'm in fear for your soul. I believe you have been tempted by heathen influences to conduct vile acts. It is my duty to try and save your soul. I fear that you will find yourself lost to the fires of purgatory if you do not repent."

Anne watched this exchange from the porch with the rest of the crowd. She almost laughed out loud to hear the very words they had used against her when the two men had forced her into this marriage.

"I am not… I do not… This is outrageous…" Daniel sputtered.

Hensley continued his pastoral attack. "Captain Jenifer, you must repent. You must submit to God's will. Let me baptize you and all the slaves today. Let me welcome you all into the one true church of our Lord and Savior Christ Jesus. Let us strike a blow against Lucifer himself today! Come join us. Come, Captain Jenifer!"

Daniel looked at the crowd of faces around him and began to capitulate. He bowed his head. Sighing, he quietly agreed to be baptized with the slaves. It was more than Anne could have hoped for. She felt like this was a dream as she watched first Daniel, then one by one all of the adult slaves lined up by the edge of the creek. They repeated the ritual verses given them by Reverend Hensley. They renounced Satan. Finally, they allowed the pastor to sprinkle them with the water he had blessed and proclaim them saved in the eyes of Christ Jesus. It took the rest of the morning to complete the rites. Twenty people allowed themselves to be saved by Jesus that day.

Anne instructed Brigid and Milly to organize a celebration meal in the gathering hall in honor of the event. Reverend Hensley was so happy with what he had achieved, he even accepted a glass of port before departing. Daniel looked grim throughout the festivities.

Once all the excitement died down, Anne sent the children to the nursery to take a nap, leaving her alone with the Captain in the library.

"Well, my lord, you truly surprised me today."

"How so? Isn't this what you had in mind?"

"I am curious. What made you do it, Captain? Did you experience an epiphany?"

"Not exactly. It just suddenly became inconvenient to be a Catholic."

"A little ranting by Reverend Hensley made you want to convert? I'm not sure I believe that."

"It seemed like a timely opportunity. I am sure it will please Governor Berkley in James City to hear from Reverend Hensley of my heartfelt submission to his Godly ministrations."

Anne was suspicious now. "You didn't have to allow the slaves to convert."

Daniel sat down at the library desk and began to play with a quill, twirling it between his fingers.

"Well, it seemed like it would make the good pastor, and you, of course, happy."

"And you will stop breeding with them now that they are Christians?" Anne asked apprehensively.

"Madam, I shall continue to exercise the right of conquest that kings and lords have done for all time. Until the law says otherwise, I will breed with my property as I see fit, including you."

"The slaves are now Christians. Breeding with any Christian against their will is rape. So, you see, it is now against the law. Slave women will have every right to bring charges against you should you persist in this atrocious practice."

"Do you really believe that magistrates who all engage in this same thing would take action against me? I think not. By the way, I've made arrangements to sell Dutch and Retta. They're a bad influence. Dutch is going to planter in Maryland and Retta to one near James City. They'll be gone by the week's end. Oh, and another thing, I just spent a good deal of time defending your name in James City. Word of your persistent buccaneering has reached the ears of the Governor."

"I am sure I do not know what you are talking about."

Daniel sniffed with derision. "There is no need for you to lie. I may not know the full extent of your crimes. I do know that if you keep it up, you'll find yourself at the end of a noose. Piracy is a hanging offence these days, you know. If I find one shred of evidence against you, I'll divorce you. You'll be sent to London for trial. Your precious daughters will be bound out. Is that clear?"

"Yes, let us be clear." Anne spoke with seething determination. "You, sir, are as deeply invested in my shipping interests as I am. You've been in it up to your neck since marrying me. Everything coming from this plantation is shipped on one of my vessels or those of my associates. If you bring charges against me, they will land on you as well."

Daniel looked intensely at Anne, trying to think of a way to put her in her place and have the last word. "Woman, I am no addle-minded fool like Edmund Scarborough. You would be wise to rethink your threats. You're on dangerous ground, my dear. Now go on and get out. I'm done with you for now. Tell Brigid I will take my dinner alone in the parlor. Oh, and I expect to see you in my bedchamber tonight. It is time we began working on a brother for young Thomas. Now get out. I am sick of the sight of ya."

Anne held her head high and left the room. After closing the door behind her she leaned against the wall and closed her eyes thinking, "Damn him. Damn him to hell."

She went through the motions of the rest of her day pushing back the fear which threatened to overcome her. She put on a brave face for everyone to see, hiding the dark thoughts in her mind. That night she complied with Daniel's commands and performed her wifely duty. This time the chore was made all the more difficult. His usual perfunctory attitude towards the sex act was replaced by punishing anger. Though he did not strike her, he seemed intent on causing her pain. When he finished, Daniel gruffly pushed Anne off the bed onto the floor then turned his back to her.

Without a word Anne, went back to her own room to clean up. She dressed and made her way to the tower, knowing that there would be no sleep that night. At first, she fought the temptation to simply get a kitchen knife and cut Daniel's throat. She wondered if she could get the slaves to rise up against Daniel now that he had been baptized alongside of them. She whispered Judith's prayer hoping it would give her courage.

"Give me constancy in my mind, that I may despise him: and fortitude that I may overthrow him. For this will be a glorious monument for thy name, when he shall fall by the hand of a woman."

Of all the things she was considering, none of her so-called *Friends and Neighbors* would be willing to join such a suicidal conspiracy. Pacing the floor, she looked once again to the horizon, thinking about her long-lost friends Uncle Star and Doctor Moon. She had long ago given up any hope of hearing from them let alone enlisting their help disappearing with the girls.

It was the thought of Alexandre that eventually sparked an idea. In his book, Anne had read of the buccaneer captains' practice of using certain herbs and minerals in the crews' food to reduce their sexual urges. Being cooped up at sea for long periods led the men to look for extreme measures to relieve their pent-up frustrations. Gang rapes and forced sodomy were known to happen and could destroy shipboard morale.

Anne wondered if she could create any of those tinctures from her own herb garden. There was a woman in the tradesmen's village who supplied the women of Gargaphia with herbal potions to prevent pregnancy. That would be very useful to have. Maybe she could recommend the other remedy as well.

Anne had begun to doubt that she was still able to conceive a child. She should have been pregnant again by now. Convincing Daniel that she was now barren would end her conjugal responsibilities but would not keep him from raping the slave women. She would need both potions.

Anne enlisted the help of Brigid who, in light of her own history with an abusive master, was eager to help. Anne sent her to see the herbalist. Brigid returned with samples and instructions on how to concoct their own supply.

"This is pennyroyal. She said you should take this only after ye have relations with the Captain. It will make yer belly ache but not too terrible. She says that you should only do this for two month's-time, or yer'll be risking barrenness. She said you could make yerself very sick if ye take too much."

"Well, I may be at the end of my child bearing years anyway. Just the same if the other herbs do their job I won't need to. What did she say about them?"

"This is saltpeter. She said to put just a little in his tea at first. Then gradually add more 'til there's two full tablespoons for every ha' pound of dry tea leaves. It will take a few weeks to take effect. As long as he keeps taking it, it'll take that many weeks to wear off if he stops."

"Do you think you can add it without Milly noticing?"

"You leave it to me, Mum. I'll make sure it gets into what she has here and whatever she travels with. It won't be in whatever she buys elsewhere, but it'll get us started. The woman also said she could get us some laudanum. If need be, we can put the master out for the night with his ale at dinner time."

So began Anne and Brigid's secret medicinal treatment of Daniel. Within three weeks Daniel began having trouble becoming aroused. He attributed this to the enmity between them. Embarrassed, he stopped asking Anne to come to his room at night. Brigid continued to secretly add the potion to the master's favorite tea which Milly continued to innocently administer to him.

By the time the next breeding season came around, Daniel, too proud to seek medical help, presumed that he had simply passed the age of fertility. He was one of those rare men who never really enjoyed sex. He saw it as one of the obligations of manhood to create life to further his family name and to advance its fortunes. Though he would never have admitted it, he was actually relieved to be done with it.

Anne found Stanley Waln a suitable bride, the daughter of the village cooper, to focus his male urges on. Daniel, in turn, promoted the Bristol Boys to serve in place of him and Stanley. The once scrawny teens had developed into strapping young men who were only too pleased to enjoy such virile tasks. Anne realized that it was not possible to tamper with the tea of every man on the plantation without being caught by her husband. She came to dread the month of September that year knowing what was happening not far away in the slave barracks.

For a while she thought that perhaps her political strategy would end the depraved practice. Much to the chagrin of Captain Jenifer and other planters, Reverend Hensley had, as Anne suggested, preached against the rights of sexual conquest over slaves. He even wrote an eloquent plea for the conversion of slaves to the Anglican faith as Anne had suggested, and sent copies to the Governor and the Archbishop of Canterbury. The newly Christian status of Gargaphia's slaves, however, did not lead to any other mass conversions in the colony. Quite the contrary.

Other planters forbade any evangelizing on their property. The law favored keeping the slaves heathen, and therefore subject to the will of their Christian betters. Planters saw any attempt to convert them as interference with their property rights. There already had been a case brought in James City where a female slave, named Elizabeth Key, had successfully brought suit, challenging the legality of holding her, a Christian, in indefinite bondage. Conversion of the slaves was a Pandora's box that could unleash slave revolts and ruin the plantation economy.

As in the past, Anne's machinations, while not always successful, had a way of taking on a life of their own. Eastern Shore slaves, talking among themselves, began to see converting to Christianity as a pathway to a better life. Some truly experienced a spiritual awakening upon hearing of the baptism of the other slaves. The more they learned about the benevolent teacher from Nazareth, the more they wanted to become his followers. Secretly, some combined their newfound beliefs with those from the old African faith. The right to openly become a Christian became one more thing that slaves dreamed of.

The seeds of freedom, no matter what variety, quietly take root and grow healthy beneath the feet of oppressors. Anne could not know the unintended consequences, good and bad, that would arise from efforts like hers to end the forced breeding of slaves. For now, she was obliged to admit defeat.

Bacon's Rebellion

About the time that the Gargaphia slaves converted to Christianity, great political tension came to a head between Virginia's gentlemen planters and their commoner neighbors. There was general disgruntlement between these groups about unsettled debts, and other class conflicts. Five years since his passing, the name of Edmund Scarborough and his abuses were invoked in the debates taking place in James City. Everyone blamed the colonial government for a litany of complaints which now included the prospect of slave owners being denied the right to breed and manage their slaves as they saw fit.

The controversy which finally brought things to a head, however, was the issue of military support for commoners. A Maryland Indian tribe called the Doges crossed Virginia's western border and tried to take back by force the land of several plantations owned by low born settlers. The Governor refused to send the militia to these settlers' aide because as commoners they were of little political consequence to him. This infuriated his wife's commoner cousin, Nathaniel Bacon, who began organizing a movement against the government. The dissenters stormed the capital forcing Governor Berkley to flee across the Chesapeake to stay with his friend John Custis on the Eastern Shore.

The news of this political turmoil reached Gargaphia on a day that was already going badly. Anne had spent her early morning hours as usual watching the sun rise from the tower when she noticed vultures circling above. The carrion eaters were not an unusual sight. Anne dismissed it, until down below one of the slaves began shrieking hysterically pointing to something on the edge of the woods by the barn.

Slave and indenture alike were superstitious lots. Animal deaths were a part of daily farm life, but to unexpectedly come across moldering remains was seen as a bad omen which would cause a big reaction. Anne calmly went down to see what was the matter thinking she would find some poor woodland creature that simply needed burying. When she rounded the corner, she was horrified to behold a dead man hanging from a tree by a red cloth. His face was purple and bloated. Below him was an overturned crate.

"Go get the Captain and Mr. Waln." Anne instructed whoever was standing next to her. She was shocked by the sight. She backed away, then turned and covered her face. When she looked up, she could see her children coming to find out what all the commotion was about.

"No! No! Go back to the house. You cannot see this." Anne stopped them, turning each one around by the shoulders as they stretched to see what was going on.

"Aww. I want to see." Little Tom complained.

"Mummy, what is it?" Arcadia chimed in.

"Nothing. Nothing I want you to see. Go on now. Go back to the house. Don't keep Brigid waiting."

"Come, children. It is one of Mother's evil deeds returned to haunt her."

"Annabella," Anne snapped. "Don't say such things!"

"Well, it's the truth isn't it? I recognize him. He used to be one of Gargaphia's regulars. And that would appear to be one of Mistress Daisy's red bed linens."

Atalanta chimed in. "Oh yes, I remember him."

"How do you know that?" Anne was horrified.

"Oh, Mother, really." Annabella sniffed "How stupid do you think we are? We were sneaking out at night to watch the shenanigans in the gathering hall through the window by the time I was nine. We know exactly what went on…"

"Girls, do as I say. Take your sister and brother out of sight. Now!!"

Annabella and Atalanta took the hands of their younger siblings and led them back to the main house passing Daniel and Stanley on the way. The men took charge, instructing some of the field hands to cut down the unfortunate fellow. They looked through his pockets and presented their master with a piece of paper they found there.

Daniel read what was written on it and grimaced.

"What does it say?" Anne asked.

"It's a man called John Stephenson. He was here the other day blathering about his indenture contract coming to an end next month. He wanted me to help him find Daisy Sheffield. I told him wherever she was, she was a bloody whore and he was better off without her. I sent him packing and told him not to come back."

"Oh, Daniel…" Anne said quietly. She was surprised at the cruel insensitivity even though she knew Stephenson's dream of starting a life with Daisy was hopeless. It had been years since she left, after all.

"This," Daniel snarled, holding up the now crumpled letter, "is what is wrong with harlotry. Whore's make men crazy with lust. The only ones at fault here are Daisy Sheffield, and you for allowing her to ply her evil trade here. Waln – get someone to bury him. And make sure you burn that blasted crimson cloth. I don't want one scrap left in the tree where the Africans can see it. We'll not get a lick of work done with them staring at that bloody thing. We'll have to notify Stephenson's master and the court. What a damn waste of my time."

Anne followed Daniel as he stalked back to the house for his breakfast alone in the parlor. As Anne and the children sat down to their breakfast in the dining room, she thought regretfully about the significance of the red cloth. Daisy liked red bed sheets because her porcelain white skin and pale golden locks made quite a visual impression against the sinful cherry colored backdrop. Daniel was not entirely wrong about the effect it had had on the besotted John Stephenson.

The Captain's voice awoke her from her dark thoughts. "I leave for the general assembly today. I won't be back for several weeks. I should have left two days ago, except I…"

A knock on the door interrupted the Captain. It was Stanley Waln.

"I am sorry to disturb you, sir, Mum…"

"What is it?" Daniel snapped.

"There's a rider here with a message from the Governor. There's trouble in James City and the… well he… I'd better let the rider in to explain."

Stanley reached through the open door and pulled a young man into the room. His face was flushed. He wore the uniform of the Governor's Cavalier guards.

"Sir, I have these orders from the Governor himself requiring the Accomack militia be mustered and brought to Arlington, the Custis plantation, in Northampton. Sir."

The boy handed Daniel the message. Daniel broke the heavy red seal and began reading.

"Milly!" he called into the kitchen. "Milly! Go get Harold and tell him to get cracking. You'll be staying here. We're not going to James City for now."

"Is there anything I can do to help?" Anne asked cautiously.

The Captain was distractedly rereading the Governor's orders. "What? No. Nothing… Don't leave Gargaphia until you hear from me that it's safe. That drunken blaggard Nathaniel Bacon's led an attack on James City."

Within the hour Daniel, his company of militiamen, and Harold rode off without further explanation. Stanley Waln had been given instruction to ride to the other plantations in Accomack to call the muster. All available troops were ordered to converge at the southern end of the peninsula to protect the Governor.

For weeks there was little news of the conflict. Anne waited anxiously to hear whether the rebellion would spread to the Eastern Shore. People were beginning to line up on either side: commoners and indentures were on one side. The Governor and fellow aristocrats were on the other, though there were a few defections. Most notable of these was Charles Scarborough who probably was still trying to distance himself from the excesses of his father. Both groups claimed loyalty to the Crown. Neither could afford to bring down the full force of the Royal Navy down on their heads.

In late September, a rider came with news that the militia would hold their ground surrounding the Custis plantation. They had received word that James City and the Governor's mansion had been ransacked and torched.

It seemed like the rebels had gotten the upper hand, until a month later. Nathaniel Bacon and his band took over the capital and began celebrating their victory with a great feast. Unfortunately, the rebel leader was so drunk he did not notice that the oysters he ate had fouled. He became sick, and not long after, Bacon died of dysentery.

This turn of events knocked the wind out of the dissident faction's sails. Their loose confederation fell apart. The Governor's Cavaliers quickly retook James City. Back on the Eastern Shore,

Berkley and his cohorts made plans to round up all the traitors for some rough justice. Before making a triumphant return across the Chesapeake, he decided to visit a few of the planters who had rallied to his side, and secure oaths of loyalty from the rest.

When Berkley's entourage arrived at Gargaphia, a great feast was prepared in the gathering hall. The mood of the household was like the old days, when Gargaphia was the social center of the county. This, however, was not to be a revel as in times past. About two dozen of Accomack's wealthiest landowners were invited to meet with the Governor. They did not bring their wives, nor was there any other female companionship provided to them.

As mistress of Gargaphia, Anne served as hostess and the lone feminine presence. The children were confined to the nursery with Annabella in charge as the oldest. Dinner was to be served well into the evening as was the custom in the capital. This gave Anne time to invite the Governor to enjoy the vibrant November sunset as seen from her tower. She and Daniel accompanied him into the loft and extolled the virtues of their plantation while sipping port.

The Governor seemed to be enjoying himself immensely. After finishing the decanter of wine almost single-handedly he asked, "Daniel, my man, be a good sport and fetch us some more of this fine port."

"Of course, my Lord," he replied.

Daniel glared at his wife from behind his superior's back and grudgingly descended the stairs. Anne knew this would be her opportunity to feather her own nest and hopefully garner some influential favor. Berkley began flirting before she had a chance to herself.

"My dear, how fortunate it is that we have time to get to know each other a little, and in such a magical setting."

With his left hand he held her right hand. With the other he stroked her cheek. Anne did not flinch, smiling sweetly at him, grateful that she was up wind of him. He emitted a cacophony of odors: halitosis, sweat, tobacco, alcohol, and heavy perfumes intended to mask it all.

He continued, "I have long wanted to meet Mistress Bluebird in person. Tell me my dear, have you been happy these last few years?"

Anne gave him the answer he was looking for. "My Lord, I have been so greatly blessed ever since receiving your wise counsel. I live well. I now have a son, and my daughters have dowries that will enable them to make fine marriages. I have you to thank for this good fortune."

The Governor had stopped listening and had begun to admire Anne's décolletage. She was wearing one of her trademark blue gowns which showed off her full round figure.

"Closing your guest house was in the best interest of the colony, but I must admit I wish I'd been here to see it in all its glory. I mean, this is a fine plantation but, well…"

"Yes, it was quite a spectacle in its time. I can just imagine you here in its prime, my Lord." Anne said as she smiled coyly.

Berkley kissed Anne's hand then looked out at the sky on fire with the colors of fall. Anne only had a few moments left to solicit the Governor for help.

"My Lord, I am so grateful for all you have done for my family. I wonder if I might offer you something in return? My eldest daughters are nearly ready for betrothal. Annabella is sixteen and her sister Atalanta is just a bit younger. Could there be some Cavaliers who would make an advantageous match, not just for them, but perhaps for you?"

The Governor was still holding her hand. She clasped it suggestively and caressed the top of his hand with her free hand. He smiled and winked at her. "You leave it to me my dear. I'll send some suitable candidates to meet you and you can take your choice."

Daniel's footsteps could be heard coming back up the stairs. Anne pulled away and changed the subject.

"God graced my path the day I received those letters from you and your beloved wife. I only wish she was here too so that I could properly thank you both. I understand she is currently visiting your London estates."

Clearing his throat Berkley replied. "Yes. Well, I believe she is setting sail for Virginia as we speak, now that the crisis has been resolved. Ah, there's a good man. Pour me another glass of that port. I was just telling your wife that this is a magical view, Jenifer."

"Mistress Anne loves it up here. I find it a bit drafty myself."

"Well, gentlemen, I am neglecting my hostess duties down below. I shall go check on our supper's progress and leave the two of you to your business." Anne made her exit hoping that Daniel would not undo any of the progress she had just made.

That night Anne was seated next to the guest of honor. She continued her charm campaign without bringing up the subject of matchmaking again. The Governor, ebullient as a result of his recent victory and the fawning attentions of Anne and her loyalist neighbors, left the Eastern Shore to face the burned ruins of James City, and prepare for the wrath of his returning wife. Lady Frances, upon seeing the wreckage of the home she had built up with so much pride, was said to have remarked that it looked worse than the aftermath of the Catholic bacchanals on Shrovetide.

Governor and Lady Berkley would spend the next year rebuilding their plantation. Despite initial promises of reform to assuage the rebels, the Governor's enemies were rounded up for retribution. Lesser offenders were heavily fined. The ring leaders were hanged, some with, some without trials. The aristocrats in the House of Burgesses passed legislation to solidify their power over the commoners. These actions threatened to generate a new wave of rebellion. The ensuing political turmoil led to Berkley being recalled by the Crown to London and replaced.

Before returning to England, however, he did not forget his promise to Anne. He had Lady Frances write to several gentlemen bachelors proposing that they visit Gargaphia to meet the Toft sisters for the purpose of considering marriage. In the spring of 1677, Anne began interviewing potential suitors and introducing them to her eldest daughters.

She allowed Annabella and Atalanta to choose their own husbands after she sat them down at the dining room table to compare dossiers she had prepared on their financial worth and prospects. She tried to counsel them about their choices as if they were business decisions.

"If you choose an older man, you are more likely to outlive him. That presents opportunities for independence or remarriage once he has died. A younger man will have greater vigor as a husband but may be more likely to require a mistress to keep him satisfied. This puts your future at risk, should he decide he likes his mistress better than you. Likewise, a handsome man is used to enjoying his flirtations and will always keep you guessing about his fidelity. Politicians and military officers are rarely home which you may find to your advantage, but that can be a lonely life."

This mercenary advice fell on deaf ears. Annabella, had reached the age where she resented her mother's authority on most subjects. She had become increasingly distant from Anne. Annabella replied with what had now become her usual disrespectful attitude.

"For goodness' sake Mother. Why would we take advice from *you* on what constitutes a good match?"

"I'm still your mother. I am only trying to give you the benefit of my experience. You can pick any but the names in this batch over here. Mark my words, they're scoundrels who'll bring you misery. These four gentlemen are well thought of throughout the colony. Any one of them will provide for you. I suggest we invite these four to call on us so that you can see if they are to your liking."

Annabella rolled her eyes replying, "I'm sure the Captain has already weeded out the bad prospects. I really don't need any advice from you. I am perfectly capable of judging who I should marry."

Ultimately, the girls were too excited about the possibility of becoming mistresses of their own plantations to think about strategic details. And besides, their mother's library full of idealistic books had them dreaming of making love matches. The young girls had romance on their minds. They fixed their sights on the most attractive gentlemen who were closest to their own age, without regard for their mother's counsel.

After several visits and some deliberations, Francis Lee was chosen for Annabella and John Osborne for Atalanta. They each were married within two months following their seventeenth birthdays. Anne happily gave them each a chest of linens, silverware, and other household items. Daniel signed over some cattle and one slave to each bride, but refused to transfer the acreage that had been set aside in their dowries until all three daughters were wed. This caused considerable tension between Anne and the new couples.

When Arcadia was finally given in marriage to Thomas Welburn just a few years later, Anne had to threaten legal action against her husband to get the property released. Captain Jenifer was forced to capitulate. He had signed a contract and it had been duly recorded with the court after all. The 5,000-acre tract between Chincoteague and Mattapenny Neck was coincidentally named *Arcadia* on Augustine Hermann's map of the colony. This was divided into equal lots, with each having some access to the coastal bay.

Anne's insistence that he live up to his promise infuriated Daniel. Though the last few years had passed surprisingly quickly, their relationship had been reduced to a series of skirmishes separated only by bitter standoffs. Out of sheer spite, he decided to retaliate for being forced to keep his promise to give up the land.

The week before Arcadia's nuptials he visited his stepdaughters' husbands. He told them he had found proof that Anne was in league with pirates, putting them all at great risk if they continued to associate with her. He claimed one of her cohorts was a notorious cutthroat, Captain Alistair Minshull, who had been executed in London several years before. He perpetuated this falsehood by including his name in the list of other pirates who actually had been hanged.

Daniel implored the young in-laws to forbid their wives from associating with Anne, and then influenced Arcadia and her fiancé to do the same. Minshull's reputation as a smuggler was well known, so Daniel had no trouble convincing them of the fictitious execution and by association of the moral failing of his longtime associate: their mother.

On Arcadia's wedding day, Annabella and Atalanta came to Gargaphia to accompany her to St. George's Chapel. The young women gathered to help her prepare and to be together in their nursery one last time. When Anne came in to tell them it was time to go, Annabella stopped her short.

"Mother, we have something to tell you. You cannot come to the church."

"What? Why…"

"I am sorry, but we need to cut ties with you altogether. Our husbands and now Thomas, they want us to be done with you – for the good of our families, our children. If you want us to have the lives you planned for us, you need to leave us alone – starting today."

Atalanta took over where her older sister left off.

"We have received word that Uncle Star was executed for piracy in London. He named you as a conspirator in his crimes. If you are charged, it will ruin the rest of us. No decent merchant will do business with our plantations."

Now Anne interrupted.

"I don't know where you got your information, but I have never heard such… Uncle Star was lost at sea during the great hurricane. Who told you he was executed?"

"Daniel" said Annabella.

"Well, he is *lying*!" Anne was furious.

Her older daughter continued. "I believe him. He says you were the one who tried to back out of our dowries. He said you didn't want to give up the land, that you had used it as collateral for a loan or something."

"That's not true. He is the one who refused to cooperate. I had to threaten to take him to court."

"Well, we believe him. If it weren't for Daniel, we never would have made respectable marriages. If it weren't for him, we would have come of age in the Gargaphia brothel. No decent family would have accepted us." Atalanta interjected.

"I never would have let that happen. I would have made sure…"

"Oh Mother, really!" Atalanta continued. "Annabella and I remember how disreputable Gargaphia was. We saw it firsthand. We saw the Colonel fornicating with barmaids in the parlor for God's sake!"

Annabella picked up where Atalanta left off.

"If Daniel had not married you, we'd all be working side by side with the Sheffield sisters. If you love us, if you love your grandchildren, you will let us build decent lives. You will stay away from us."

"Arcadia," Anne turned to her youngest daughter tearfully. "Do *you* want me to stay away from your wedding?"

Arcadia was crying too.

"Yes, Mother. Thomas says I must never see you after today. He would not marry me unless I promised."

"Daniel has twisted everything. Annabella, Atalanta, you remember Uncle Star. You loved him. Don't you remember all the gifts he brought you?"

"That doesn't mean he wasn't a pirate." Annabella interrupted.

"I certainly remember him behaving like an animal with the serving wenches. His conviction does not surprise me in the least. Face it, he was a bad influence on you, Mother." Atalanta added.

Annabella continued the condemnation. "It wasn't just Uncle Star. Everything was a lie, a subterfuge. All your sweetness towards us was just a mask over the real evil in you. You pretended to raise us as good Christians, yet on every All Saints Day – of all days – you conducted heathen rites. You think we did not know? You're lucky that piracy and keeping a brothel are all you were accused of. You could have been burned on a stake for that witchcraft. We are lucky to have survived a childhood with you. We are done with you."

"I can't believe you want to do this." Anne began to weep. "Everything I have done all these years was for the three of you. I did everything I could to give you a happy childhood, a good life. My only wish was to assure that you had a better chance than I had. I gave you a better future."

Annabella stood firm. "Mother, you put that future at risk every day with your devious schemes. We've had to watch you lie and cheat our whole lives. I thank God every day that a gentleman Cavalier like Daniel Jenifer came into our lives. He was the best father we could have asked for. We owe our respectability to him. I only hope that he gets young Tom away from you as soon as possible."

"How can you say that? Don't you know of *his* evil acts? He never cared about you. He wanted to have you bound out. He was always threatening to… I have always loved you. *I love you.* Please, my darlings, please listen to me…" Anne tried to hug and kiss her daughters. They pushed her away. They were done talking. Without another word they helped Arcadia gather her things to make their departure from Gargaphia.

There was nothing left for Ann to do, except climb the tower and watch her entire family leave in the carriage for the wedding without her. In her anger and devastation, she paced the floor. Wicked responses to this terrible turn of events rushed through her mind: murder, suicide, making her own false accusation against Daniel in court. She imagined her daughters mortified faces watching the trial.

This thought made her weep uncontrollably until she dismissed the idea altogether. This would only make the rift between her and her girls worse. She had no idea how to respond to this turn of events. Even prayer was useless. When Anne finally came back downstairs, she told Brigid what had happened. The two women held each other and cried. They had both lost their beloved daughters that day.

For weeks, Anne did not speak and refused to be in Daniel's presence. Finally, he left to attend to business on his Maryland plantation. The couple's uneasy marriage of convenience was now one of estranged contempt. From then on, Daniel stayed at Gargaphia for just a few days at a time and only when absolutely necessary.

A few months later, in May of 1687, Daniel had one more piece of property that he co-owned with Anne which he wanted to sell: Chiconessex. Anne had resisted selling it for some time for sentimental reasons. She had even suggested selling Gargaphia and letting her live there. Daniel, wanting to punish her, would not relent.

Now she had run out of objections and any energy to resist. Though the transfer of deeds still required her signature, her property rights were lost the day she married. Anne had no choice but to comply. All her land in Virginia had been sold except this and Gargaphia. Daniel brought the settlement papers to the library for her to sign and made an announcement that she had long dreaded.

"That, my dear, concludes the business between us. I will no longer be returning to Gargaphia and its cursed past. I'll once again make my Maryland plantation my primary residence. You and Brigid can live out your days here. I am taking the other slaves and the indentures to my Maryland plantation. Waln and the Bristol boys are moving the livestock to the barrier island up north. They don't require fencing there and… Well, never mind that is none of your concern. I am here to tell you that Tom will be coming with me. He will receive a proper Jesuit education in St. Mary's City which will help him become a good Christian without the stain of your past following him."

Anne said nothing at first. Plantation business was all there ever really had been between them. She would certainly not miss him, but she would miss her son. Tom was the only family she really had, now that her daughters had forsaken her.

Sadly, it was too late for that relationship as well. Like many boys of that time, the older he got, the less he wanted his mother's company, preferring that of his father. Daniel, for all his faults, had been an attentive caring parent. He spent time with the boy, teaching him to ride and hunt. Like many planters, Daniel was a practiced surveyor, a skill which he passed on to his son. They spent long hours together contentedly poring over maps.

There was no disharmony between Anne and her son. He had no memory of the Gargaphia revels to hold against her. But he craved the approval of his father, who taught him that the company of women was a detriment to one's manhood. Daniel had indoctrinated him into the philosophy that simply by virtue of his gender, even at his young age, his discernment was superior to that of his mother. Women were to be admired for their beauty but otherwise tolerated as a necessary evil. As much as Anne loved Tom, she knew that she had lost him long ago.

"A Jesuit education? So, you are converting back to Catholicism and making Tom do so as well?"

"In fact, I never really left it. I think you will remember that my so-called conversion was a matter of show to prevent a riot, which was caused by you. My son is ready to become a faithful follower of the one true church of Christ. I don't really care whether you approve or not."

"When will you bring him back to Gargaphia?"

"As long as you are here, never."

"After all this time, you still think I am a corrupting influence?"

"Now more than ever. I won't have your buccaneering infecting him."

"I've never involved any of the children in anything that would do them harm."

Daniel was dismayed that she could still exasperate him.

"Your mind is so twisted from the truth you cannot even see it. You are a disgrace. Your children will never be able to hold their heads up unless they disown you completely. You couldn't be satisfied simply being a good mother, could you? Your life of comfort here was never enough. I've given up trying to understand your sinful ways."

Anne responded bitterly. "Maybe if I wasn't living under the constant threat of having everything ripped away from me, I wouldn't have had to make my own fortune."

"Admit it." Daniel said. "You are just as immoral as the Colonel was. You, and your daughters, profited from his misdeeds just as much as he did. Surely you must realize that you've condemned their souls by making them complicit in your own evil affairs. Do you even care that they are bound for Purgatory?"

"I can justify all that I have done because it has been for their sake." Anne replied. "I only did what a mother is meant to do. I have assured that all my children were raised in better circumstances than I was. They live in fine homes with servants to care for them. Their children will be brought up in comfort and privilege far from the depravation I have seen. I hope they won't have to dance with the devil to keep them safe as I have had to do. In time, I hope they will come to understand what women like me have to do to survive in the cruel world of men. I just hope I have taught them well enough to triumph over their own hardships.

"My children will all have to find their own destiny. You've done your best to make sure I no longer play a part in it. If you've won anything you've won that. Perhaps I am corrupt. Perhaps the path that led me here has been littered with poor excuses. Nothing you can say will make me regret doing what I have had to do."

"And what of your soul?" Daniel sneered. *"For what shall it profit a man, if he shall gain the whole world, and lose his own soul?"*

Daniel stood over her seeming to look deeply into Anne's eyes to see if she understood what he was saying. She did understand and it made her furious.

"*You* are quoting scripture? You see to your salvation and I will see to my own, you hypocrite. When I die, God our Father will sort out the good and evil in me. My faith is strong enough to leave it in his capable hands. How is your faith, sir? What made you think you could wash the stain of marrying a whore off your precious piety?"

Daniel looked away from Anne and spoke quietly.

"I thought the sacred marriage rite would cleanse you of your sins. I thought I could reform you. I thought you would be grateful to be saved. I did not realize that you were irredeemable."

Ann shook her head sadly.

"Don't you know one sinner cannot reform another? You have just as much to atone for as I do. You may not have lusted after my body. Your lust was much worse than that. You forced me into this marriage just to steal my property and all the power that went with it. You condemn me so you don't have to admit that you are a thief. You did all this to take what was mine. A sin is not absolved just because it is made against a sinner. You wanted to have what you did not rightfully earn on your own. You broke God's commandments. Thou shalt not steal, Daniel. Thou shalt not covet Daniel. God hated coveting so much he said it three times: thy neighbor's house, thy neighbor's wife, thy neighbor's belongings. Have you confessed your coveting and your thievery to a priest? These are mortal sins, Daniel. It may not be possible for him to absolve you. Your heart is as black as the blackest sin there is. You and Edmund Scarborough will burn together in hell."

The color drained from Daniel's face. Anne knew her daggers had struck him at his own corrupt core.

She smiled as she stepped closer to him and whispered, "I will probably join you both to spend eternity in Hell. I really don't care. I just hope the Devil gives us separate corners there, as I have already lived in this Hell with you long enough."

Anne stepped away from her husband, whose ashen face was now burning red with anger. Turning her back on him she held her head high and said the last words he would ever hear from her.

"You may go now. Tom is waiting for you to steal him away. He is the last thing you will ever take from me."

Daniel stalked out of the room. Anne knew there was nothing she could do to prevent Tom from leaving. Youthful exuberance made him oblivious to how going might affect his mother. The boy was excited to finally get to travel beyond the borders of the plantation to experience the manly adventures awaiting him.

Despite the verbal sparring with Daniel, Anne knew she was beaten. With resignation she bade her son farewell and presented him with a silver compass she had been saving for his twentieth name's day. She had had it engraved: "Wherever you go my love will always be with you. Mother"

Tom thanked her and kissed her on the cheek. With that he and Daniel, and their entourage, rode off leaving only a plume of dust behind them. Anne was finally free from the conventions of marriage and servitude. Yet she still felt as bound to them as ever.

The once bustling life at Gargaphia had become a ghostly shell of its former existence. The halls echoed with eerie lonely emptiness. Her hardworking faithful servant, Brigid, was dying. She had been declining for a long time as she suffered from terrible painful arthritis. Too weak to perform her chores, Brigid spent most days seated by a window in the kitchen mumbling about missing the children. She had loved them as if they were her own.

Anne spent her days nursing Brigid, who lingered on throughout the summer. She died in her sleep early that August. It took Anne two days to dig her a plot in the yard where other servants had been laid to rest. She saddled the one horse left to her and went to Reverend Hensley to arrange funeral rites. He came back with her, did his pastoral duty, then helped fill Brigid's grave. He left quickly thereafter, declining Anne's hospitality, offering no words of consolation.

On All Saints Day in 1687, Anne held a ribbon blessing as she had done so many times before. There was no longer anyone to disapprove and she needed the ritual more than ever. She prepared several sprigs of lavender tied with blue ribbon. The largest of these was to honor Brigid. She made sprigs for Anna Hack Boote, Giles Ishim, and his wife Rachel, who had all recently gone on to meet their maker. She also made a sprig for Captain Minshull and Alexandre Lorentz. They had disappeared from her life so long ago. Daniel's vicious lie had forced her to accept that only death could have prevented their return.

Anne took the dory out in the channel alone, just before sunset. One by one she gently laid her ceremonial offerings in the water then recited the words of the ritual.

"To our guardian angels we plead, carry our love on soft sea breezes to our cherished Mother Mary and sweet Christ Jesus, that they might wrap our beloveds Alistair, Alexandre, Giles, Rachel, Anna, and our dear, dear Brigid… Wrap them in your holy embrace, that they might be with us always, that they and the angels might guide us and watch over us. We bless these ribbons and send them on their way with all our love and devotion. Amen."

The sky was ablaze in every shade of yellow, orange, red and purple. The sound of the nearby surf mixed in a strange requiem symphony with the plaintive honking wails of a flock of geese that had settled in the lagoon. Anne sat weeping in the skiff until darkness overtook daylight. Then, she slowly rowed back up the creek to face a bleak winter of grief.

The Persistent Buccaneer

Gargaphia was now a desperately lonely place, filled with as many troubling memories as happy ones. Isolation made Anne fearful. An undefended Gargaphia would provide great temptation to thieves. It would not be long before gossips spread the news that Scarborough's pirate queen was unprotected and guarding some fantastical treasure all by herself. Anne remembered Maude's advice to her back at Chiconessex. She began sleeping with a large kitchen knife on the table next to her bed, for fear some ruffian might try to attack her in her sleep. She carried it with her as she walked around the empty buildings daily, making sure squatters had not tried to move in.

Though winter felt like an eternity, Anne used her chilly confinement to do what she had always done: to make plans. She would start her life over somewhere else. She enlisted the help of the few allies she still had in her *Friends and Neighbors* ledger in getting messages to and from her ship captains. They helped her only out of obligation or pity. Her past kindness and fair dealing entitled her to their secret assistance, but not to public displays of friendship. Her knowledge of their own secrets made her a threat. Worst of all, she had the taint of criminality. They did not want it to rub off on them. They were glad to help her leave.

Anne made arrangements to sell one of her ships. She used the proceeds to buy a house in the town of Lewes northward in Pennsylvania. The government there had been somewhat dysfunctional since its Quaker proprietor, William Penn, had returned to his estates in England three years prior. Adept criminals had an easy time of plying their trade there by paying off corrupt officials concealed among the famously ethical Quakers. Anne had been assured by a few smuggling contacts in that region, that this was a place she could live comfortably while concealing her illicit business affairs.

Anne weighed heavily what if anything she should tell her family about her plan to escape from Virginia. In the end she decided not to tell them anything. She would leave them, most of her personal possessions, and her past behind her.

On the appointed day, Anne dragged a heavy trunk of clothes, linens, and books to the dock. She almost capsized the skiff as she pulled it in. She then went back to the house for a second chest. She considered setting the building ablaze but decided it would take too much work. Instead, she took one last look around before walking out leaving the door wide open behind her.

Anne rowed through the winding creek out into the channel, then put down the oars letting the tide pull the dory swiftly out to sea. Before she knew what was happening, she lost sight of the shoreline. The wind had picked up raising waves as tall as she was. She began to row again trying desperately to turn the boat southward towards her destination, the sailing ketch *Providence*, which she could see from the top of the swells, though it seemed like it was miles away.

It was still early morning. Despite the breeze, the sun beat down on Anne, sapping her energy. Her arms were unused to such hard labor. They ached. She was already tired from dragging her trunks from the house to the dock. The coins and jewels she had sewn into her bodice were jabbing into her ribs. Her skirts were already getting wet. They were hot and heavy. She began to feel dizzy as the boat bobbed up and down. She wished she had brought a jug of cider.

Each time the dory got to the crest of a wave she turned to look for the *Providence*. It was growing larger and it had raised just one of her sails. She wanted to believe it was sailing closer to her. She kept rowing as long as she could until, exhausted, she lay back in the dory and prayed that the *Providence* would get to her before the books in her trunk were ruined by the salt water.

Anne shielded her eyes from the sun with her left arm and waited. She thought of her beloved children and how she missed them. She began to weep a little, but bit her lip to distract her mind from her sorrows.

Anne must have laid like that for more than an hour when she started to hear the sound of men shouting. Then came the sounds of oars slapping the water. For a moment she thought she was dreaming, but indeed the voices were those of sailors from the *Providence*. She sat up, wiped her face and watched them coming to rescue her.

One of the men jumped into her boat and tied it off to the other dory which towed her to the side of the ketch. The men on deck threw down a great net which the sailor on Anne's boat loaded with her trunks. Once her things were in it, he tied it tight so nothing would fall out. Before she knew what was happening the man grabbed her by the waist with one arm. He used the other to hold on to a large rope tied to the net. He pulled her to his side as he planted one foot in the webbing. With much shouting the men above winched them up to the main deck. There Captain Simon Jansen greeted her.

This was the first time Anne had met the middle-aged man with a thick grey and white mane and full beard. Their business relationship had been conducted all these years through intermediaries. He was short and stocky but fit, with tanned skin, sparkling blue eyes, and a broad flashing smile. His small gold hoop earrings and captain's attire completed the picture of the adventurer Anne expected him to be.

"Welcome aboard your ship, Mistress Anne. You've owned her a long time. Now you will finally get to sail on her." Jansen said, bowing deep while removing his hat with a great flourish.

"Aye, I'm glad to be here and to finally meet you in person. I thank you and your men for catching up with me so quickly. I wasn't sure I wouldn't be swept out to oblivion."

She looked out over the rail and saw that her now empty skiff had been set adrift.

"We never would have let that happen." Jansen smiled. "We had our eye on you since before you left the creek. Now we'll be off. By the morrow we'll be settling you into your new home."

"It's been over thirty years since I've been to sea." Anne mused. "This time I'll be charting my own course."

Anne and Captain Jansen talked at length on their brief voyage north to Lewes. They gossiped about people they both knew like Anna Hack Boote and a variety of other merchants and sea captains. She learned that he knew both Uncle Star and Dr. Moon, and thought highly of them. He said that he had not heard of Minshull's execution and doubted it was true. Jansen had heard that Minshull had given up his ship and was a harbor master somewhere. He did not know where. It made Anne happy to imagine Uncle Star living out his days swapping stories with visiting captains on some tropical island.

Simon was full of amusing anecdotes about his life and travels. The Dutchman had been at sea since he became a cabin boy sailing out of Rotterdam at the age of twelve. His indenture with the Dutch East India Company brought him to the colonies where he rose through the ranks to captain his own ship. Anne found him to be good company. He reminded her of Uncle Star.

Simon, in turn, seemed to be anxious to please her. He was genuinely proud of all he had done to help her start her new life. He described in detail the new home he had procured for her. The property had belonged to a Swedish family who had abandoned it when they were beset by misfortune several years before.

The journey and their conversations came to a swift end when they reached their destination on Delaware Bay. The flat landscape there was very much like that of Virginia. On the carriage ride from the harbor past marshes, farms, and forests, Anne noticed bluebirds flitting from tree to tree.

"This is a good omen." she thought. "It's as if they followed me from Chiconessex."

Jansen had employed a woman named Martha to do the housework. She was about Anne's age, large and sturdy, with brown hair and green eyes. The Captain had also hired a young man to help with more substantial labor and provide some masculine security. Douglas was a tall blond who said very little.

Anne did not hold an indenture contract with either of them. She preferred instead to give them room and board with a small stipend. Anne was determined not to hold anyone in any form of bondage ever again. These servants were free to go at any time. She hoped good living and working conditions would be enough to inspire loyalty.

Anne's new home was known as Swede's Haven. The tract was bounded by a creek on the southwest and on the east by a thick forest. A path through it led to great towering sand dunes on the cape facing the Delaware Bay on one side and the Atlantic Ocean on the other. The entire property of three hundred square acres would afford Anne the convenience of living close to the town yet provide the privacy she required to do her business.

The cropland surrounding the house had been leased to a neighbor. There was a large barn for livestock, a chicken coop, a drying shed, and a fenced kitchen garden.

The main house was brick with three stories. It had four bedrooms, a large parlor, dining room, and a winter kitchen. The servants' quarters were above the summer kitchen in a separate building. The furnishings were simpler than those at Gargaphia, but they were of good quality.

The feature that Anne liked the best was the widow's walk, a cupola on the main house reached by a ladder from the attic. This small square room had windows on all sides providing a view not unlike the tower at Gargaphia. Though dunes and trees obstructed a clear view of the beaches, with her spyglass Anne could easily watch both the bay and the ocean for approaching ships. All in all, the property was charming. It would suit her needs very well.

Captain Jansen stayed on the farm for two weeks after their arrival, to help Anne get settled and arrange for any improvements she required. His next assignment was to carry passengers and produce to Hispaniola and return with sugar cane and rum. Before he left, Simon spread the word Anne was available for scrivening business. He likewise let privateers working area waters know that she was an ally, warning them not to give her any trouble.

All this was done in a covert manner so as not to alert authorities that Anne Toft was still alive and well in another colony. Anne was now presenting herself as a sea captain's widow: "Mistress Anne Newcastle" also known as "Mrs. Alexandre Newcastle." Alexandre stood for Dr. Lorentz, the only man she had come close to truly loving. Newcastle was chosen in admiration of author Margaret Cavendish, Duchess of Newcastle-upon-Tyne.

Captain Jansen also advised Anne about whom she could and could not trust locally. The county High Sheriff, Stephen Rodney was incorruptible, and should not be crossed. The harbormaster Richard Winder, however, was known to receive bribes. He and Anne already had a business relationship through captains like Simon. For a small price he looked the other way when contraband was unloaded on the docks in defiance of royal embargos. He likewise ignored passenger lists and travel writs that were clearly forged. He drew the line however, at any tolerance of thieving cutthroats who occasionally raided the town, violently attacking innocent settlers.

Piracy was becoming more and more common on the waters between New England and the Caribbean, making life along those coasts increasingly dangerous. Anne came quickly to understand that the Lewes community was very much like her birthplace – Robin Hood's Bay. Most of the residents were in some way complicit with pirate activities. Many merely wanted to insure their own personal protection. Others bought stolen goods or contraband. A few were actively engaged in the illicit commerce. For them smuggling was just their way of life.

Anne, with her own proclivities for buccaneering, fit right in. She mostly kept to herself minding her own business. Meanwhile, certain neighbors were thankful to find out that she could be counted on not to meddle in their unlawful affairs. Anne continued to benefit from her shipping interests both legitimate and otherwise, without any interference.

She was especially glad to no longer be constrained by church authority. Sussex County was presently owned by a Quaker proprietor who believed in religious toleration. Only Christian men could vote, but there was no requirement to attend services or tithe. Each person could exercise their own religious conscience. Anne still prayed daily, but she did not miss the requirements of the Anglican Church which she blamed in part for the forced marriage which ultimately resulted in the loss of her daughters.

Though they had rejected her, she tried to stay informed about her family through her smuggling network back in Accomack. Anne learned that her children had presumed she died accidently when she took the boat out. Though her disappearance was briefly the subject of outrageous rumors, Anne was quickly forgotten. There was no body to bury, so no one went to the trouble to have her declared dead in church or court records. Her notorious past had rendered her passing too uncomfortable an event to officially recognize.

The thought that no one seemed to miss her made Anne feel particularly low. It called into question every decision she had made. Eventually she stopped asking her cohorts for news of Accomack. Remorse was the cost Anne had paid for her freedom.

Anne returned to her old routines and tried to enjoy her new life. She filled her days with reading, needle work, accounting, and a little gardening. She often took walks, climbing over the tall dunes to stroll along the shoreline. Though her waking hours were peaceful, at night her lifelong insomnia continued to afflict her. Nightmares replaying her last meeting with her estranged children frequently drove her from her bed to the widow's walk. The rhythm of her life had not changed, only its location.

Anne's scrivening work allowed her to get news and meet her neighbors. It did not take long for people to find out that a wealthy widow was living among them. Suitors soon came calling. Anne made it clear that she was not interested in entertaining proposals. She had not ruled out the possibility of remarrying. However, as much as she hated him, she could not deny to herself that she was still married to Daniel. She was not really free. More importantly, her troubled past made her cynical about future relationships.

Busyness made life pass quickly, as it always had. Five years following her departure from Gargaphia had passed in May of 1693 when word of the passing of Daniel Jenifer reached Anne. He had been felled by pneumonia that previous February. With that also came the news that his stepdaughter Atalanta had died as had his stepdaughter Annabella's child Rebecca during an epidemic of fever two years prior. Anne no longer existed in the minds of her family in Virginia, so of course no one had thought to contact her.

For the next few months Anne vacillated between her grief and self-recrimination for abandoning her children. Racked with guilt because she had stopped asking about her family, she kept trying to work out if there might be a way to be part of their lives now that Daniel was gone. Could they ever forgive her for all the ways she had failed them?

Ultimately, fear of stories about her being dredged up made her decide that it was in her children's best interest to remain dead to them. She did not know how to bear this reality. There was no one she could turn to for comfort. She began to exist in a state of numbness. This was not just grief. This was a profound lack of purpose. What was the point of this life, if she had no one to share it with, if no one needed her?

By fall, Anne's greying hair had turned completely white. When she looked in the mirror, she saw her Granny looking back at her. The old nightmare of seeing her grandmother arrested and thrown from the bluff over Robin Hood's Bay returned. Night after night Anne saw the two of them being cast into the watery abyss. The only thing that would pull her out of this emotional quagmire was another disaster.

One day in mid-October, while Anne was perched in her widow's walk, she saw that a storm was approaching from the south. Anne had Douglas bring the livestock into the barn then sent him to the harbormaster to warn the town that a gale would soon hit. She and Martha, began closing shutters. By the time Douglas had returned they had finished bringing inside anything that could be caught by the wind.

Together, the three of them settled in the kitchen to wait out the storm. They talked about other bad weather they had endured. The wind howled and roared like some ungodly demon. The house shook causing dishes to rattle in their cabinets. At the height of gale, the frightened band held hands and prayed for deliverance. Anne and her servants were confined this way for five days and four nights.

When they were finally able to go back outside, they found that only the barn had sustained serious damage. A large section of its roof was lost and had fallen through, killing one of the cows inside. Several chickens were missing. Cedar shingles were lying everywhere. The kitchen garden looked as though it had been plowed under. Cord wood, which had been stacked to dry for winter, was scattered about the yard.

Anne was relieved. It could have been much worse. She got busy planning what needed to be done. After some initial cleanup was completed, she sent Martha and Douglas to check on their neighbors to see how they might help each other. The worst hit area in Lewes was the harbor itself. One ship had sunk, while another had lost its main mast and most of its rigging. Some of the smaller docks had been wrenched from their pilings. Up and down the coast the hurricane had altered the course of several rivers. New ocean inlets had been cut while others had been closed. Many farm fields had been flooded. Luck had been on Anne's side. Swede's Haven was relatively unscathed.

Fall storms continued to hit the region in the weeks that followed. Though the weather was not ideal, when All Saints Day arrived Anne could not allow the occasion to pass without saying goodbye to her daughter and granddaughter. She prepared a lavender sprig to use in a ribbon blessing for them. Late that afternoon Anne left the house without telling anyone where she was going. The servants were busy with their chores. She expected to be back before they noticed she was gone. She wanted her ritual to be private.

When she came out of the woods onto the dunes, the smell of salt water and fish washed over her, mingling with the smell of the dried lavender in her hands. The sky was grey, darkened by thick clouds. Despite a stiff breeze, fog was settling on the land around her, obscuring the view of the nearby cape. The only sound was the muted din of countless coursing waves. Even a nearby flock of gulls sat silently transfixed in vigilant meditation.

The dirty brown surf was still roiling from a squall that had passed by earlier that morning. A steady wind raised white caps on the waves of the outgoing tide. Puffs of foam broke free from large frothy mounds building up along the waterline, floating through the air until they disintegrated.

Anne walked up to the water's edge and tossed her ceremonial bouquet eastward. Before she could begin her prayer, the wind caught it and blew it back on to the beach. She picked it up and tried again. Still it did not even touch the water. Once more she threw it as hard as she could. Once more it landed behind her in the sand.

Determined to complete her sacred rite, she gathered the sprig up and walked out knee deep into the surf. The water felt strangely warm against the chilled air. Anne took another step forward to lay her offering in the water. Suddenly she found herself in waves up to her chest. Determined to complete her mission she began to recite the ribbon blessing as she tried to find her footing.

"To our guardian angels we plead, carry our love on soft sea breezes to our cherished Mother Mary and sweet Christ Jesus, that they might wrap our beloved Atalanta and Rebecca…"

At that moment a large breaker rose up before Anne like a giant fist. She looked curiously at the towering wall of ocean, oddly paralyzed by the sight of it. Before she realized what was happening the churning waters crashed down around her. Her skirts quickly became one with the swift impersonal current, swirling her under and away from shore. Anne did not have time to cry out or even fight for her life, only to wonder if the sea fairies would carry her off to Mother Mary and Christ Jesus and reunite her with all those she had loved and lost.

Afterword

Today on Virginia's Eastern Shore, the small town known as Gargatha is all that remains of the tradesmen's village associated with the Gargaphia plantation. To the east, in an area known as Gargathy Neck, farmland and housing developments can be found where the infamous guest house once stood. The inlet of nearby Gargathy Bay still leads to the ocean and an isolated barrier island inhabited only by wildlife. These derivations of the name Gargaphia having evolved from the changing accents of Accomack's residents are all that remain to remind people of the fabled plantation.

In the early days of the colonies, every business transaction, dispute, and death, was documented in local court records. Churches kept track of weddings and births. So, though most people were illiterate, many settlers left a paper trail. In 1653 one "An Toft" was recorded with that same spelling as an indentured servant to two different masters at the same time in the emigration rolls of James City, Virginia. This may or may not be the "widow Anne Toft" we next hear about on Virginia's Eastern Shore purchasing 800 acres of land from Colonel Edmund Scarborough at the age of 17. The relationship between Anne and Edmund was well documented after that. Because she could read and write, and because of her association with Scarborough, Anne's name can be found throughout court documents of the era as a participant in and witness to a variety of dealings.

Those ledger entries are all that is left to memorialize Anne Toft. She disappeared from the historical record at the age of 44, following the 1687 sale of Chiconessex which she, and her then husband Daniel Jenifer, registered in Accomack County Court.

It was not uncommon then for people in the colony to die at that relatively young age. It was strange that her passing was not recorded in church or court documents when so many lesser known characters from that community were. Not even her children seemed to have been led to mark her passing in any permanent way.

Anne Toft was, however, remarkable for her time. She must have been lovely. Edmund Scarborough clearly thought she was a catch. It was rare for anyone, let alone a woman, to know how to read and write. An unmarried female who exercised free agency, conducting business with such great success, was even rarer. Beauty and brains used with such power is noteworthy in any age.

Anne had three daughters with Edmund. They actually did name them Atalanta, Annabella, and Arcadia. The young women each met the conditions of the dowry agreed to by their mother and stepfather. They were good girls till the age of seventeen and accepted marriage proposals from respectable men. They split five thousand acres of coastal Virginia farmland between them once they all were wed. Two of them were widowed and remarried at least once, Atalanta twice. They each had several children.

Anne's only son, Daniel of St. Thomas Jenifer, took over the plantation at Gargaphia and had a son named after him who became a doctor. He in turn had his own namesake who became a well-known Maryland politician and a signer of the U.S. Constitution. He lived near Annapolis, Maryland. There is even an elementary school named for him. An unmarried idealist, when this last Daniel died with no children, he manumitted all of his slaves through his will.

Anne Toft's story remains relevant not only for the truths it tells us about our country's origins and the role women played in it. Whatever the unwritten facts may actually be, the record shows that for a while this Mistress Toft mastered the art of tenacious adaptation in a time of dynamic change.

Some of the people whom the characters in this book are based on, may not have been as terrible as they are portrayed herein. I certainly don't mean to cast aspersions on anyone's ancestors. I have no proof that their real-life counterparts engaged in any of the despicable acts that brought drama to my fiction. Likewise, it could be that Anne Toft was actually an innocent pawn used and discarded by the men in her life. Then again, maybe she really was a terrible person and I was too easy on her.

My novel Gargaphia makes a lot of assumptions about her character in order to tell a story that goes beyond who she really was. If we give Anne the benefit of the doubt, she seems to tell us that the path to corruption is littered with poor excuses disguised as good intentions. The crazy but true facts of her life seemed to inspire questions about what it looks like to be complicit in the evil happening all around us. How do we resist the temptations it presents? How do we find the courage to stop it?

We are not to blame for the sins of our ancestors. We are, however, fated to bear the consequences of them. The roots of society's greatest problems today, reach far back to the sins of the past. Imagining the lives of those people so long ago, from the vantage point of the future, helps us to ask: How will history view the consequences of our actions? What fiction will we inspire?

About The Author

Dana Kester-McCabe is the author of *The Delmarva School of Art*, a book celebrating creativity on the Delmarva Peninsula. She served as host, executive producer, writer, and photographer for the Delmarva Almanac, a local online culture magazine and a radio show on NPR stations WSCL and WSDL in Salisbury, Maryland.

Dana is also an artist with over forty years of creative experience in graphic design, media production, and painting. A lifelong active member of the Religious Society of Friends (the Quakers), and the mother of two grown children, she lives with her husband on the Eastern Shore of Maryland.

Other Books By This Author

The Delmarva School of Art

The Seeker's Field Guide To Exploring Spirituality

A Book Of Seeds

Find out more at moonshell.net

CPSIA information can be obtained
at www.ICGtesting.com
Printed in the USA
LVHW012057280720
661667LV00001B/10

9 781087 871431